RUGRATS™

BUILDING BLOCKS

kaboom!™

RUGRATS: BUILDING BLOCKS, September 2019. Published by KaBOOM!, a division of Boom Entertainment, Inc. © 2019 Viacom International Inc. All Rights Reserved. Nickelodeon, Rugrats and all related titles, logos, and characters are trademarks of Viacom International Inc. Originally published in single magazine form as RUGRATS: R IS FOR REPTAR No. 1, and RUGRATS: C IS FOR CHANUKAH No. 1 © 2018 Viacom International Inc. Created by Klasky, Csupo and Germain. All Rights Reserved. KaBOOM!™ and the KaBOOM! logo are trademarks of Boom Entertainment, Inc., registered in various countries and categories. All characters, events, and institutions depicted herein are fictional. Any similarity between any of the names, characters, persons, events, and/or institutions in this publication to actual names, characters, and persons, whether living or dead, events, and/or institutions is unintended and purely coincidental. KaBOOM! does not read or accept unsolicited submissions of ideas, stories, or artwork.

BOOM! Studios, 5670 Wilshire Boulevard, Suite 400, Los Angeles, CA 90036-5679. Printed in China. First Printing.

ISBN: 978-1-68415-460-9, eISBN: 978-1-64144-577-1

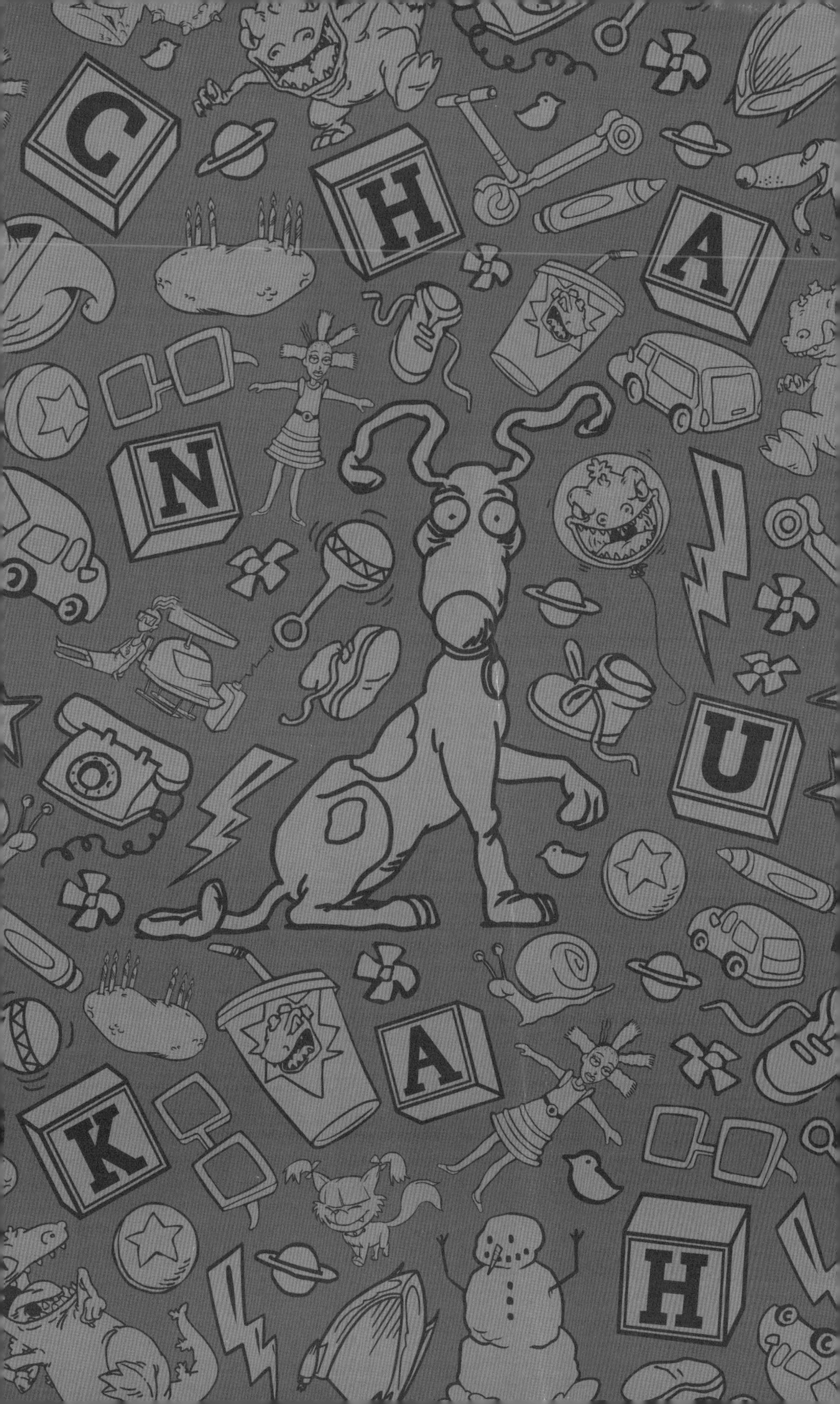
C
H
A
N
U
A
K
H

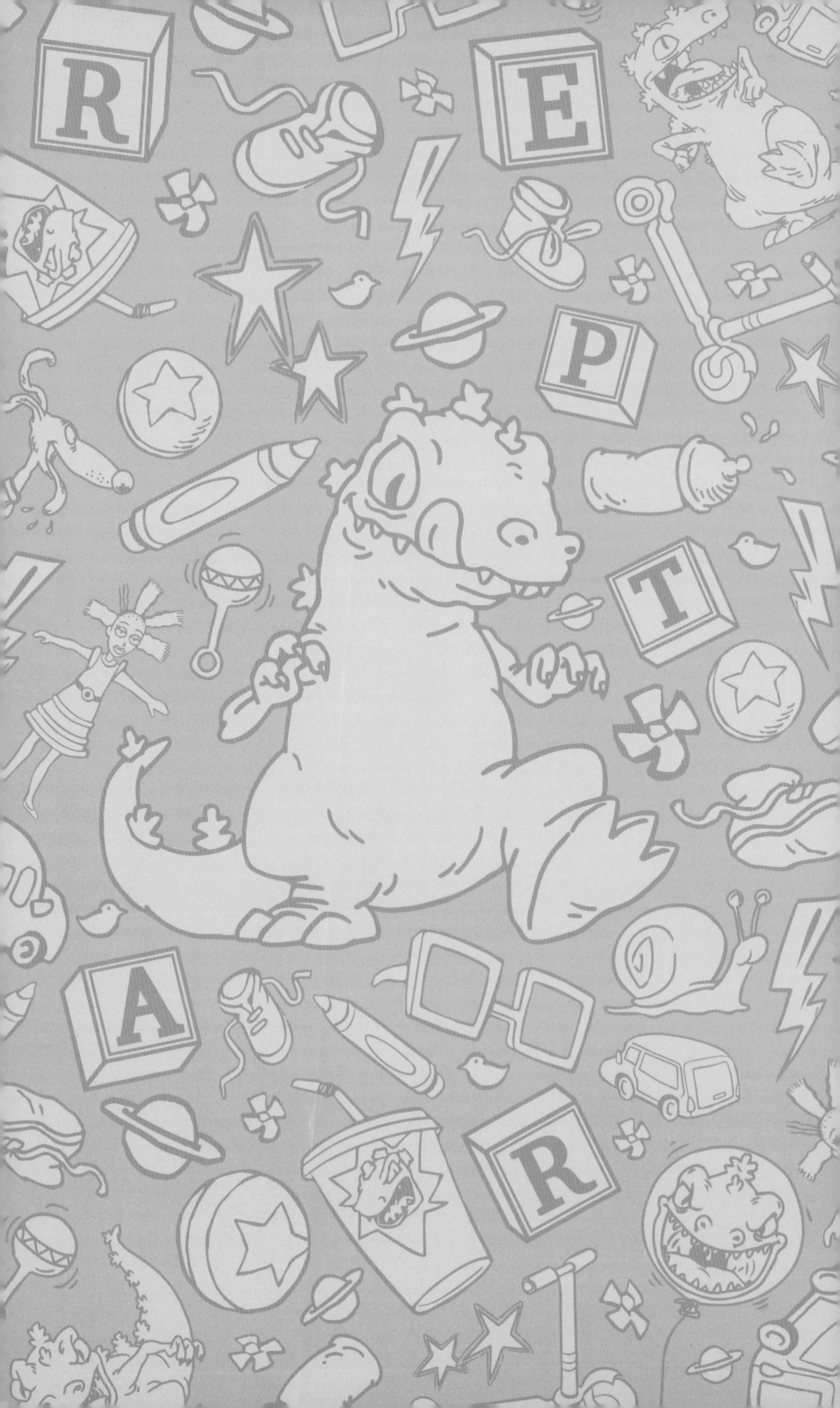
R
E
P
T
A
R

"R" IS FOR REPTAR

WRITTEN BY
NICOLE ANDELFINGER

"WORLD WAR REPTAR"
ILLUSTRATED BY
ESDRAS CRISTOBAL

"LI'L REPTARS"
ILLUSTRATED AND LETTERED BY
SARAH WEBB

"SUPER CYNTHIA"
ILLUSTRATED BY
BRITTNEY WILLIAMS
COLORED BY
JOANA LAFUENTE

"BEAUTY AND THE REPTAR"
ILLUSTRATED BY
LAURA LANGSTON

"TOMMY & REPTAR"
ILLUSTRATED BY
ILARIA CATALANI
COLORED BY
FRED C. STRESING & MEG CASEY

LETTERED BY
JIM CAMPBELL

"C" IS FOR CHANUKAH

WRITTEN BY
DANIEL KIBBLESMITH & CULLEN CRAWFORD

ILLUSTRATED BY
KATE SHERRON

LETTERED BY
JIM CAMPBELL

COVER BY
JORGE CORONA

DESIGNER
MARIE KRUPINA

EDITOR
MATTHEW LEVINE

SPECIAL THANKS TO
**JOAN HILTY, LINDA LEE, JAMES SALERNO
AND THE WONDERFUL TEAM AT NICKELODEON.**

"R" IS FOR REPTAR

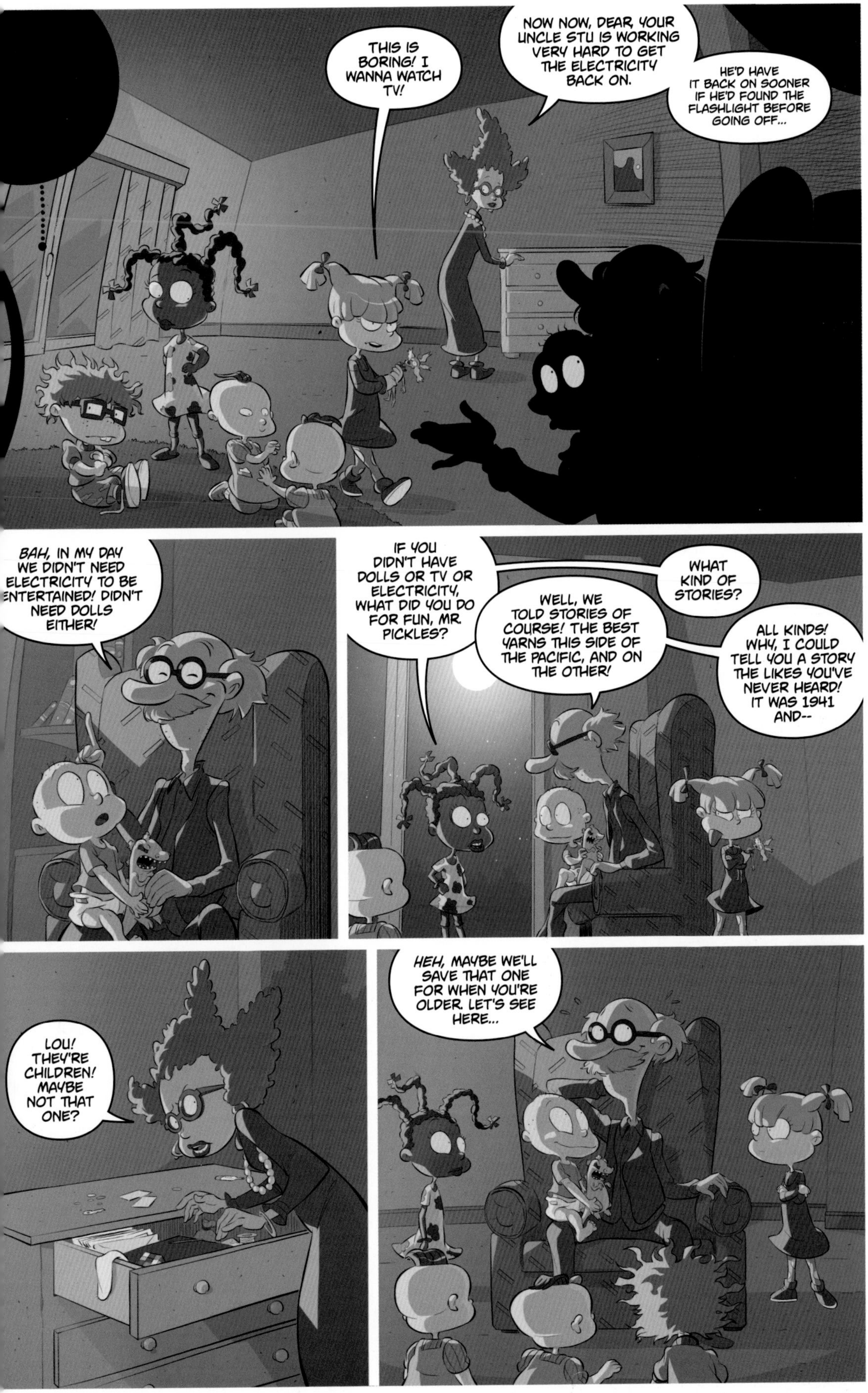
THIS IS BORING! I WANNA WATCH TV!
NOW NOW, DEAR, YOUR UNCLE STU IS WORKING VERY HARD TO GET THE ELECTRICITY BACK ON.
HE'D HAVE IT BACK ON SOONER IF HE'D FOUND THE FLASHLIGHT BEFORE GOING OFF...
BAH, IN MY DAY WE DIDN'T NEED ELECTRICITY TO BE ENTERTAINED! DIDN'T NEED DOLLS EITHER!
IF YOU DIDN'T HAVE DOLLS OR TV OR ELECTRICITY, WHAT DID YOU DO FOR FUN, MR. PICKLES?
WELL, WE TOLD STORIES OF COURSE! THE BEST YARNS THIS SIDE OF THE PACIFIC, AND ON THE OTHER!
WHAT KIND OF STORIES?
ALL KINDS! WHY, I COULD TELL YOU A STORY THE LIKES YOU'VE NEVER HEARD! IT WAS 1941 AND--
LOU! THEY'RE CHILDREN! MAYBE NOT THAT ONE?
HEH, MAYBE WE'LL SAVE THAT ONE FOR WHEN YOU'RE OLDER. LET'S SEE HERE...

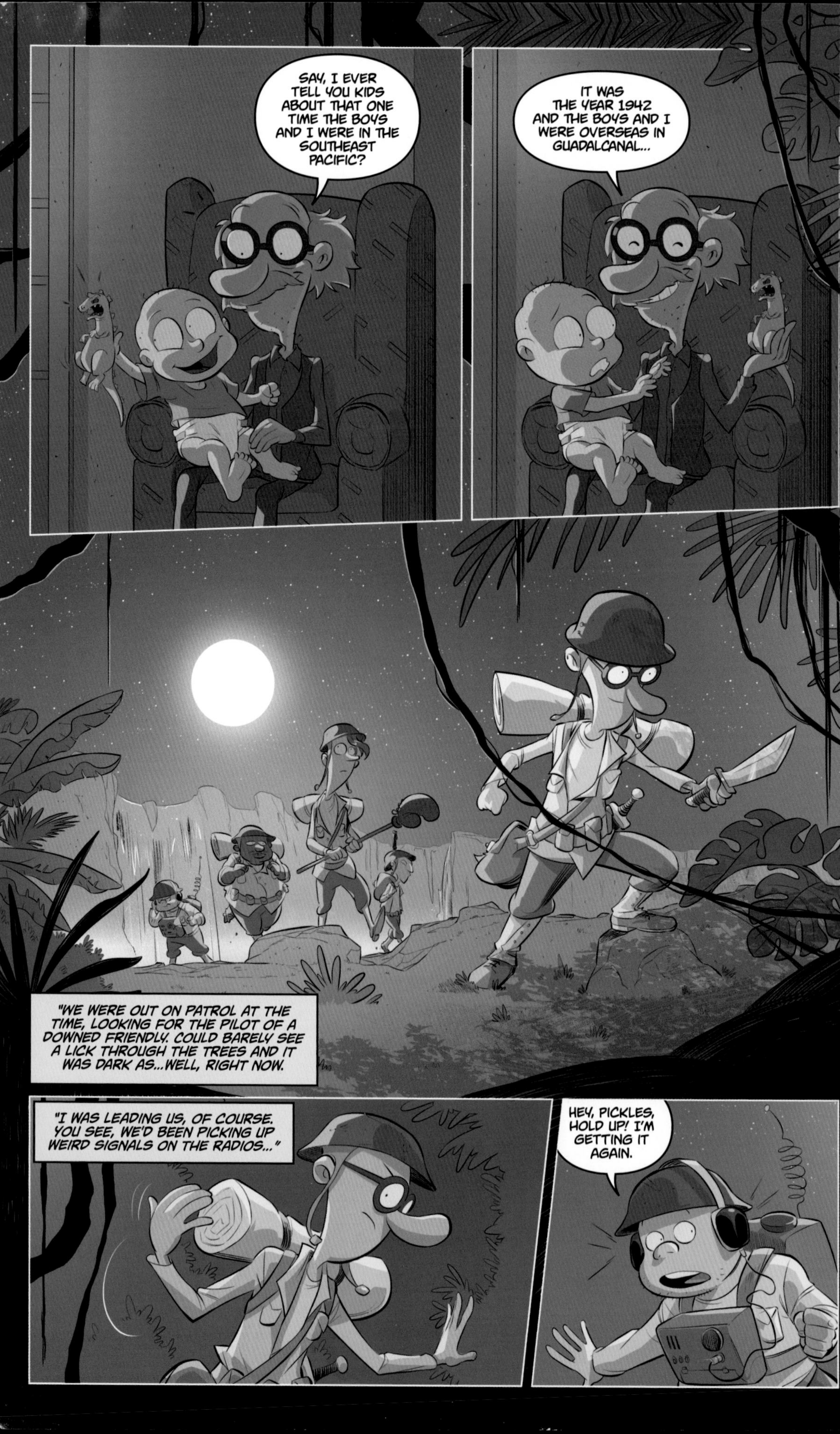
SAY, I EVER TELL YOU KIDS ABOUT THAT ONE TIME THE BOYS AND I WERE IN THE SOUTHEAST PACIFIC?
IT WAS THE YEAR 1942 AND THE BOYS AND I WERE OVERSEAS IN GUADALCANAL...
"WE WERE OUT ON PATROL AT THE TIME, LOOKING FOR THE PILOT OF A DOWNED FRIENDLY. COULD BARELY SEE A LICK THROUGH THE TREES AND IT WAS DARK AS...WELL, RIGHT NOW.
"I WAS LEADING US, OF COURSE. YOU SEE, WE'D BEEN PICKING UP WEIRD SIGNALS ON THE RADIOS..."
HEY, PICKLES, HOLD UP! I'M GETTING IT AGAIN.

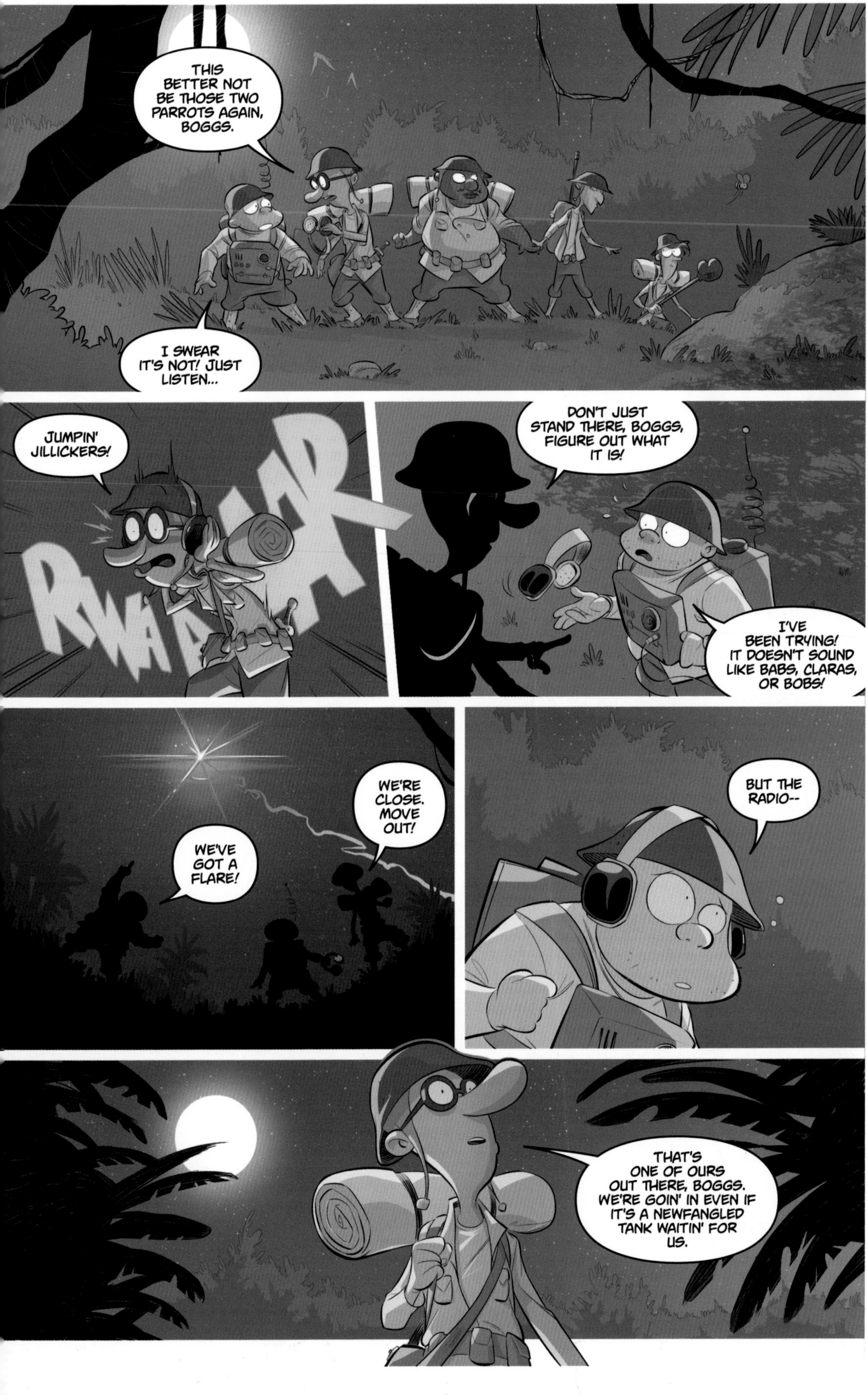
THIS BETTER NOT BE THOSE TWO PARROTS AGAIN, BOGGS.
I SWEAR IT'S NOT! JUST LISTEN...
JUMPIN' JILLICKERS!
RWAAAR
DON'T JUST STAND THERE, BOGGS, FIGURE OUT WHAT IT IS!
I'VE BEEN TRYING! IT DOESN'T SOUND LIKE BABS, CLARAS, OR BOBS!
WE'VE GOT A FLARE!
WE'RE CLOSE. MOVE OUT!
BUT THE RADIO--
THAT'S ONE OF OURS OUT THERE, BOGGS. WE'RE GOIN' IN EVEN IF IT'S A NEWFANGLED TANK WAITIN' FOR US.

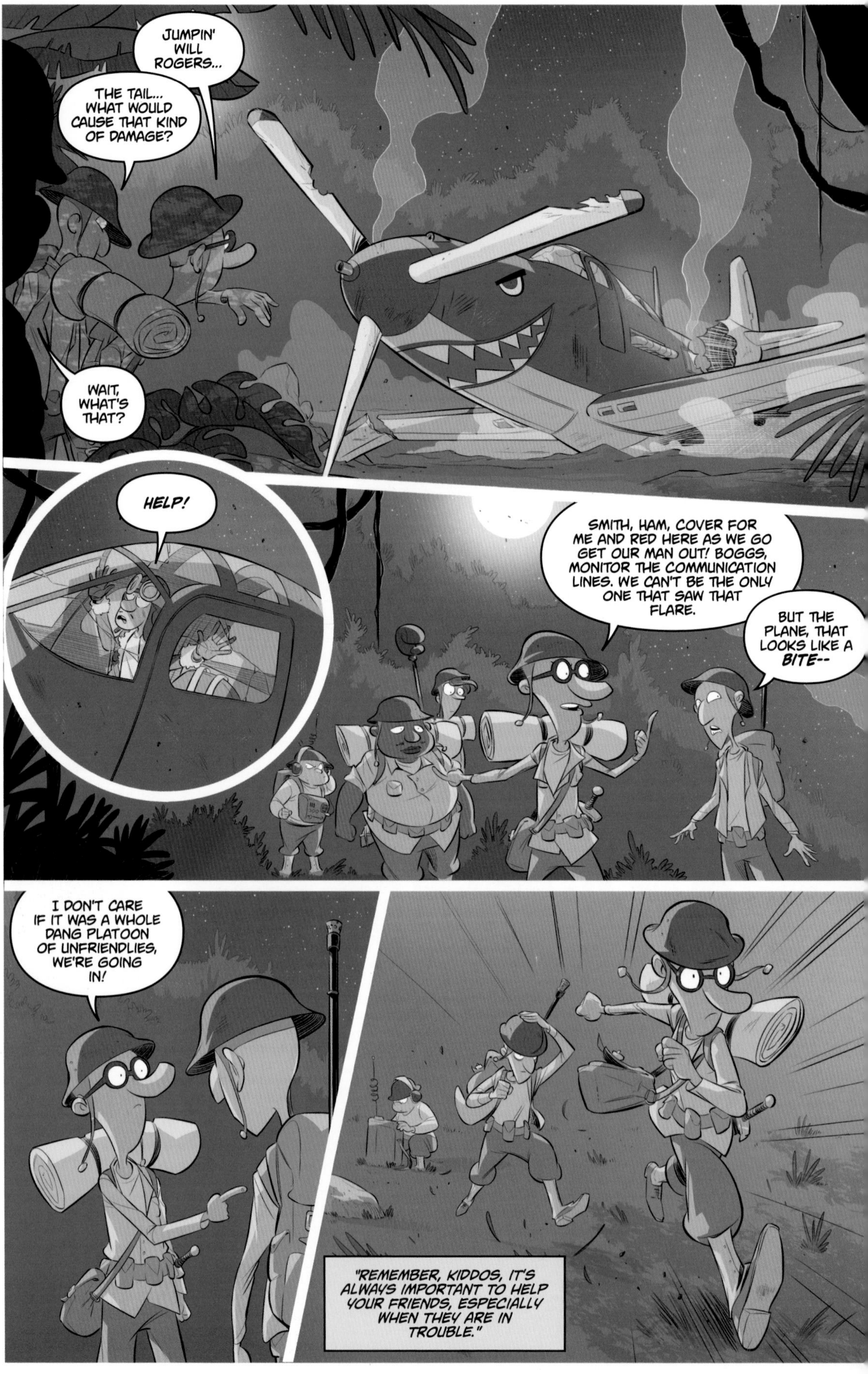
JUMPIN' WILL ROGERS...
THE TAIL... WHAT WOULD CAUSE THAT KIND OF DAMAGE?
WAIT, WHAT'S THAT?
HELP!
SMITH, HAM, COVER FOR ME AND RED HERE AS WE GO GET OUR MAN OUT! BOGGS, MONITOR THE COMMUNICATION LINES. WE CAN'T BE THE ONLY ONE THAT SAW THAT FLARE.
BUT THE PLANE, THAT LOOKS LIKE A *BITE*--
I DON'T CARE IF IT WAS A WHOLE DANG PLATOON OF UNFRIENDLIES, WE'RE GOING IN!
"REMEMBER, KIDDOS, IT'S ALWAYS IMPORTANT TO HELP YOUR FRIENDS, ESPECIALLY WHEN THEY ARE IN TROUBLE."

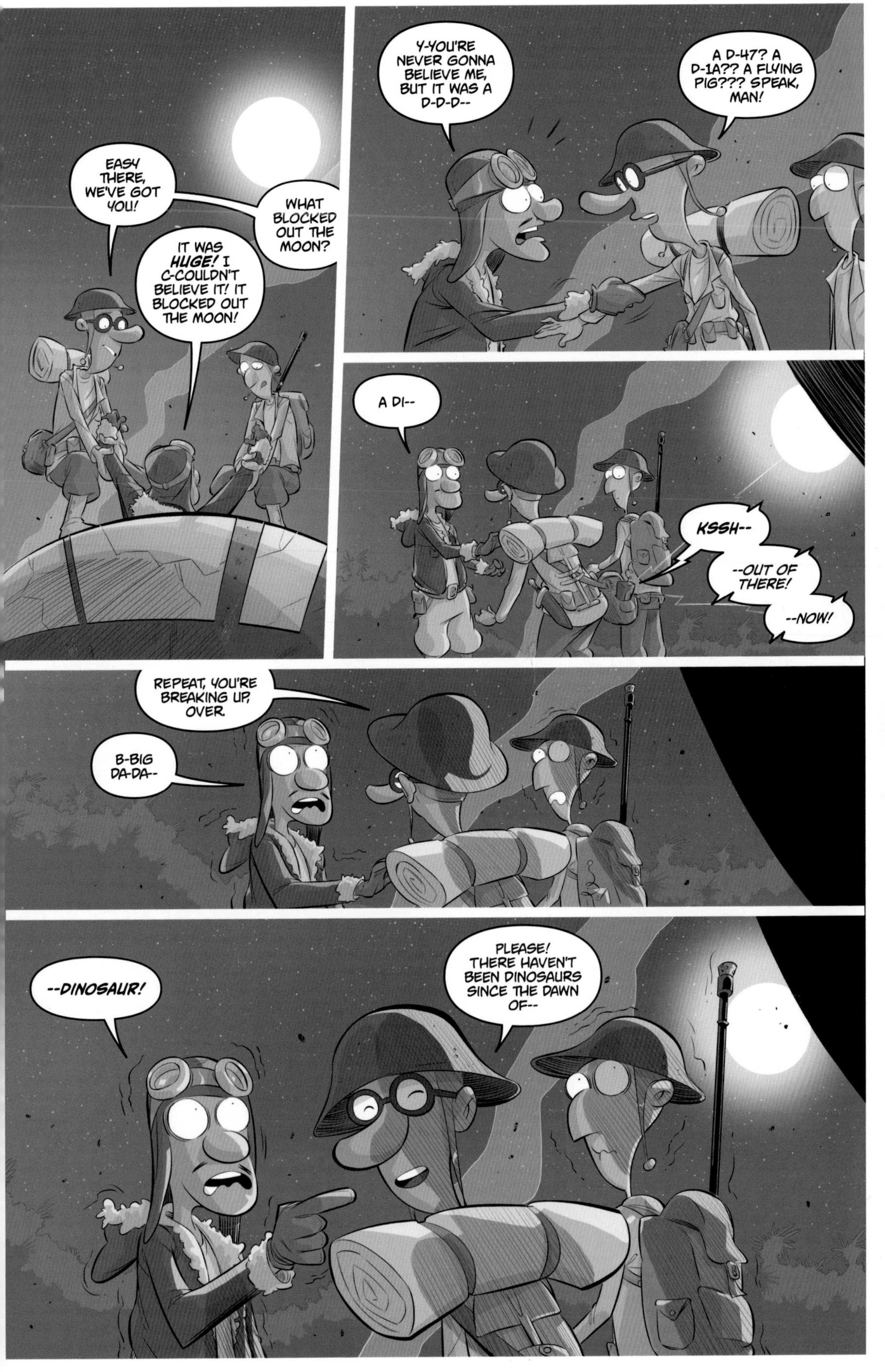

EASY THERE, WE'VE GOT YOU!
WHAT BLOCKED OUT THE MOON?
IT WAS HUGE! I C-COULDN'T BELIEVE IT! IT BLOCKED OUT THE MOON!
Y-YOU'RE NEVER GONNA BELIEVE ME, BUT IT WAS A D-D-D--
A D-47? A D-1A?? A FLYING PIG??? SPEAK, MAN!
A DI--
KSSH--
--OUT OF THERE!
--NOW!
REPEAT, YOU'RE BREAKING UP, OVER.
B-BIG DA-DA--
--DINOSAUR!
PLEASE! THERE HAVEN'T BEEN DINOSAURS SINCE THE DAWN OF--

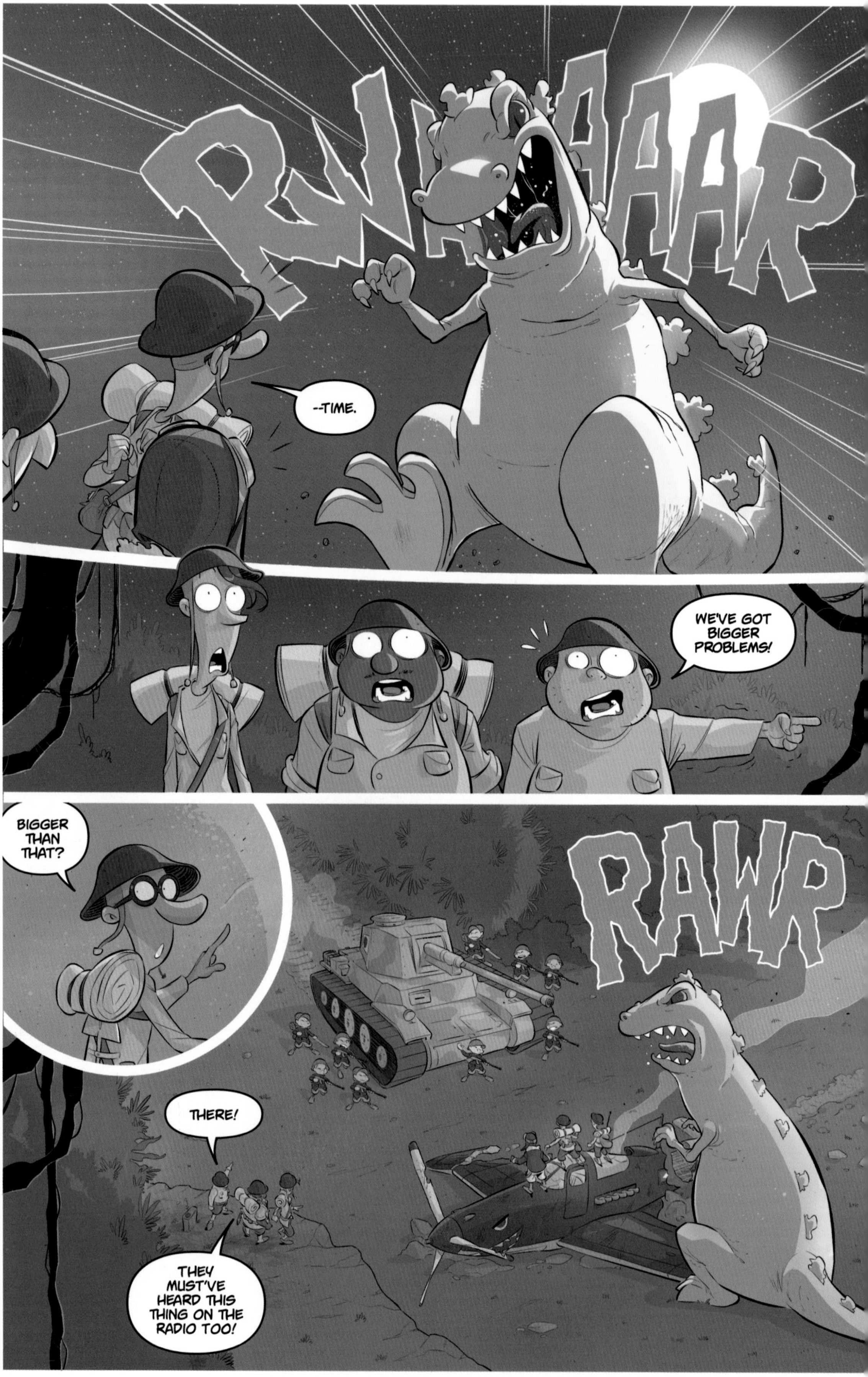
RWAAAAR
--TIME.
WE'VE GOT BIGGER PROBLEMS!
BIGGER THAN THAT?
RAWR
THERE!
THEY MUST'VE HEARD THIS THING ON THE RADIO TOO!

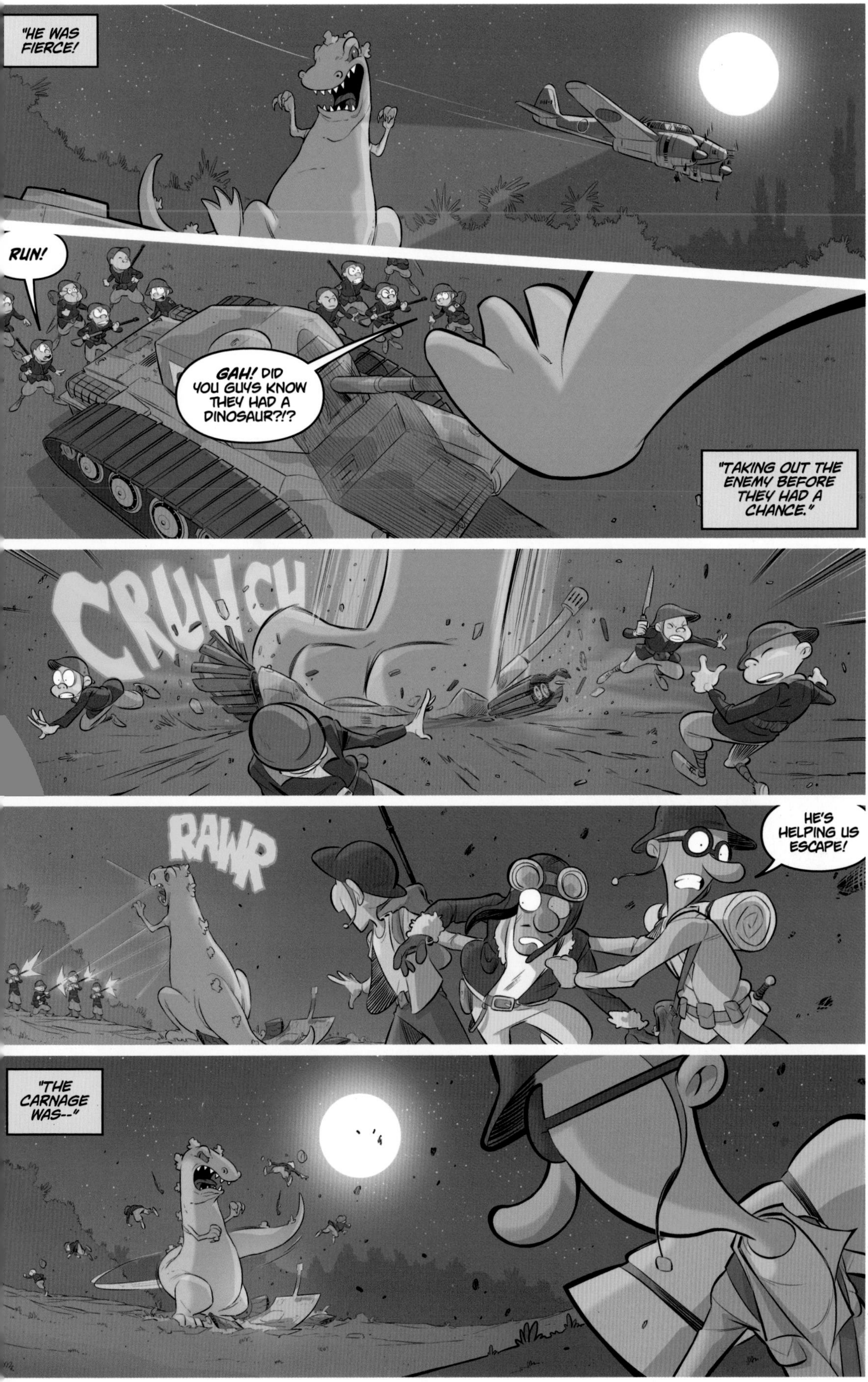
"HE WAS FIERCE!
RUN!
GAH! DID YOU GUYS KNOW THEY HAD A DINOSAUR?!?
"TAKING OUT THE ENEMY BEFORE THEY HAD A CHANCE."
CRUNCH
RAWR
HE'S HELPING US ESCAPE!
"THE CARNAGE WAS--"

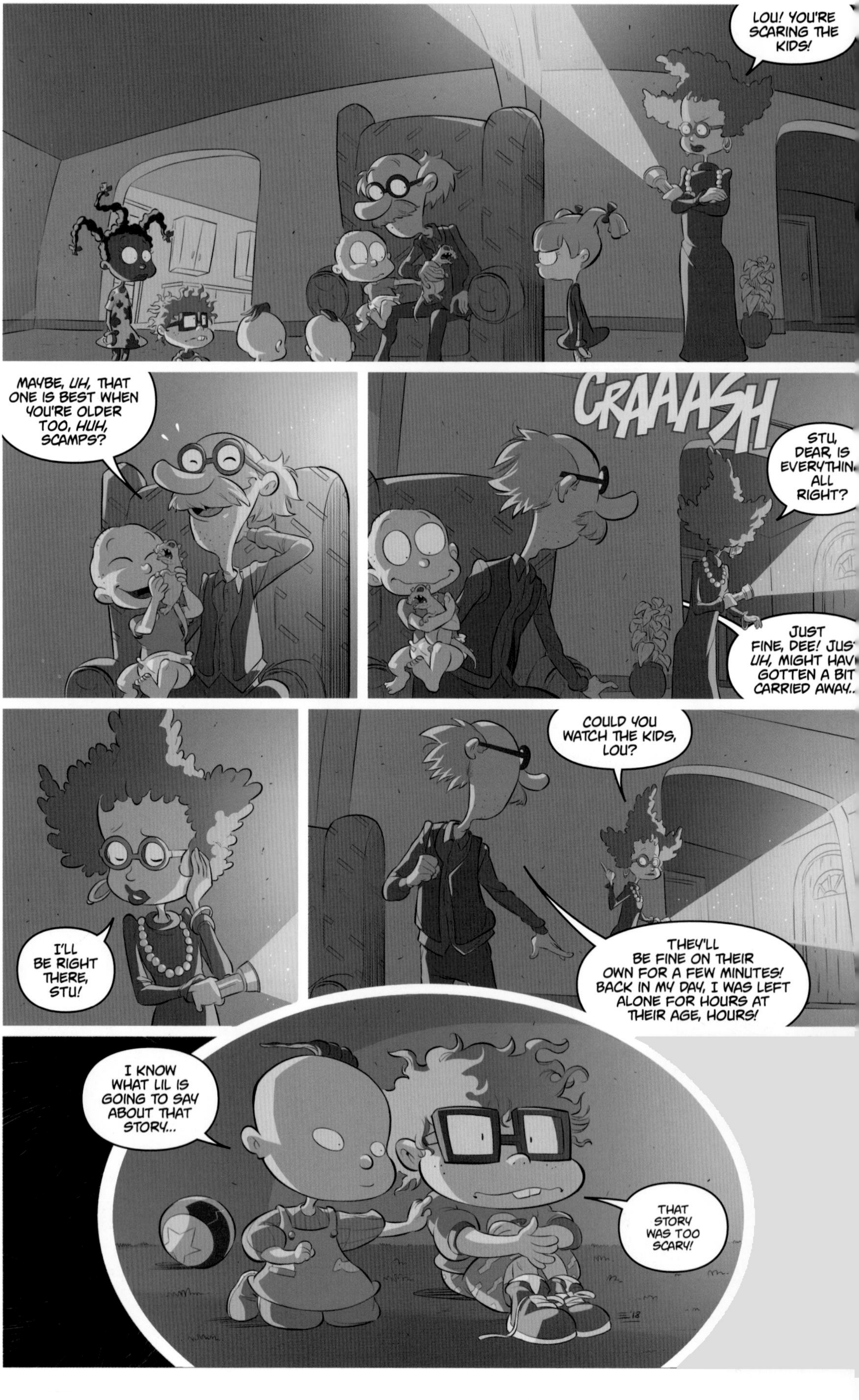
LOU! YOU'RE SCARING THE KIDS!
MAYBE, UH, THAT ONE IS BEST WHEN YOU'RE OLDER TOO, HUH, SCAMPS?
CRAAASH
STU, DEAR, IS EVERYTHIN ALL RIGHT?
JUST FINE, DEE! JUS UH, MIGHT HAV GOTTEN A BIT CARRIED AWAY...
I'LL BE RIGHT THERE, STU!
COULD YOU WATCH THE KIDS, LOU?
THEY'LL BE FINE ON THEIR OWN FOR A FEW MINUTES! BACK IN MY DAY, I WAS LEFT ALONE FOR HOURS AT THEIR AGE, HOURS!
I KNOW WHAT LIL IS GOING TO SAY ABOUT THAT STORY...
THAT STORY WAS TOO SCARY!

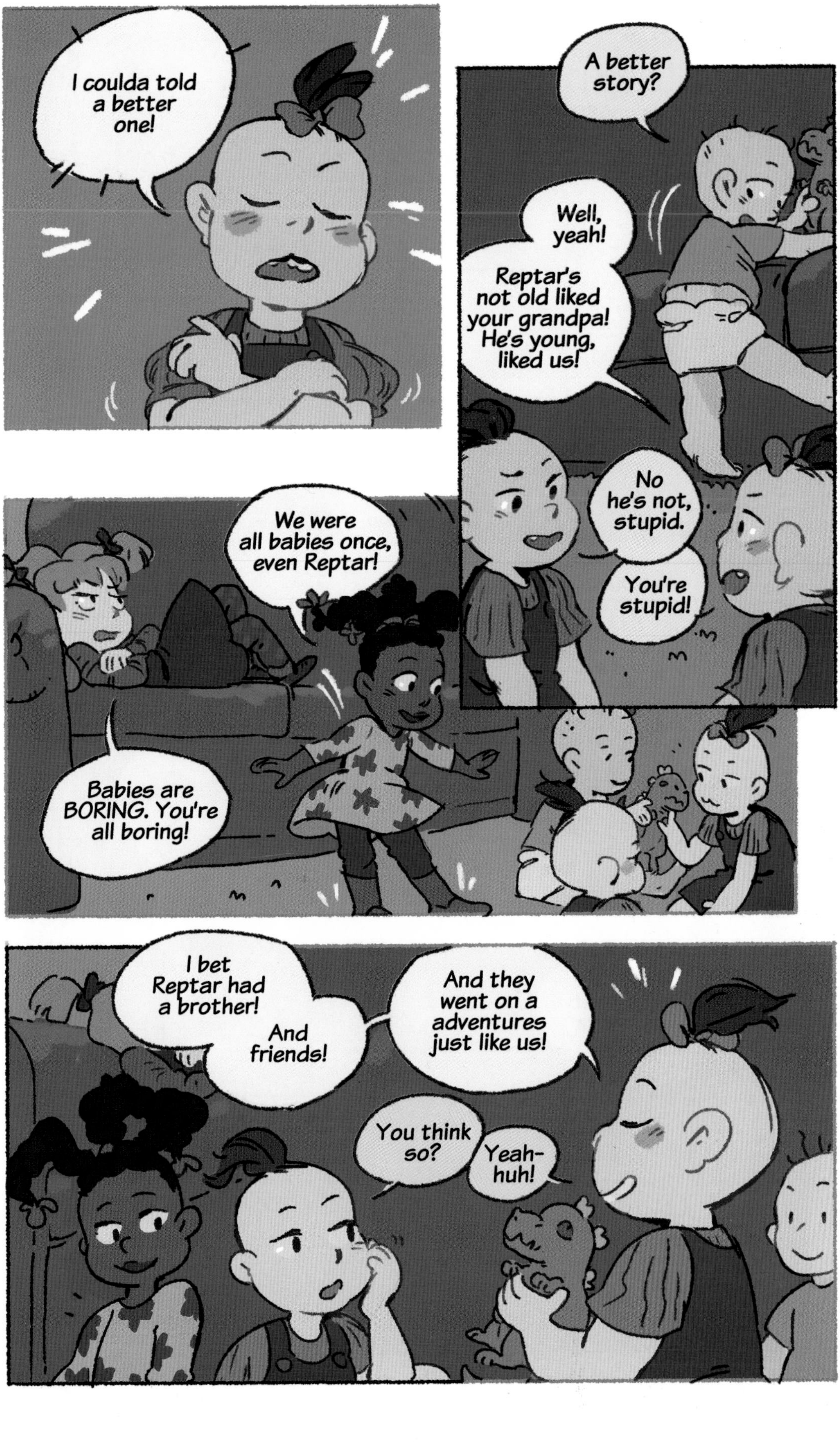

I coulda told a better one!
A better story?
Well, yeah!
Reptar's not old liked your grandpa! He's young, liked us!
No he's not, stupid.
You're stupid!
We were all babies once, even Reptar!
Babies are BORING. You're all boring!
I bet Reptar had a brother!
And friends!
And they went on a adventures just like us!
You think so?
Yeah-huh!

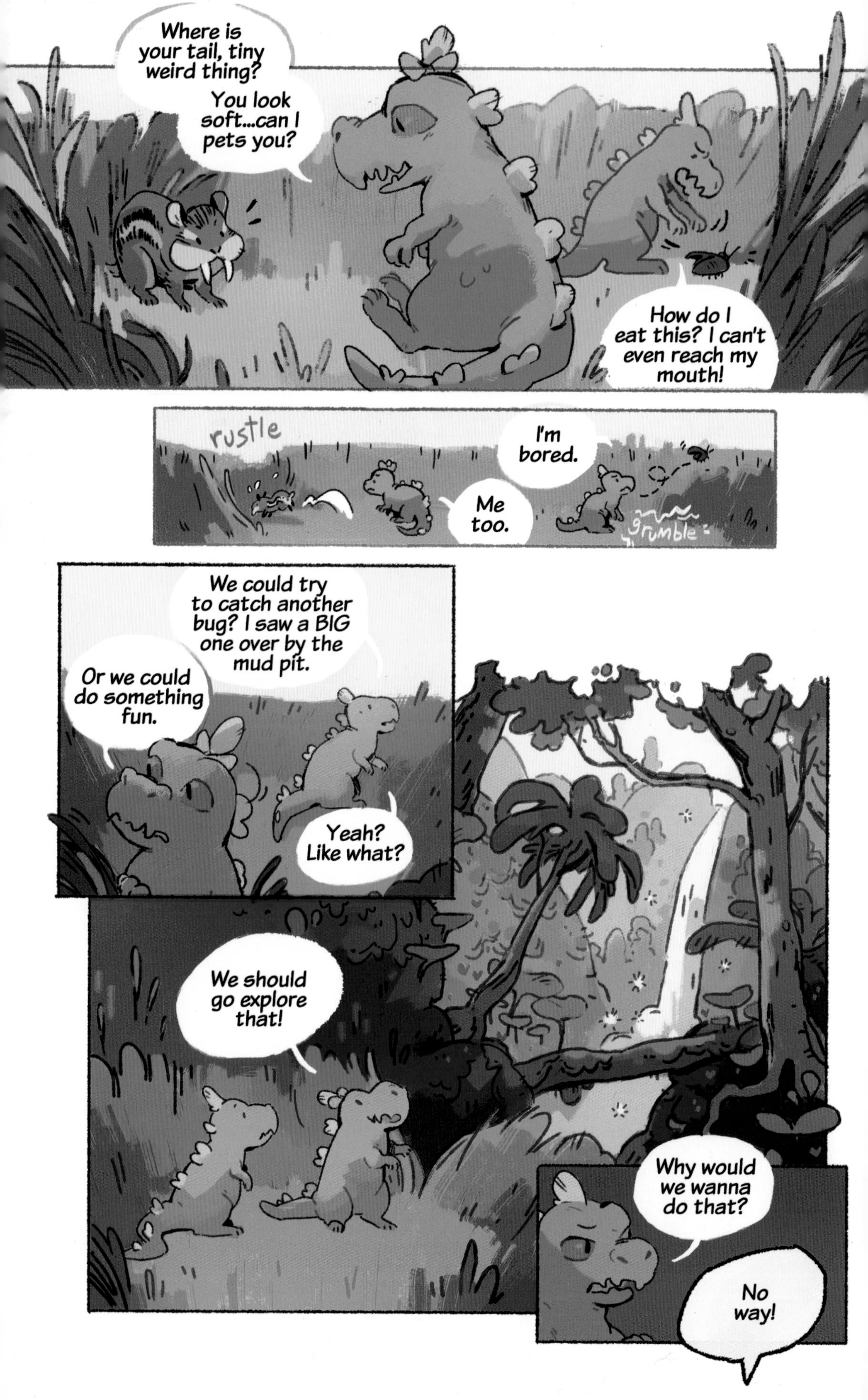
Where is your tail, tiny weird thing?
You look soft...can I pets you?
How do I eat this? I can't even reach my mouth!
rustle
I'm bored.
Me too.
grumble
We could try to catch another bug? I saw a BIG one over by the mud pit.
Or we could do something fun.
Yeah? Like what?
We should go explore that!
Why would we wanna do that?
No way!

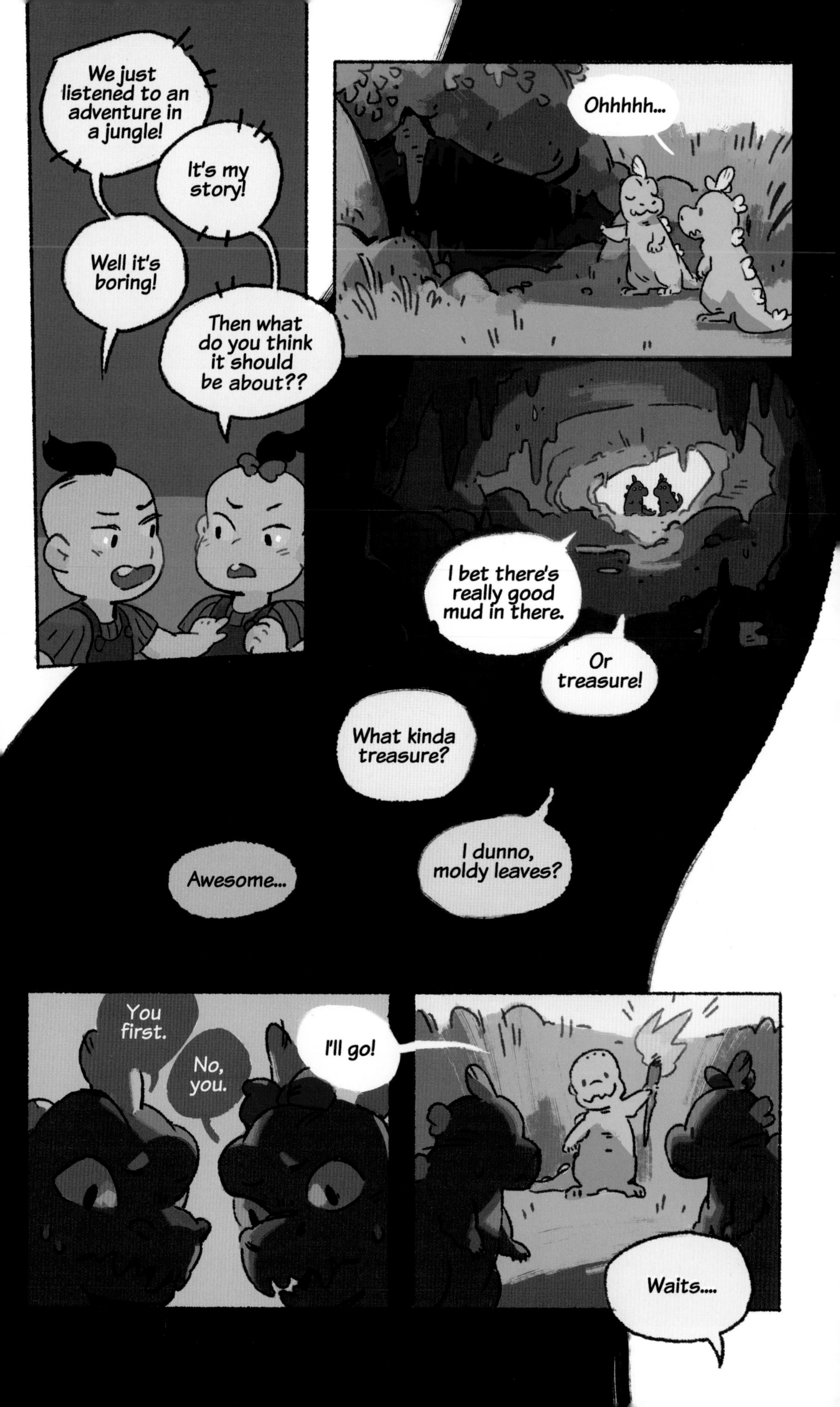

We just listened to an adventure in a jungle!
It's my story!
Well it's boring!
Then what do you think it should be about??
Ohhhhh...
I bet there's really good mud in there.
Or treasure!
What kinda treasure?
I dunno, moldy leaves?
Awesome...
You first.
No, you.
I'll go!
Waits....

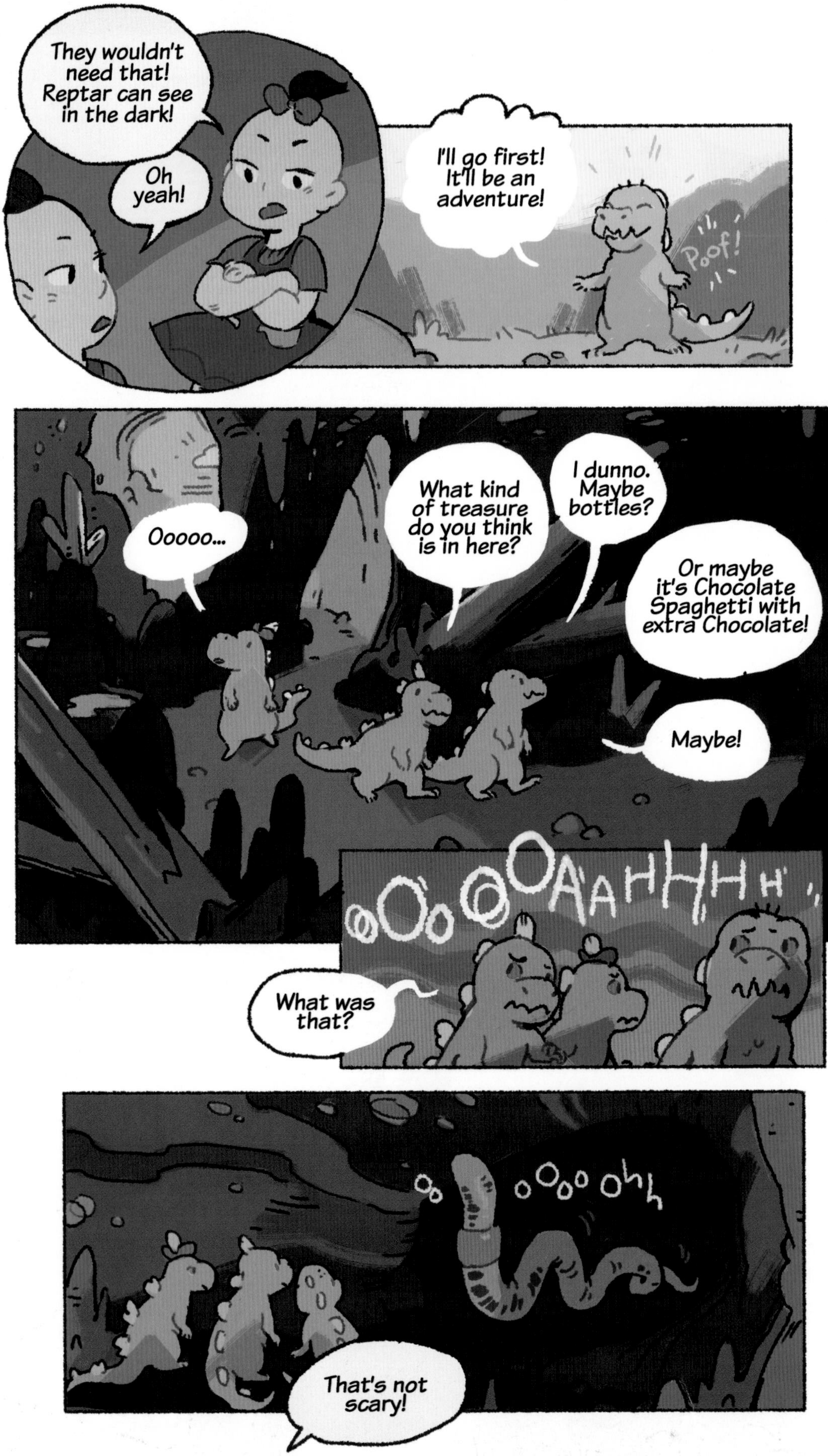
They wouldn't need that! Reptar can see in the dark!
Oh yeah!
I'll go first! It'll be an adventure!
Poof!
Ooooo...
What kind of treasure do you think is in here?
I dunno. Maybe bottles?
Or maybe it's Chocolate Spaghetti with extra Chocolate!
Maybe!
OOOOOOAAHHHHH
What was that?
oo oOoo ohh
That's not scary!

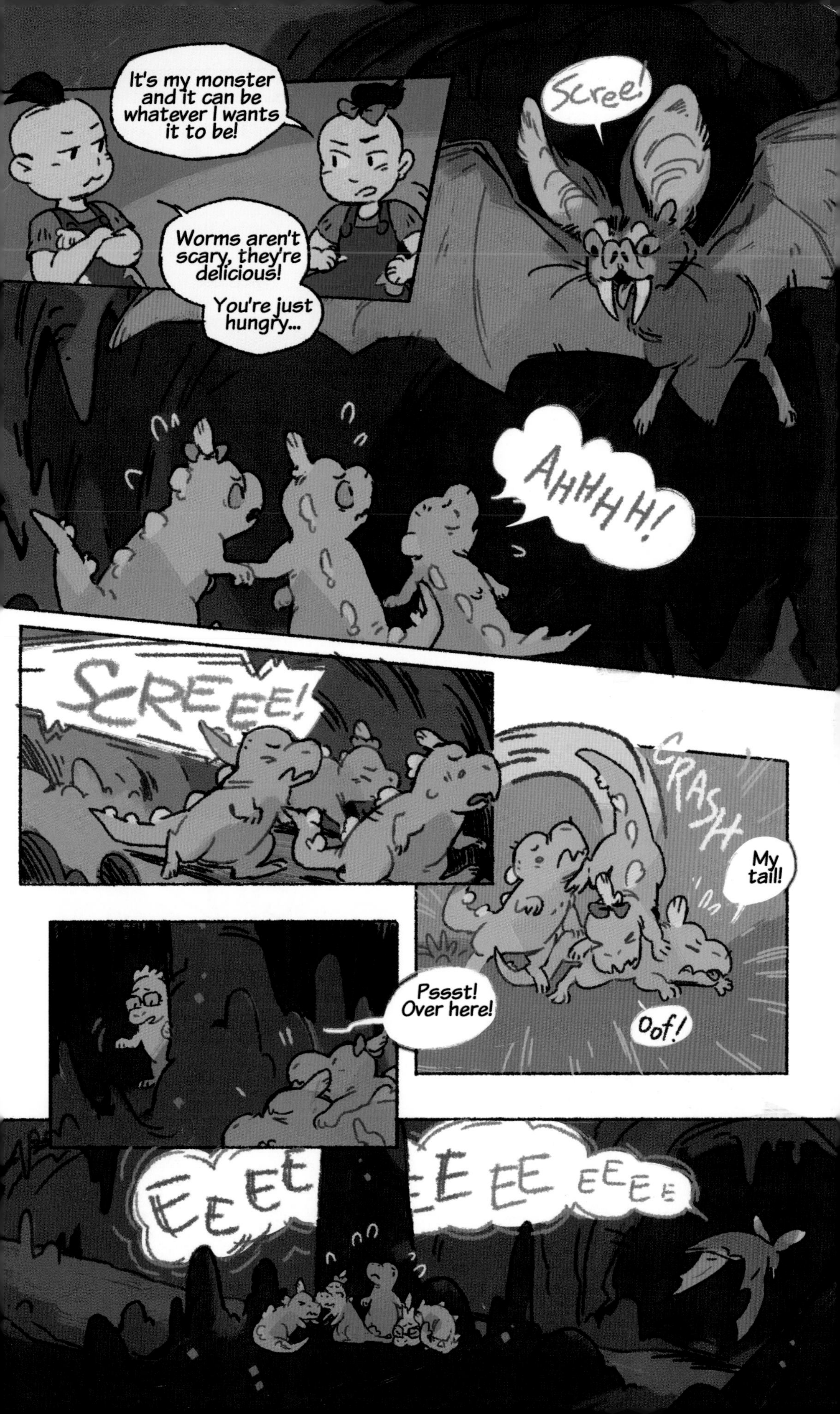

It's my monster and it can be whatever I wants it to be!
Worms aren't scary, they're delicious!
You're just hungry...
Scree!
AHHHH!
SCREEE!
CRASH
My tail!
Oof!
Pssst! Over here!
EEEEEEEEEEEE

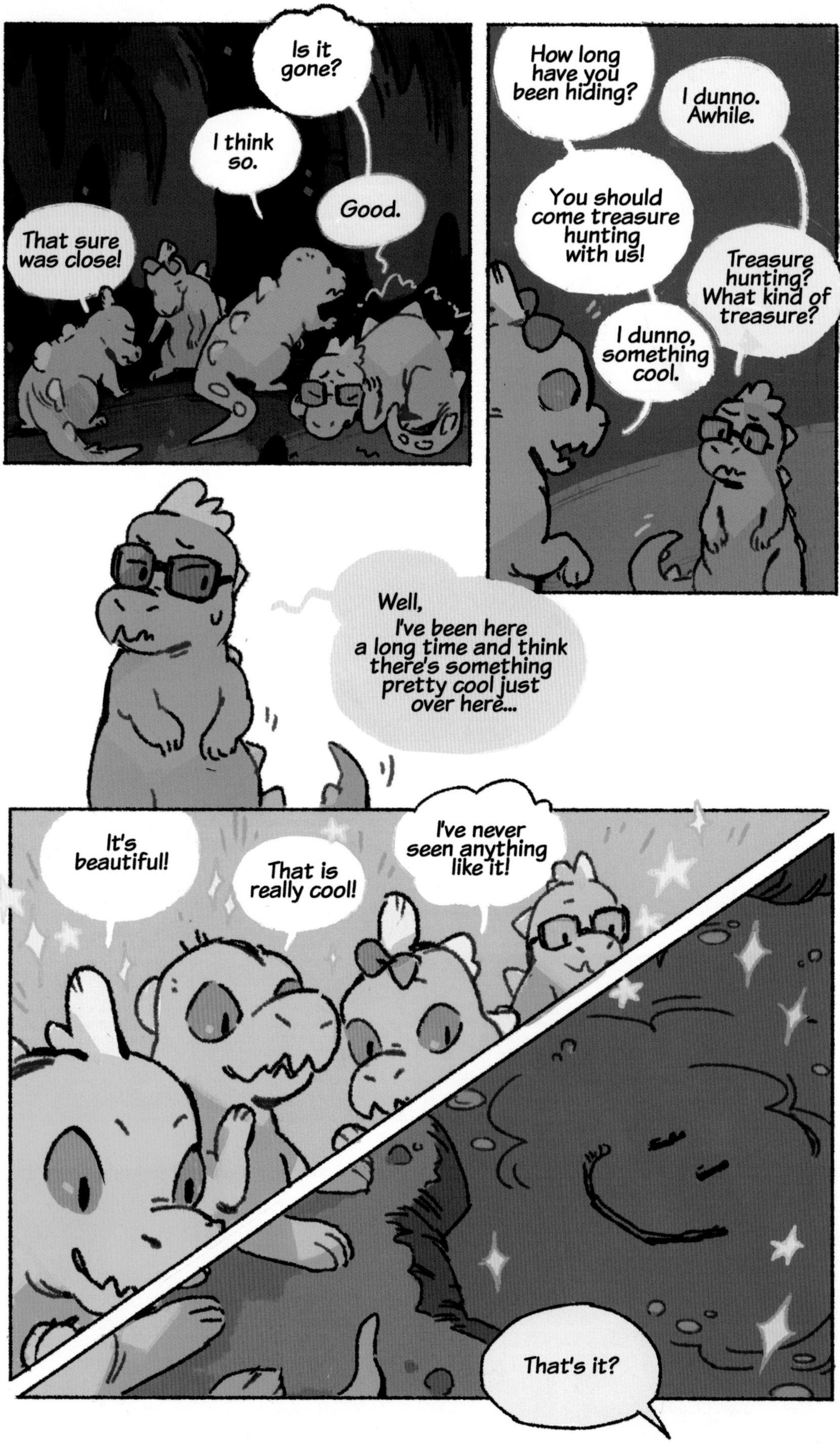
That sure was close!
I think so.
Is it gone?
Good.
How long have you been hiding?
I dunno. Awhile.
You should come treasure hunting with us!
Treasure hunting? What kind of treasure?
I dunno, something cool.
Well, I've been here a long time and think there's something pretty cool just over here...
It's beautiful!
That is really cool!
I've never seen anything like it!
That's it?

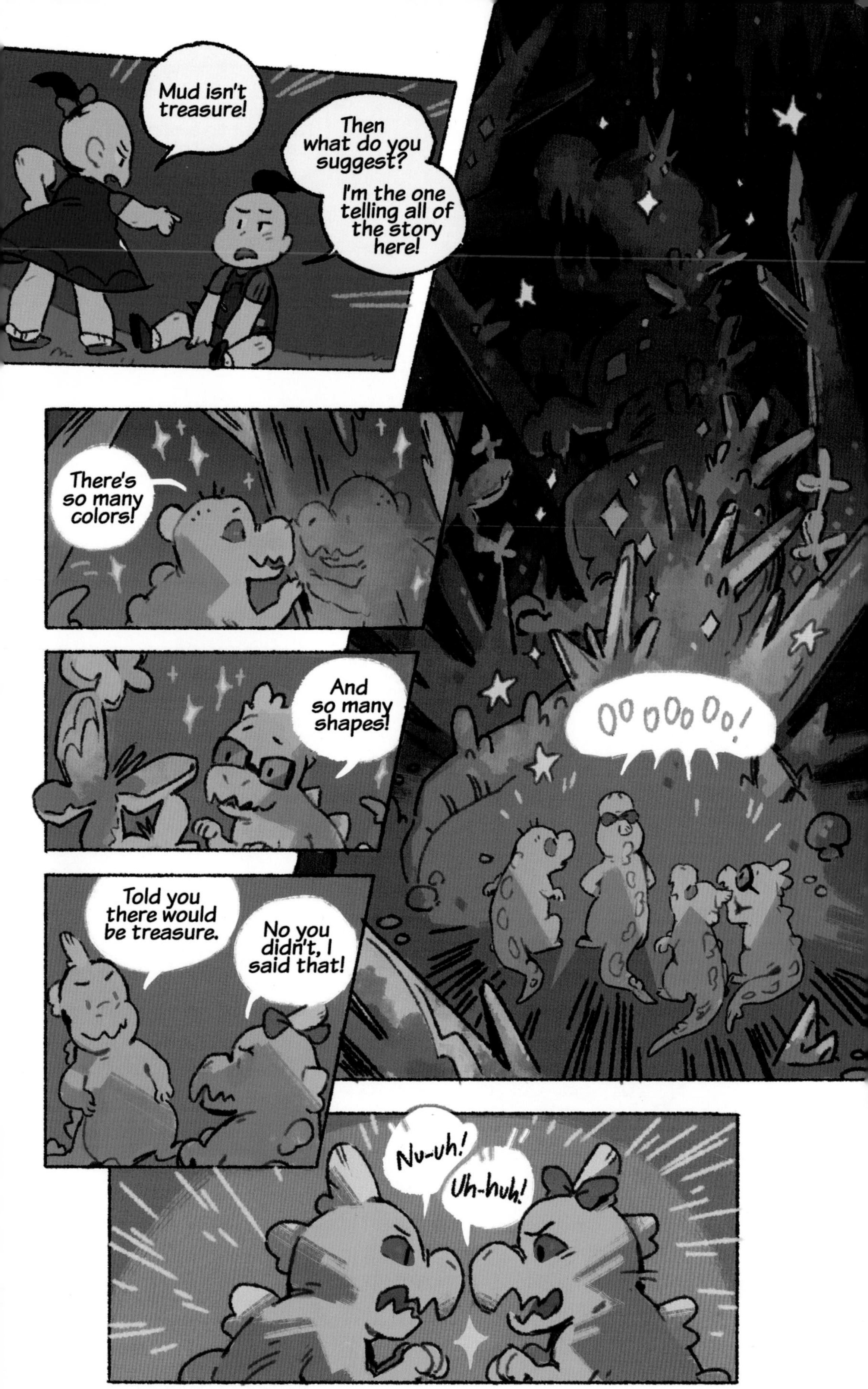
Mud isn't treasure!
Then what do you suggest?
I'm the one telling all of the story here!
There's so many colors!
And so many shapes!
Oo ooo oo!
Told you there would be treasure.
No you didn't, I said that!
Nu-uh!
Uh-huh!

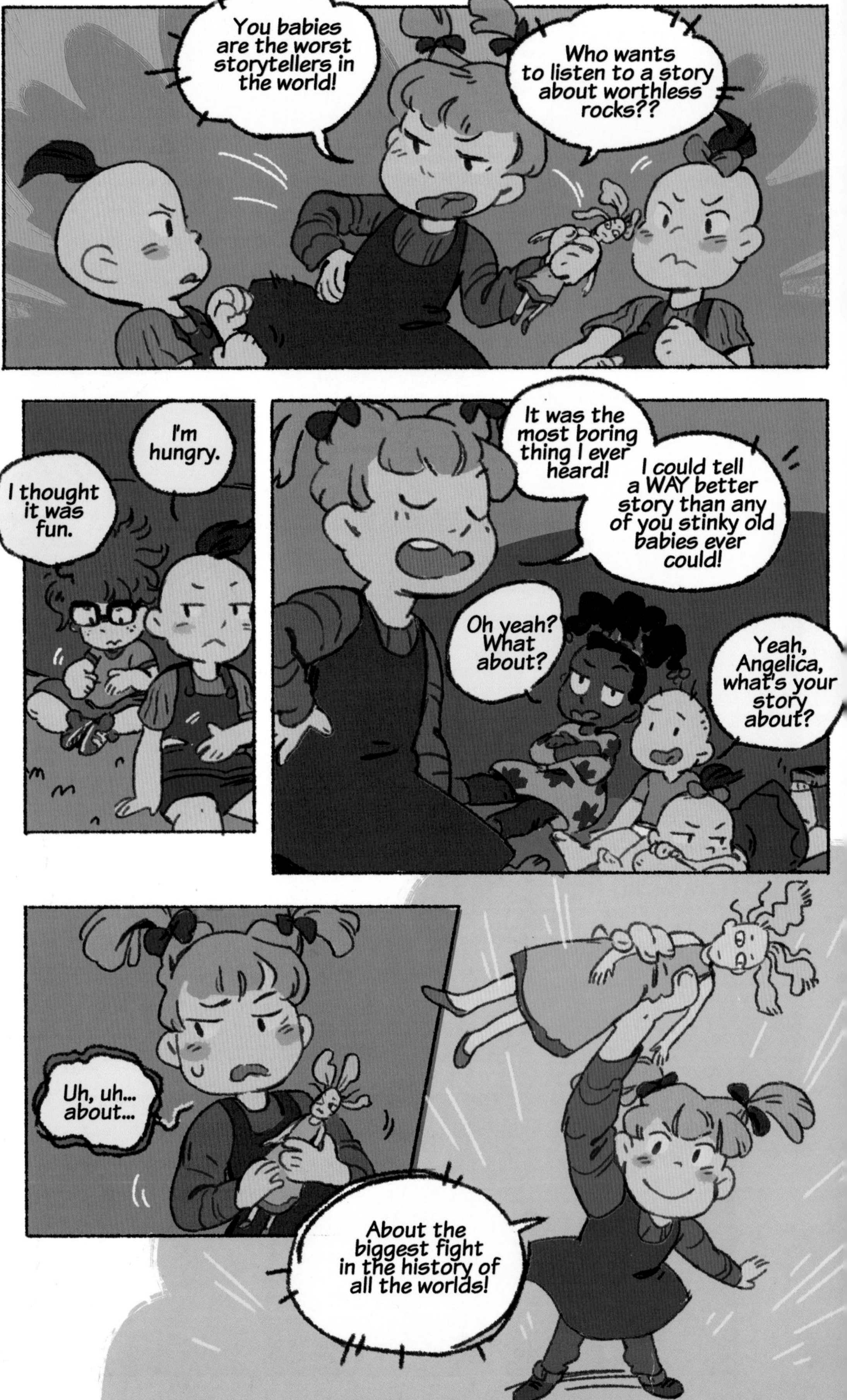

You babies are the worst storytellers in the world!
Who wants to listen to a story about worthless rocks??
I'm hungry.
I thought it was fun.
It was the most boring thing I ever heard!
I could tell a WAY better story than any of you stinky old babies ever could!
Oh yeah? What about?
Yeah, Angelica, what's your story about?
Uh, uh... about...
About the biggest fight in the history of all the worlds!

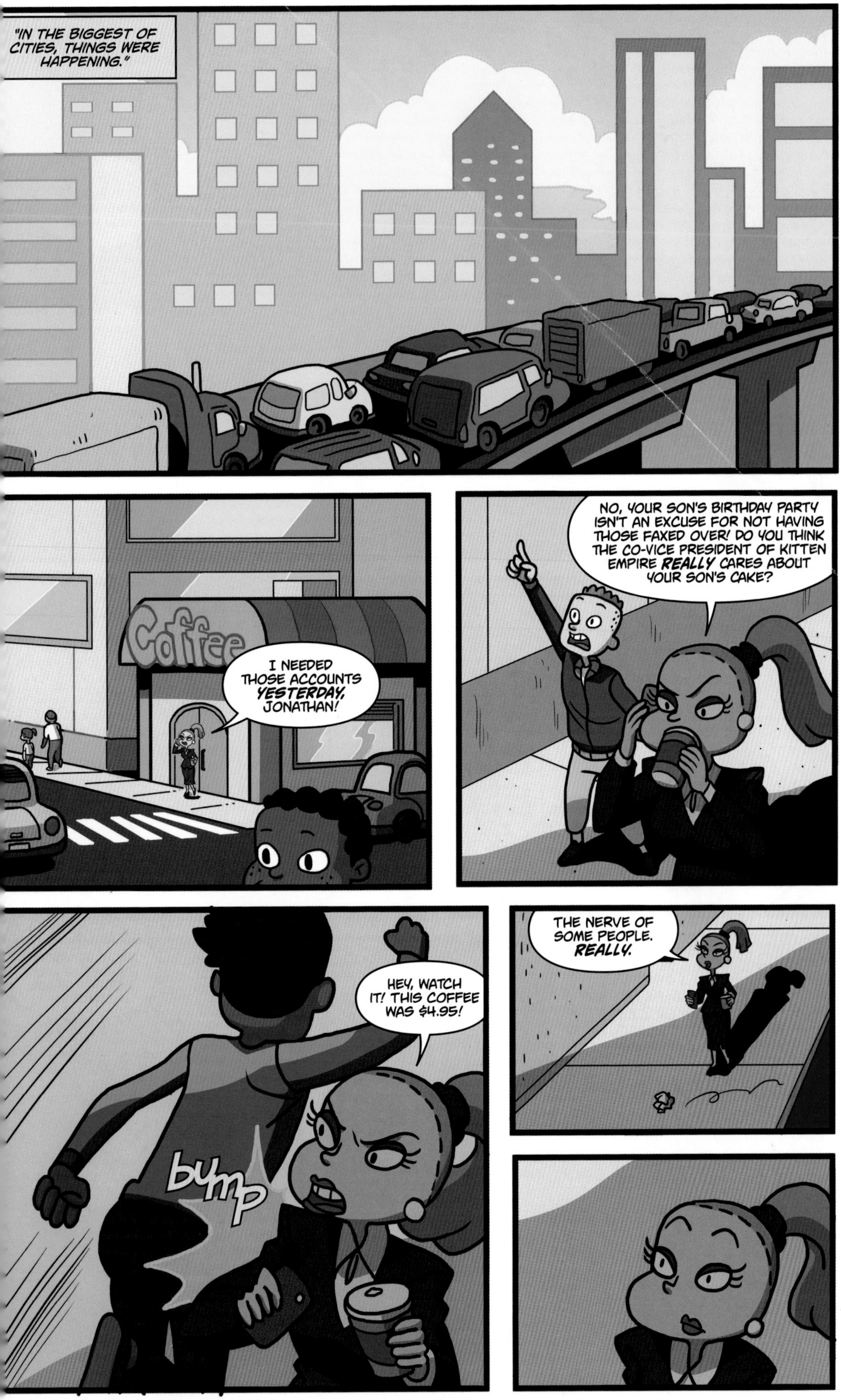
"IN THE BIGGEST OF CITIES, THINGS WERE HAPPENING."
Coffee
I NEEDED THOSE ACCOUNTS *YESTERDAY,* JONATHAN!
NO, YOUR SON'S BIRTHDAY PARTY ISN'T AN EXCUSE FOR NOT HAVING THOSE FAXED OVER! DO YOU THINK THE CO-VICE PRESIDENT OF KITTEN EMPIRE *REALLY* CARES ABOUT YOUR SON'S CAKE?
HEY, WATCH IT! THIS COFFEE WAS $4.95!
bump
THE NERVE OF SOME PEOPLE. *REALLY.*

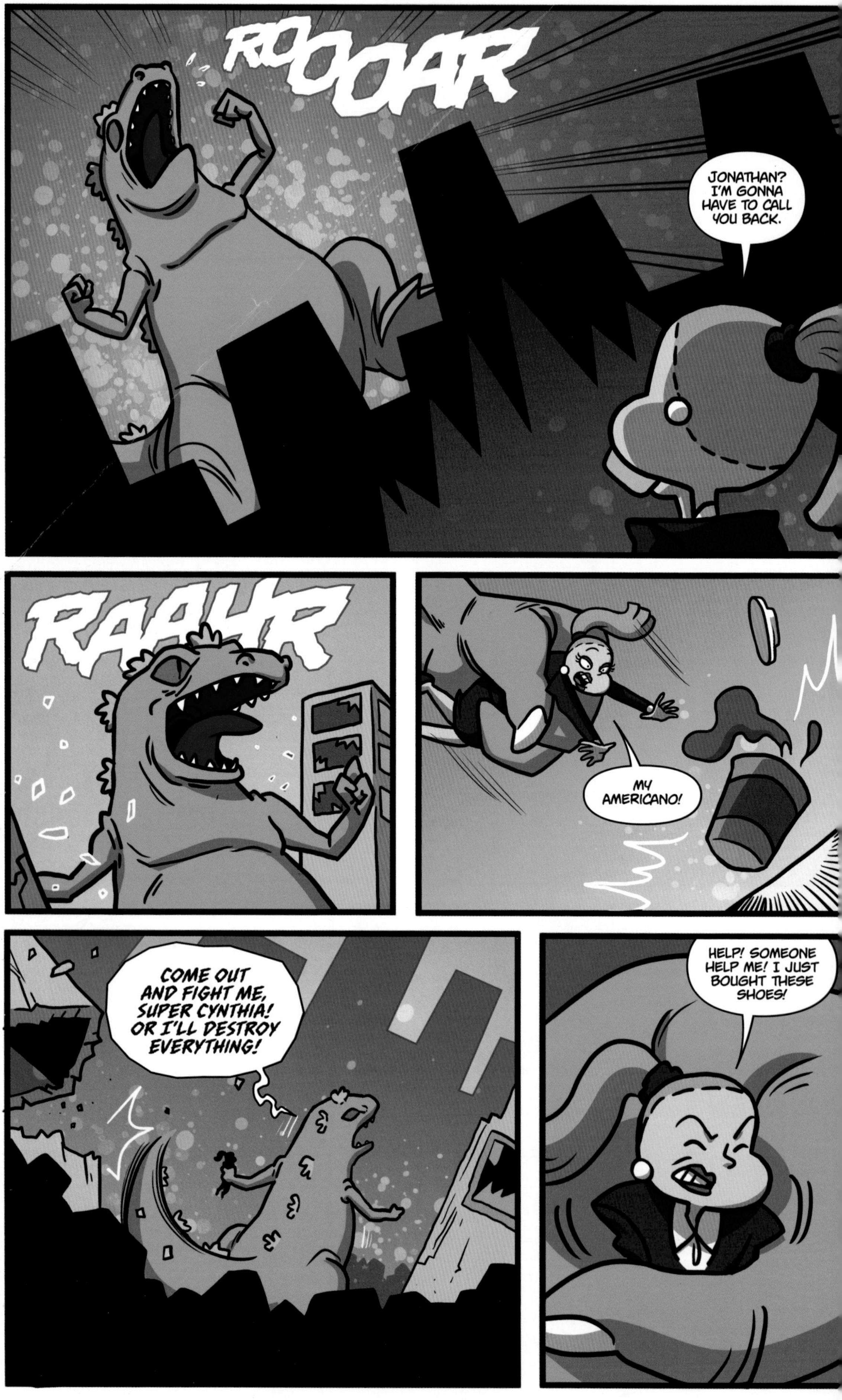
ROOOAR
JONATHAN? I'M GONNA HAVE TO CALL YOU BACK.
RAAHR
MY AMERICANO!
COME OUT AND FIGHT ME, SUPER CYNTHIA! OR I'LL DESTROY EVERYTHING!
HELP! SOMEONE HELP ME! I JUST BOUGHT THESE SHOES!

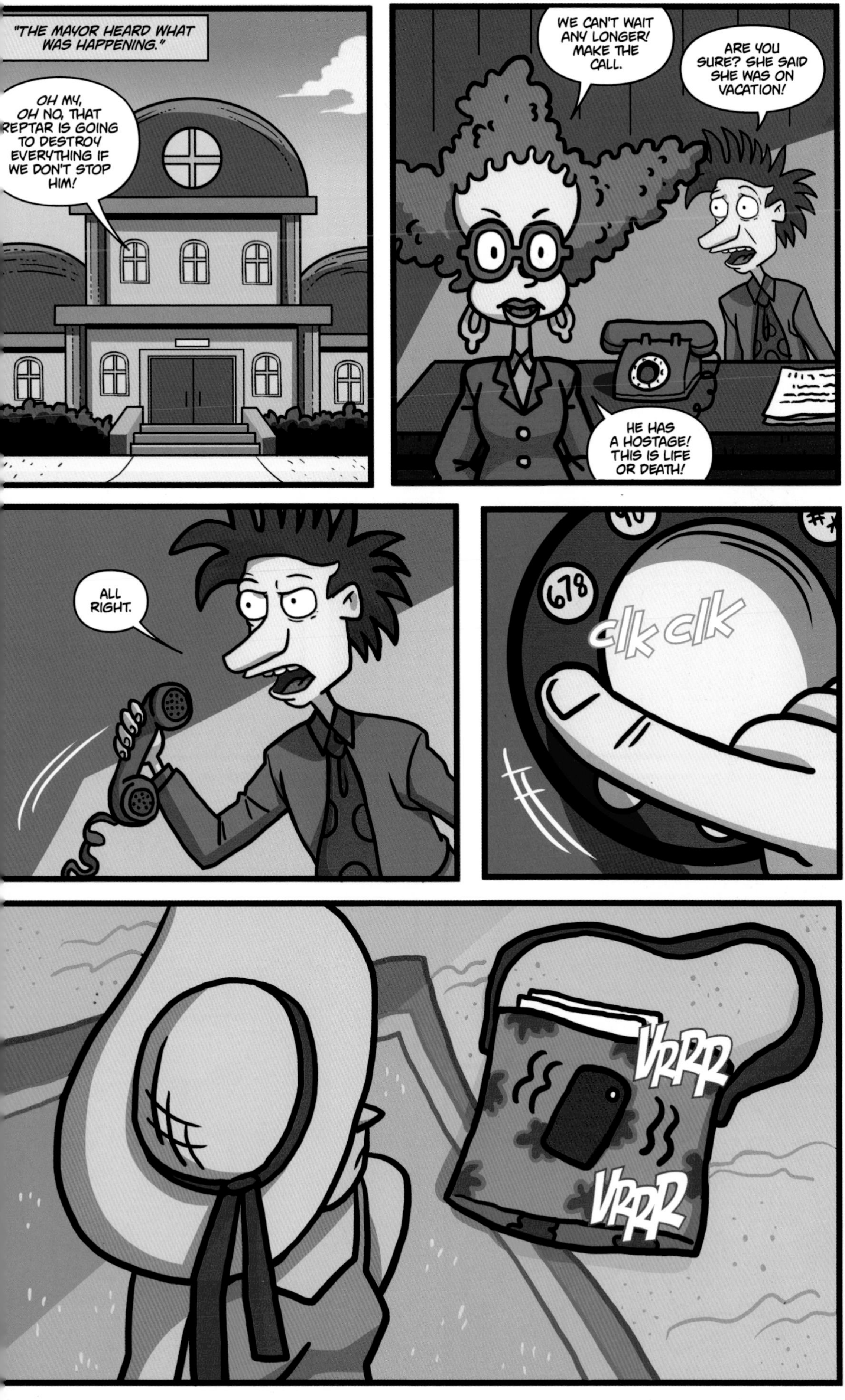

"THE MAYOR HEARD WHAT WAS HAPPENING."
OH MY, OH NO, THAT REPTAR IS GOING TO DESTROY EVERYTHING IF WE DON'T STOP HIM!
WE CAN'T WAIT ANY LONGER! MAKE THE CALL.
ARE YOU SURE? SHE SAID SHE WAS ON VACATION!
HE HAS A HOSTAGE! THIS IS LIFE OR DEATH!
ALL RIGHT.
678
clk clk
VRRRR
VRRRR

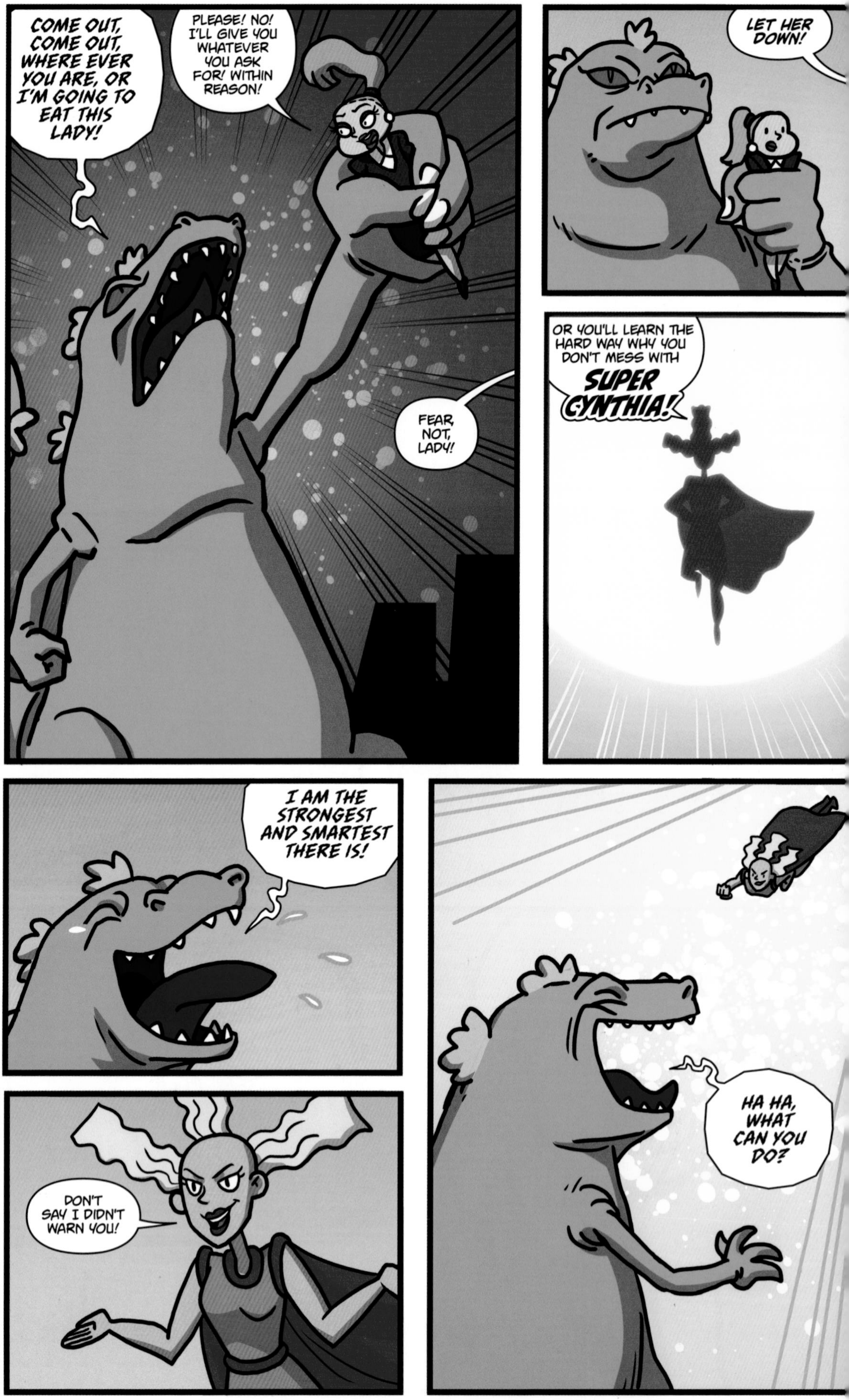
COME OUT, COME OUT, WHERE EVER YOU ARE, OR I'M GOING TO EAT THIS LADY!
PLEASE! NO! I'LL GIVE YOU WHATEVER YOU ASK FOR! WITHIN REASON!
FEAR, NOT, LADY!
LET HER DOWN!
OR YOU'LL LEARN THE HARD WAY WHY YOU DON'T MESS WITH
SUPER CYNTHIA!
I AM THE STRONGEST AND SMARTEST THERE IS!
HA HA, WHAT CAN YOU DO?
DON'T SAY I DIDN'T WARN YOU!

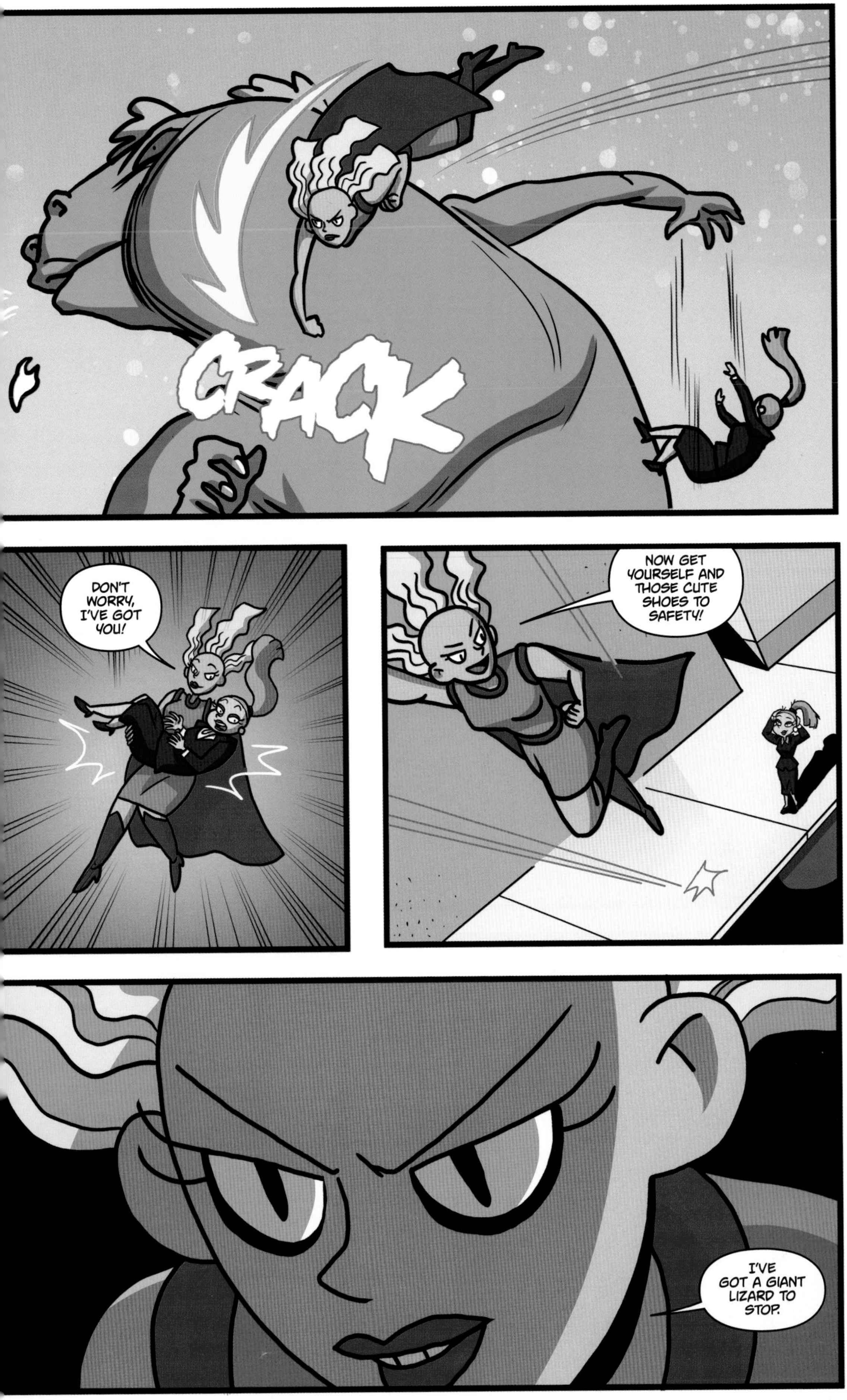
CRACK
DON'T WORRY, I'VE GOT YOU!
NOW GET YOURSELF AND THOSE CUTE SHOES TO SAFETY!
I'VE GOT A GIANT LIZARD TO STOP.

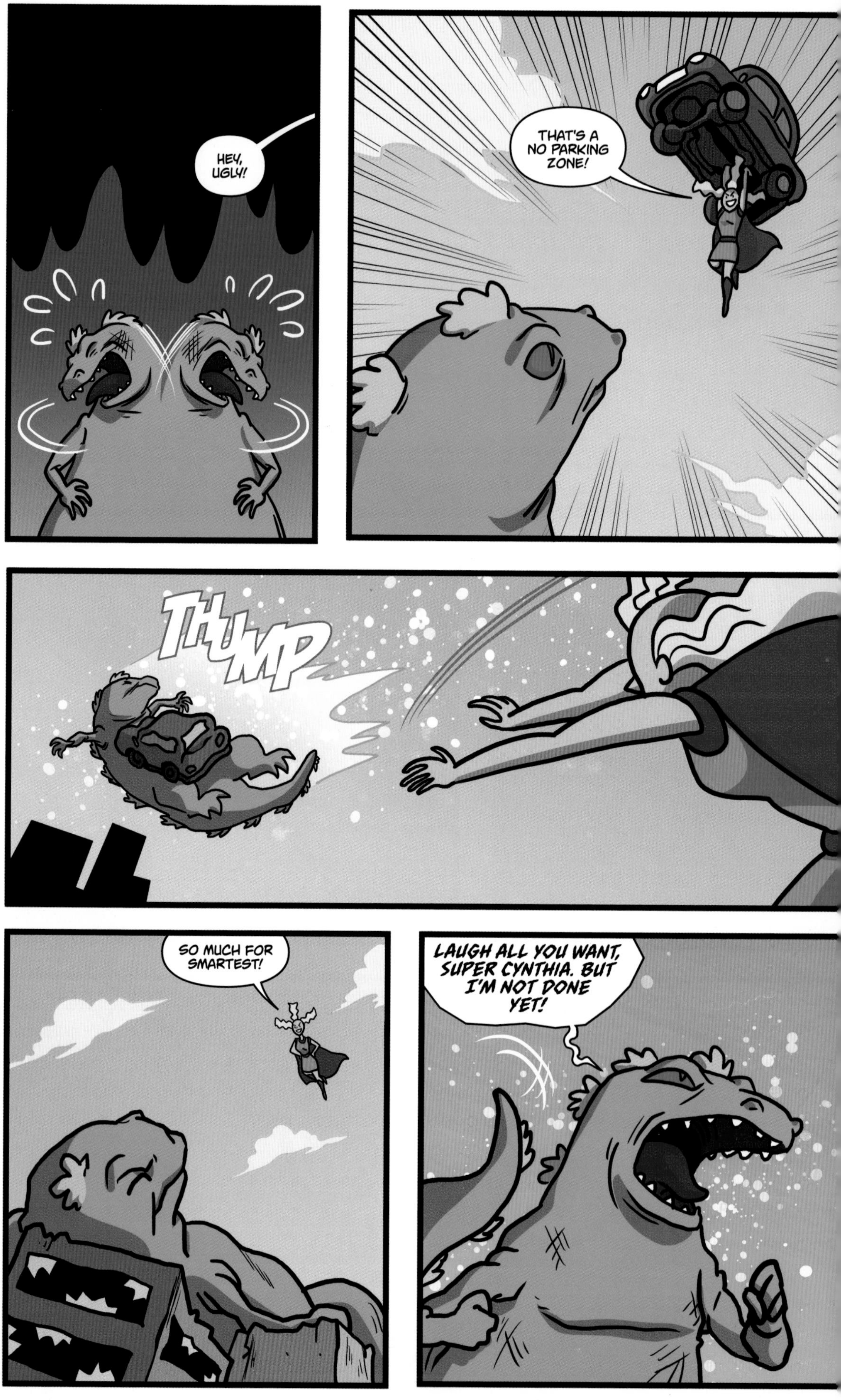
HEY, UGLY!
THAT'S A NO PARKING ZONE!
THUMP
SO MUCH FOR SMARTEST!
LAUGH ALL YOU WANT, SUPER CYNTHIA. BUT I'M NOT DONE YET!

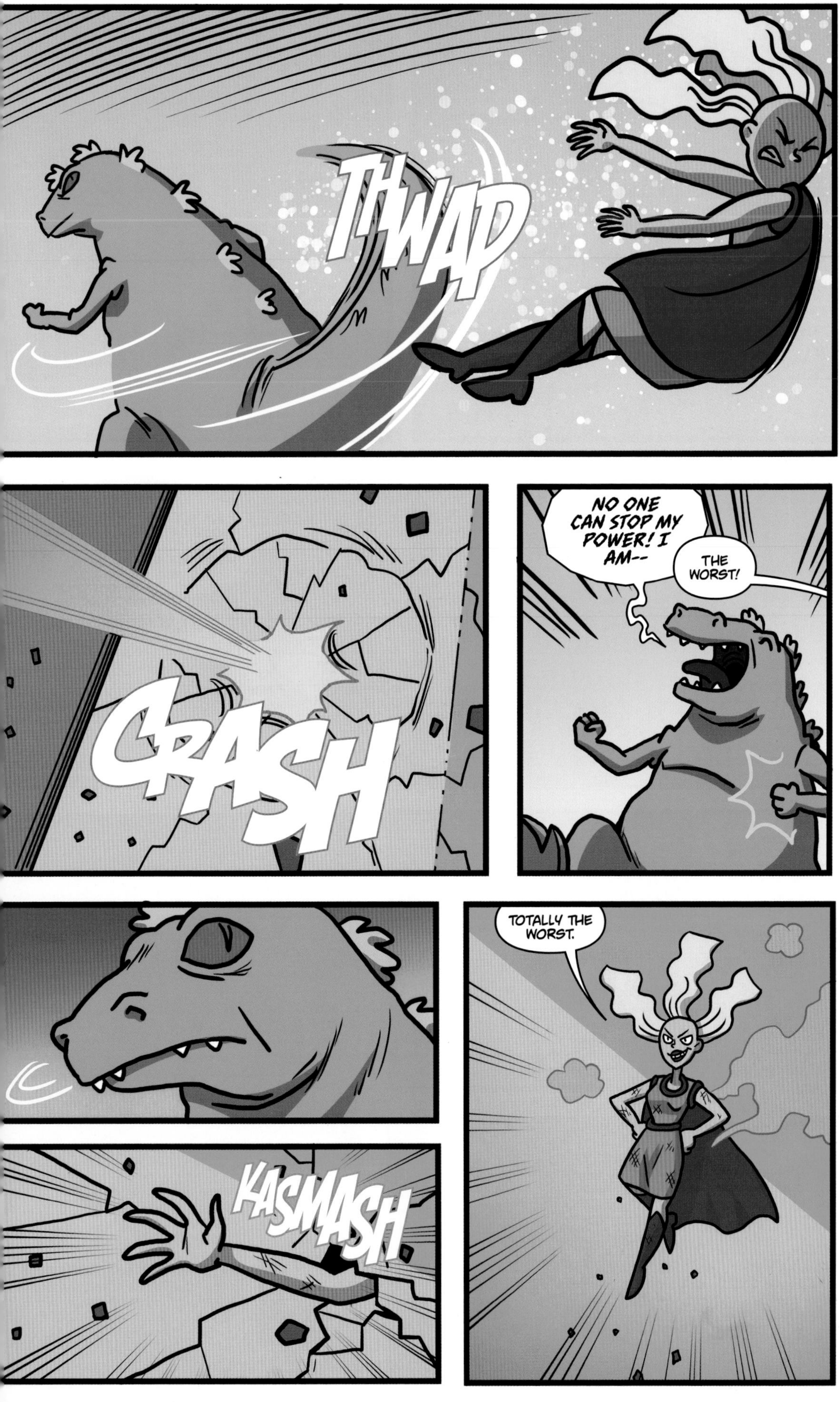

THWAP
CRASH
NO ONE CAN STOP MY POWER! I AM--
THE WORST!
KASMASH
TOTALLY THE WORST.

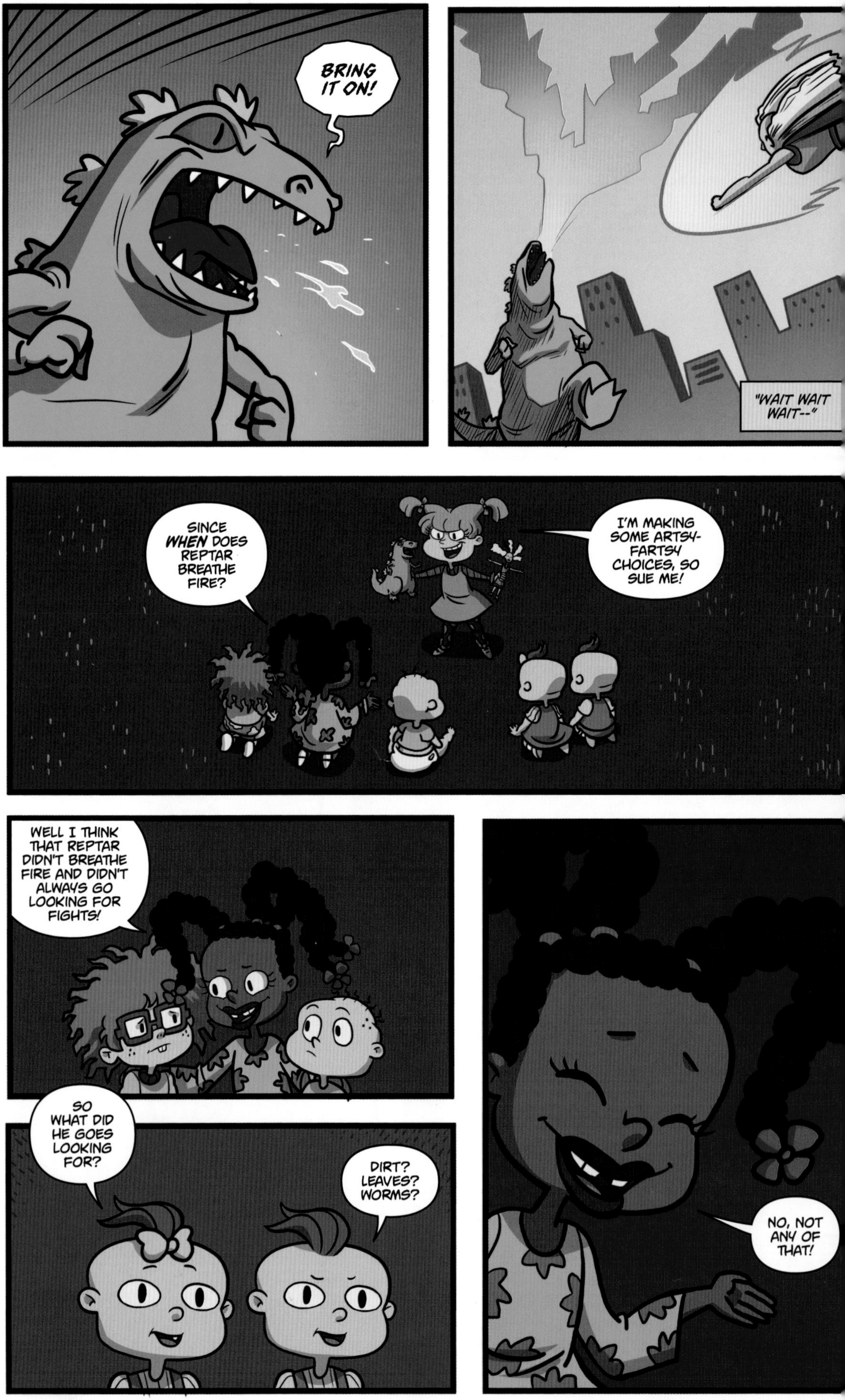

BRING IT ON!
"WAIT WAIT WAIT--"
SINCE WHEN DOES REPTAR BREATHE FIRE?
I'M MAKING SOME ARTSY-FARTSY CHOICES, SO SUE ME!
WELL I THINK THAT REPTAR DIDN'T BREATHE FIRE AND DIDN'T ALWAYS GO LOOKING FOR FIGHTS!
SO WHAT DID HE GOES LOOKING FOR?
DIRT? LEAVES? WORMS?
NO, NOT ANY OF THAT!

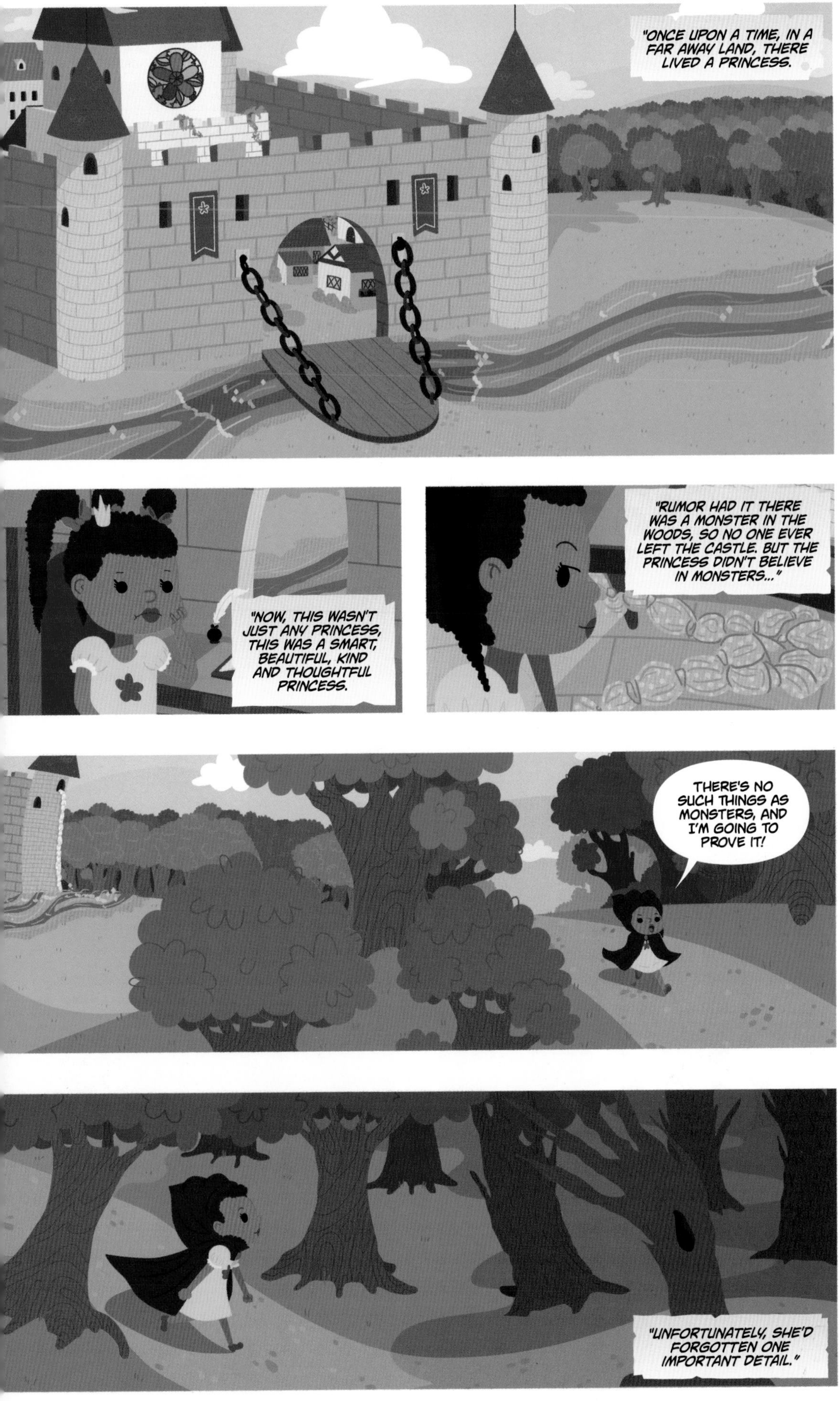
"ONCE UPON A TIME, IN A FAR AWAY LAND, THERE LIVED A PRINCESS.
"NOW, THIS WASN'T JUST ANY PRINCESS, THIS WAS A SMART, BEAUTIFUL, KIND AND THOUGHTFUL PRINCESS.
"RUMOR HAD IT THERE WAS A MONSTER IN THE WOODS, SO NO ONE EVER LEFT THE CASTLE. BUT THE PRINCESS DIDN'T BELIEVE IN MONSTERS..."
THERE'S NO SUCH THINGS AS MONSTERS, AND I'M GOING TO PROVE IT!
"UNFORTUNATELY, SHE'D FORGOTTEN ONE IMPORTANT DETAIL."

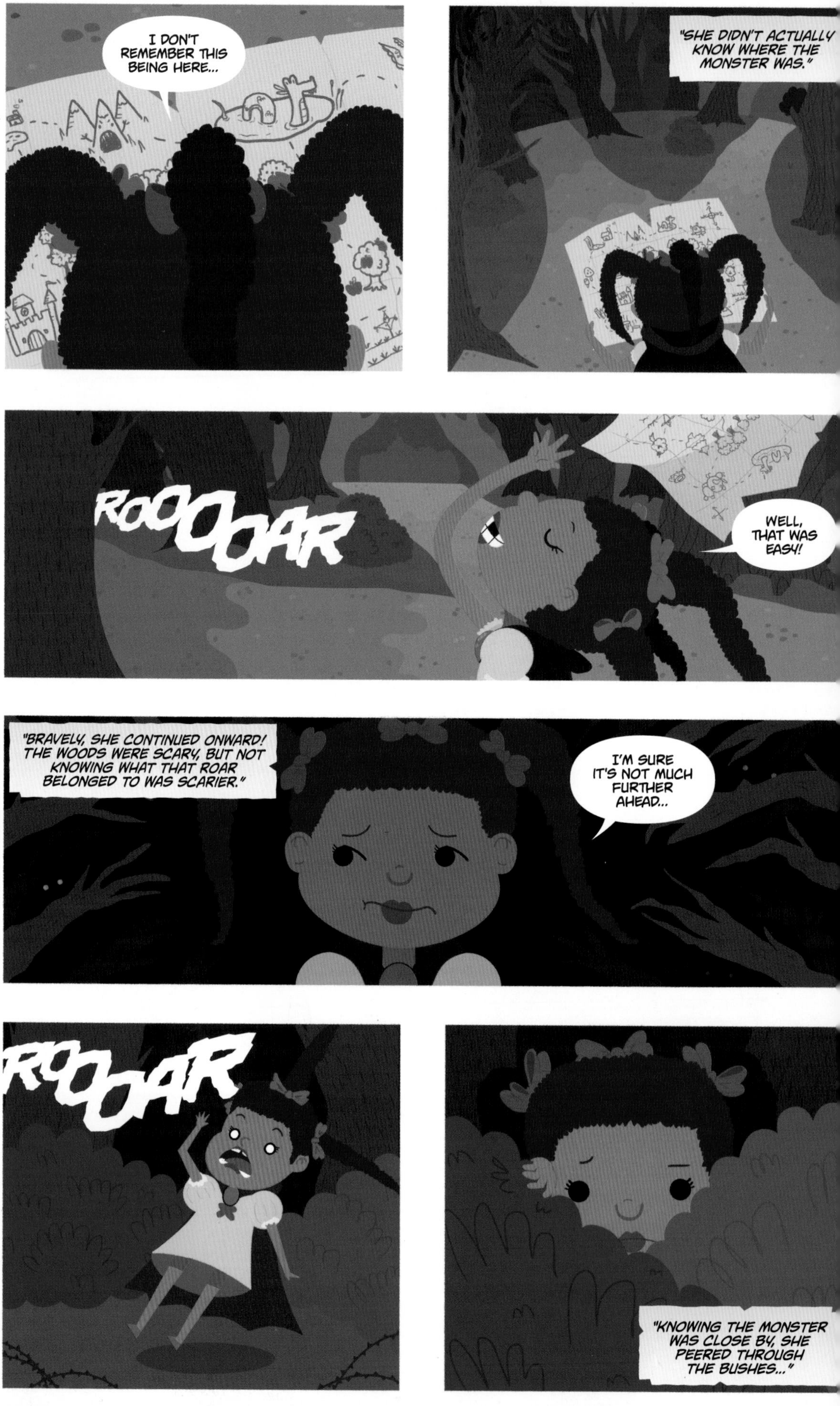

I DON'T REMEMBER THIS BEING HERE...
"SHE DIDN'T ACTUALLY KNOW WHERE THE MONSTER WAS."
ROOOOAR
WELL, THAT WAS EASY!
"BRAVELY, SHE CONTINUED ONWARD! THE WOODS WERE SCARY, BUT NOT KNOWING WHAT THAT ROAR BELONGED TO WAS SCARIER."
I'M SURE IT'S NOT MUCH FURTHER AHEAD...
ROOOAR
"KNOWING THE MONSTER WAS CLOSE BY, SHE PEERED THROUGH THE BUSHES..."

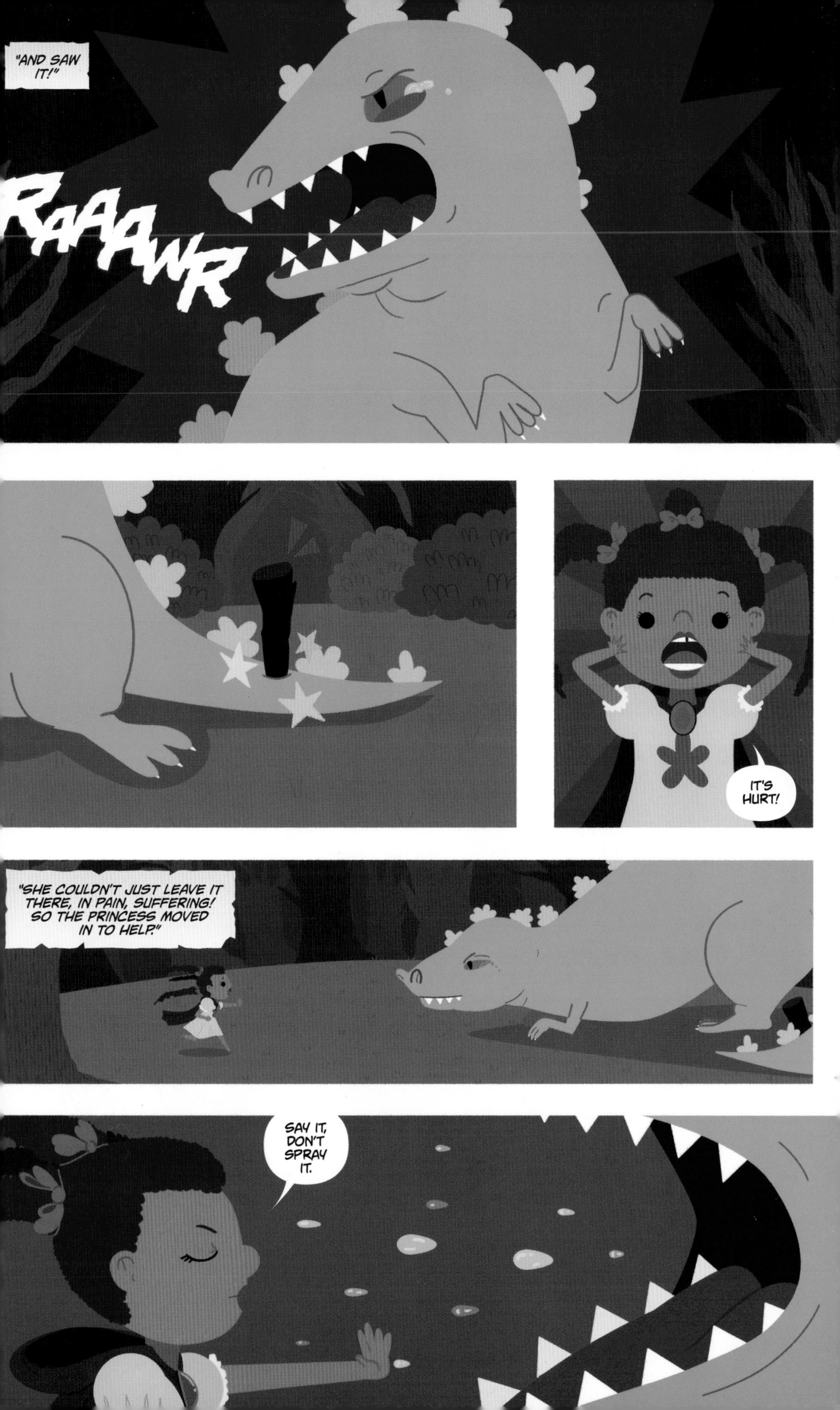
"AND SAW IT!"
RAAAWR
IT'S HURT!
"SHE COULDN'T JUST LEAVE IT THERE, IN PAIN, SUFFERING! SO THE PRINCESS MOVED IN TO HELP."
SAY IT, DON'T SPRAY IT.

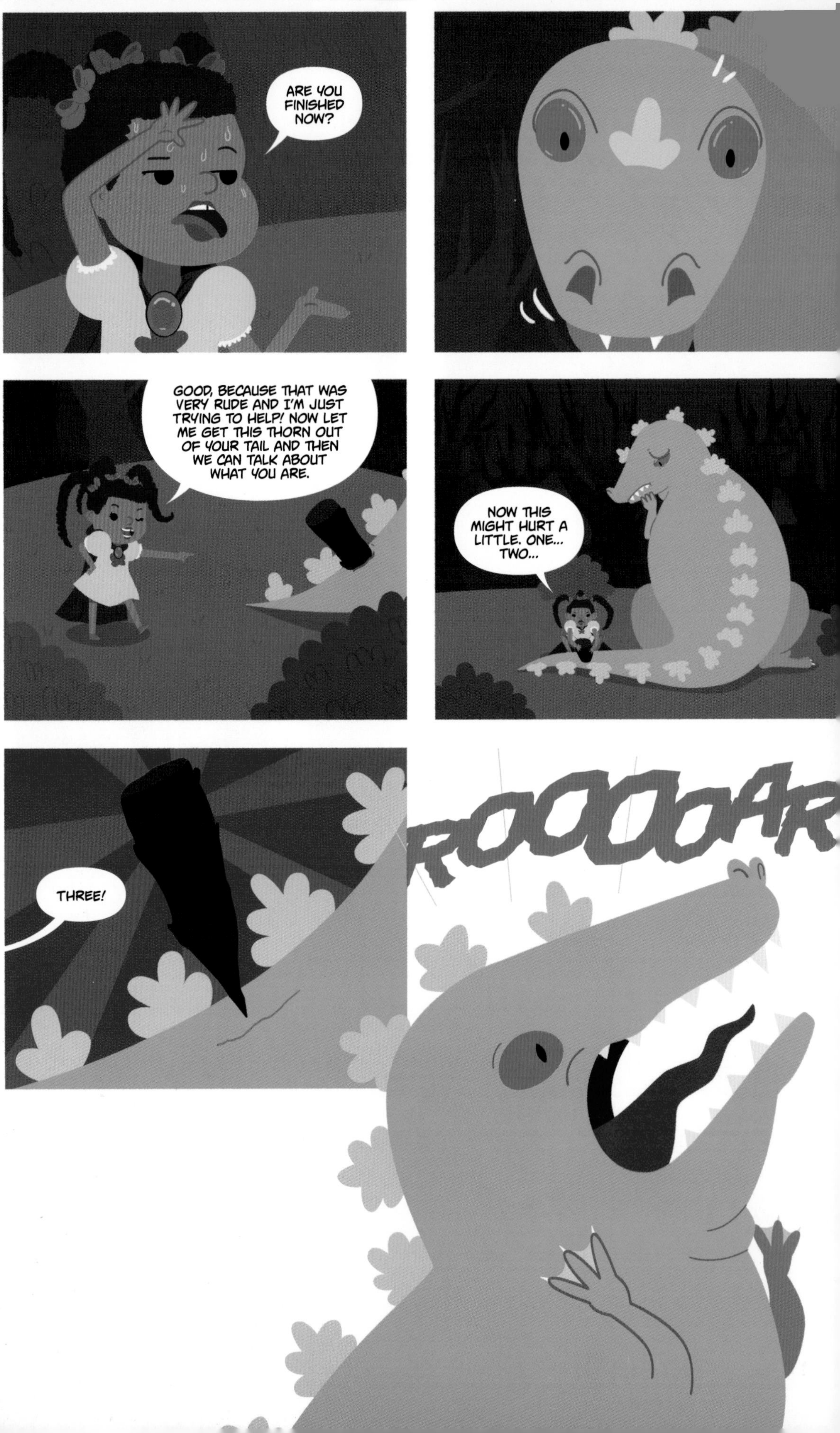
ARE YOU FINISHED NOW?
GOOD, BECAUSE THAT WAS VERY RUDE AND I'M JUST TRYING TO HELP! NOW LET ME GET THIS THORN OUT OF YOUR TAIL AND THEN WE CAN TALK ABOUT WHAT YOU ARE.
NOW THIS MIGHT HURT A LITTLE. ONE... TWO...
THREE!
ROOOOAR

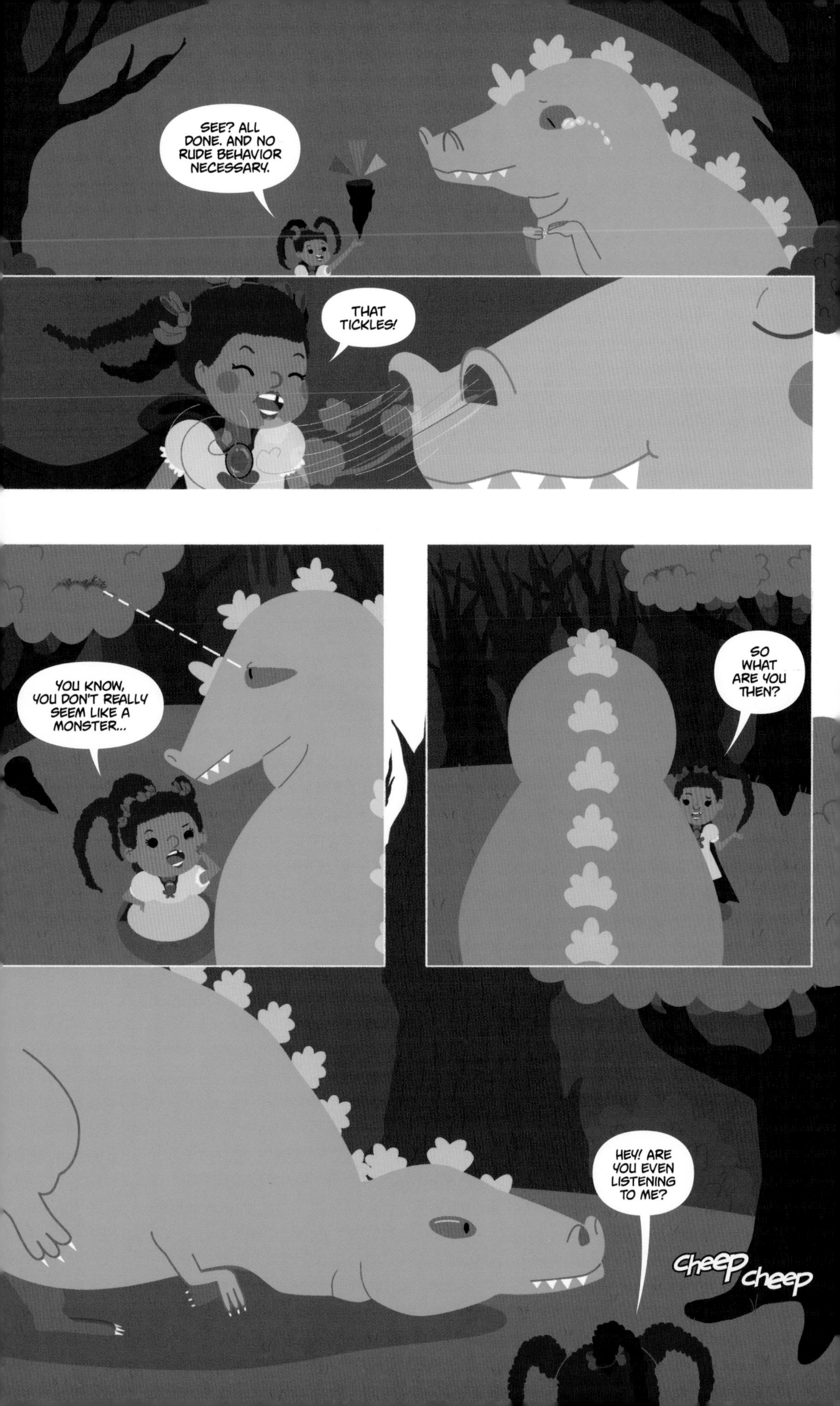

SEE? ALL DONE. AND NO RUDE BEHAVIOR NECESSARY.
THAT TICKLES!
YOU KNOW, YOU DON'T REALLY SEEM LIKE A MONSTER...
SO WHAT ARE YOU THEN?
HEY! ARE YOU EVEN LISTENING TO ME?
CHEEP CHEEP

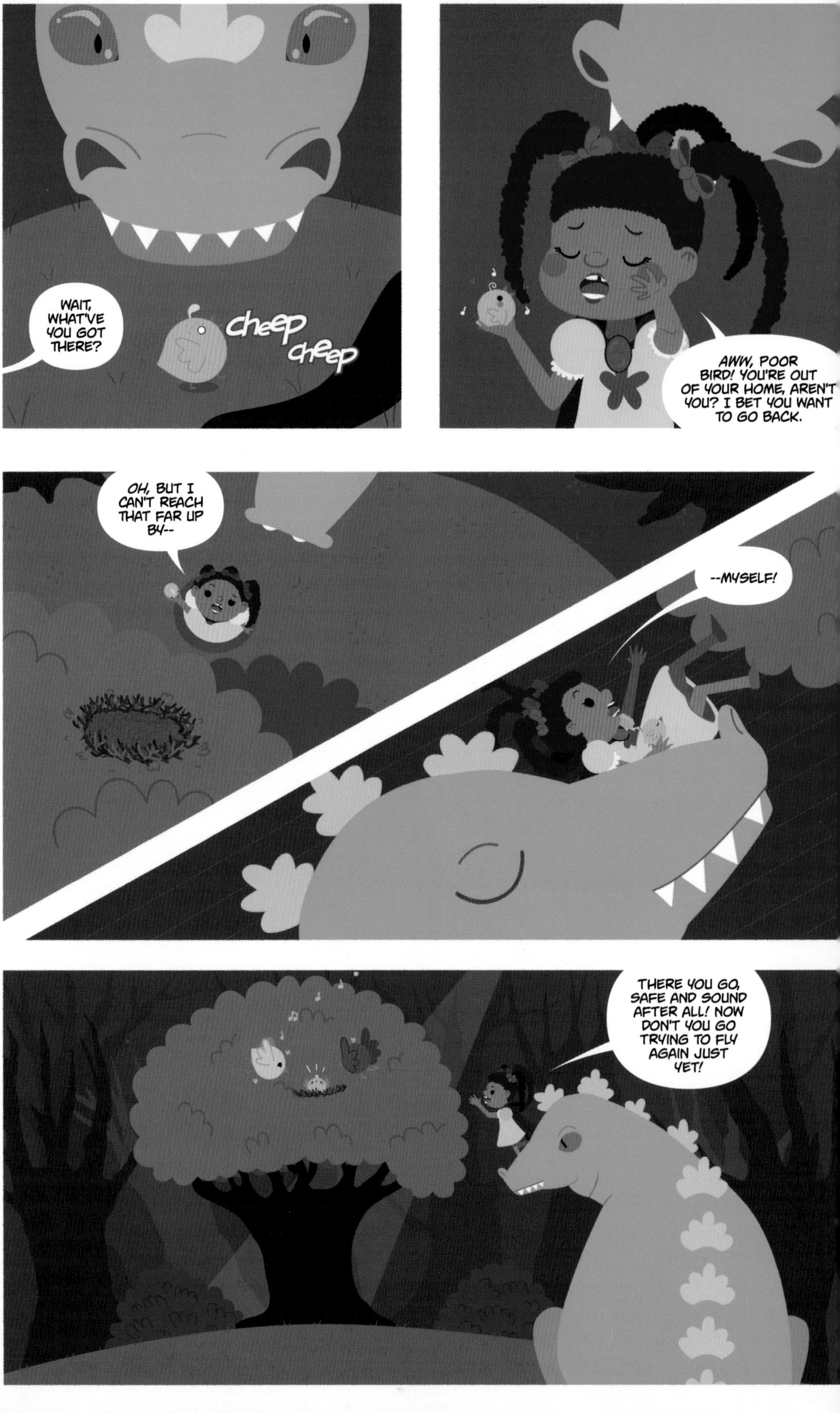
WAIT, WHAT'VE YOU GOT THERE?
cheep cheep
AWW, POOR BIRD! YOU'RE OUT OF YOUR HOME, AREN'T YOU? I BET YOU WANT TO GO BACK.
OH, BUT I CAN'T REACH THAT FAR UP BY--
--MYSELF!
THERE YOU GO, SAFE AND SOUND AFTER ALL! NOW DON'T YOU GO TRYING TO FLY AGAIN JUST YET!

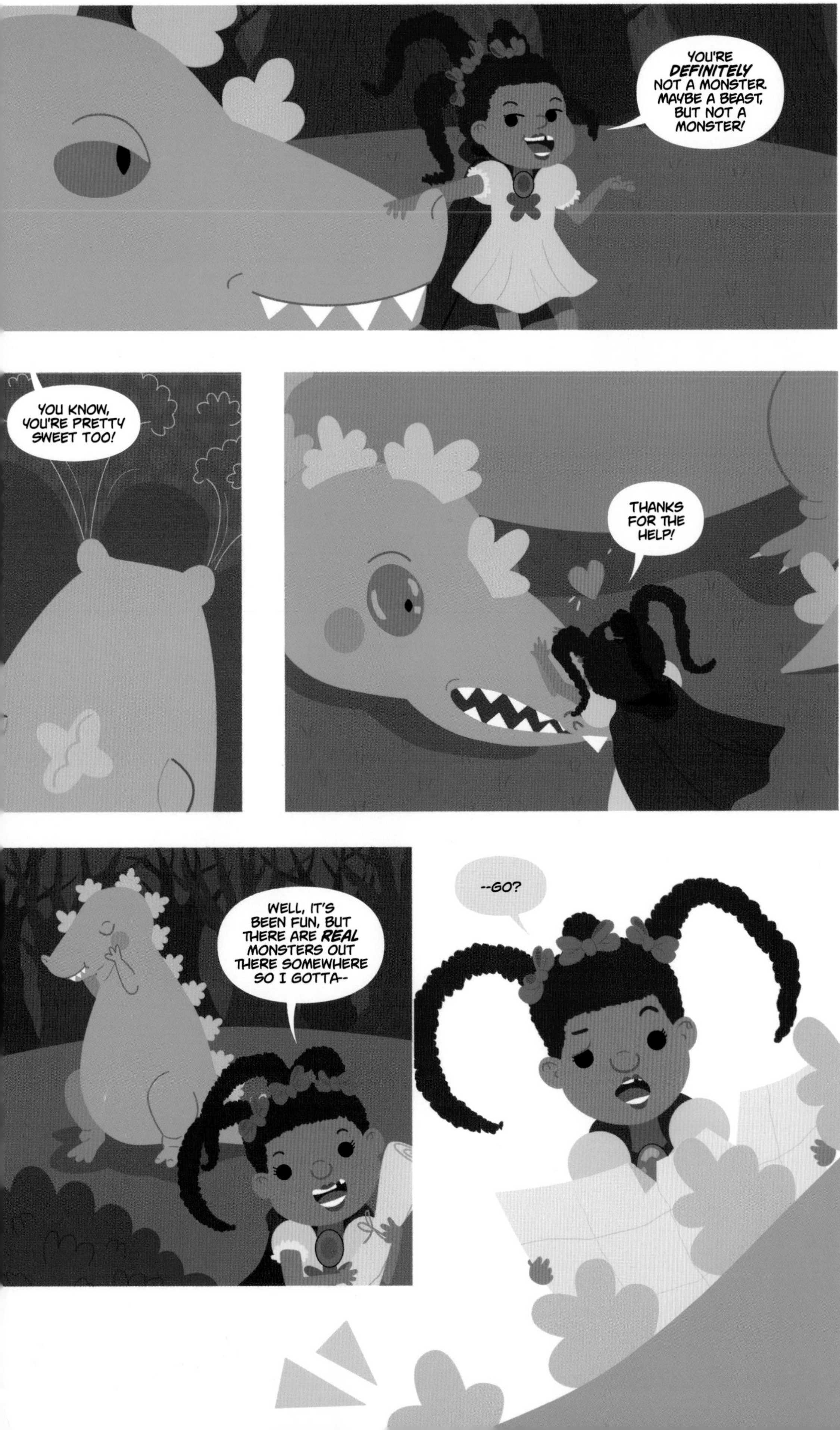
YOU'RE *DEFINITELY* NOT A MONSTER. MAYBE A BEAST, BUT NOT A MONSTER!
YOU KNOW, YOU'RE PRETTY SWEET TOO!
THANKS FOR THE HELP!
WELL, IT'S BEEN FUN, BUT THERE ARE *REAL* MONSTERS OUT THERE SOMEWHERE SO I GOTTA--
--GO?

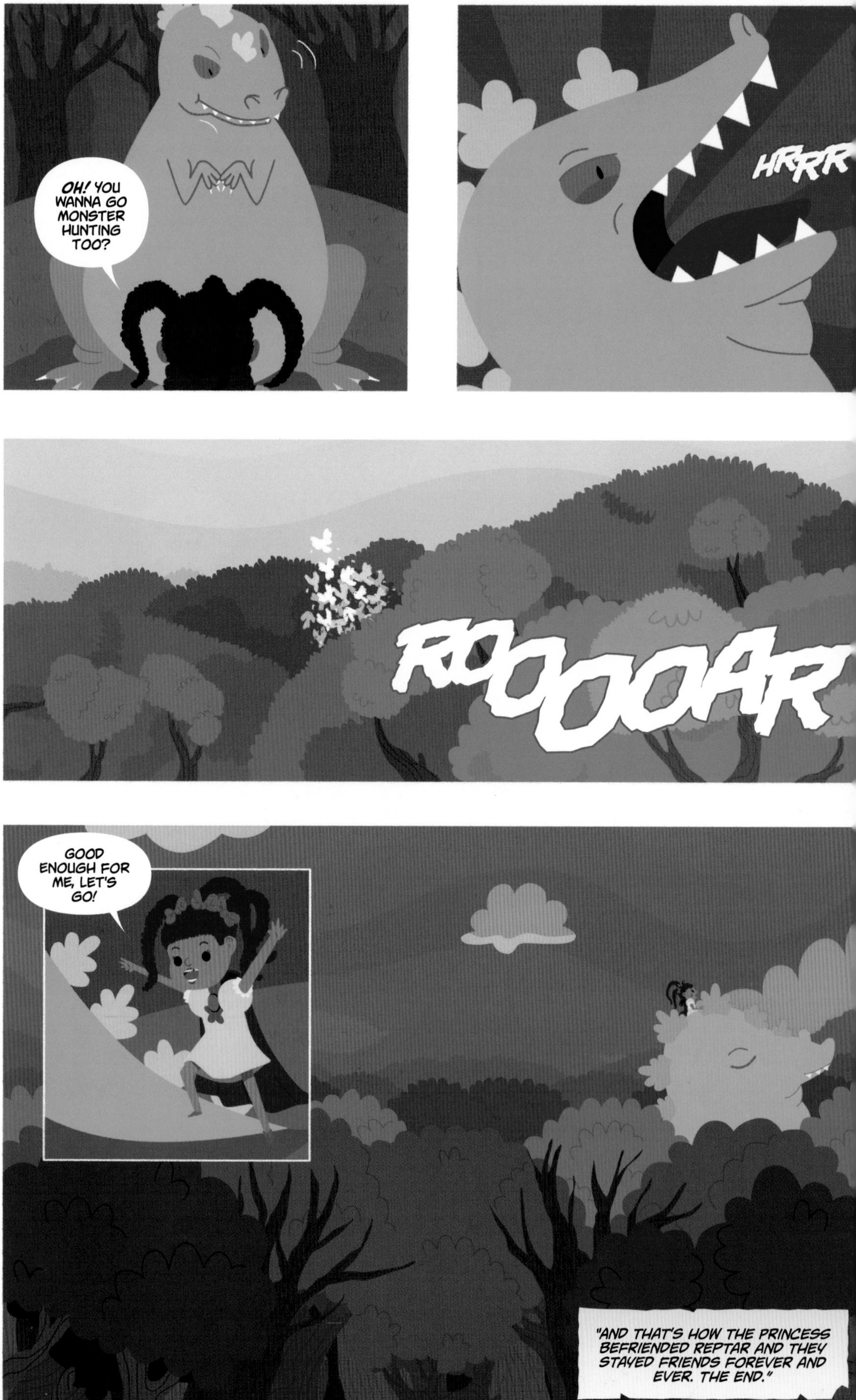
OH! YOU WANNA GO MONSTER HUNTING TOO?
HRRR
ROOOOAR
GOOD ENOUGH FOR ME, LET'S GO!
"AND THAT'S HOW THE PRINCESS BEFRIENDED REPTAR AND THEY STAYED FRIENDS FOREVER AND EVER. THE END."

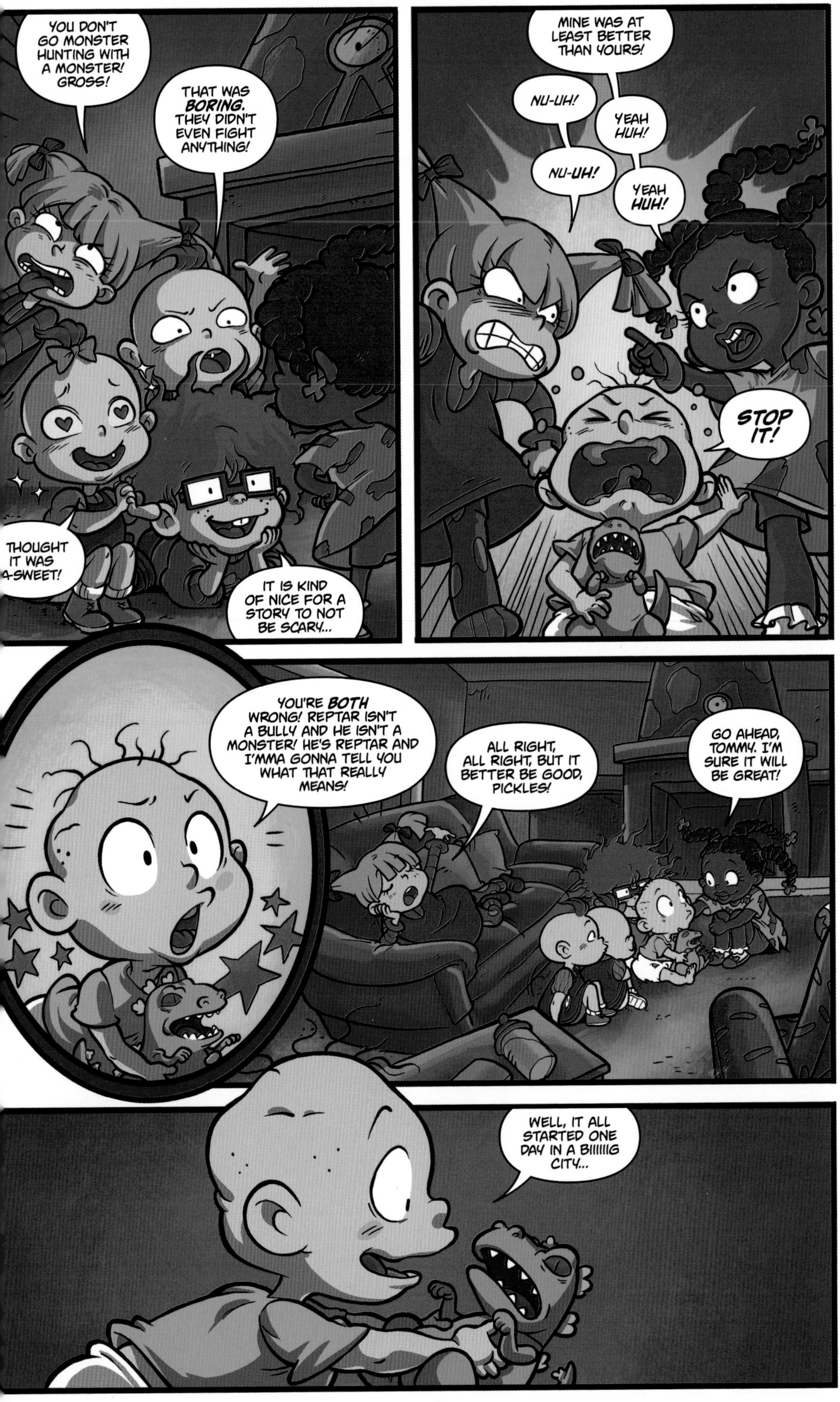
YOU DON'T GO MONSTER HUNTING WITH A MONSTER! GROSS!
THAT WAS **BORING**. THEY DIDN'T EVEN FIGHT ANYTHING!
THOUGHT IT WAS A-SWEET!
IT IS KIND OF NICE FOR A STORY TO NOT BE SCARY...
MINE WAS AT LEAST BETTER THAN YOURS!
NU-UH!
YEAH HUH!
NU-**UH!**
YEAH **HUH!**
STOP IT!
YOU'RE **BOTH** WRONG! REPTAR ISN'T A BULLY AND HE ISN'T A MONSTER! HE'S REPTAR AND I'MMA GONNA TELL YOU WHAT THAT REALLY MEANS!
ALL RIGHT, ALL RIGHT, BUT IT BETTER BE GOOD, PICKLES!
GO AHEAD, TOMMY. I'M SURE IT WILL BE GREAT!
WELL, IT ALL STARTED ONE DAY IN A BIIIIIIG CITY...

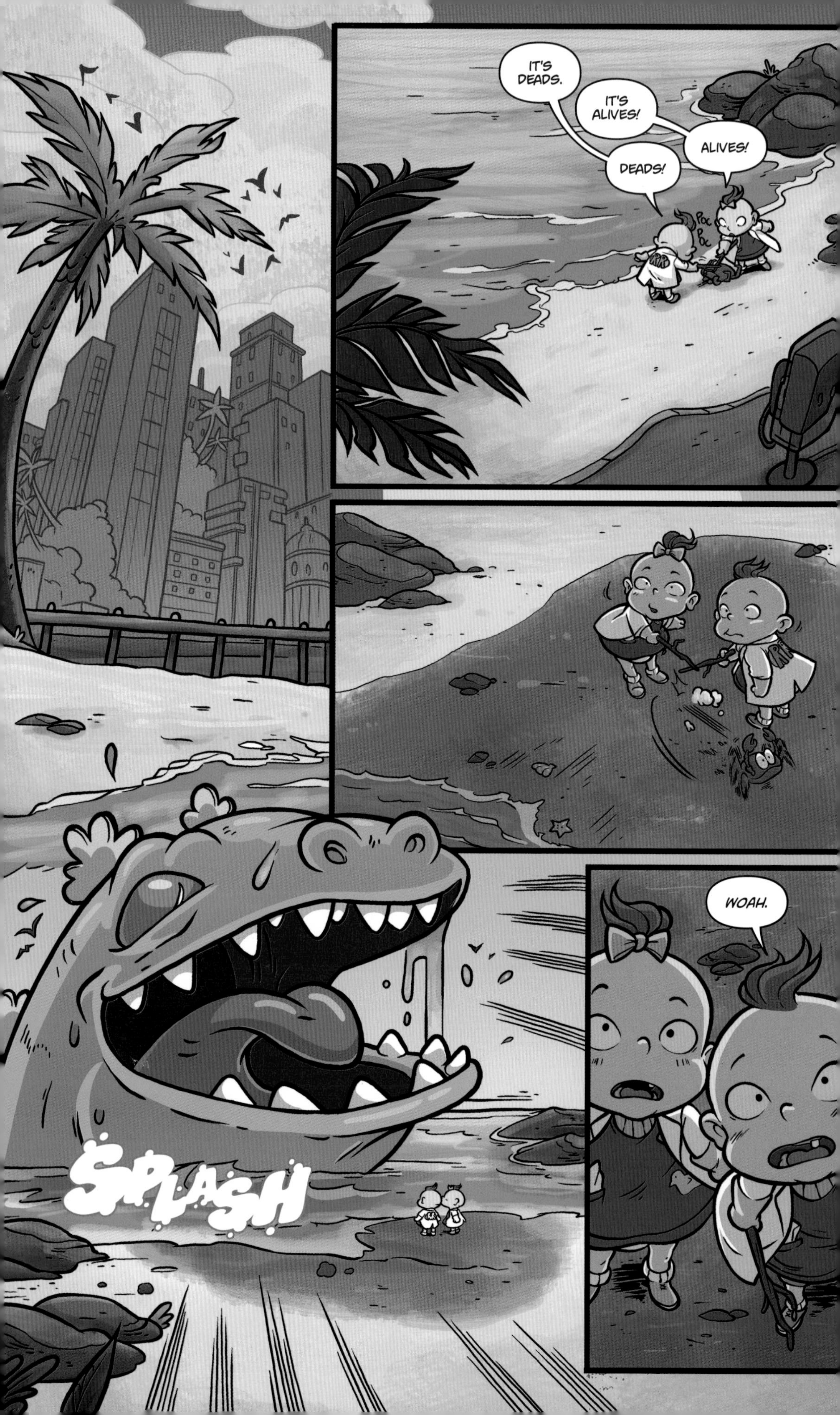
IT'S DEADS.
IT'S ALIVES!
DEADS!
ALIVES!
POC POC
SPLASH
WOAH.

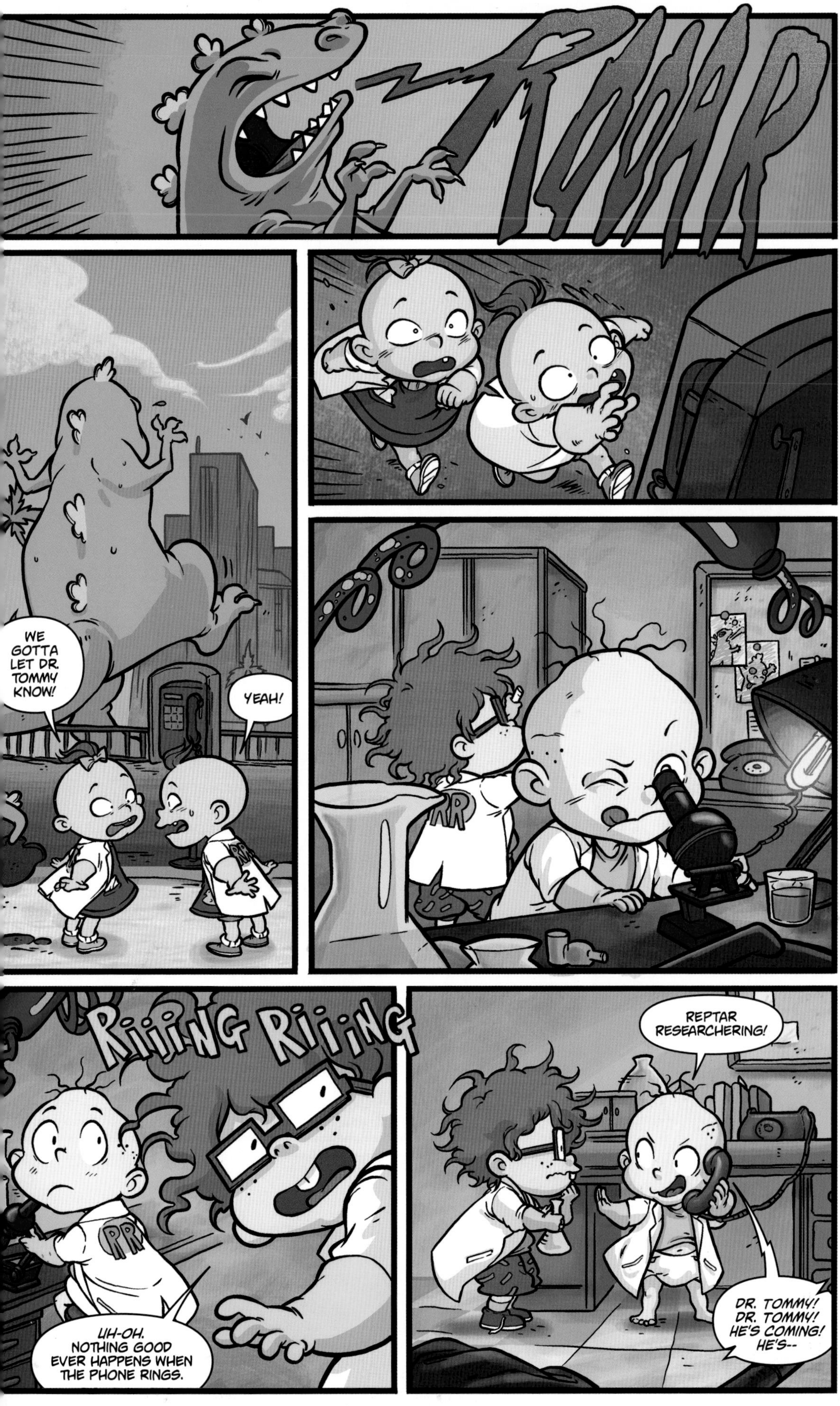

ROOAR
WE GOTTA LET DR. TOMMY KNOW!
YEAH!
RIIING RIIING
UH-OH. NOTHING GOOD EVER HAPPENS WHEN THE PHONE RINGS.
REPTAR RESEARCHERING!
DR. TOMMY! DR. TOMMY! HE'S COMING! HE'S--

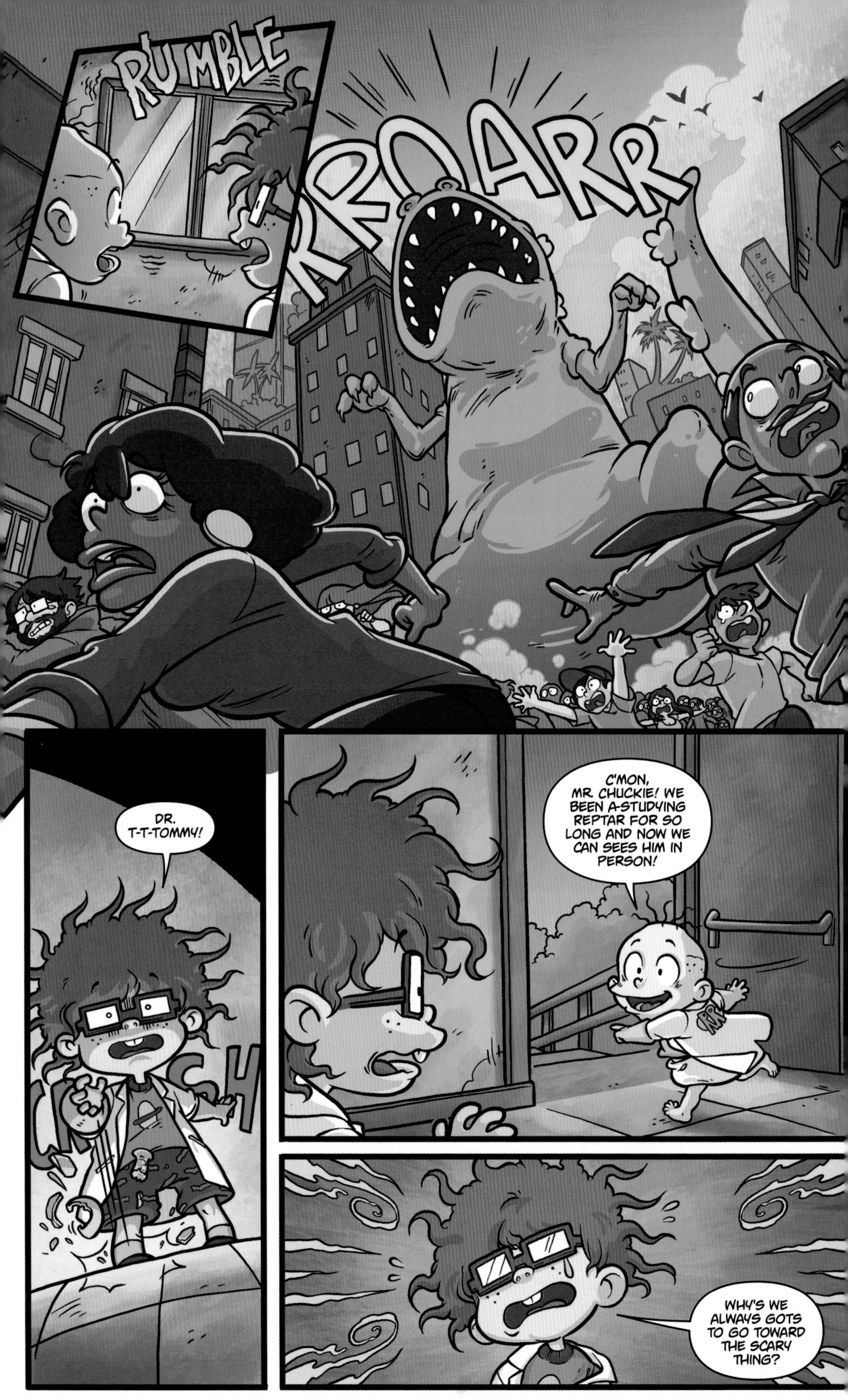
RUMBLE
RROARR
DR. T-T-TOMMY!
C'MON, MR. CHUCKIE! WE BEEN A-STUDYING REPTAR FOR SO LONG AND NOW WE CAN SEES HIM IN PERSON!
WHY'S WE ALWAYS GOTS TO GO TOWARD THE SCARY THING?

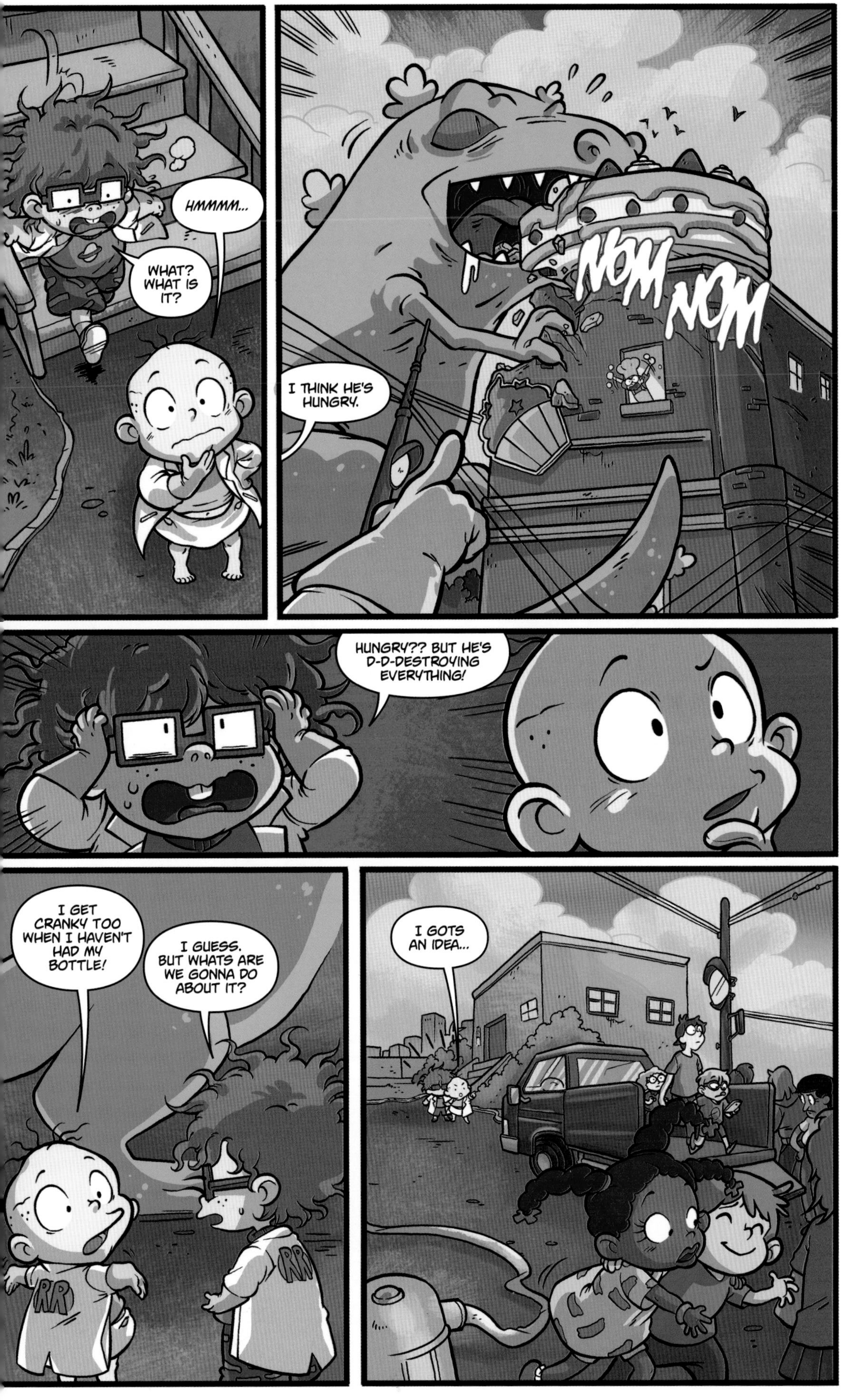
HMMMM...
WHAT? WHAT IS IT?
I THINK HE'S HUNGRY.
NOM NOM
HUNGRY?? BUT HE'S D-D-DESTROYING EVERYTHING!
I GET CRANKY TOO WHEN I HAVEN'T HAD MY BOTTLE!
I GUESS. BUT WHATS ARE WE GONNA DO ABOUT IT?
I GOTS AN IDEA...

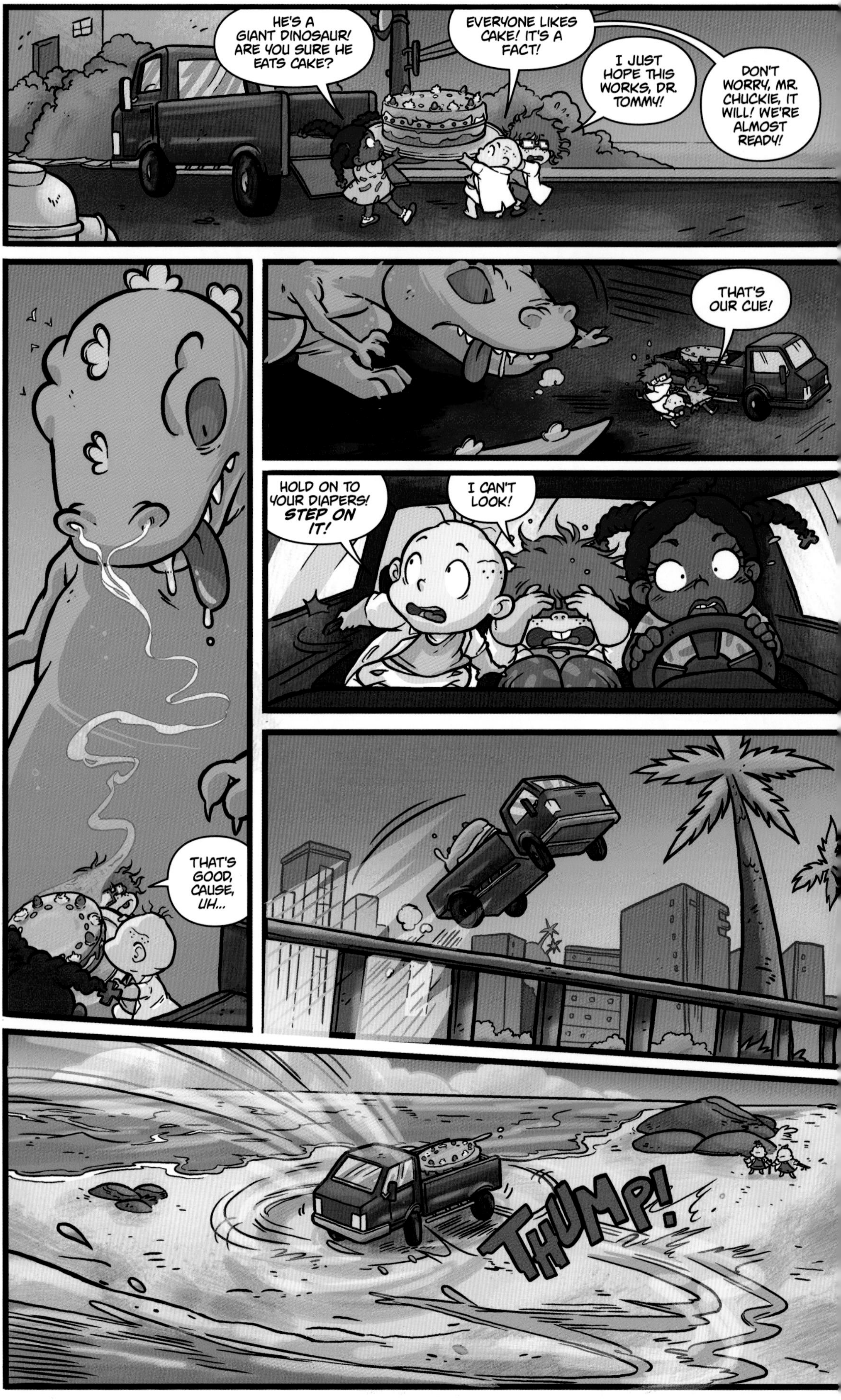

HE'S A GIANT DINOSAUR! ARE YOU SURE HE EATS CAKE?
EVERYONE LIKES CAKE! IT'S A FACT!
I JUST HOPE THIS WORKS, DR. TOMMY!
DON'T WORRY, MR. CHUCKIE, IT WILL! WE'RE ALMOST READY!
THAT'S GOOD, CAUSE, UH...
THAT'S OUR CUE!
HOLD ON TO YOUR DIAPERS! STEP ON IT!
I CAN'T LOOK!
THUMP!

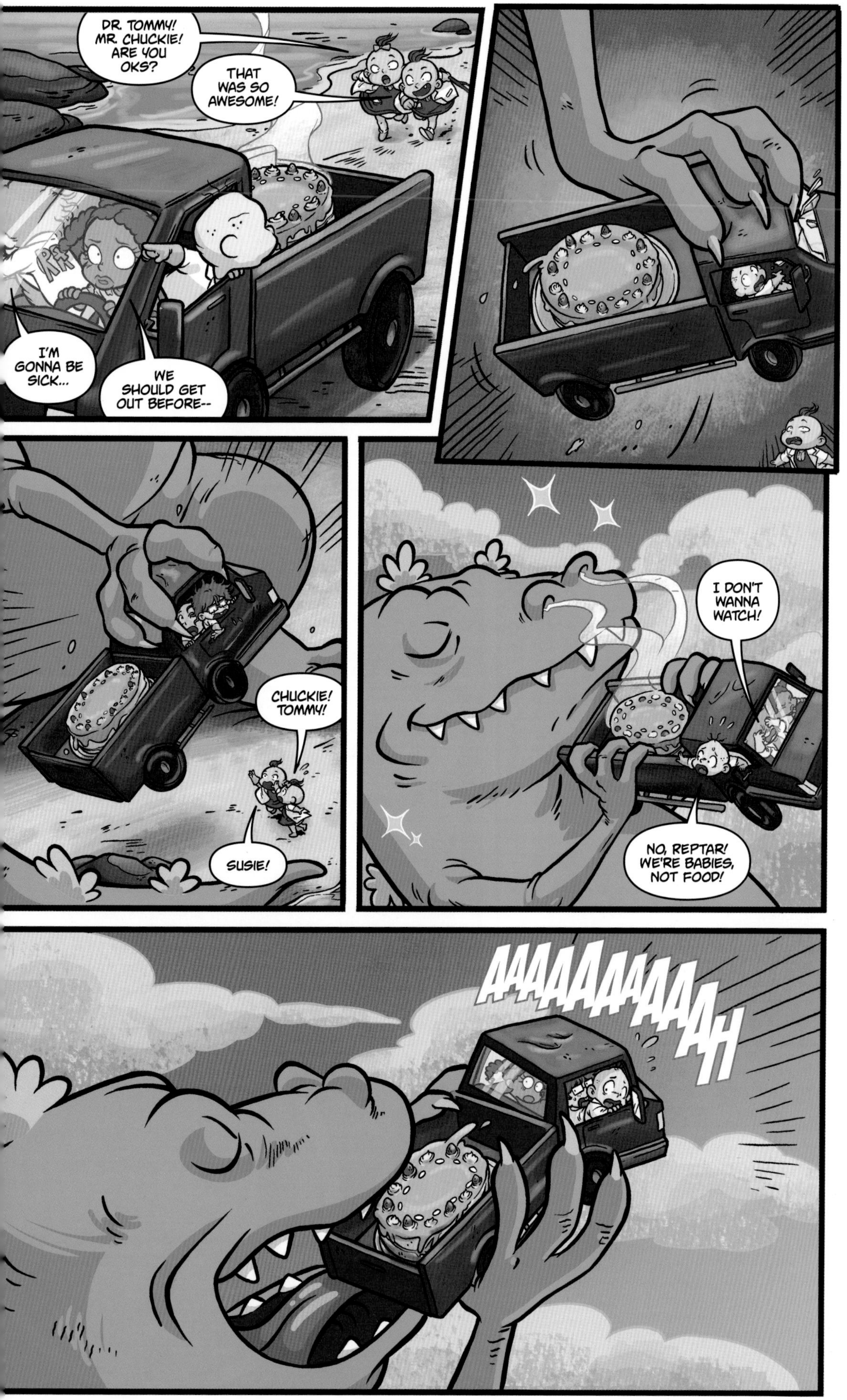
DR. TOMMY! MR. CHUCKIE! ARE YOU OKS?
THAT WAS SO AWESOME!
I'M GONNA BE SICK...
WE SHOULD GET OUT BEFORE--
CHUCKIE! TOMMY!
SUSIE!
I DON'T WANNA WATCH!
NO, REPTAR! WE'RE BABIES, NOT FOOD!
AAAAAAAAAAAH

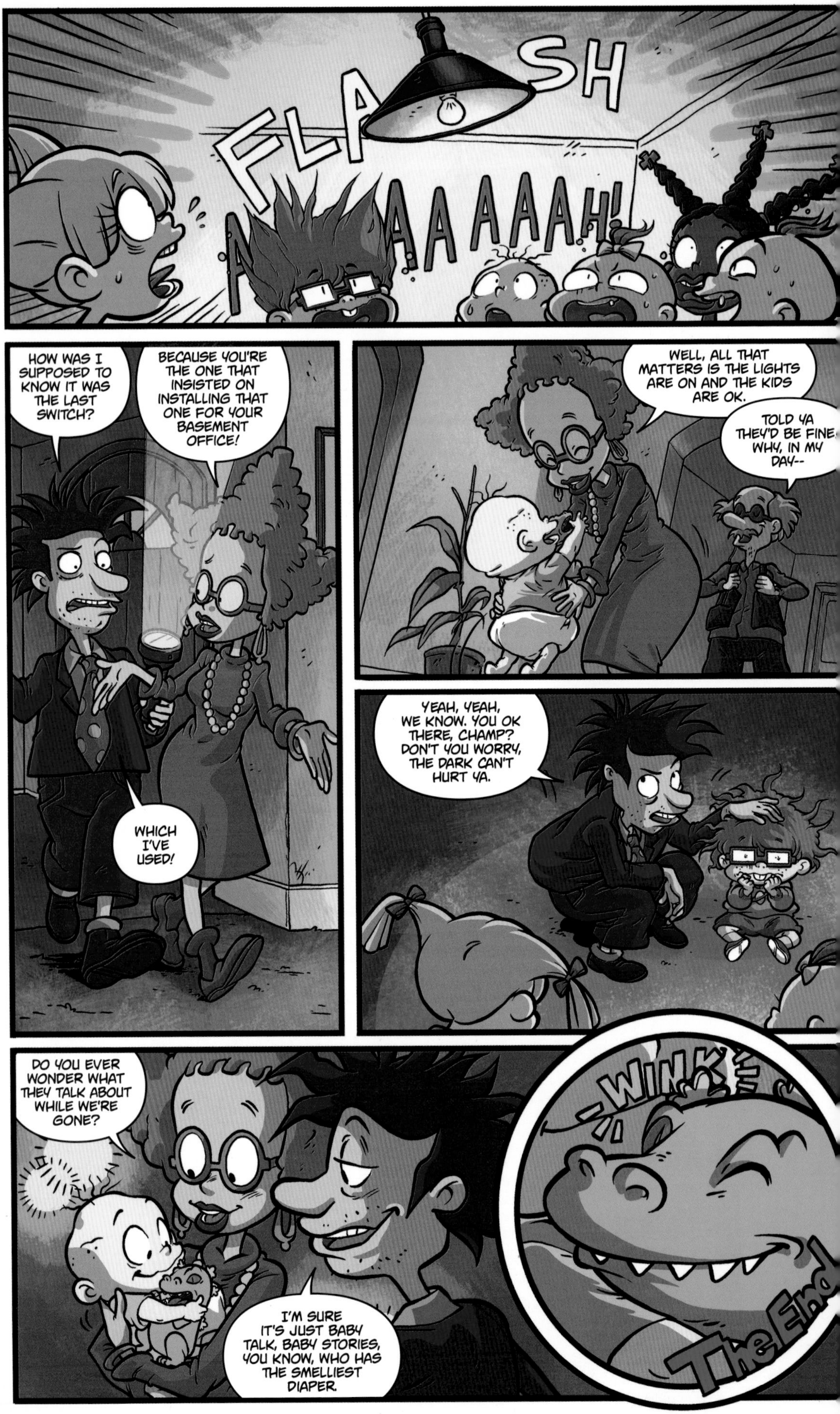
FLASH
AAAAAAH!
HOW WAS I SUPPOSED TO KNOW IT WAS THE LAST SWITCH?
BECAUSE YOU'RE THE ONE THAT INSISTED ON INSTALLING THAT ONE FOR YOUR BASEMENT OFFICE!
WHICH I'VE USED!
WELL, ALL THAT MATTERS IS THE LIGHTS ARE ON AND THE KIDS ARE OK.
TOLD YA THEY'D BE FINE. WHY, IN MY DAY--
YEAH, YEAH, WE KNOW. YOU OK THERE, CHAMP? DON'T YOU WORRY, THE DARK CAN'T HURT YA.
DO YOU EVER WONDER WHAT THEY TALK ABOUT WHILE WE'RE GONE?
I'M SURE IT'S JUST BABY TALK, BABY STORIES, YOU KNOW, WHO HAS THE SMELLIEST DIAPER.
-WINK-
The End

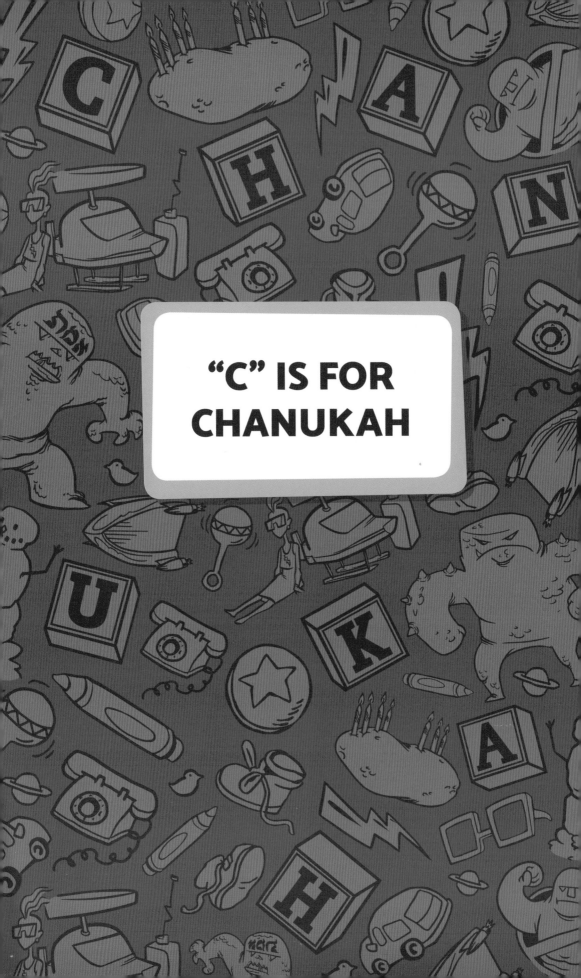

"C" IS FOR CHANUKAH

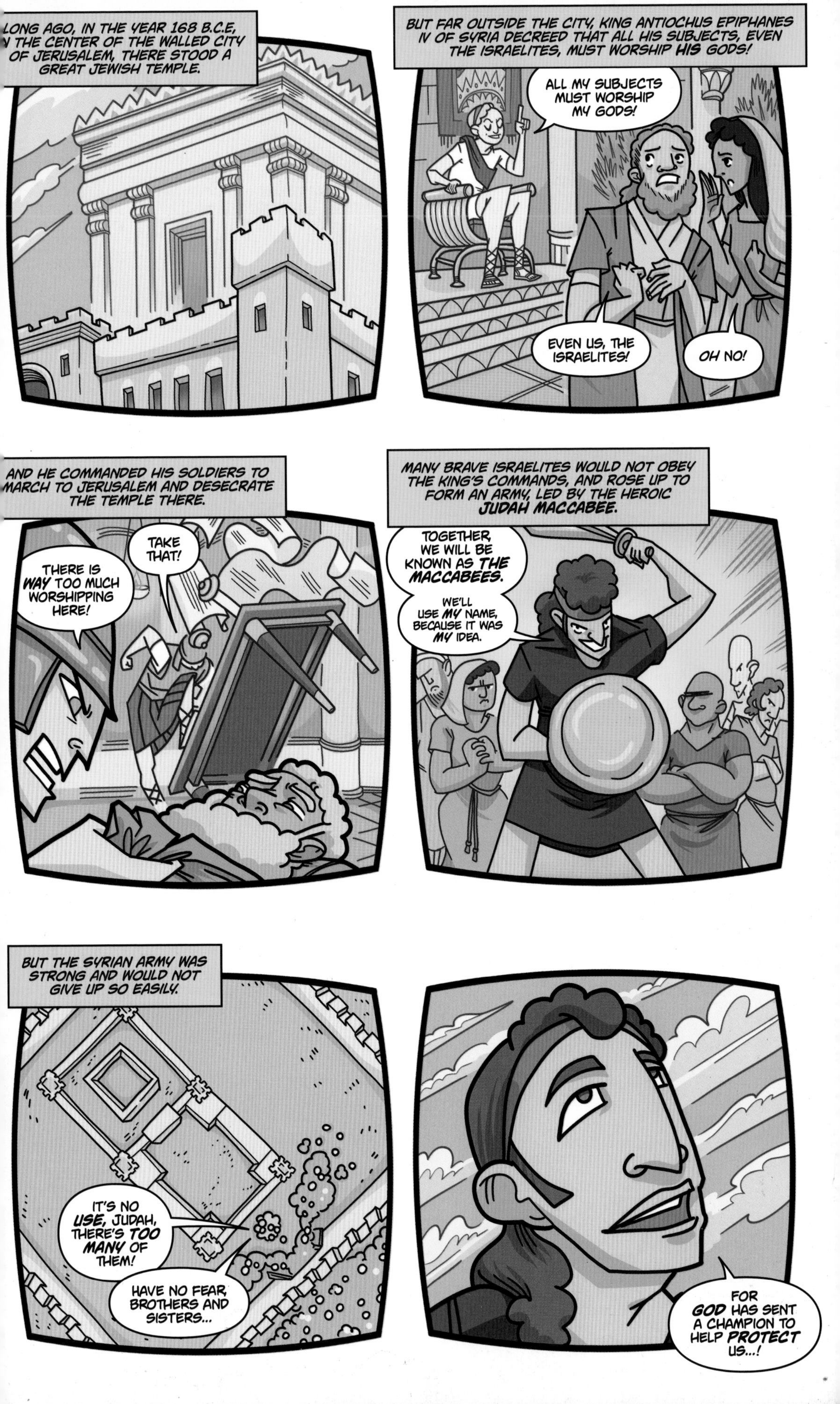

LONG AGO, IN THE YEAR 168 B.C.E,
N THE CENTER OF THE WALLED CITY
OF JERUSALEM, THERE STOOD A
GREAT JEWISH TEMPLE.
BUT FAR OUTSIDE THE CITY, KING ANTIOCHUS EPIPHANES IV OF SYRIA DECREED THAT ALL HIS SUBJECTS, EVEN THE ISRAELITES, MUST WORSHIP HIS GODS!
ALL MY SUBJECTS MUST WORSHIP MY GODS!
EVEN US, THE ISRAELITES!
OH NO!
AND HE COMMANDED HIS SOLDIERS TO MARCH TO JERUSALEM AND DESECRATE THE TEMPLE THERE.
THERE IS WAY TOO MUCH WORSHIPPING HERE!
TAKE THAT!
MANY BRAVE ISRAELITES WOULD NOT OBEY THE KING'S COMMANDS, AND ROSE UP TO FORM AN ARMY, LED BY THE HEROIC JUDAH MACCABEE.
TOGETHER, WE WILL BE KNOWN AS THE MACCABEES.
WE'LL USE MY NAME, BECAUSE IT WAS MY IDEA.
BUT THE SYRIAN ARMY WAS STRONG AND WOULD NOT GIVE UP SO EASILY.
IT'S NO USE, JUDAH, THERE'S TOO MANY OF THEM!
HAVE NO FEAR, BROTHERS AND SISTERS...
FOR GOD HAS SENT A CHAMPION TO HELP PROTECT US...!

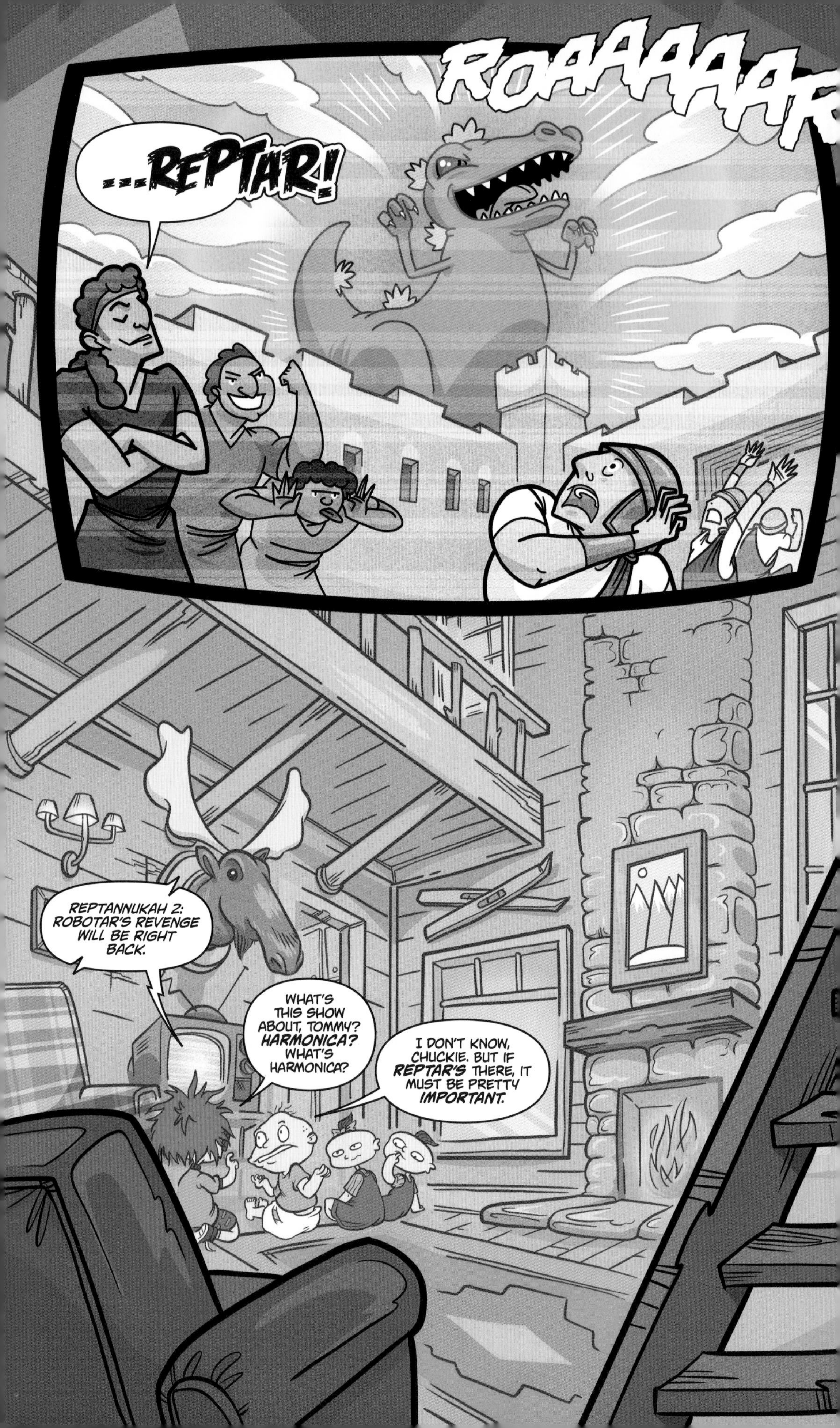

ROAAAAAAR
...REPTAR!
REPTANNUKAH 2: ROBOTAR'S REVENGE WILL BE RIGHT BACK.
WHAT'S THIS SHOW ABOUT, TOMMY? HARMONICA? WHAT'S HARMONICA?
I DON'T KNOW, CHUCKIE. BUT IF REPTAR'S THERE, IT MUST BE PRETTY IMPORTANT.

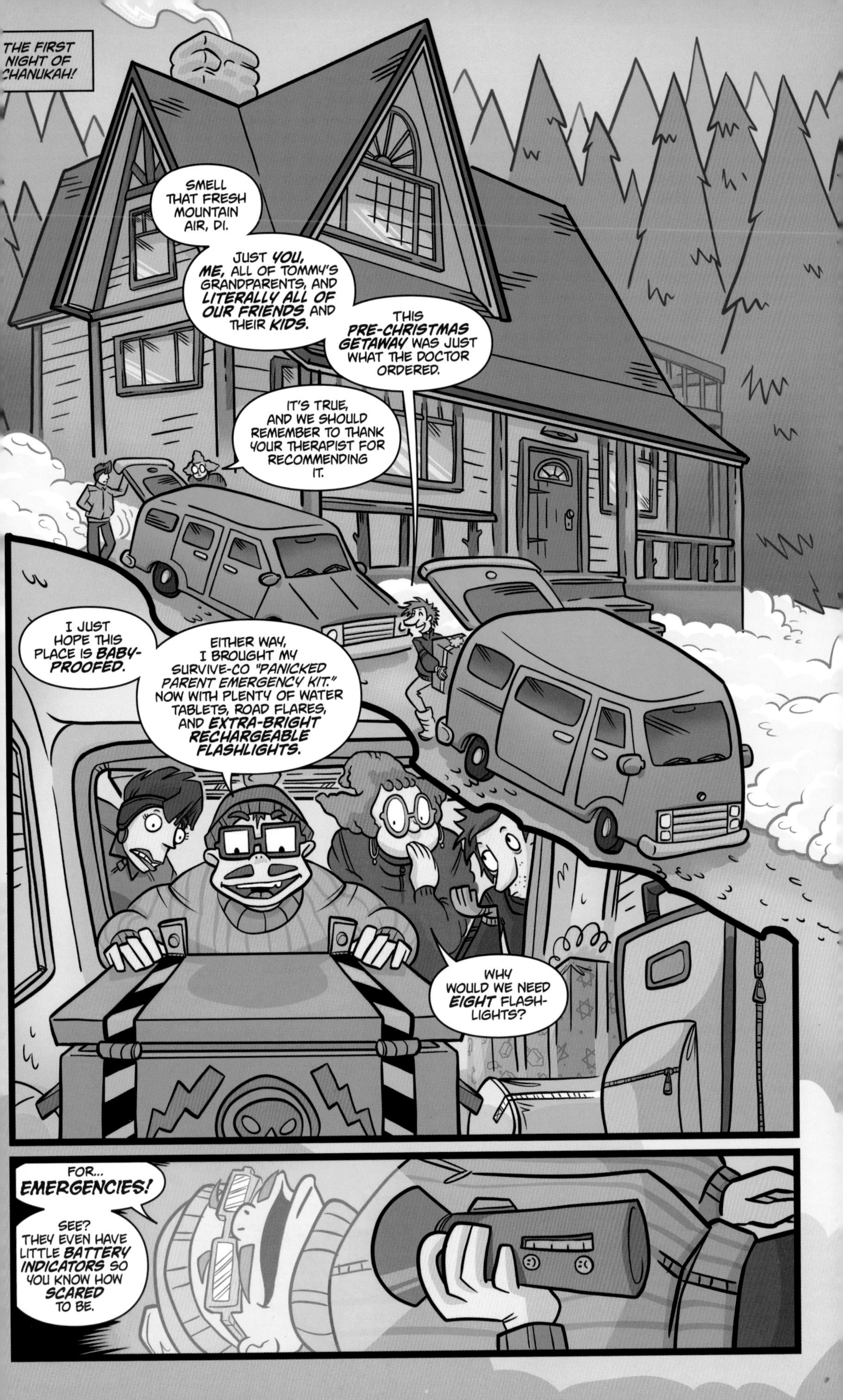

THE FIRST NIGHT OF CHANUKAH!
SMELL THAT FRESH MOUNTAIN AIR, DI.
JUST YOU, ME, ALL OF TOMMY'S GRANDPARENTS, AND LITERALLY ALL OF OUR FRIENDS AND THEIR KIDS.
THIS PRE-CHRISTMAS GETAWAY WAS JUST WHAT THE DOCTOR ORDERED.
IT'S TRUE, AND WE SHOULD REMEMBER TO THANK YOUR THERAPIST FOR RECOMMENDING IT.
I JUST HOPE THIS PLACE IS BABY-PROOFED.
EITHER WAY, I BROUGHT MY SURVIVE-CO "PANICKED PARENT EMERGENCY KIT." NOW WITH PLENTY OF WATER TABLETS, ROAD FLARES, AND EXTRA-BRIGHT RECHARGEABLE FLASHLIGHTS.
WHY WOULD WE NEED EIGHT FLASH-LIGHTS?
FOR... EMERGENCIES!
SEE? THEY EVEN HAVE LITTLE BATTERY INDICATORS SO YOU KNOW HOW SCARED TO BE.

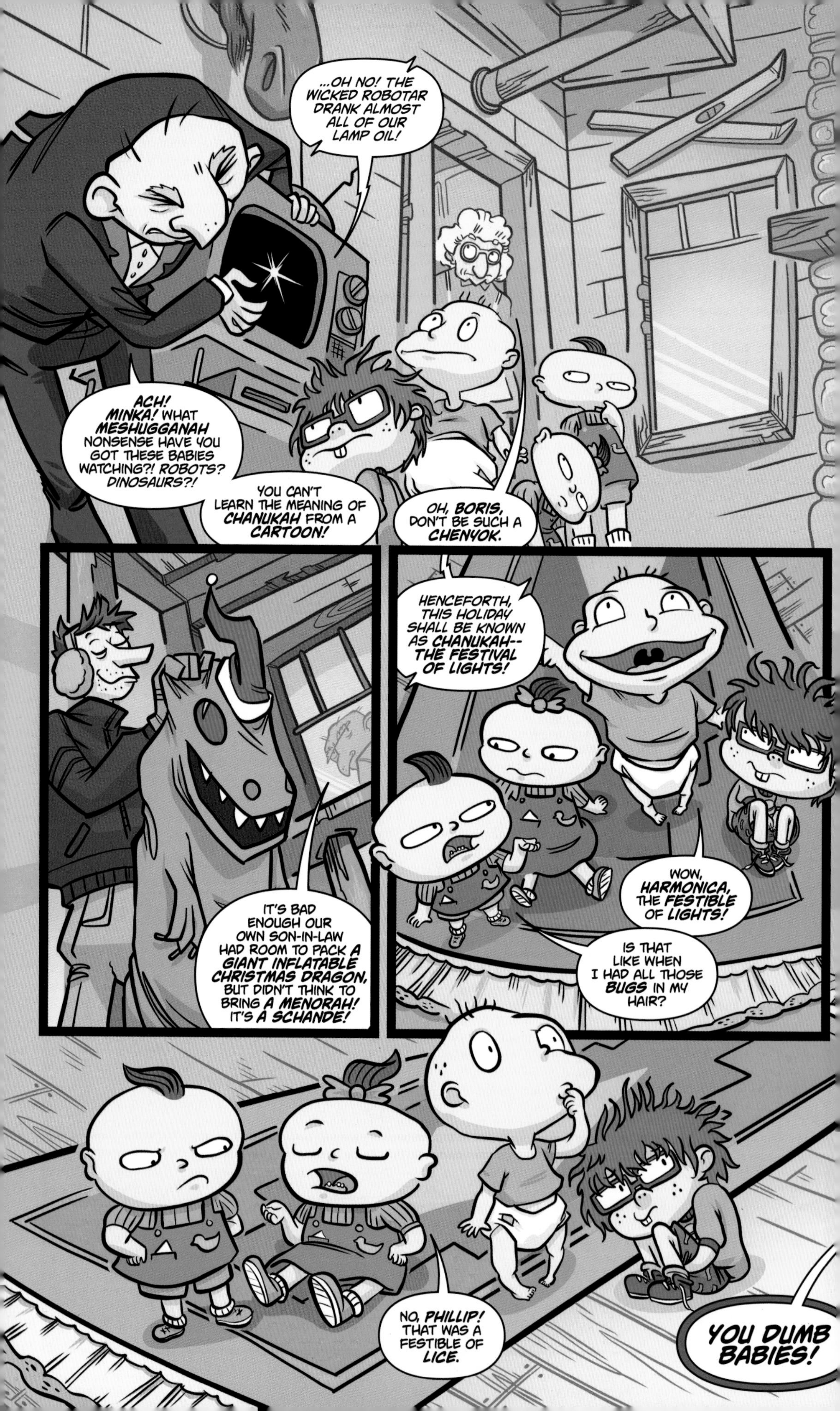
...OH NO! THE WICKED ROBOTAR DRANK ALMOST ALL OF OUR LAMP OIL!
ACH! MINKA! WHAT MESHUGGANAH NONSENSE HAVE YOU GOT THESE BABIES WATCHING?! ROBOTS? DINOSAURS?!
YOU CAN'T LEARN THE MEANING OF CHANUKAH FROM A CARTOON!
OH, BORIS, DON'T BE SUCH A CHENYOK.
IT'S BAD ENOUGH OUR OWN SON-IN-LAW HAD ROOM TO PACK A GIANT INFLATABLE CHRISTMAS DRAGON, BUT DIDN'T THINK TO BRING A MENORAH! IT'S A SCHANDE!
HENCEFORTH, THIS HOLIDAY SHALL BE KNOWN AS CHANUKAH-- THE FESTIVAL OF LIGHTS!
WOW, HARMONICA, THE FESTIBLE OF LIGHTS!
IS THAT LIKE WHEN I HAD ALL THOSE BUGS IN MY HAIR?
NO, PHILLIP! THAT WAS A FESTIBLE OF LICE.
YOU DUMB BABIES!

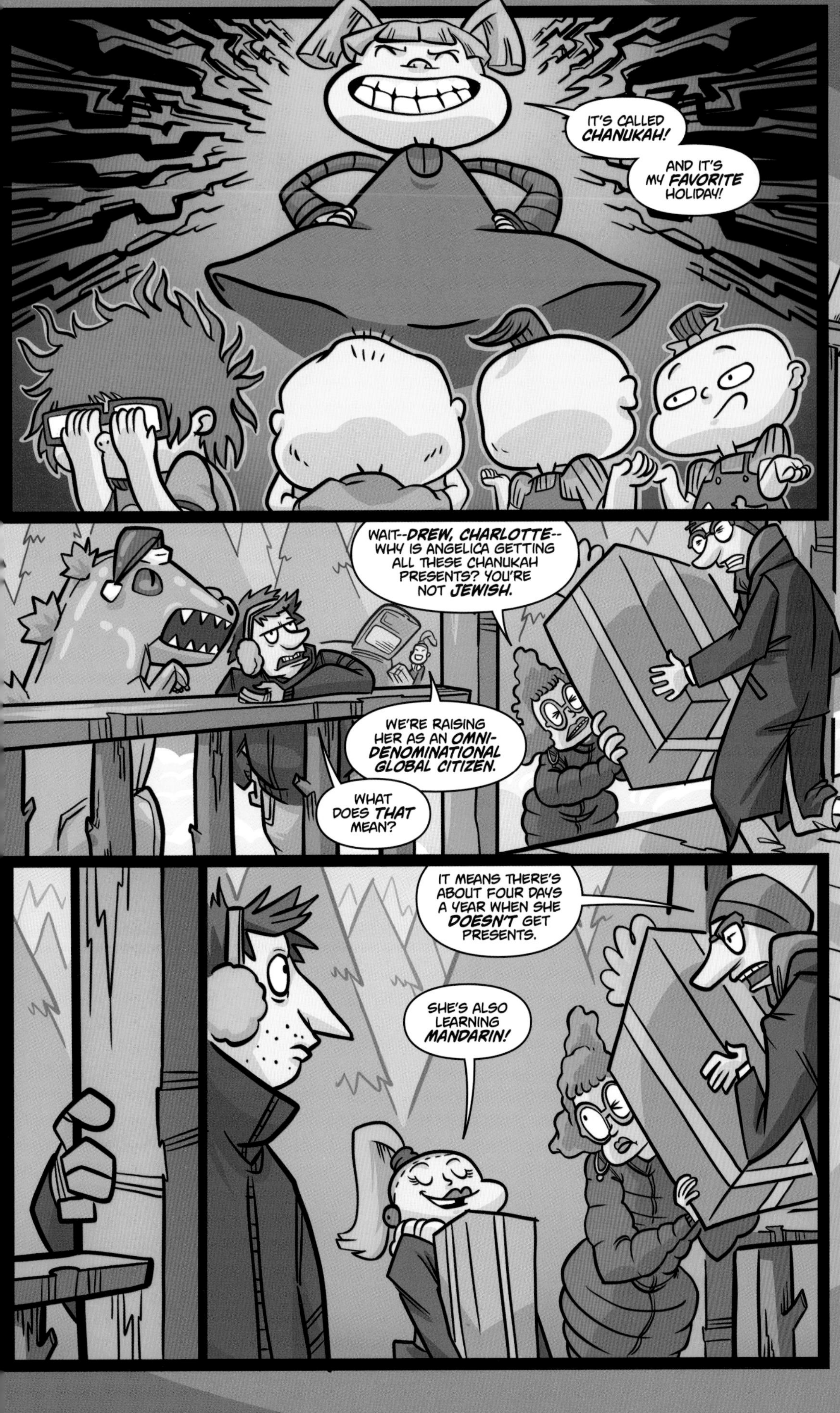
IT'S CALLED CHANUKAH!
AND IT'S MY FAVORITE HOLIDAY!
WAIT--DREW, CHARLOTTE-- WHY IS ANGELICA GETTING ALL THESE CHANUKAH PRESENTS? YOU'RE NOT JEWISH.
WE'RE RAISING HER AS AN OMNI-DENOMINATIONAL GLOBAL CITIZEN.
WHAT DOES THAT MEAN?
IT MEANS THERE'S ABOUT FOUR DAYS A YEAR WHEN SHE DOESN'T GET PRESENTS.
SHE'S ALSO LEARNING MANDARIN!

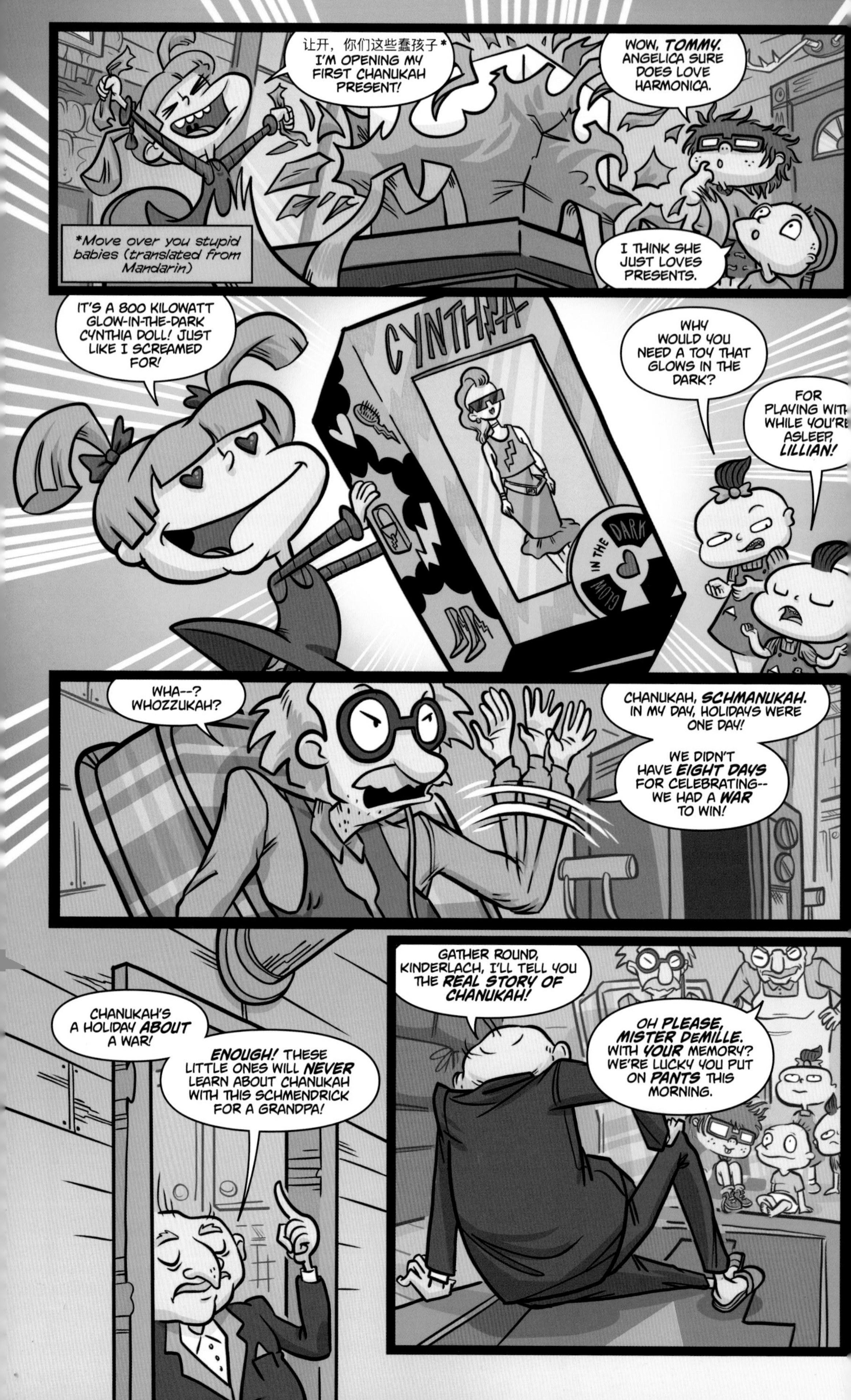

让开，你们这些蠢孩子* I'M OPENING MY FIRST CHANUKAH PRESENT!
*Move over you stupid babies (translated from Mandarin)
WOW, TOMMY. ANGELICA SURE DOES LOVE HARMONICA.
I THINK SHE JUST LOVES PRESENTS.
IT'S A 800 KILOWATT GLOW-IN-THE-DARK CYNTHIA DOLL! JUST LIKE I SCREAMED FOR!
CYNTHIA
GLOW IN THE DARK
WHY WOULD YOU NEED A TOY THAT GLOWS IN THE DARK?
FOR PLAYING WITH WHILE YOU'RE ASLEEP, LILLIAN!
WHA--? WHOZZUKAH?
CHANUKAH, SCHMANUKAH. IN MY DAY, HOLIDAYS WERE ONE DAY!
WE DIDN'T HAVE EIGHT DAYS FOR CELEBRATING-- WE HAD A WAR TO WIN!
CHANUKAH'S A HOLIDAY ABOUT A WAR!
ENOUGH! THESE LITTLE ONES WILL NEVER LEARN ABOUT CHANUKAH WITH THIS SCHMENDRICK FOR A GRANDPA!
GATHER ROUND, KINDERLACH, I'LL TELL YOU THE REAL STORY OF CHANUKAH!
OH PLEASE, MISTER DEMILLE. WITH YOUR MEMORY? WE'RE LUCKY YOU PUT ON PANTS THIS MORNING.

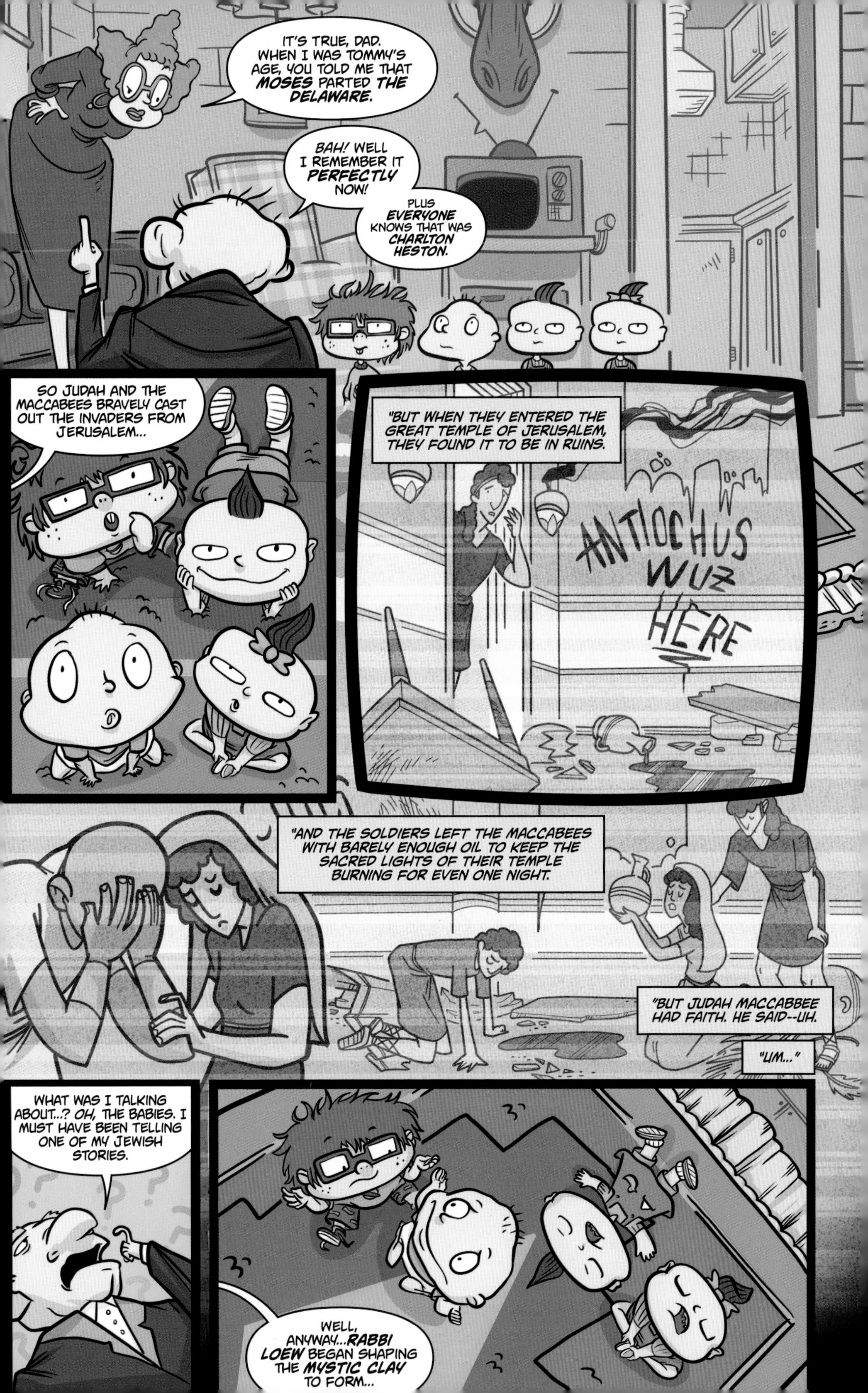
IT'S TRUE, DAD. WHEN I WAS TOMMY'S AGE, YOU TOLD ME THAT MOSES PARTED THE DELAWARE.
BAH! WELL I REMEMBER IT PERFECTLY NOW!
PLUS EVERYONE KNOWS THAT WAS CHARLTON HESTON.
SO JUDAH AND THE MACCABEES BRAVELY CAST OUT THE INVADERS FROM JERUSALEM...
"BUT WHEN THEY ENTERED THE GREAT TEMPLE OF JERUSALEM, THEY FOUND IT TO BE IN RUINS.
ANTIOCHUS WUZ HERE
"AND THE SOLDIERS LEFT THE MACCABEES WITH BARELY ENOUGH OIL TO KEEP THE SACRED LIGHTS OF THEIR TEMPLE BURNING FOR EVEN ONE NIGHT.
"BUT JUDAH MACCABBEE HAD FAITH. HE SAID--UH.
"UM..."
WHAT WAS I TALKING ABOUT...? OH, THE BABIES. I MUST HAVE BEEN TELLING ONE OF MY JEWISH STORIES.
WELL, ANYWAY...RABBI LOEW BEGAN SHAPING THE MYSTIC CLAY TO FORM...

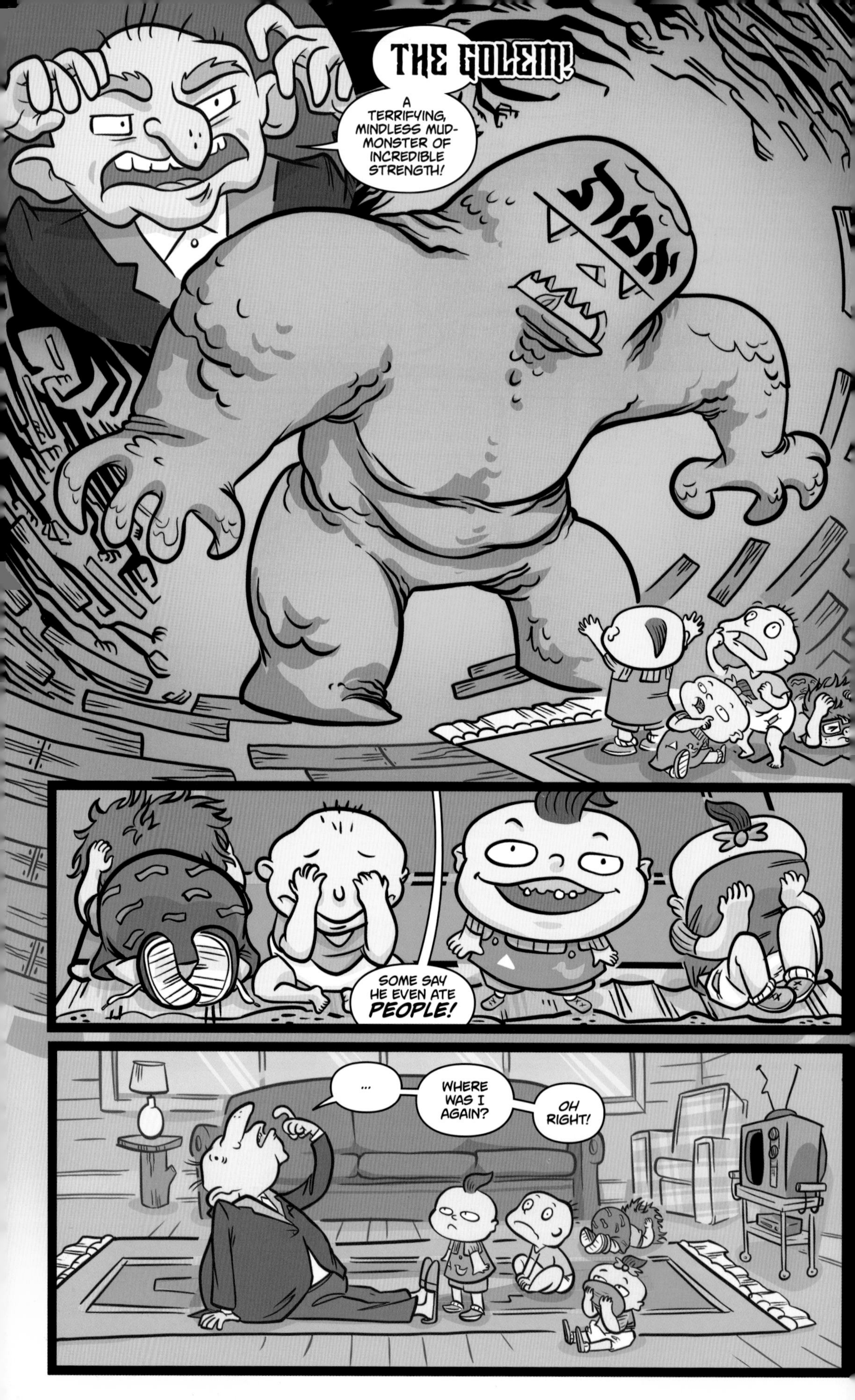

THE GOLEM!
A TERRIFYING, MINDLESS MUD-MONSTER OF INCREDIBLE STRENGTH!
SOME SAY HE EVEN ATE PEOPLE!
...
WHERE WAS I AGAIN?
OH RIGHT!

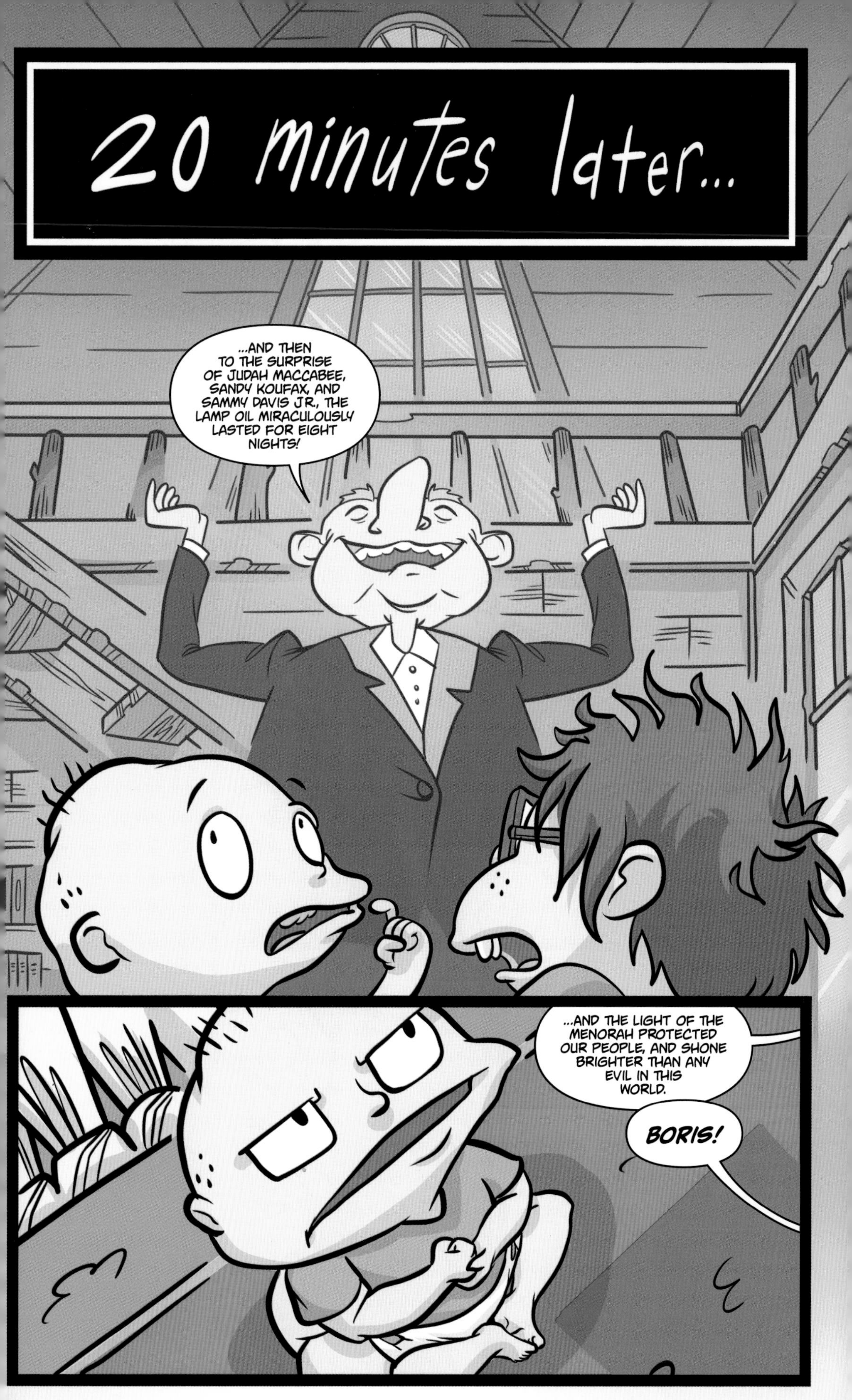
20 minutes later...
...AND THEN TO THE SURPRISE OF JUDAH MACCABEE, SANDY KOUFAX, AND SAMMY DAVIS JR., THE LAMP OIL MIRACULOUSLY LASTED FOR EIGHT NIGHTS!
...AND THE LIGHT OF THE MENORAH PROTECTED OUR PEOPLE, AND SHONE BRIGHTER THAN ANY EVIL IN THIS WORLD.
BORIS!

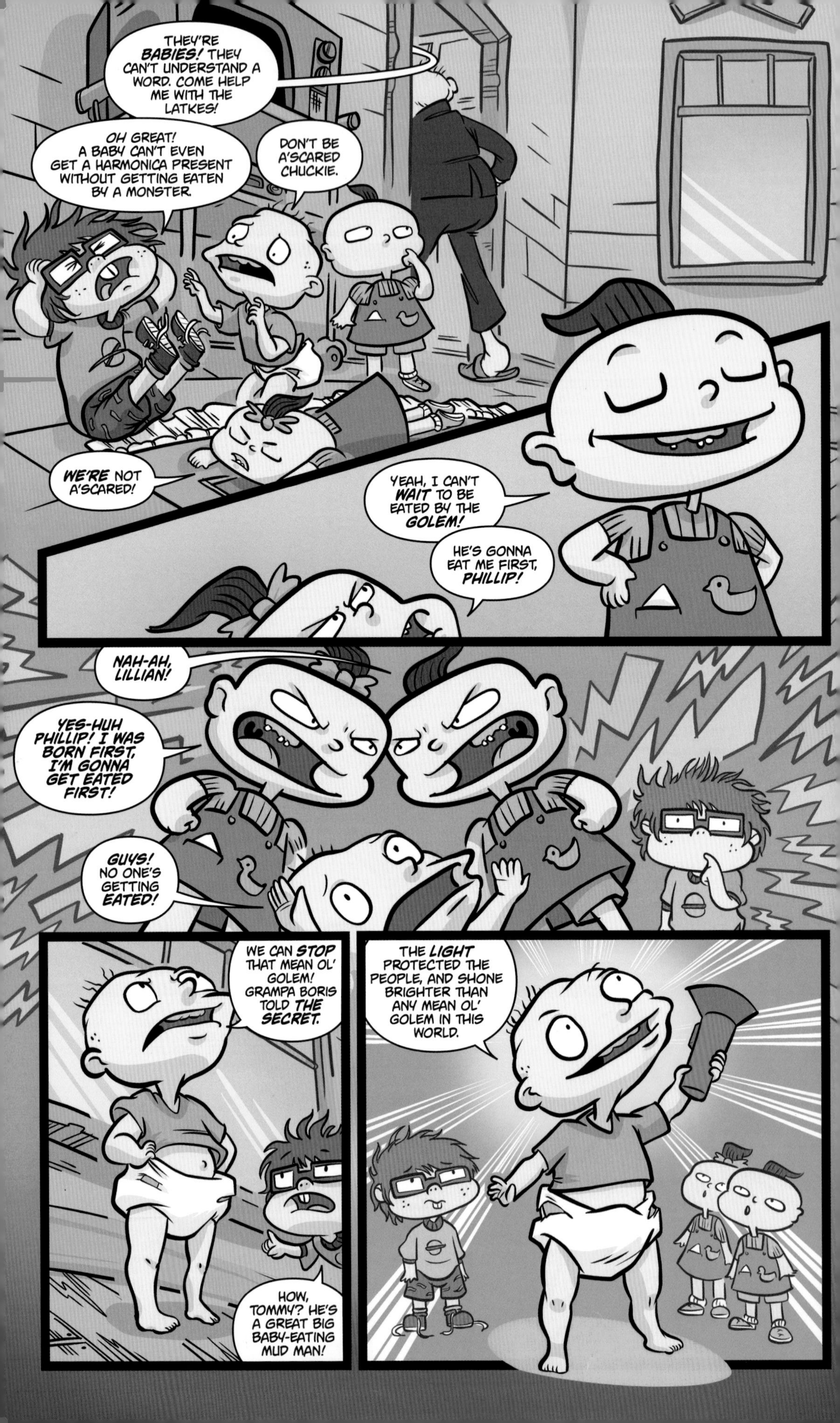
THEY'RE BABIES! THEY CAN'T UNDERSTAND A WORD. COME HELP ME WITH THE LATKES!
OH GREAT! A BABY CAN'T EVEN GET A HARMONICA PRESENT WITHOUT GETTING EATEN BY A MONSTER.
DON'T BE A'SCARED CHUCKIE.
WE'RE NOT A'SCARED!
YEAH, I CAN'T WAIT TO BE EATED BY THE GOLEM!
HE'S GONNA EAT ME FIRST, PHILLIP!
NAH-AH, LILLIAN!
YES-HUH PHILLIP! I WAS BORN FIRST, I'M GONNA GET EATED FIRST!
GUYS! NO ONE'S GETTING EATED!
WE CAN STOP THAT MEAN OL' GOLEM! GRAMPA BORIS TOLD THE SECRET.
HOW, TOMMY? HE'S A GREAT BIG BABY-EATING MUD MAN!
THE LIGHT PROTECTED THE PEOPLE, AND SHONE BRIGHTER THAN ANY MEAN OL' GOLEM IN THIS WORLD.

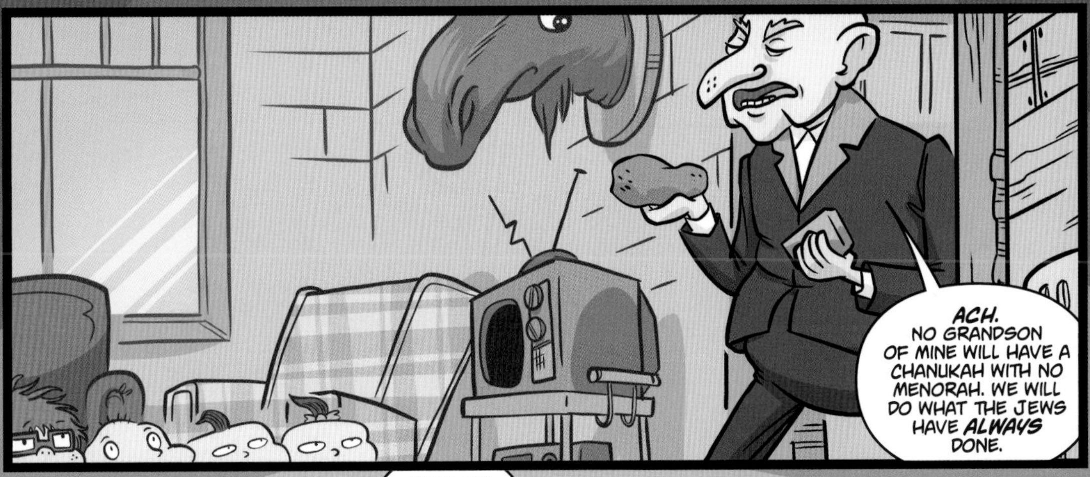
ACH. NO GRANDSON OF MINE WILL HAVE A CHANUKAH WITH NO MENORAH. WE WILL DO WHAT THE JEWS HAVE ALWAYS DONE.

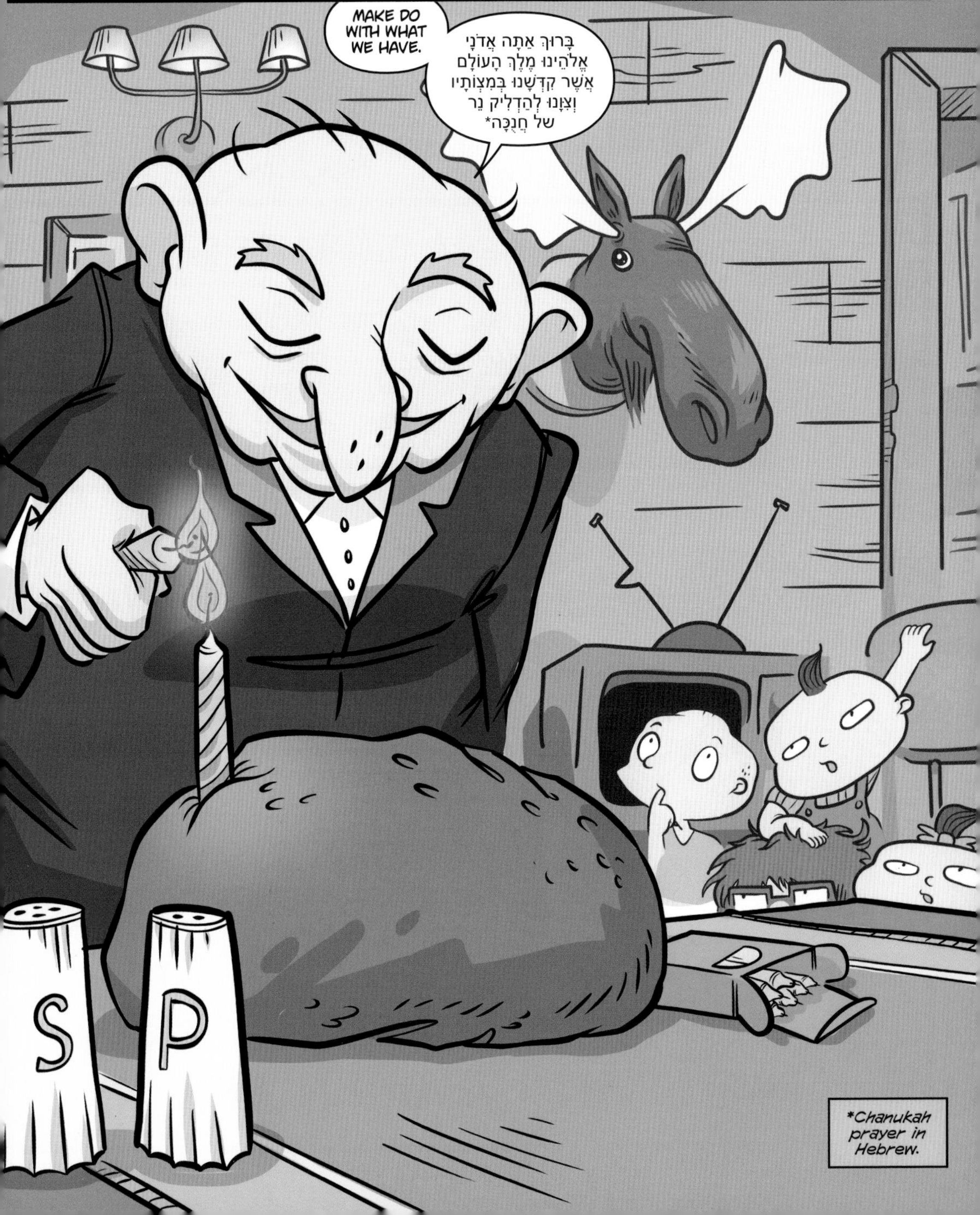
MAKE DO WITH WHAT WE HAVE.
בָּרוּךְ אַתָּה אֲדֹנָי
אֱלֹהֵינוּ מֶלֶךְ הָעוֹלָם
אֲשֶׁר קִדְּשָׁנוּ בְּמִצְוֹתָיו
וְצִוָּנוּ לְהַדְלִיק נֵר
של חֲנֻכָּה*
S
P
*Chanukah prayer in Hebrew.

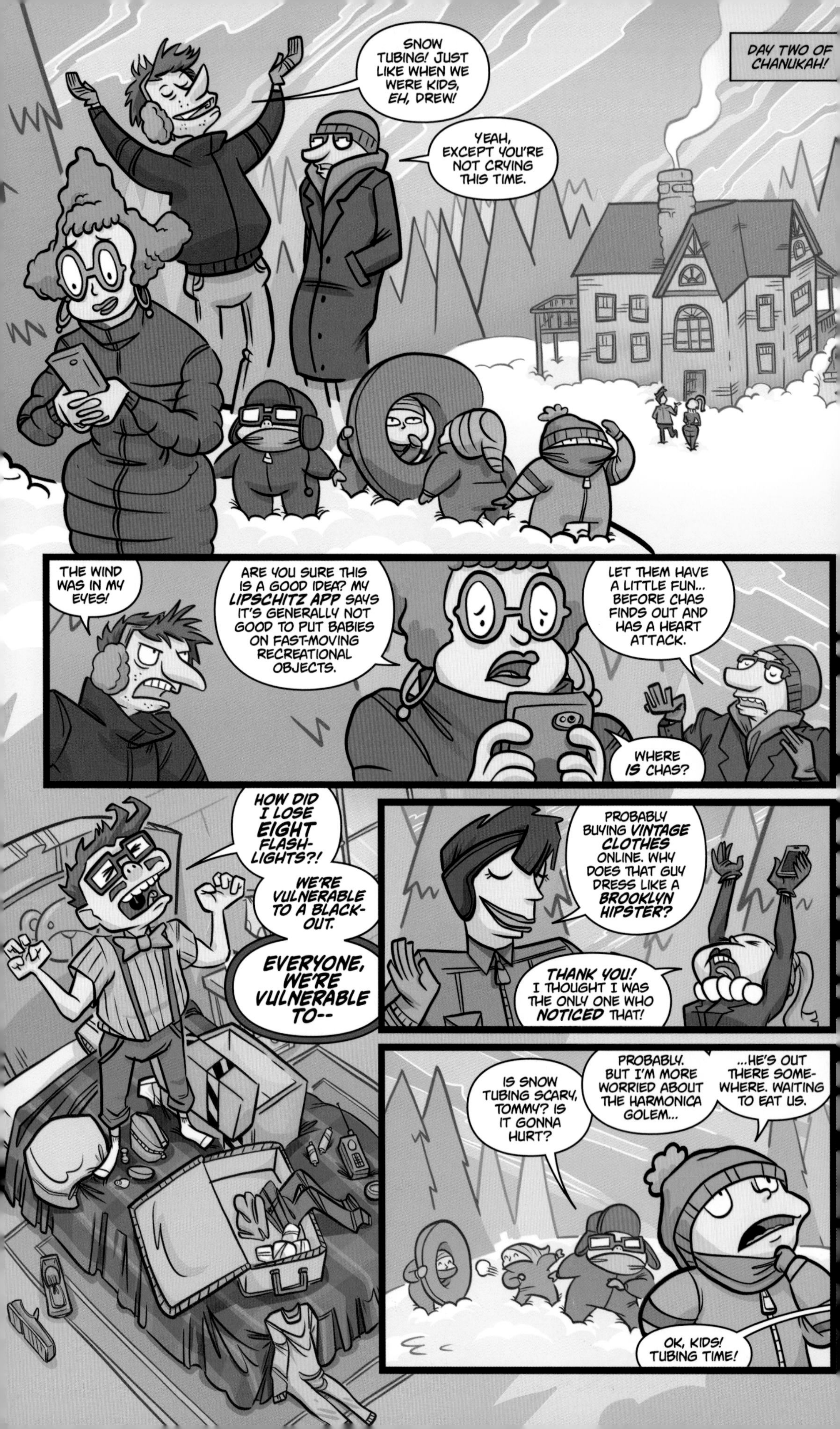
DAY TWO OF CHANUKAH!
SNOW TUBING! JUST LIKE WHEN WE WERE KIDS, EH, DREW!
YEAH, EXCEPT YOU'RE NOT CRYING THIS TIME.
THE WIND WAS IN MY EYES!
ARE YOU SURE THIS IS A GOOD IDEA? MY LIPSCHITZ APP SAYS IT'S GENERALLY NOT GOOD TO PUT BABIES ON FAST-MOVING RECREATIONAL OBJECTS.
LET THEM HAVE A LITTLE FUN... BEFORE CHAS FINDS OUT AND HAS A HEART ATTACK.
WHERE IS CHAS?
HOW DID I LOSE EIGHT FLASH-LIGHTS?!
WE'RE VULNERABLE TO A BLACK-OUT.
EVERYONE, WE'RE VULNERABLE TO--
PROBABLY BUYING VINTAGE CLOTHES ONLINE. WHY DOES THAT GUY DRESS LIKE A BROOKLYN HIPSTER?
THANK YOU! I THOUGHT I WAS THE ONLY ONE WHO NOTICED THAT!
IS SNOW TUBING SCARY, TOMMY? IS IT GONNA HURT?
PROBABLY. BUT I'M MORE WORRIED ABOUT THE HARMONICA GOLEM...
...HE'S OUT THERE SOME-WHERE. WAITING TO EAT US.
OK, KIDS! TUBING TIME!

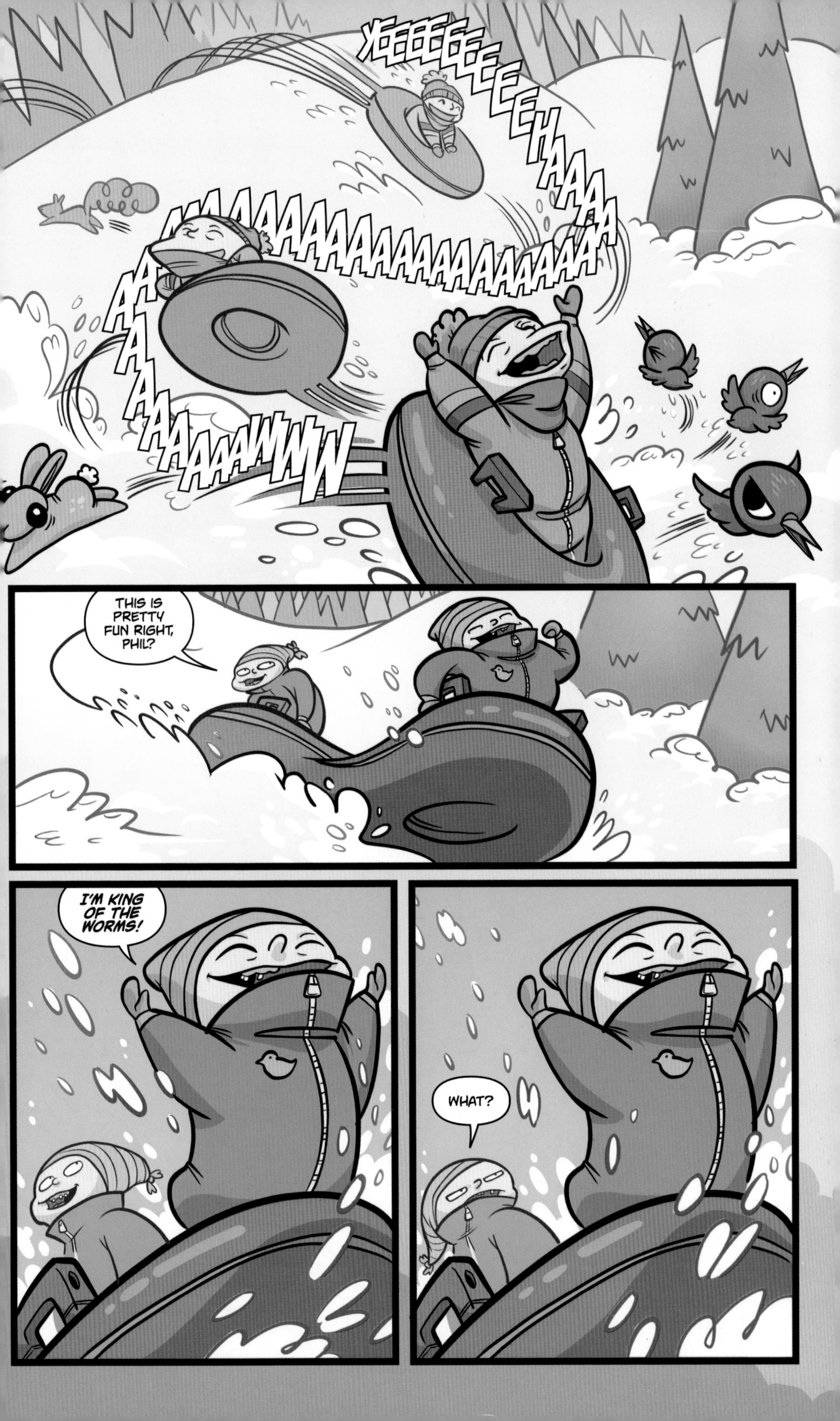
YEEEEEEEEEEEHAAAAA
AAAAAAAAAAAAAAAAAAAAAAAAAAAAAWWW
THIS IS PRETTY FUN RIGHT, PHIL?
I'M KING OF THE WORMS!
WHAT?

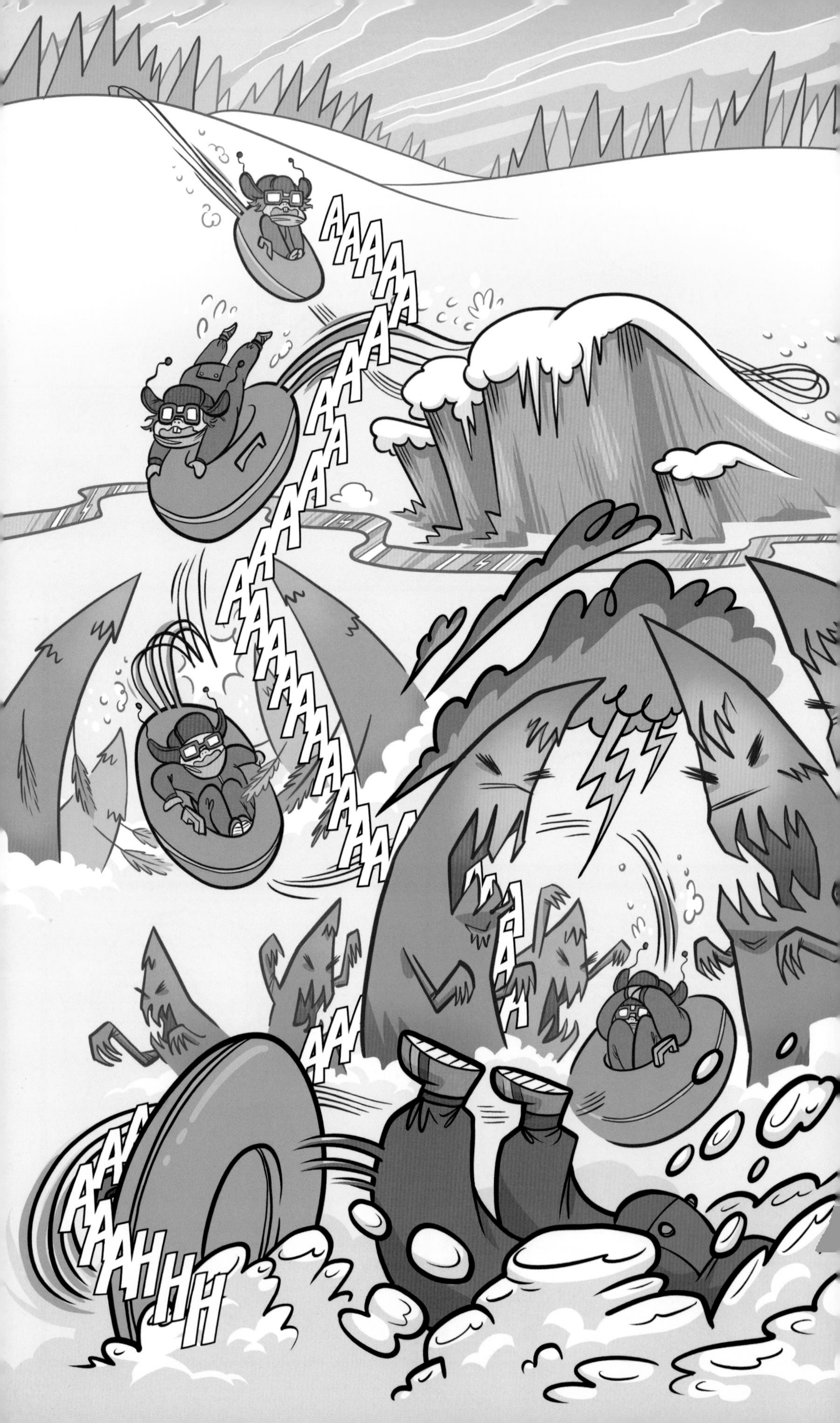
AAAAAAAAAAAAAAAAAAAAAAAAAAA
AAAA
AAAAHHHH

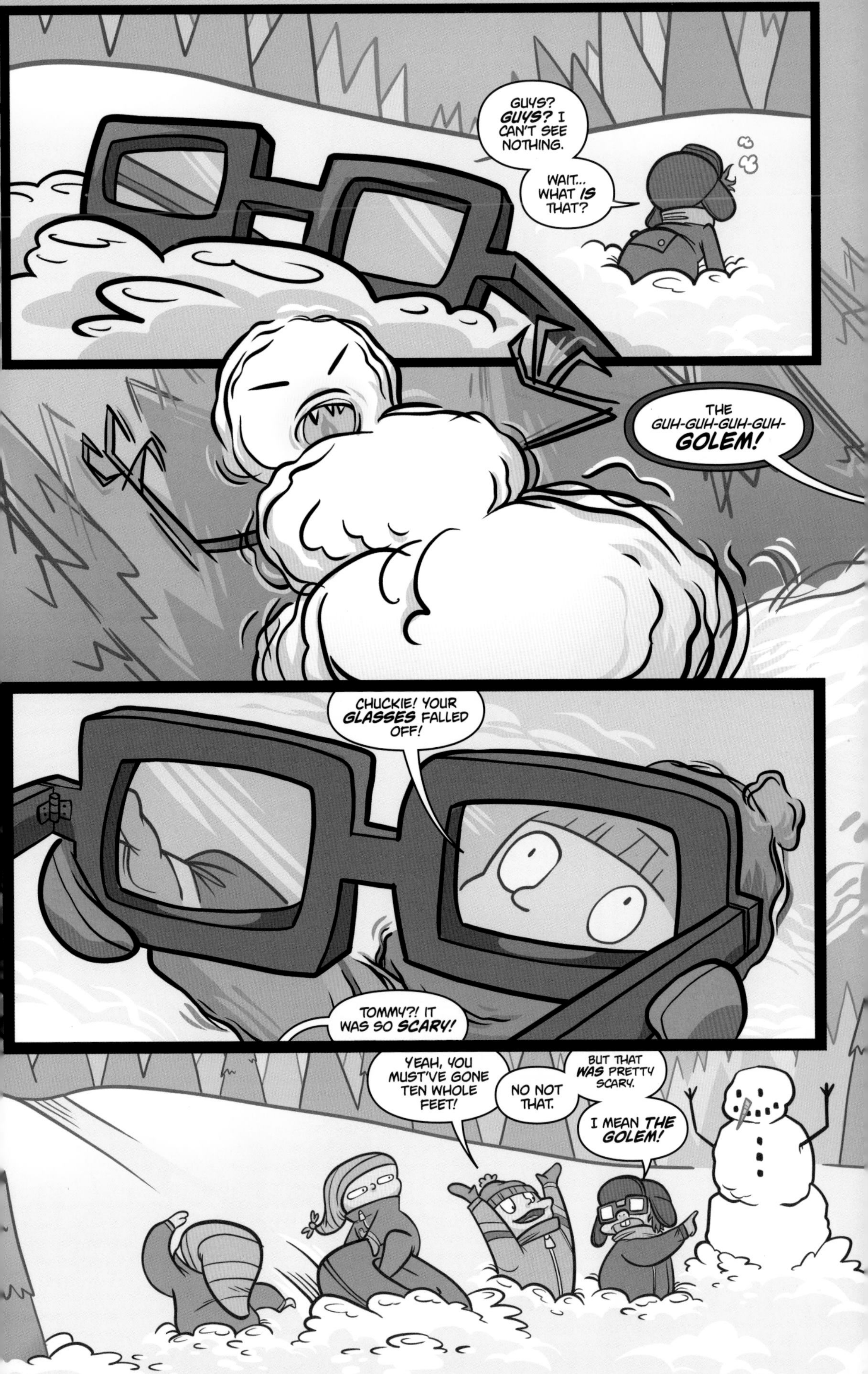
GUYS? GUYS? I CAN'T SEE NOTHING.
WAIT... WHAT IS THAT?
THE GUH-GUH-GUH-GUH-GOLEM!
CHUCKIE! YOUR GLASSES FALLED OFF!
TOMMY?! IT WAS SO SCARY!
YEAH, YOU MUST'VE GONE TEN WHOLE FEET!
NO NOT THAT.
BUT THAT WAS PRETTY SCARY.
I MEAN THE GOLEM!

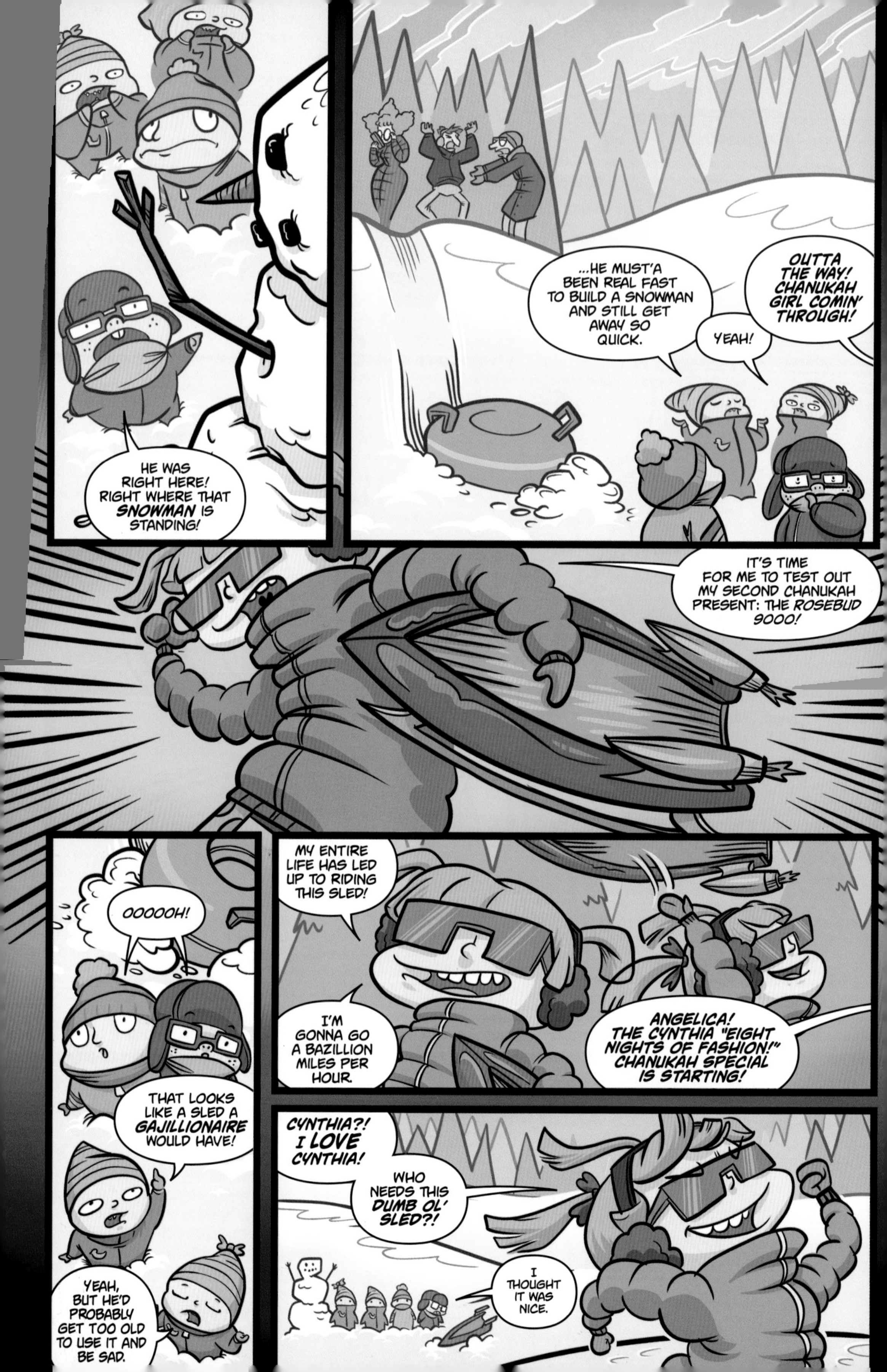
HE WAS RIGHT HERE! RIGHT WHERE THAT SNOWMAN IS STANDING!
...HE MUST'A BEEN REAL FAST TO BUILD A SNOWMAN AND STILL GET AWAY SO QUICK.
YEAH!
OUTTA THE WAY! CHANUKAH GIRL COMIN' THROUGH!
IT'S TIME FOR ME TO TEST OUT MY SECOND CHANUKAH PRESENT: THE ROSEBUD 9000!
OOOOOH!
THAT LOOKS LIKE A SLED A GAJILLIONAIRE WOULD HAVE!
YEAH, BUT HE'D PROBABLY GET TOO OLD TO USE IT AND BE SAD.
MY ENTIRE LIFE HAS LED UP TO RIDING THIS SLED!
I'M GONNA GO A BAZILLION MILES PER HOUR.
ANGELICA! THE CYNTHIA "EIGHT NIGHTS OF FASHION!" CHANUKAH SPECIAL IS STARTING!
CYNTHIA?! I LOVE CYNTHIA!
WHO NEEDS THIS DUMB OL' SLED?!
I THOUGHT IT WAS NICE.

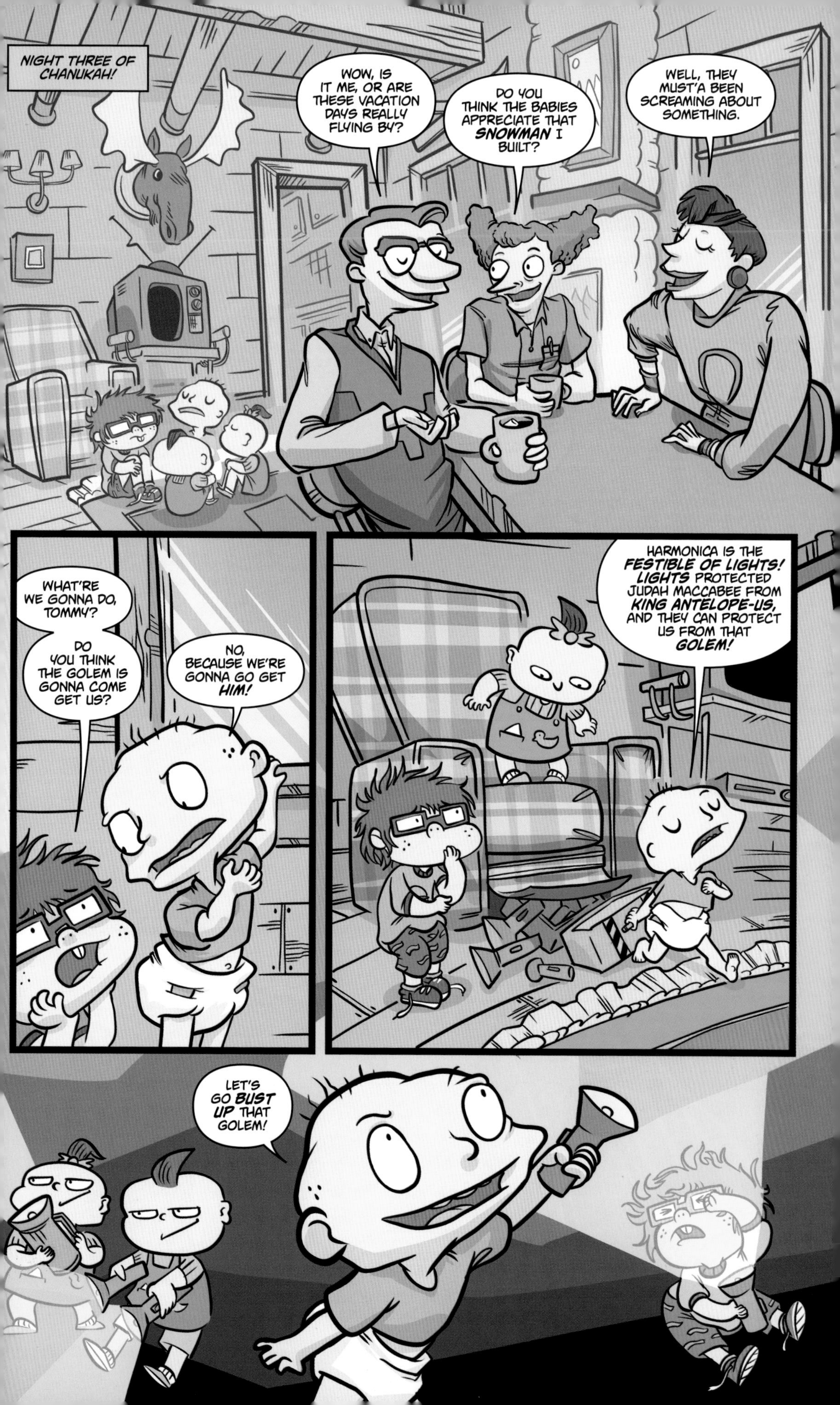
NIGHT THREE OF CHANUKAH!
WOW, IS IT ME, OR ARE THESE VACATION DAYS REALLY FLYING BY?
DO YOU THINK THE BABIES APPRECIATE THAT SNOWMAN I BUILT?
WELL, THEY MUST'A BEEN SCREAMING ABOUT SOMETHING.
WHAT'RE WE GONNA DO, TOMMY?
DO YOU THINK THE GOLEM IS GONNA COME GET US?
NO, BECAUSE WE'RE GONNA GO GET HIM!
HARMONICA IS THE FESTIBLE OF LIGHTS! LIGHTS PROTECTED JUDAH MACCABEE FROM KING ANTELOPE-US, AND THEY CAN PROTECT US FROM THAT GOLEM!
LET'S GO BUST UP THAT GOLEM!

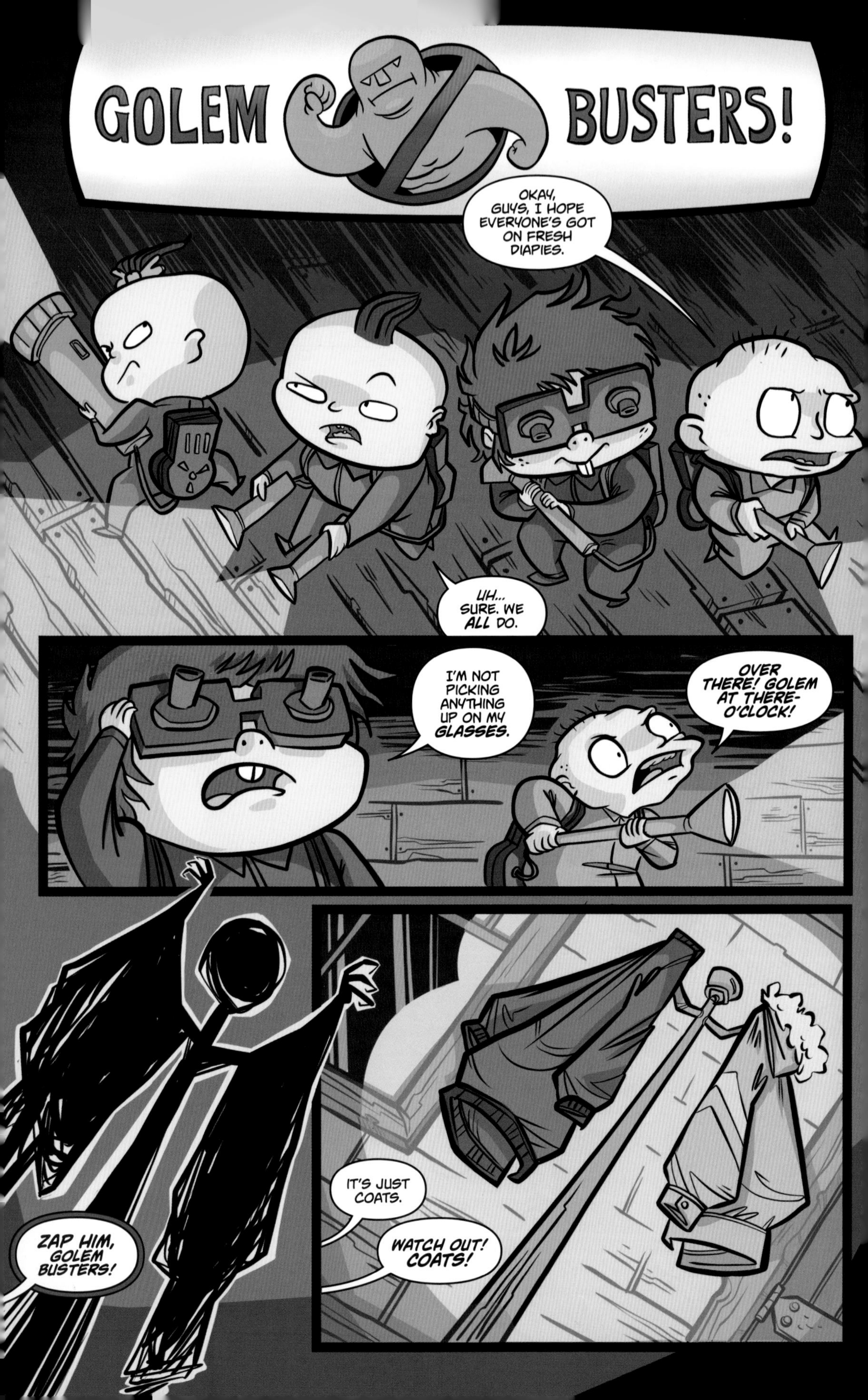
GOLEM BUSTERS!
OKAY, GUYS, I HOPE EVERYONE'S GOT ON FRESH DIAPIES.
UH... SURE. WE ALL DO.
I'M NOT PICKING ANYTHING UP ON MY GLASSES.
OVER THERE! GOLEM AT THERE-O'CLOCK!
IT'S JUST COATS.
WATCH OUT! COATS!
ZAP HIM, GOLEM BUSTERS!

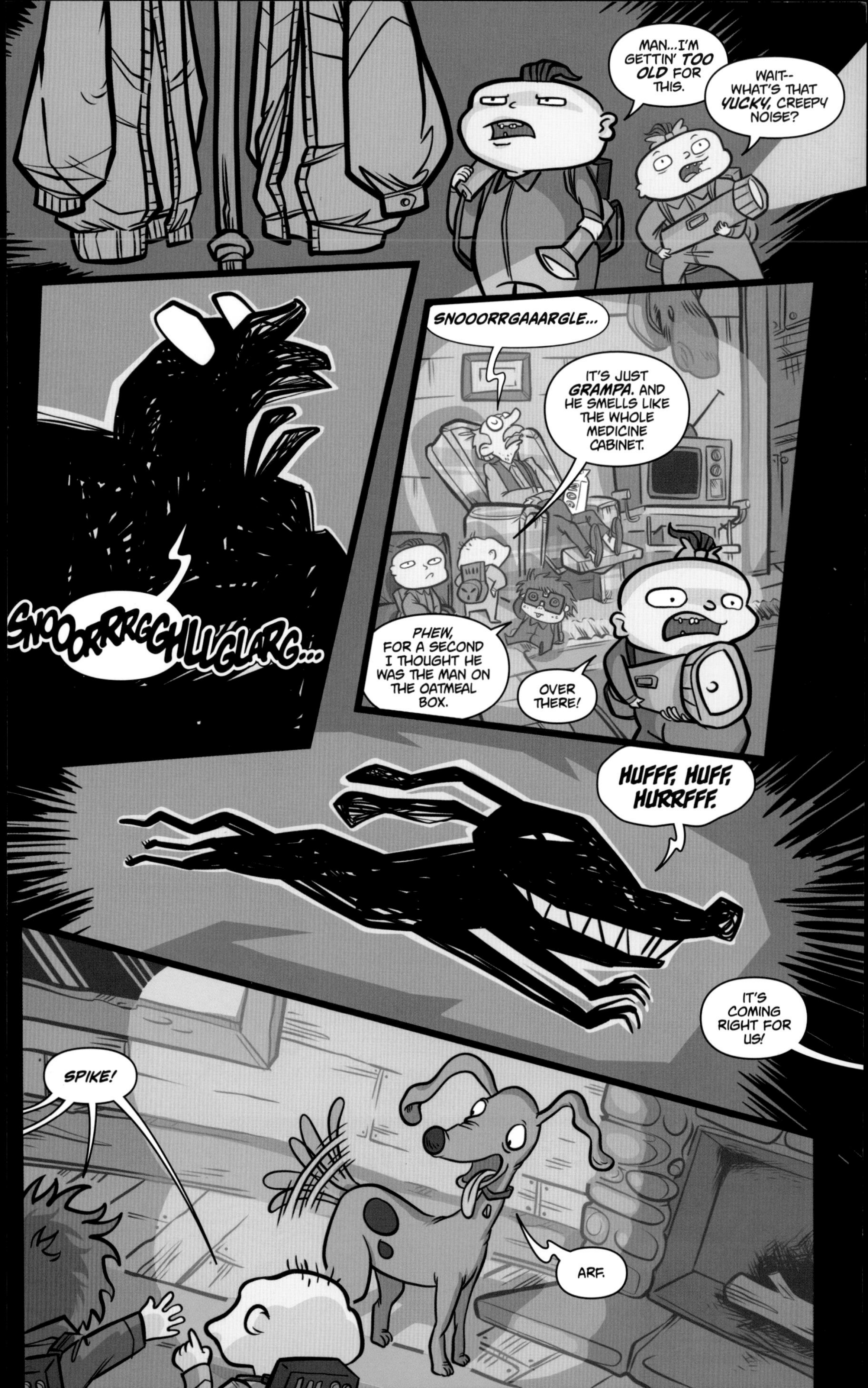
MAN...I'M GETTIN' TOO OLD FOR THIS.
WAIT-- WHAT'S THAT YUCKY, CREEPY NOISE?
SNOOORRRGGHLLGLARG...
SNOOORRGAAARGLE...
IT'S JUST GRAMPA. AND HE SMELLS LIKE THE WHOLE MEDICINE CABINET.
PHEW, FOR A SECOND I THOUGHT HE WAS THE MAN ON THE OATMEAL BOX.
OVER THERE!
HUFFF, HUFF, HURRFFF.
IT'S COMING RIGHT FOR US!
SPIKE!
ARF.

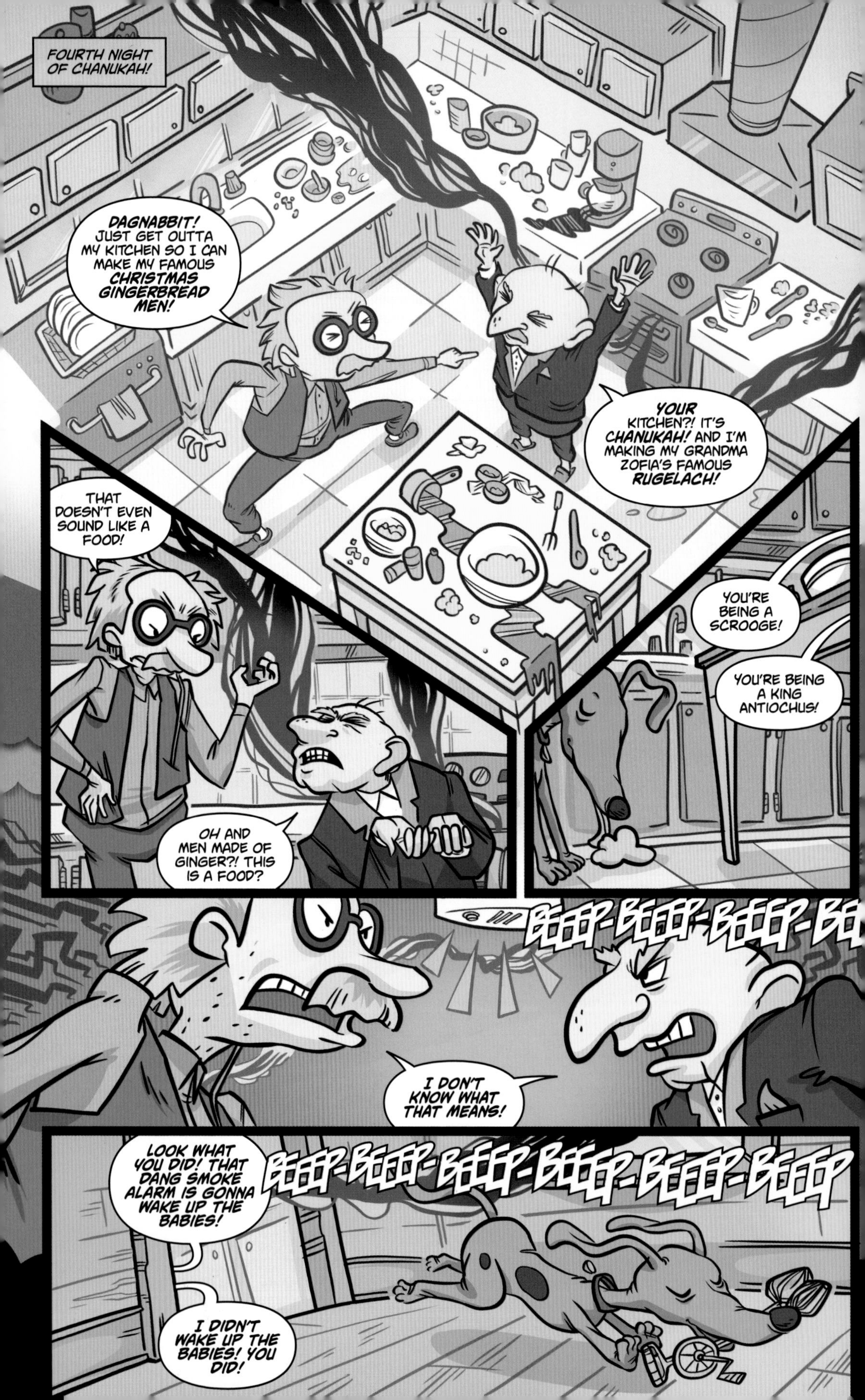
FOURTH NIGHT OF CHANUKAH!
DAGNABBIT! JUST GET OUTTA MY KITCHEN SO I CAN MAKE MY FAMOUS CHRISTMAS GINGERBREAD MEN!
YOUR KITCHEN?! IT'S CHANUKAH! AND I'M MAKING MY GRANDMA ZOFIA'S FAMOUS RUGELACH!
THAT DOESN'T EVEN SOUND LIKE A FOOD!
OH AND MEN MADE OF GINGER?! THIS IS A FOOD?
YOU'RE BEING A SCROOGE!
YOU'RE BEING A KING ANTIOCHUS!
BEEEP-BEEEP-BEEEP-BEEEP-BE
I DON'T KNOW WHAT THAT MEANS!
LOOK WHAT YOU DID! THAT DANG SMOKE ALARM IS GONNA WAKE UP THE BABIES!
BEEEP-BEEEP-BEEEP-BEEEP-BEEEP-BEEEP
I DIDN'T WAKE UP THE BABIES! YOU DID!

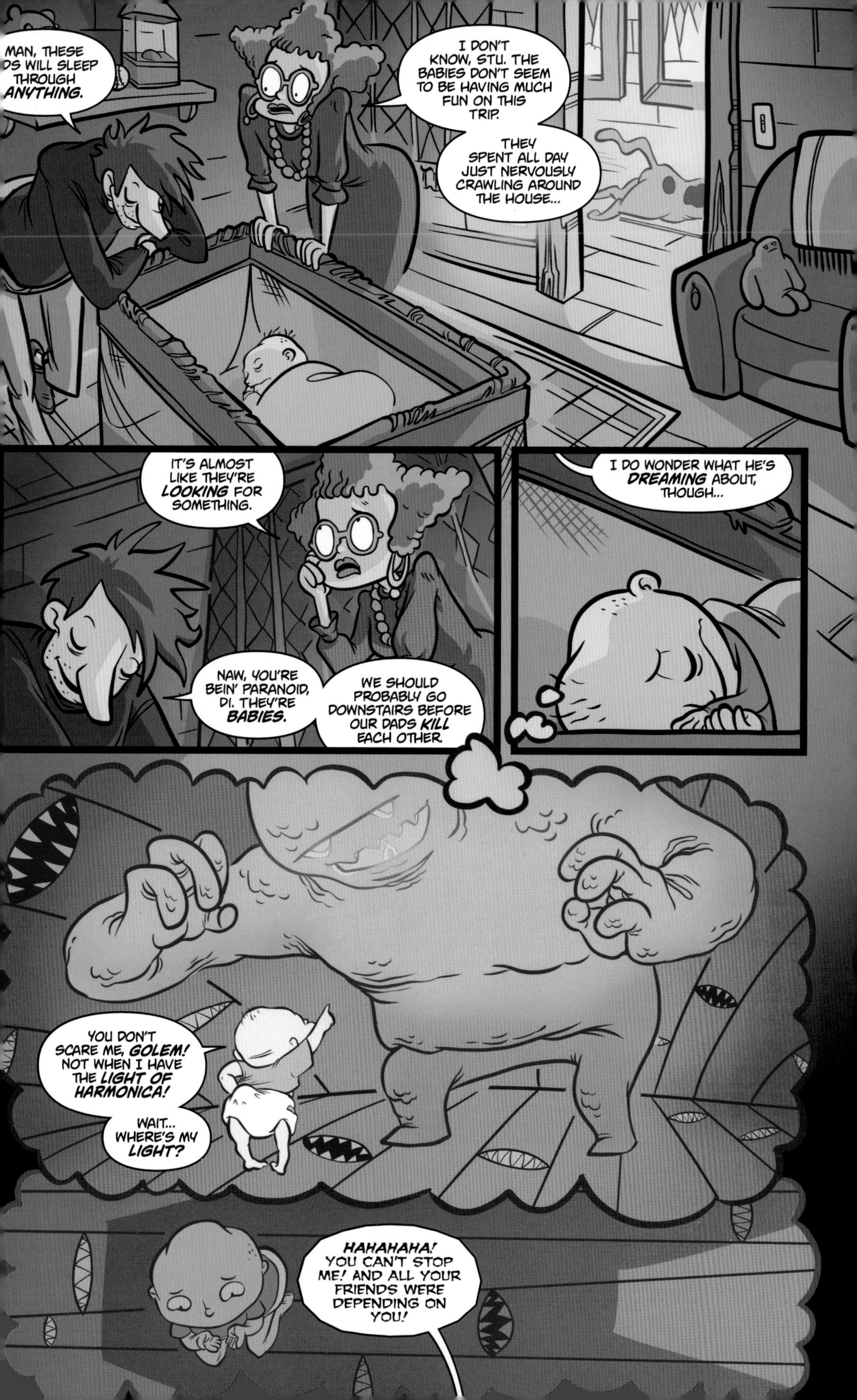
MAN, THESE DS WILL SLEEP THROUGH ANYTHING.
I DON'T KNOW, STU. THE BABIES DON'T SEEM TO BE HAVING MUCH FUN ON THIS TRIP.
THEY SPENT ALL DAY JUST NERVOUSLY CRAWLING AROUND THE HOUSE...
IT'S ALMOST LIKE THEY'RE LOOKING FOR SOMETHING.
NAW, YOU'RE BEIN' PARANOID, DI. THEY'RE BABIES.
WE SHOULD PROBABLY GO DOWNSTAIRS BEFORE OUR DADS KILL EACH OTHER.
I DO WONDER WHAT HE'S DREAMING ABOUT, THOUGH...
YOU DON'T SCARE ME, GOLEM! NOT WHEN I HAVE THE LIGHT OF HARMONICA!
WAIT... WHERE'S MY LIGHT?
HAHAHAHA! YOU CAN'T STOP ME! AND ALL YOUR FRIENDS WERE DEPENDING ON YOU!

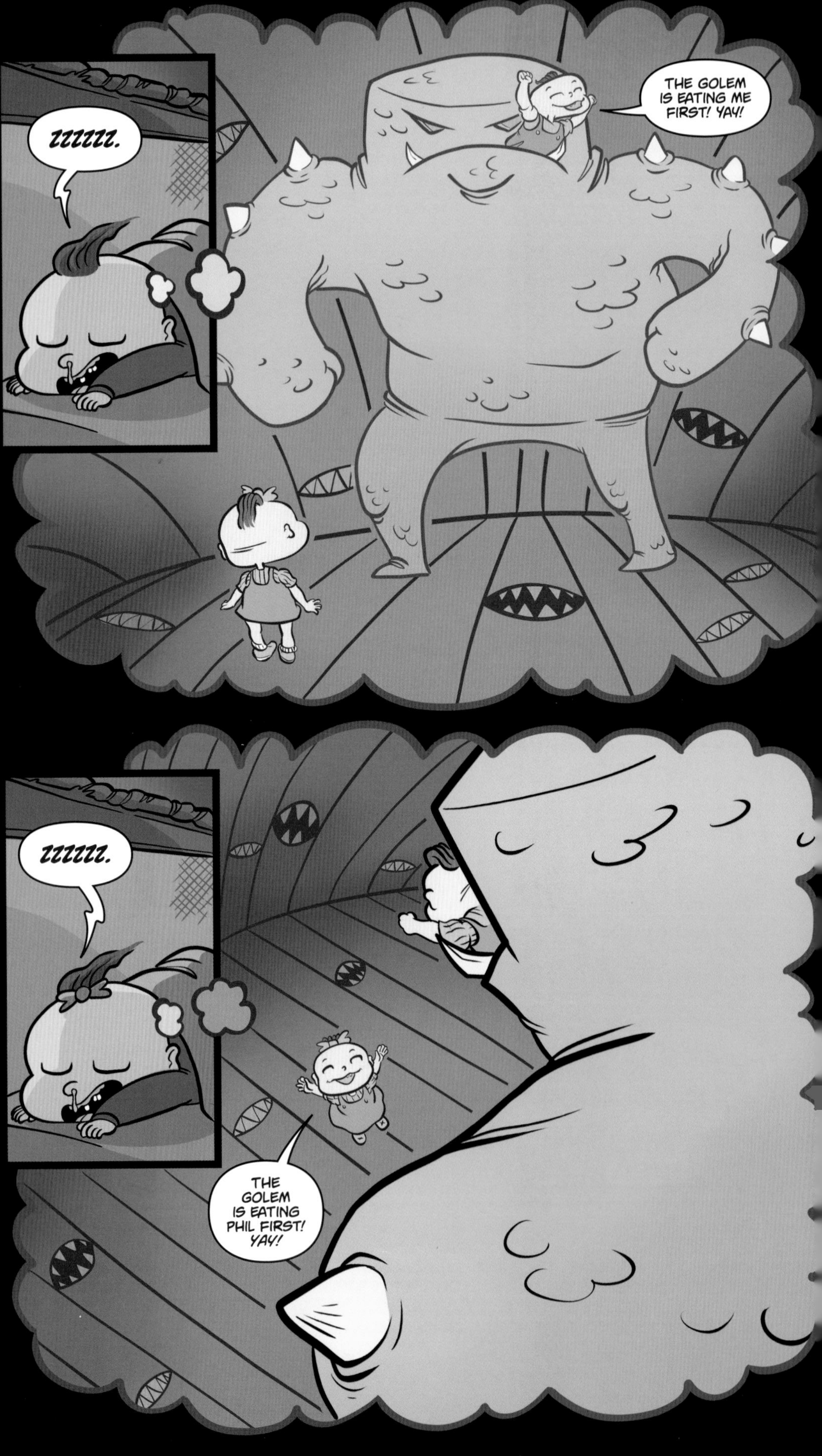
ZZZZZZ.
THE GOLEM IS EATING ME FIRST! YAY!
ZZZZZZ.
THE GOLEM IS EATING PHIL FIRST! YAY!

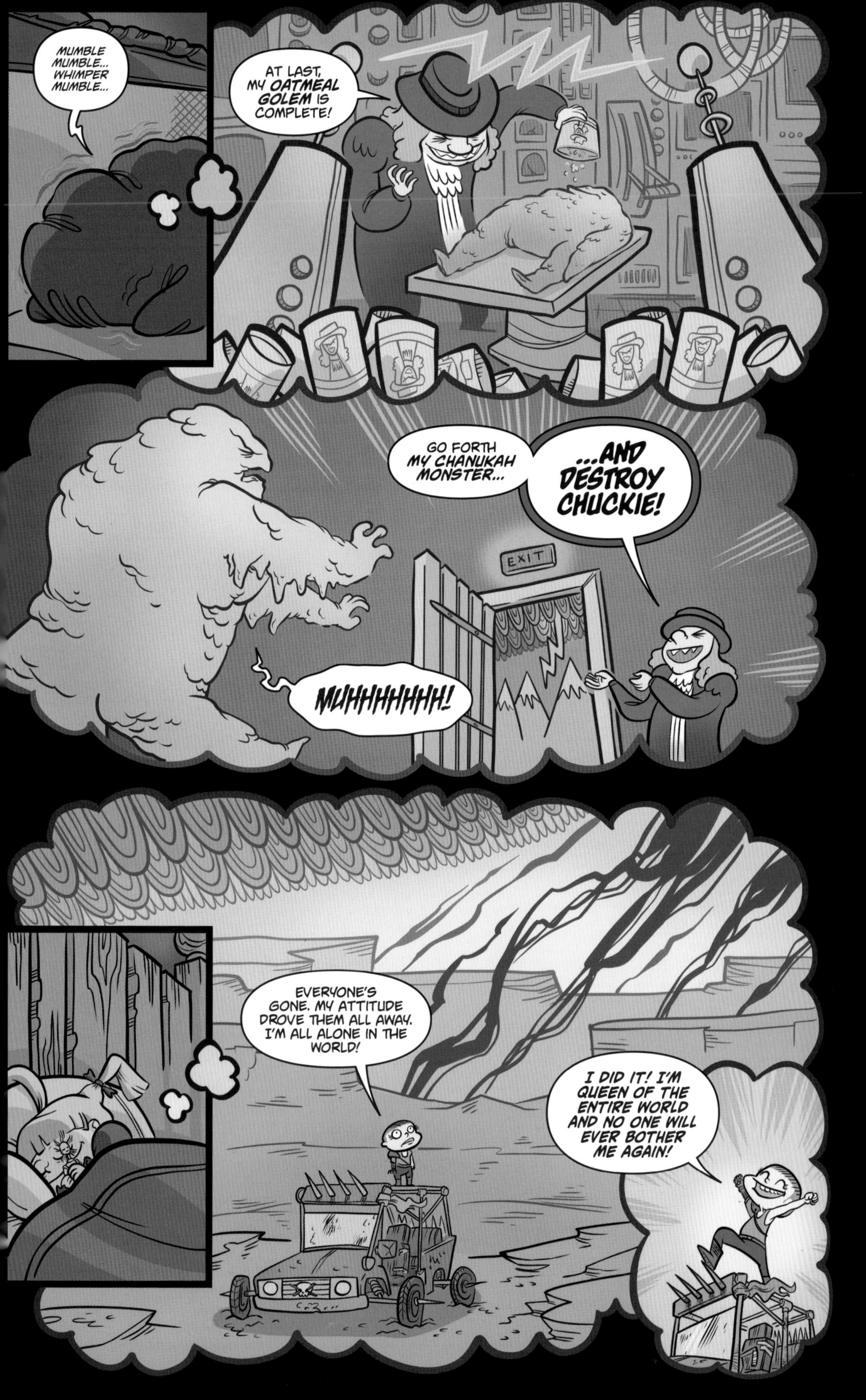
MUMBLE MUMBLE... WHIMPER MUMBLE...
AT LAST, MY OATMEAL GOLEM IS COMPLETE!
GO FORTH MY CHANUKAH MONSTER...
...AND DESTROY CHUCKIE!
EXIT
MUHHHHHHH!
EVERYONE'S GONE. MY ATTITUDE DROVE THEM ALL AWAY. I'M ALL ALONE IN THE WORLD!
I DID IT! I'M QUEEN OF THE ENTIRE WORLD AND NO ONE WILL EVER BOTHER ME AGAIN!

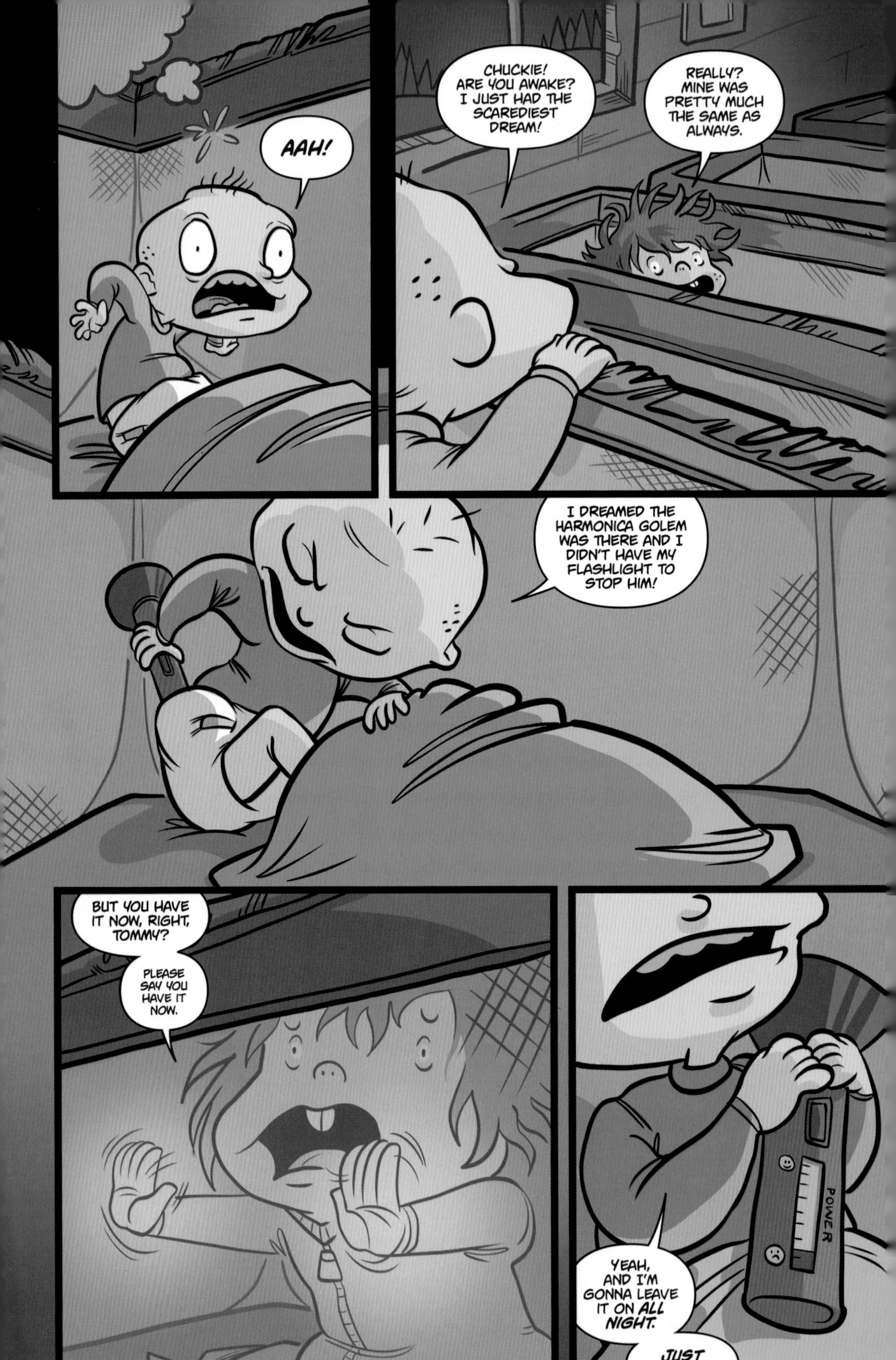
AAH!
CHUCKIE! ARE YOU AWAKE? I JUST HAD THE SCAREDIEST DREAM!
REALLY? MINE WAS PRETTY MUCH THE SAME AS ALWAYS.
I DREAMED THE HARMONICA GOLEM WAS THERE AND I DIDN'T HAVE MY FLASHLIGHT TO STOP HIM!
BUT YOU HAVE IT NOW, RIGHT, TOMMY?
PLEASE SAY YOU HAVE IT NOW.
POWER
YEAH, AND I'M GONNA LEAVE IT ON ALL NIGHT.
JUST IN CASE.

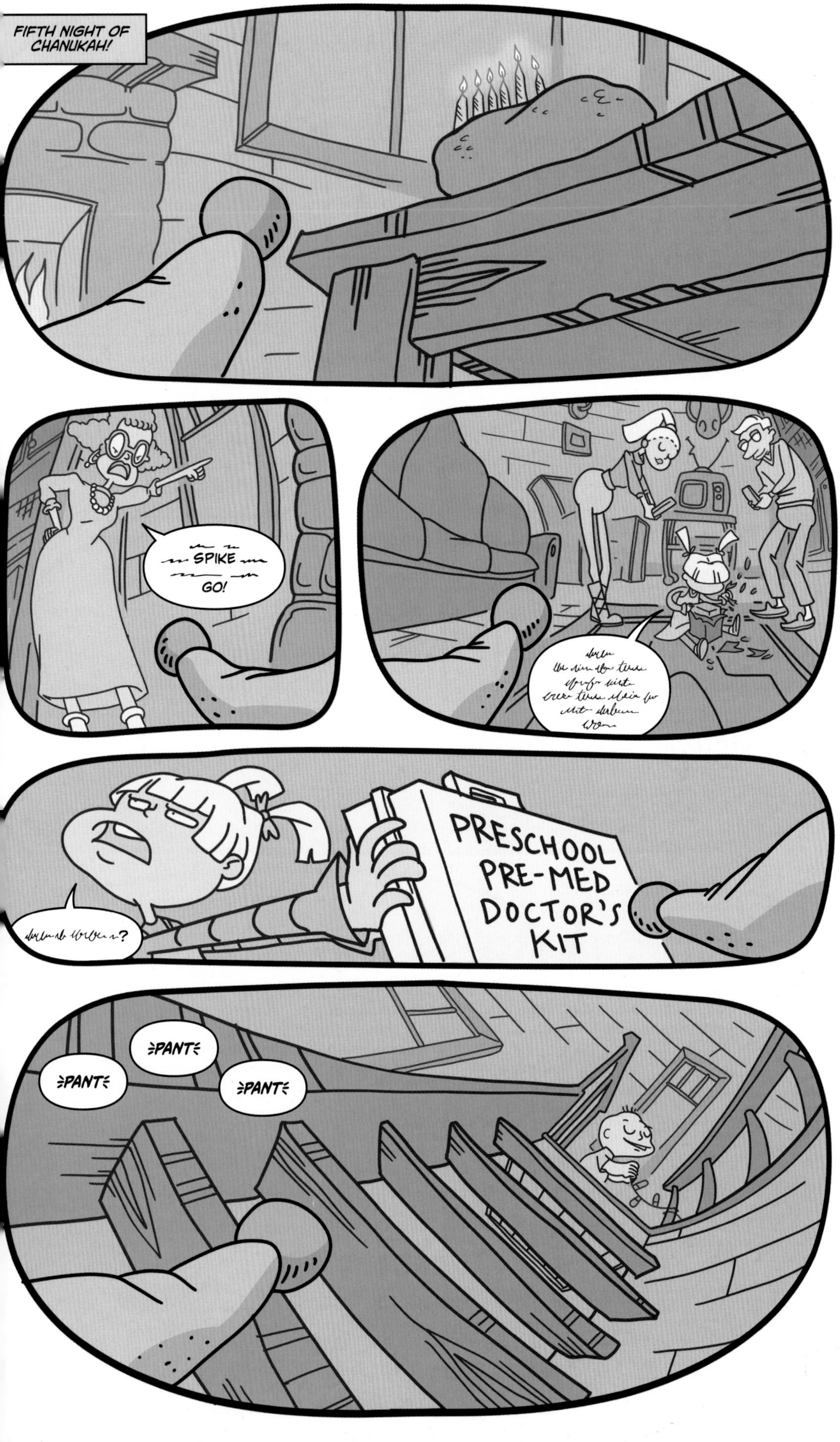
FIFTH NIGHT OF CHANUKAH!
SPIKE
GO!
PRESCHOOL PRE-MED DOCTOR'S KIT
PANT
PANT
PANT

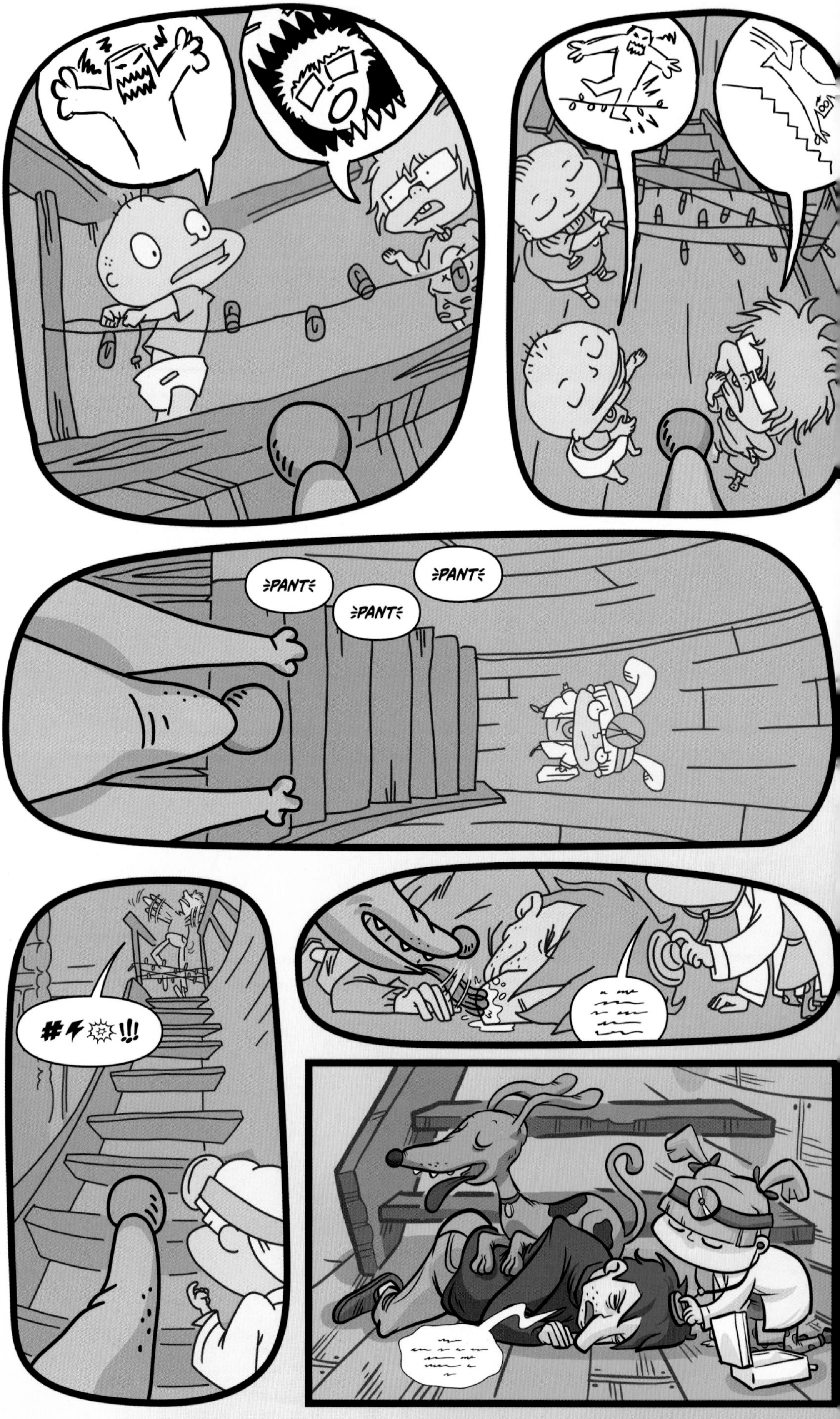
PANT
PANT
PANT

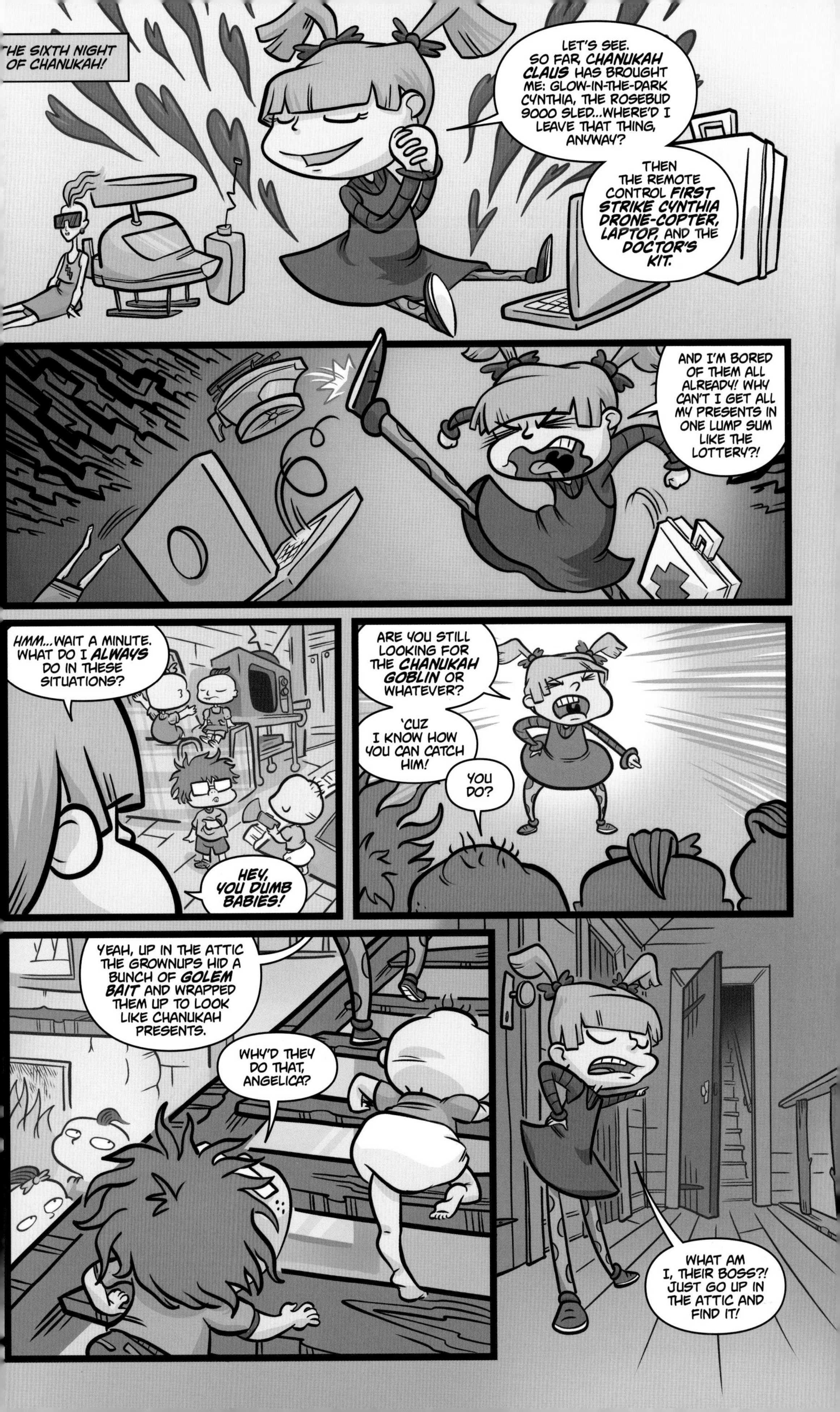
THE SIXTH NIGHT OF CHANUKAH!
LET'S SEE. SO FAR, CHANUKAH CLAUS HAS BROUGHT ME: GLOW-IN-THE-DARK CYNTHIA, THE ROSEBUD 9000 SLED...WHERE'D I LEAVE THAT THING, ANYWAY?
THEN THE REMOTE CONTROL FIRST STRIKE CYNTHIA DRONE-COPTER, LAPTOP, AND THE DOCTOR'S KIT.
AND I'M BORED OF THEM ALL ALREADY! WHY CAN'T I GET ALL MY PRESENTS IN ONE LUMP SUM LIKE THE LOTTERY?!
HMM...WAIT A MINUTE. WHAT DO I ALWAYS DO IN THESE SITUATIONS?
HEY, YOU DUMB BABIES!
ARE YOU STILL LOOKING FOR THE CHANUKAH GOBLIN OR WHATEVER?
'CUZ I KNOW HOW YOU CAN CATCH HIM!
YOU DO?
YEAH, UP IN THE ATTIC THE GROWNUPS HID A BUNCH OF GOLEM BAIT AND WRAPPED THEM UP TO LOOK LIKE CHANUKAH PRESENTS.
WHY'D THEY DO THAT, ANGELICA?
WHAT AM I, THEIR BOSS?! JUST GO UP IN THE ATTIC AND FIND IT!

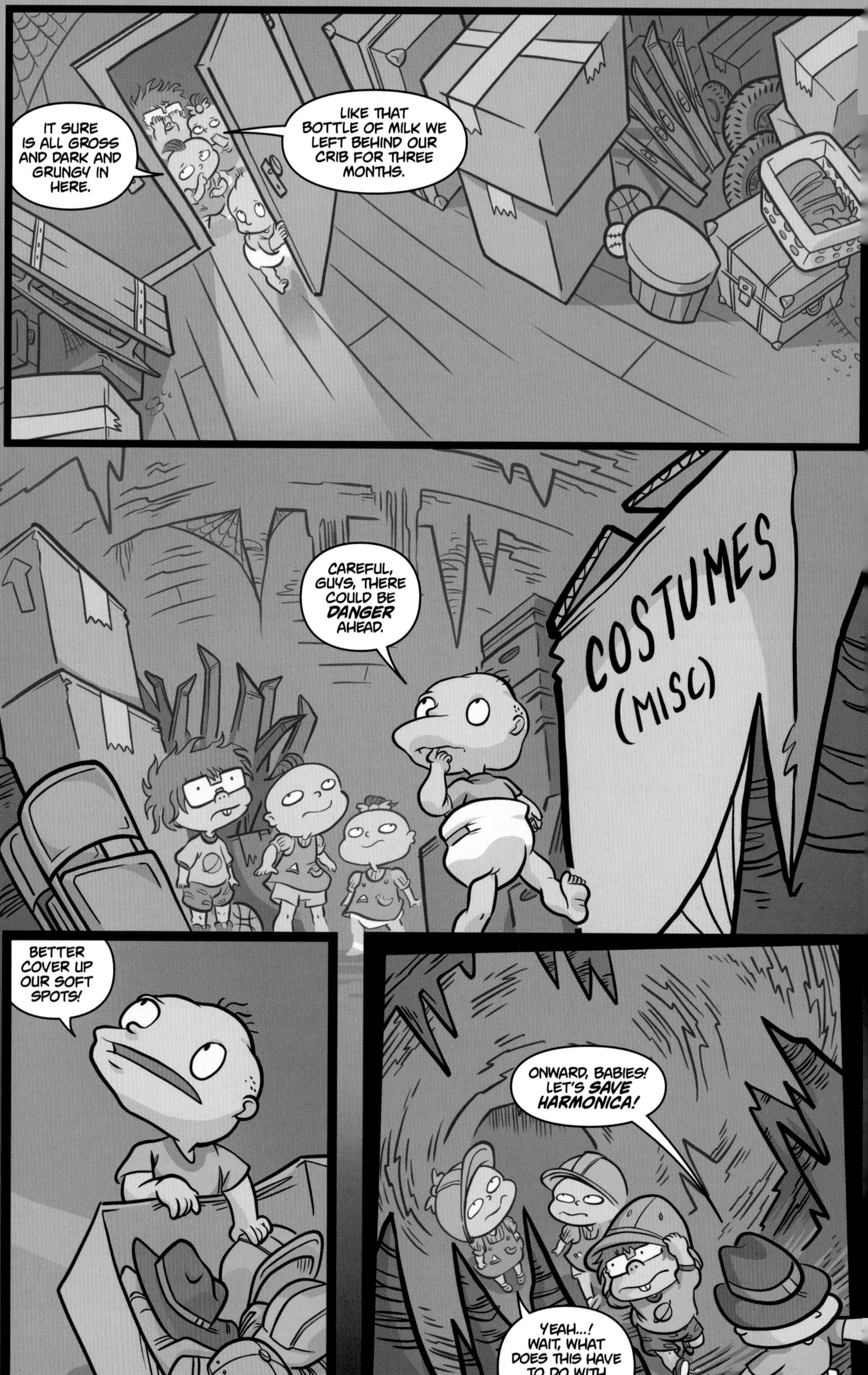
IT SURE IS ALL GROSS AND DARK AND GRUNGY IN HERE.
LIKE THAT BOTTLE OF MILK WE LEFT BEHIND OUR CRIB FOR THREE MONTHS.
CAREFUL, GUYS, THERE COULD BE DANGER AHEAD.
COSTUMES (MISC)
BETTER COVER UP OUR SOFT SPOTS!
ONWARD, BABIES! LET'S SAVE HARMONICA!
YEAH...! WAIT, WHAT DOES THIS HAVE TO DO WITH HARMONICA AGAIN?

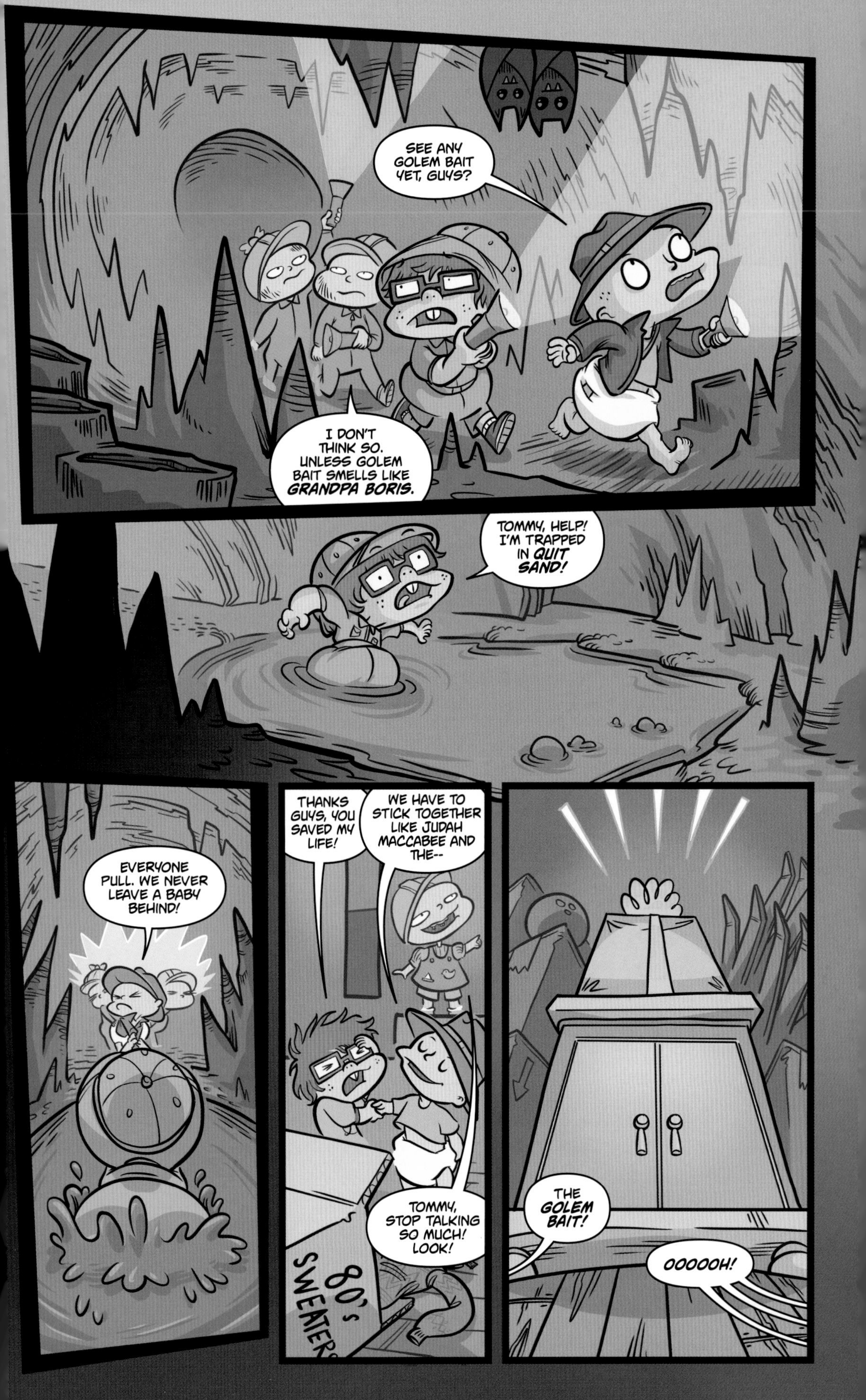
SEE ANY GOLEM BAIT YET, GUYS?
I DON'T THINK SO. UNLESS GOLEM BAIT SMELLS LIKE GRANDPA BORIS.
TOMMY, HELP! I'M TRAPPED IN QUIT SAND!
EVERYONE PULL. WE NEVER LEAVE A BABY BEHIND!
THANKS GUYS, YOU SAVED MY LIFE!
WE HAVE TO STICK TOGETHER LIKE JUDAH MACCABEE AND THE--
TOMMY, STOP TALKING SO MUCH! LOOK!
80'S SWEATERS
THE GOLEM BAIT!
OOOOOH!

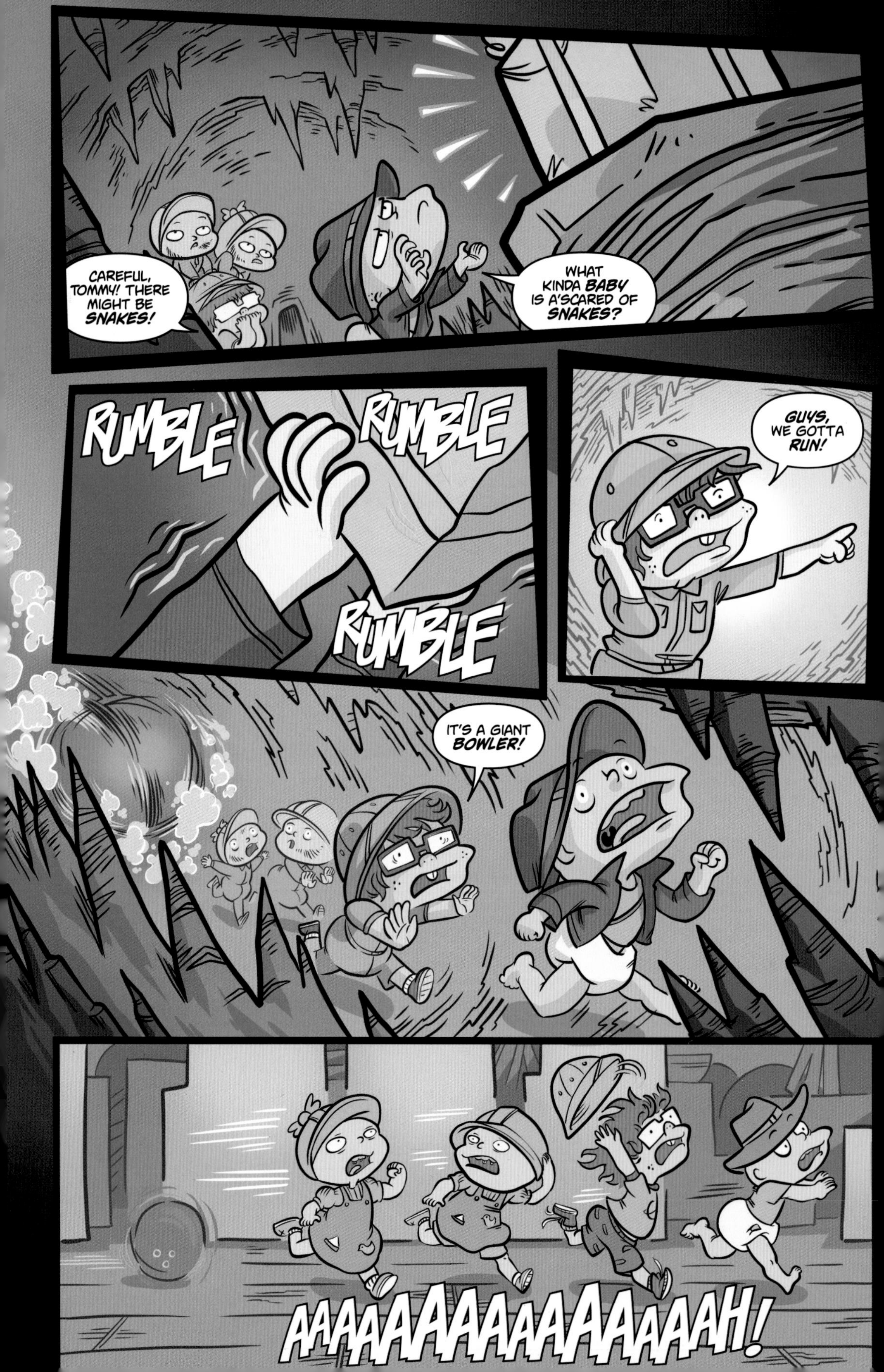
CAREFUL, TOMMY! THERE MIGHT BE SNAKES!
WHAT KINDA BABY IS A'SCARED OF SNAKES?
RUMBLE
RUMBLE
RUMBLE
GUYS, WE GOTTA RUN!
IT'S A GIANT BOWLER!
AAAAAAAAAAAAAAAAH!

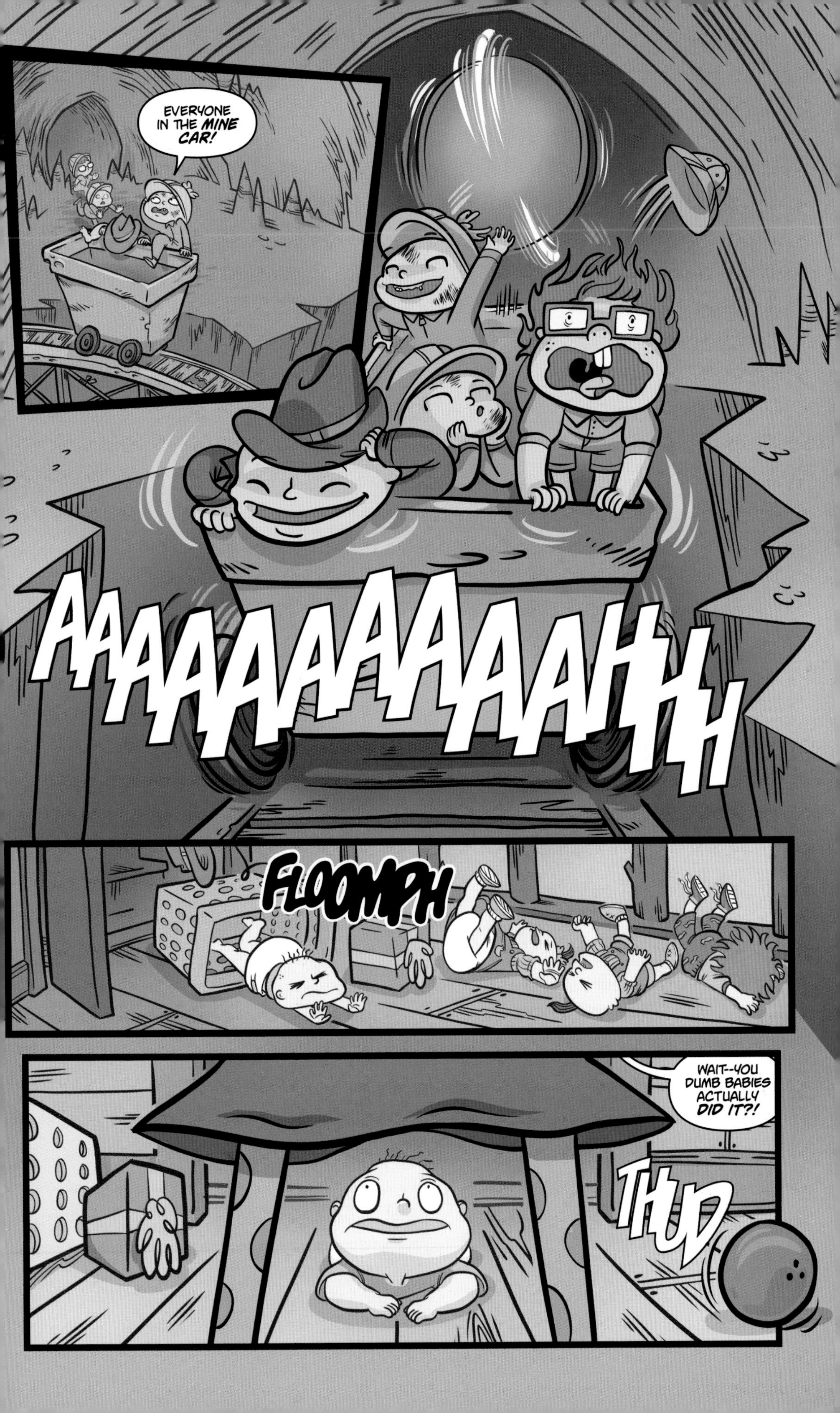
EVERYONE IN THE MINE CAR!
AAAAAAAAAAAHHH
FLOOMPH
WAIT--YOU DUMB BABIES ACTUALLY DID IT?!
THUD

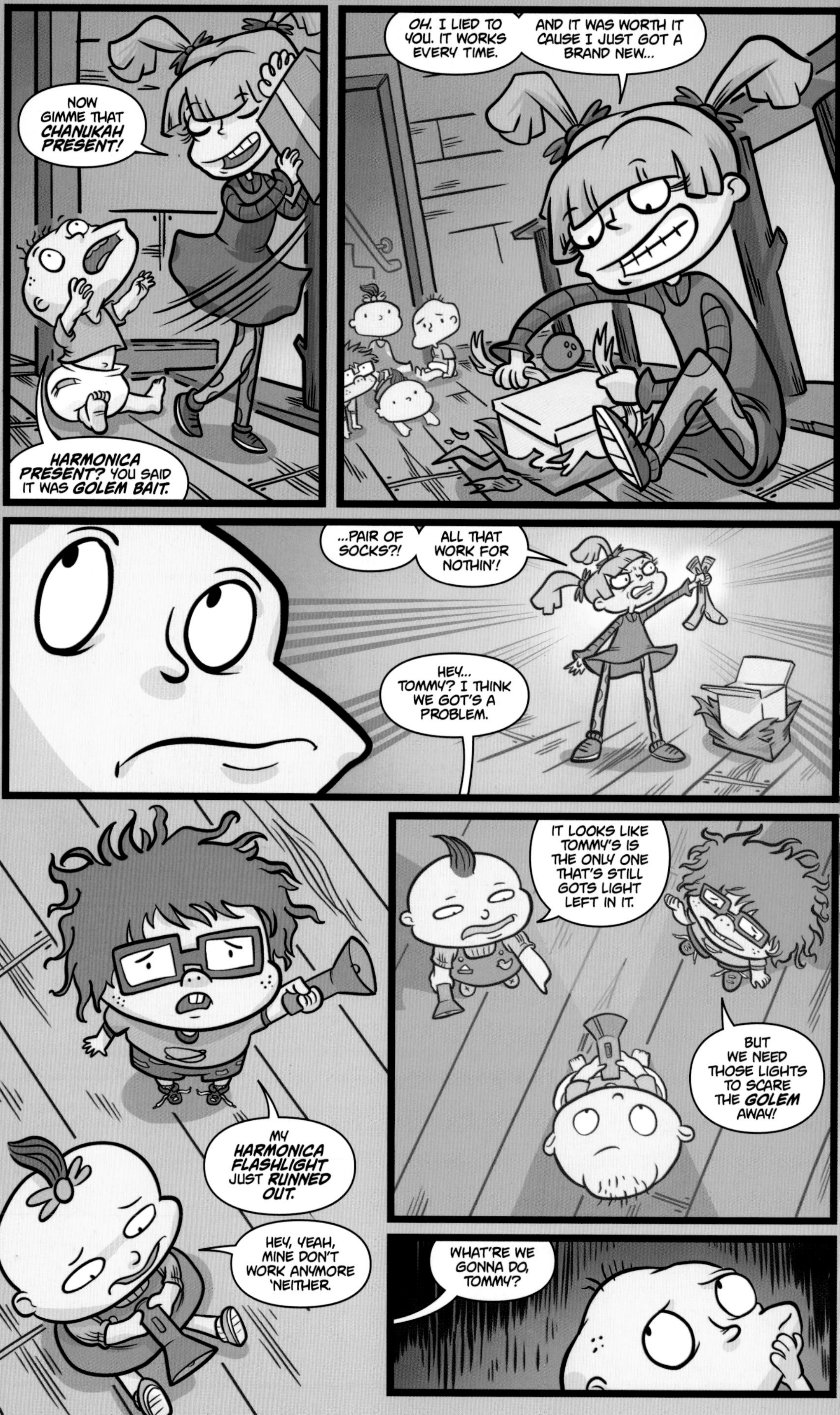
NOW GIMME THAT CHANUKAH PRESENT!
HARMONICA PRESENT? YOU SAID IT WAS GOLEM BAIT.
OH. I LIED TO YOU. IT WORKS EVERY TIME.
AND IT WAS WORTH IT CAUSE I JUST GOT A BRAND NEW...
...PAIR OF SOCKS?!
ALL THAT WORK FOR NOTHIN'!
HEY... TOMMY? I THINK WE GOT'S A PROBLEM.
MY HARMONICA FLASHLIGHT JUST RUNNED OUT.
HEY, YEAH, MINE DON'T WORK ANYMORE 'NEITHER.
IT LOOKS LIKE TOMMY'S IS THE ONLY ONE THAT'S STILL GOTS LIGHT LEFT IN IT.
BUT WE NEED THOSE LIGHTS TO SCARE THE GOLEM AWAY!
WHAT'RE WE GONNA DO, TOMMY?

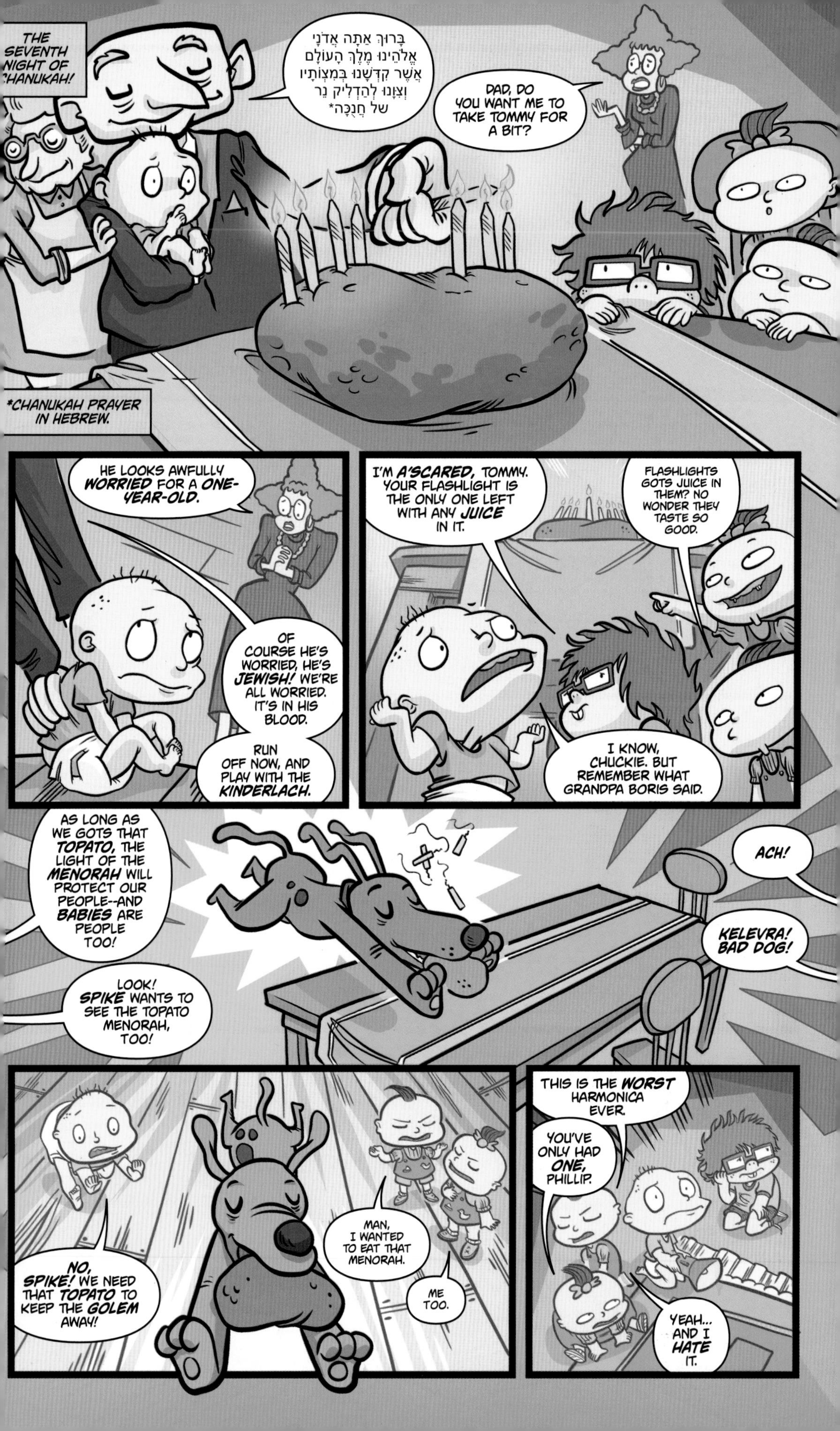
THE SEVENTH NIGHT OF CHANUKAH!
בָּרוּךְ אַתָּה אֲדֹנָי
אֱלֹהֵינוּ מֶלֶךְ הָעוֹלָם
אֲשֶׁר קִדְּשָׁנוּ בְּמִצְוֹתָיו
וְצִוָּנוּ לְהַדְלִיק נֵר
שֶׁל חֲנֻכָּה*
DAD, DO YOU WANT ME TO TAKE TOMMY FOR A BIT?
*CHANUKAH PRAYER IN HEBREW.
HE LOOKS AWFULLY WORRIED FOR A ONE-YEAR-OLD.
OF COURSE HE'S WORRIED, HE'S JEWISH! WE'RE ALL WORRIED. IT'S IN HIS BLOOD.
RUN OFF NOW, AND PLAY WITH THE KINDERLACH.
I'M A'SCARED, TOMMY. YOUR FLASHLIGHT IS THE ONLY ONE LEFT WITH ANY JUICE IN IT.
FLASHLIGHTS GOTS JUICE IN THEM? NO WONDER THEY TASTE SO GOOD.
I KNOW, CHUCKIE. BUT REMEMBER WHAT GRANDPA BORIS SAID.
AS LONG AS WE GOTS THAT TOPATO, THE LIGHT OF THE MENORAH WILL PROTECT OUR PEOPLE--AND BABIES ARE PEOPLE TOO!
LOOK! SPIKE WANTS TO SEE THE TOPATO MENORAH, TOO!
ACH!
KELEVRA! BAD DOG!
NO, SPIKE! WE NEED THAT TOPATO TO KEEP THE GOLEM AWAY!
MAN, I WANTED TO EAT THAT MENORAH.
ME TOO.
THIS IS THE WORST HARMONICA EVER.
YOU'VE ONLY HAD ONE, PHILLIP.
YEAH... AND I HATE IT.

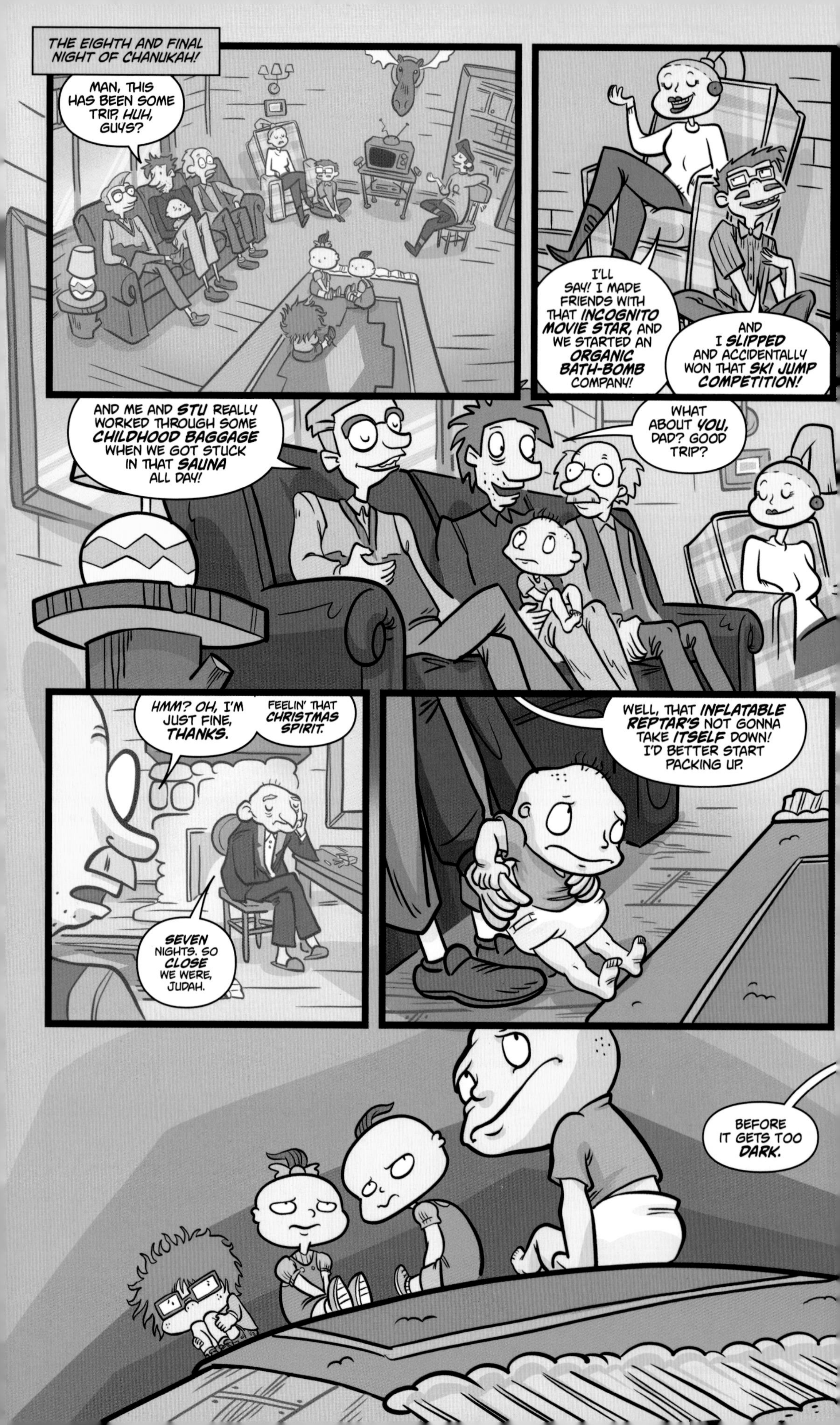
THE EIGHTH AND FINAL NIGHT OF CHANUKAH!
MAN, THIS HAS BEEN SOME TRIP, HUH, GUYS?
I'LL SAY! I MADE FRIENDS WITH THAT INCOGNITO MOVIE STAR, AND WE STARTED AN ORGANIC BATH-BOMB COMPANY!
AND I SLIPPED AND ACCIDENTALLY WON THAT SKI JUMP COMPETITION!
AND ME AND STU REALLY WORKED THROUGH SOME CHILDHOOD BAGGAGE WHEN WE GOT STUCK IN THAT SAUNA ALL DAY!
WHAT ABOUT YOU, DAD? GOOD TRIP?
HMM? OH, I'M JUST FINE, THANKS.
FEELIN' THAT CHRISTMAS SPIRIT.
SEVEN NIGHTS. SO CLOSE WE WERE, JUDAH.
WELL, THAT INFLATABLE REPTAR'S NOT GONNA TAKE ITSELF DOWN! I'D BETTER START PACKING UP.
BEFORE IT GETS TOO DARK.

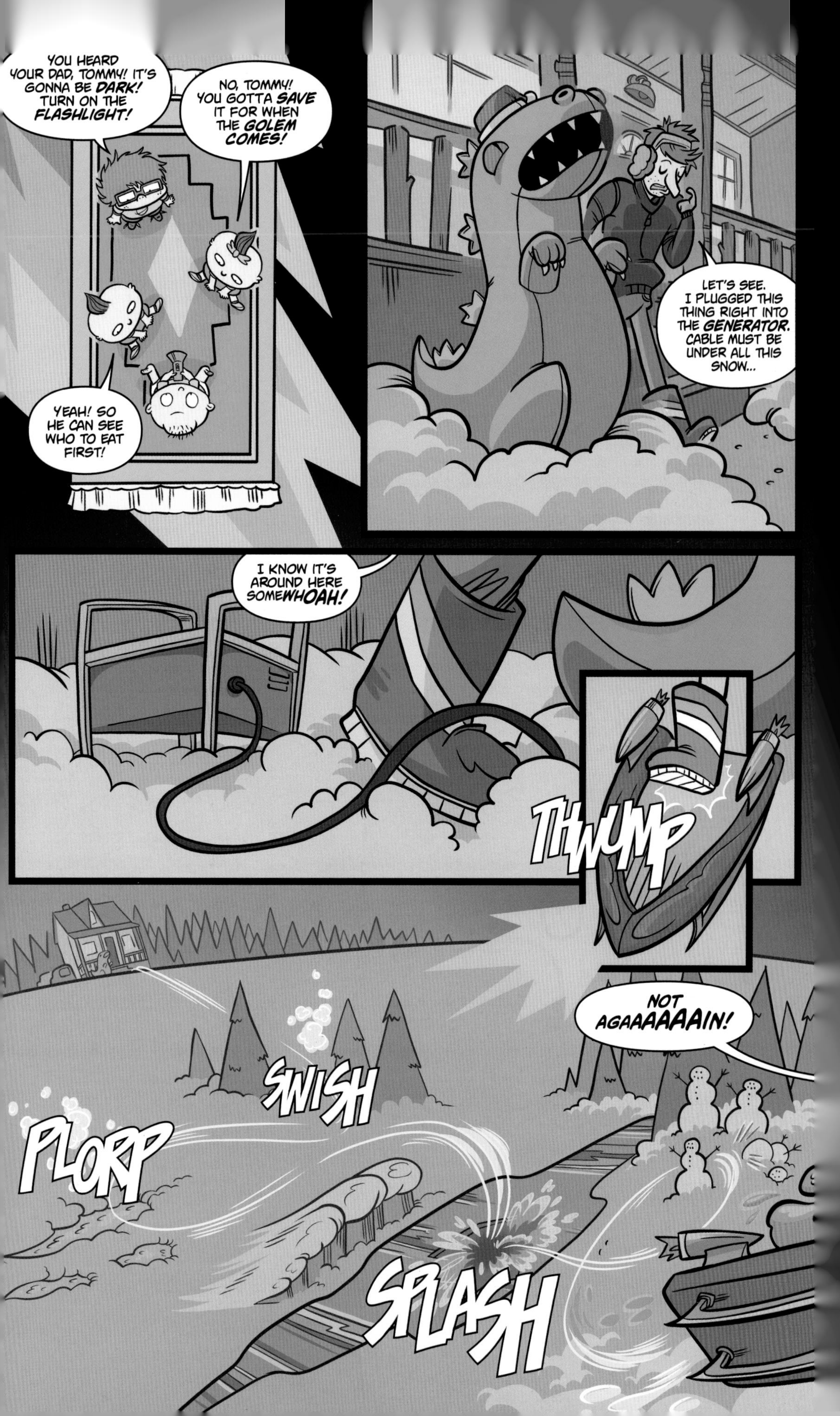

YOU HEARD YOUR DAD, TOMMY! IT'S GONNA BE DARK! TURN ON THE FLASHLIGHT!
NO, TOMMY! YOU GOTTA SAVE IT FOR WHEN THE GOLEM COMES!
YEAH! SO HE CAN SEE WHO TO EAT FIRST!
LET'S SEE. I PLUGGED THIS THING RIGHT INTO THE GENERATOR. CABLE MUST BE UNDER ALL THIS SNOW...
I KNOW IT'S AROUND HERE SOMEWHOAH!
THWUMP
NOT AGAAAAAAIN!
SWISH
PLORP
SPLASH

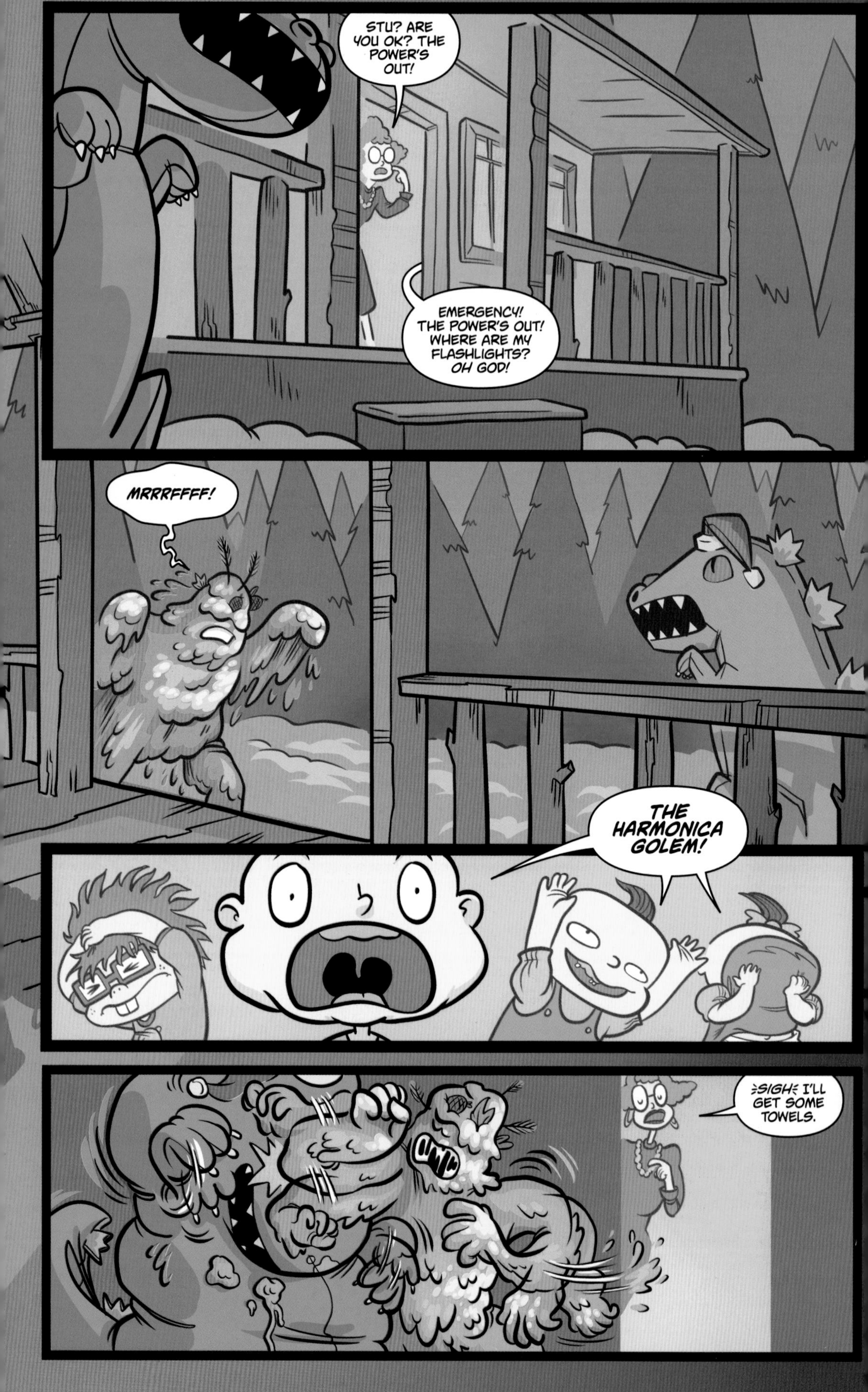
STU? ARE YOU OK? THE POWER'S OUT!
EMERGENCY! THE POWER'S OUT! WHERE ARE MY FLASHLIGHTS? OH GOD!
MRRRFFFF!
THE HARMONICA GOLEM!
SIGH I'LL GET SOME TOWELS.

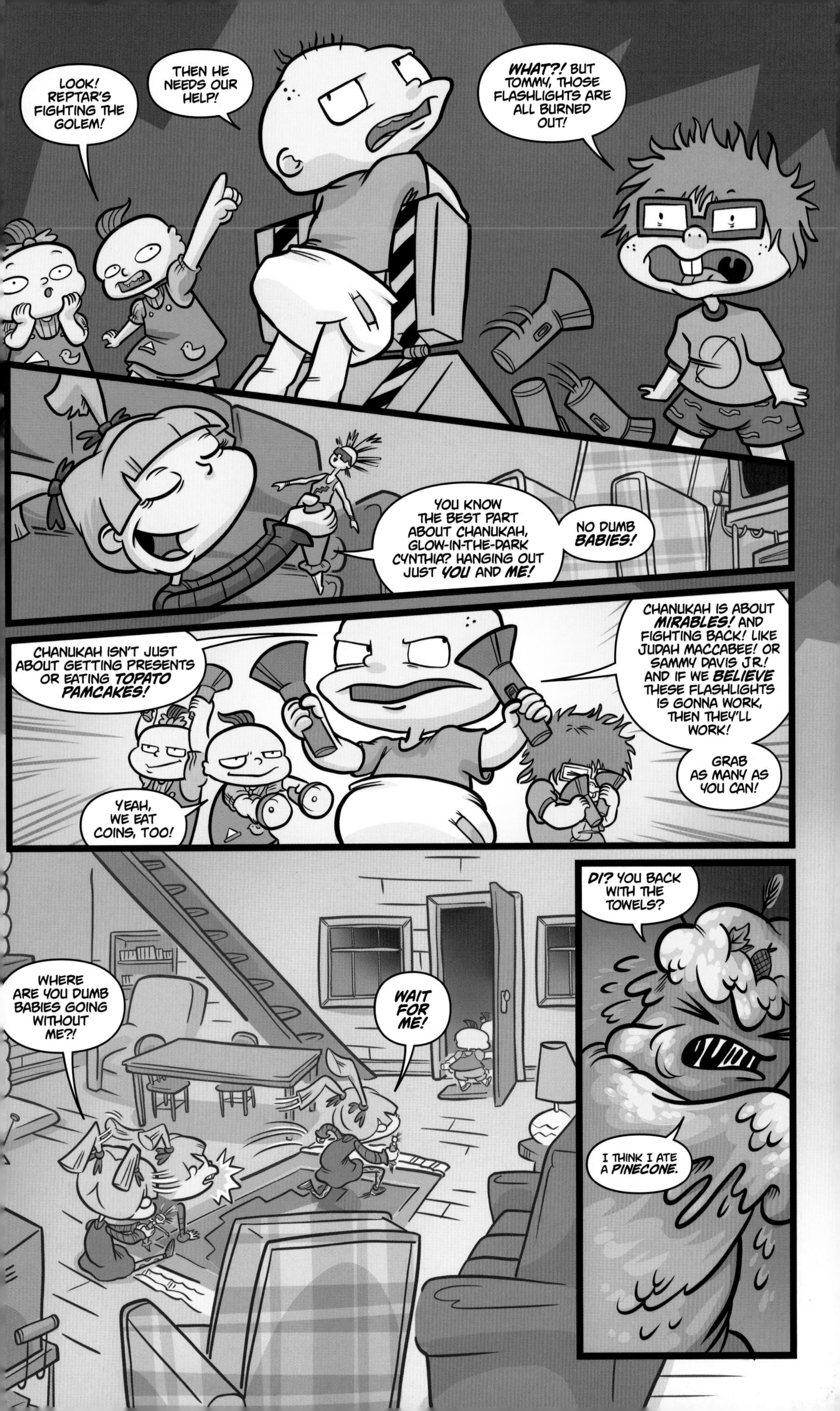

LOOK! REPTAR'S FIGHTING THE GOLEM!
THEN HE NEEDS OUR HELP!
WHAT?! BUT TOMMY, THOSE FLASHLIGHTS ARE ALL BURNED OUT!
YOU KNOW THE BEST PART ABOUT CHANUKAH, GLOW-IN-THE-DARK CYNTHIA? HANGING OUT JUST YOU AND ME!
NO DUMB BABIES!
CHANUKAH ISN'T JUST ABOUT GETTING PRESENTS OR EATING TOPATO PAMCAKES!
CHANUKAH IS ABOUT MIRABLES! AND FIGHTING BACK! LIKE JUDAH MACCABEE! OR SAMMY DAVIS JR.! AND IF WE BELIEVE THESE FLASHLIGHTS IS GONNA WORK, THEN THEY'LL WORK!
GRAB AS MANY AS YOU CAN!
YEAH, WE EAT COINS, TOO!
WHERE ARE YOU DUMB BABIES GOING WITHOUT ME?!
WAIT FOR ME!
DI? YOU BACK WITH THE TOWELS?
I THINK I ATE A PINECONE.

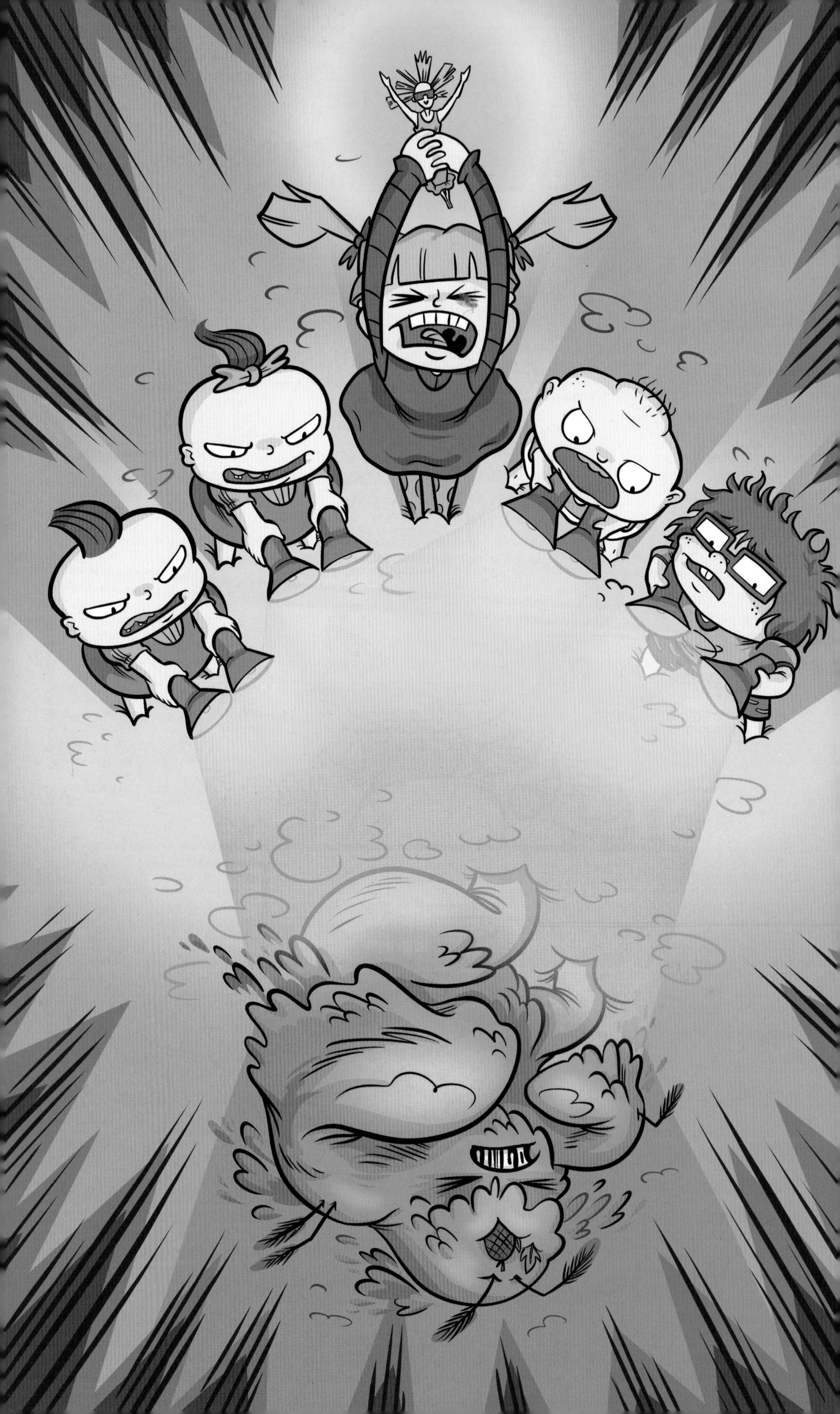

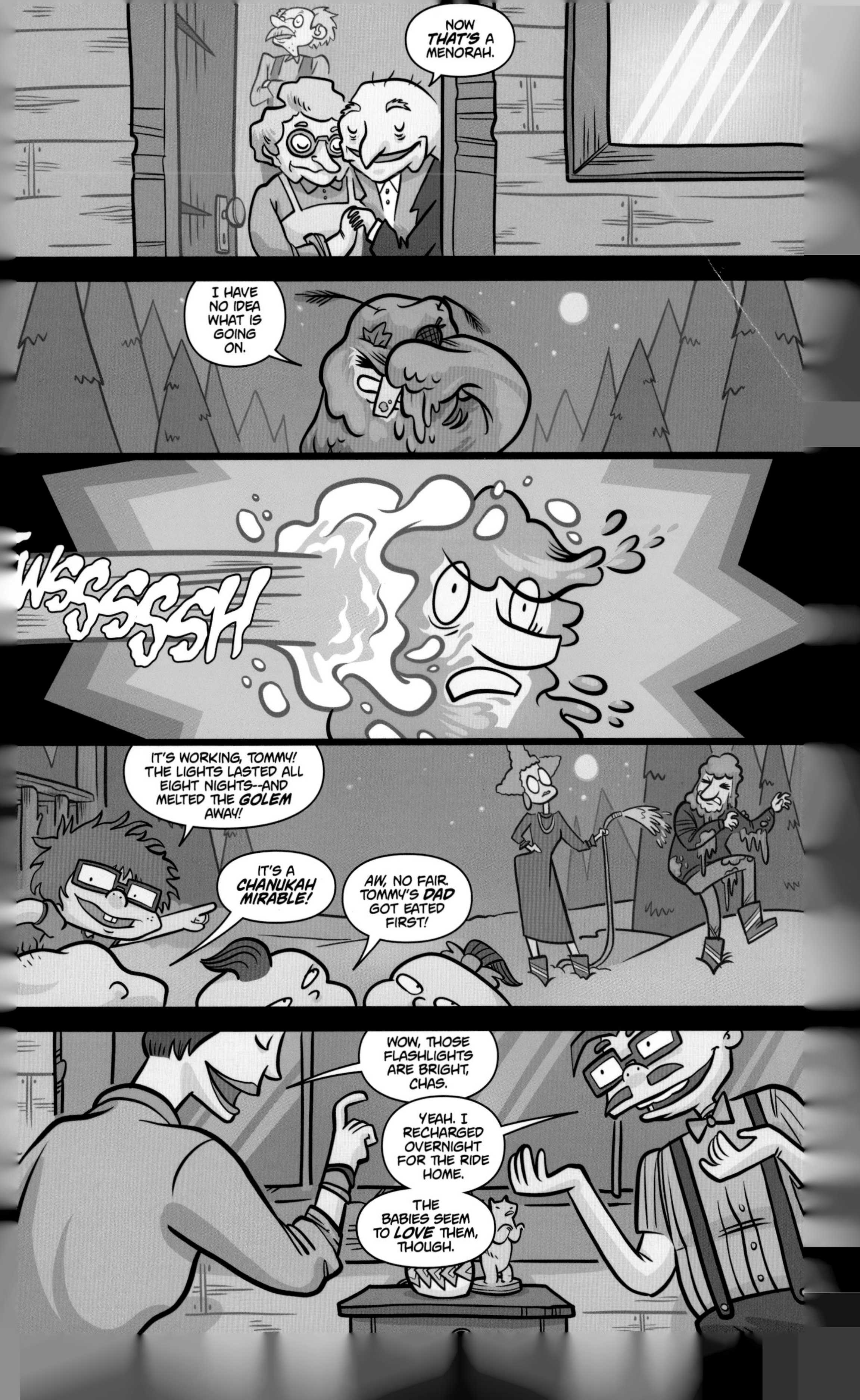
NOW THAT'S A MENORAH.
I HAVE NO IDEA WHAT IS GOING ON.
WSSSSSH
IT'S WORKING, TOMMY! THE LIGHTS LASTED ALL EIGHT NIGHTS--AND MELTED THE GOLEM AWAY!
IT'S A CHANUKAH MIRABLE!
AW, NO FAIR. TOMMY'S DAD GOT EATED FIRST!
WOW, THOSE FLASHLIGHTS ARE BRIGHT, CHAS.
YEAH. I RECHARGED OVERNIGHT FOR THE RIDE HOME.
THE BABIES SEEM TO LOVE THEM, THOUGH.

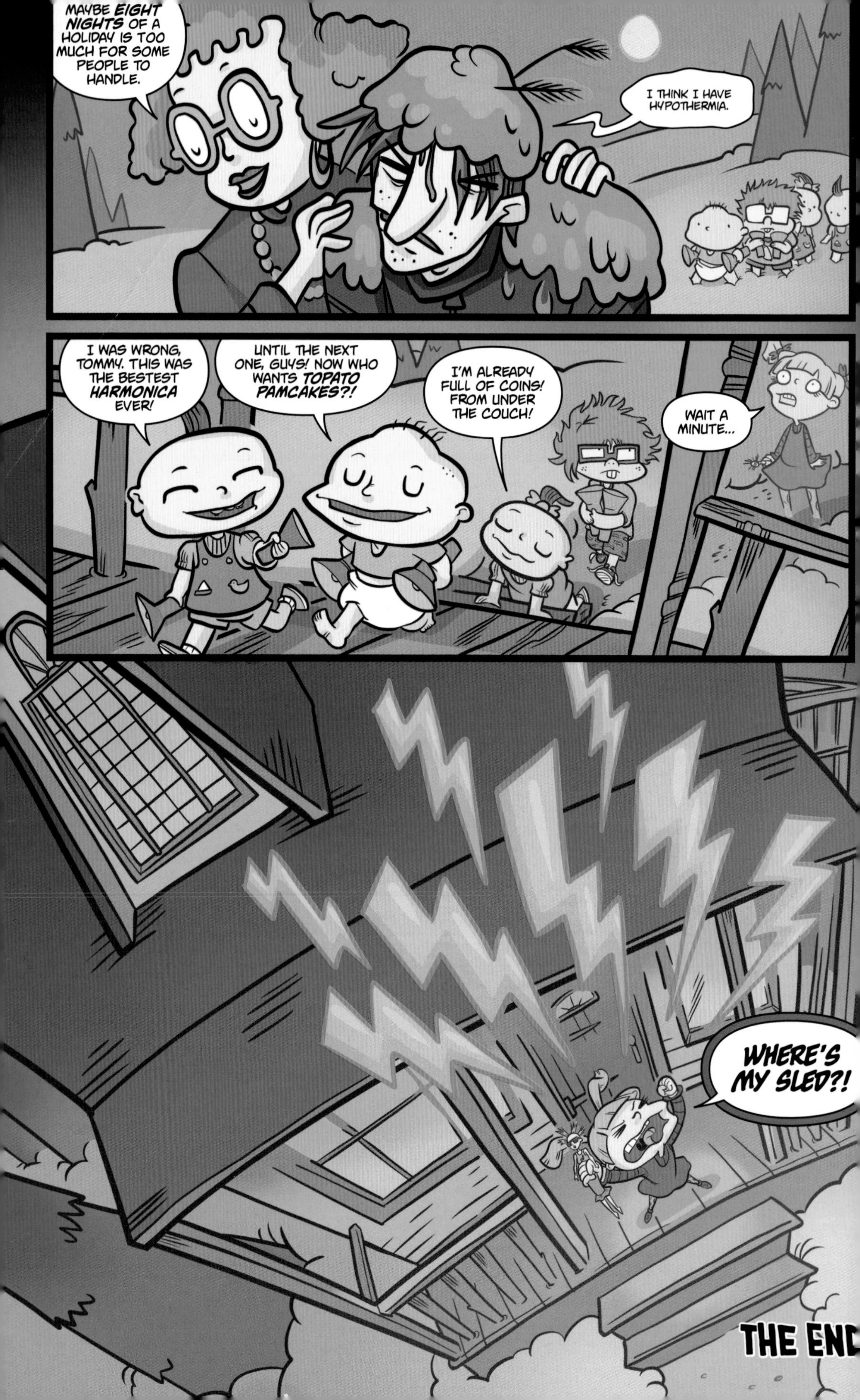
MAYBE EIGHT NIGHTS OF A HOLIDAY IS TOO MUCH FOR SOME PEOPLE TO HANDLE.
I THINK I HAVE HYPOTHERMIA.
I WAS WRONG, TOMMY. THIS WAS THE BESTEST HARMONICA EVER!
UNTIL THE NEXT ONE, GUYS! NOW WHO WANTS TOPATO PAMCAKES?!
I'M ALREADY FULL OF COINS! FROM UNDER THE COUCH!
WAIT A MINUTE...
WHERE'S MY SLED?!
THE END

COVER
GALLERY

“R” IS FOR REPTAR COVER BY **SAVANNAH GANUCHEAU**

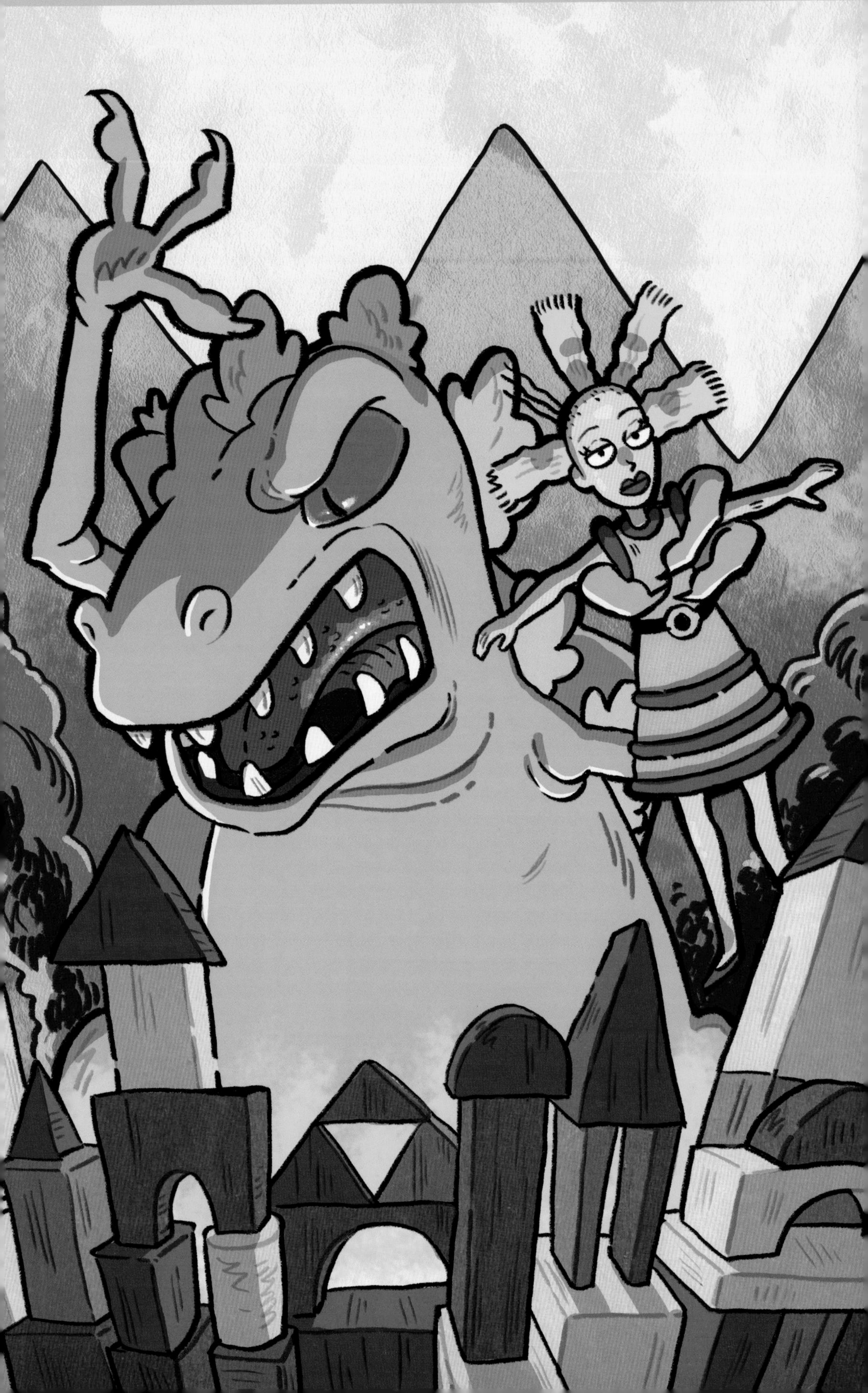

"R" IS FOR REPTAR VARIANT COVER BY **MATT FRANK**

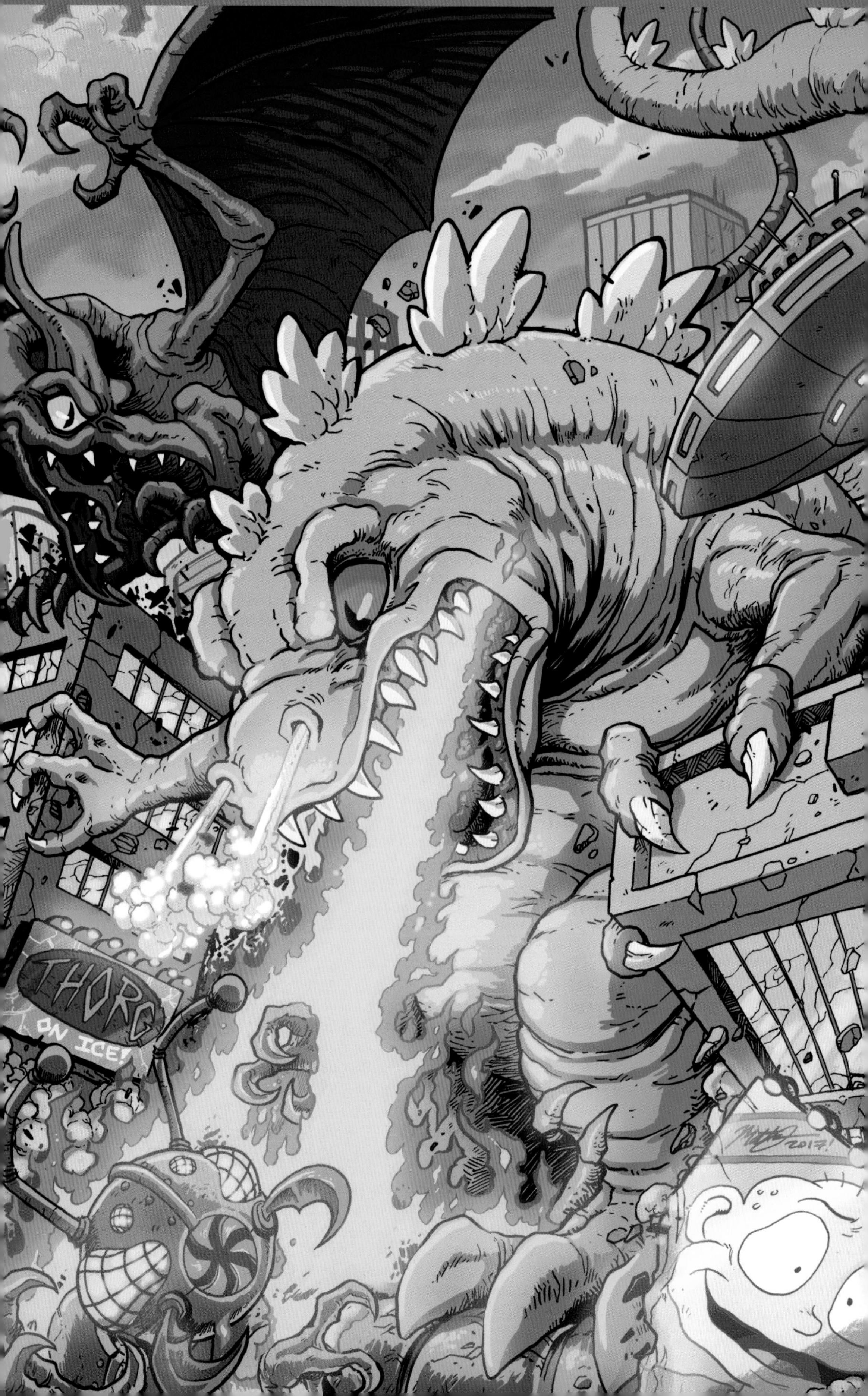
THORG
ON ICE!

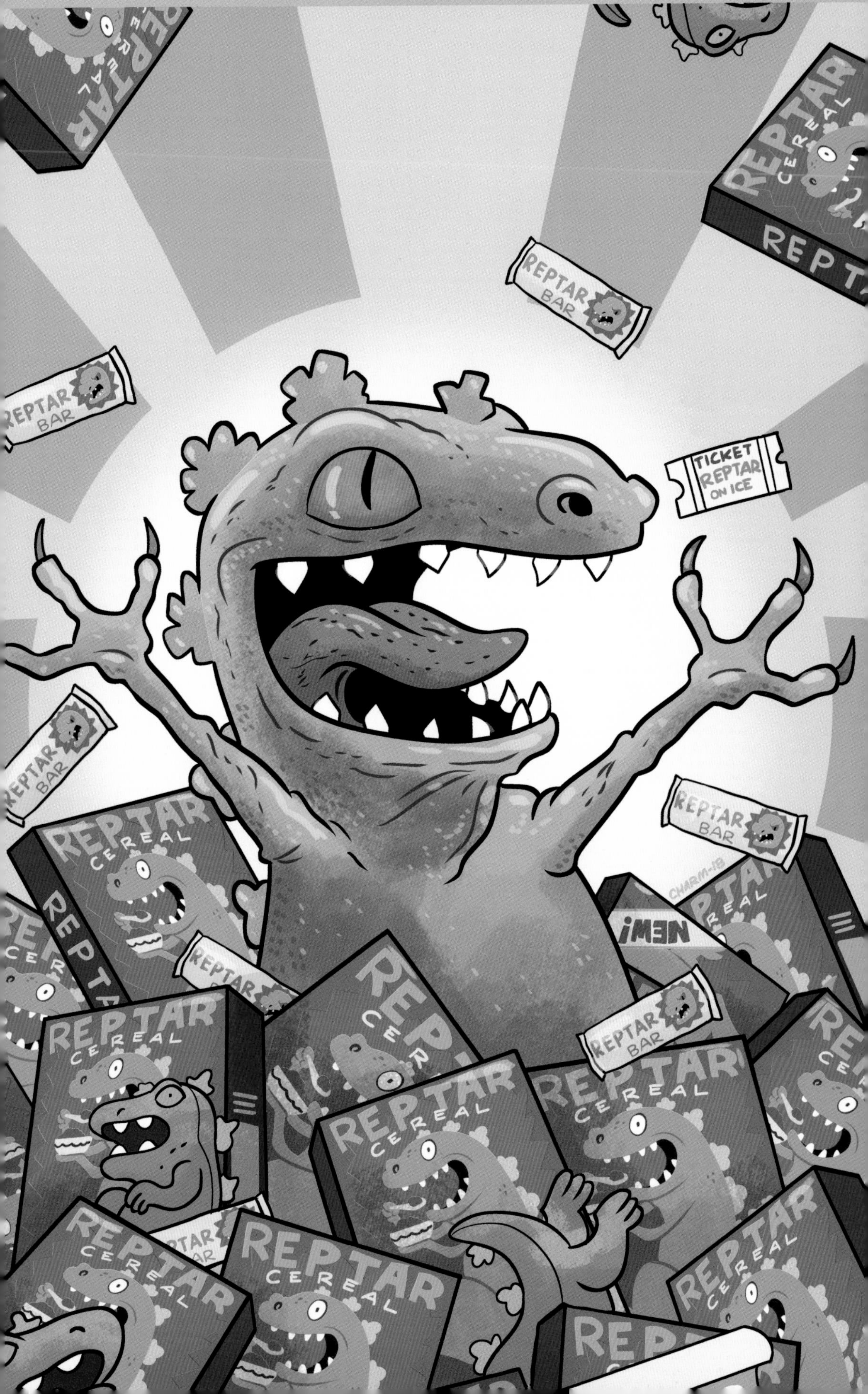
REPTAR CEREAL
REPTAR BAR
TICKET REPTAR ON ICE
REPTAR BAR
REPTAR BAR
REPTAR CEREAL
REPTAR
REPTAR BAR
CHARM-18
NEW!
REPTAR CEREAL
REPTAR BAR
REPTAR CEREAL
REPTAR CEREAL

"C" IS FOR CHANUKAH COVER BY **CHRYSTIN GARLAND**

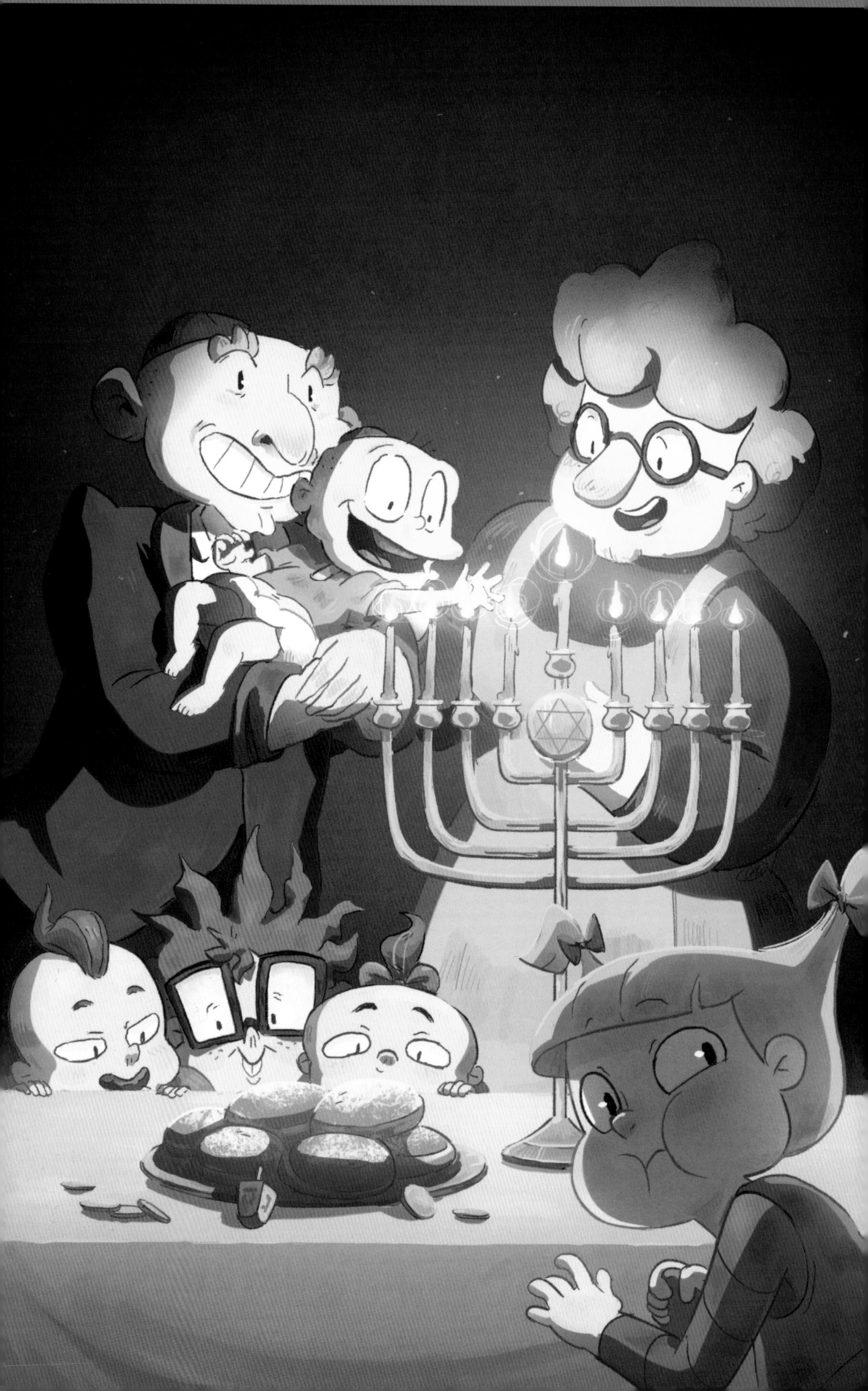

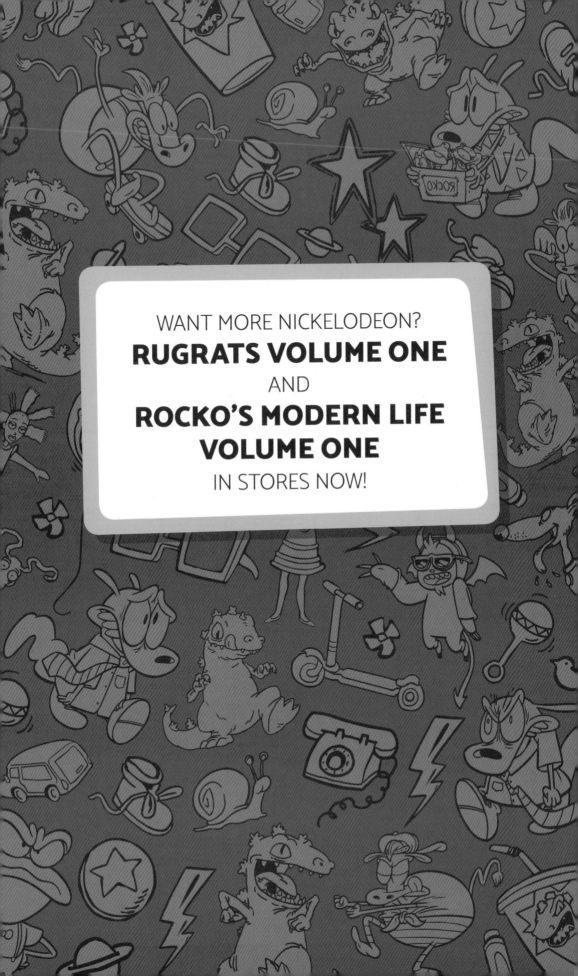

WANT MORE NICKELODEON?
RUGRATS VOLUME ONE
AND
**ROCKO'S MODERN LIFE
VOLUME ONE**
IN STORES NOW!

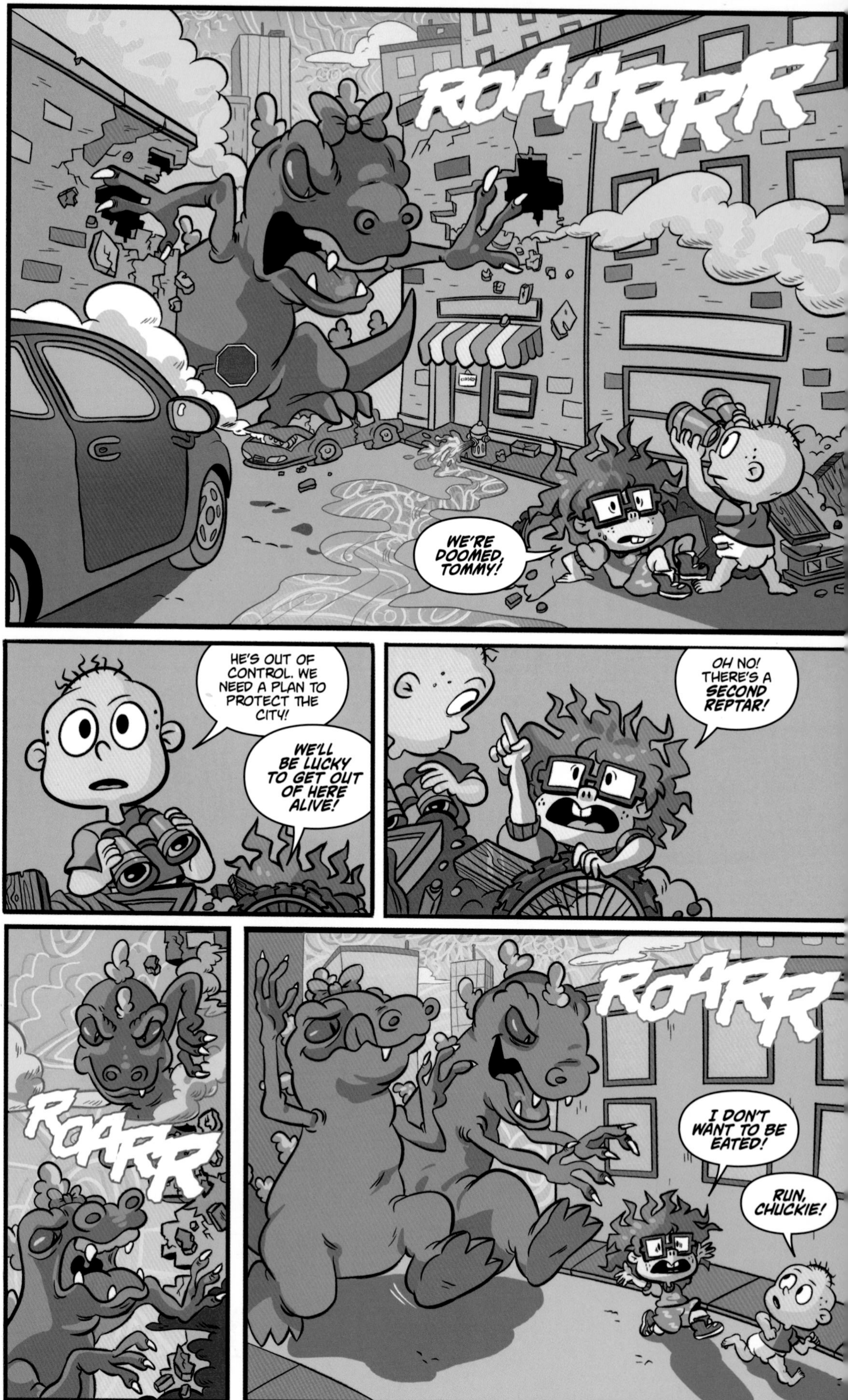
ROAAARRR
WE'RE DOOMED, TOMMY!
HE'S OUT OF CONTROL. WE NEED A PLAN TO PROTECT THE CITY!
WE'LL BE LUCKY TO GET OUT OF HERE ALIVE!
OH NO! THERE'S A SECOND REPTAR!
ROARR
ROARR
I DON'T WANT TO BE EATED!
RUN, CHUCKIE!

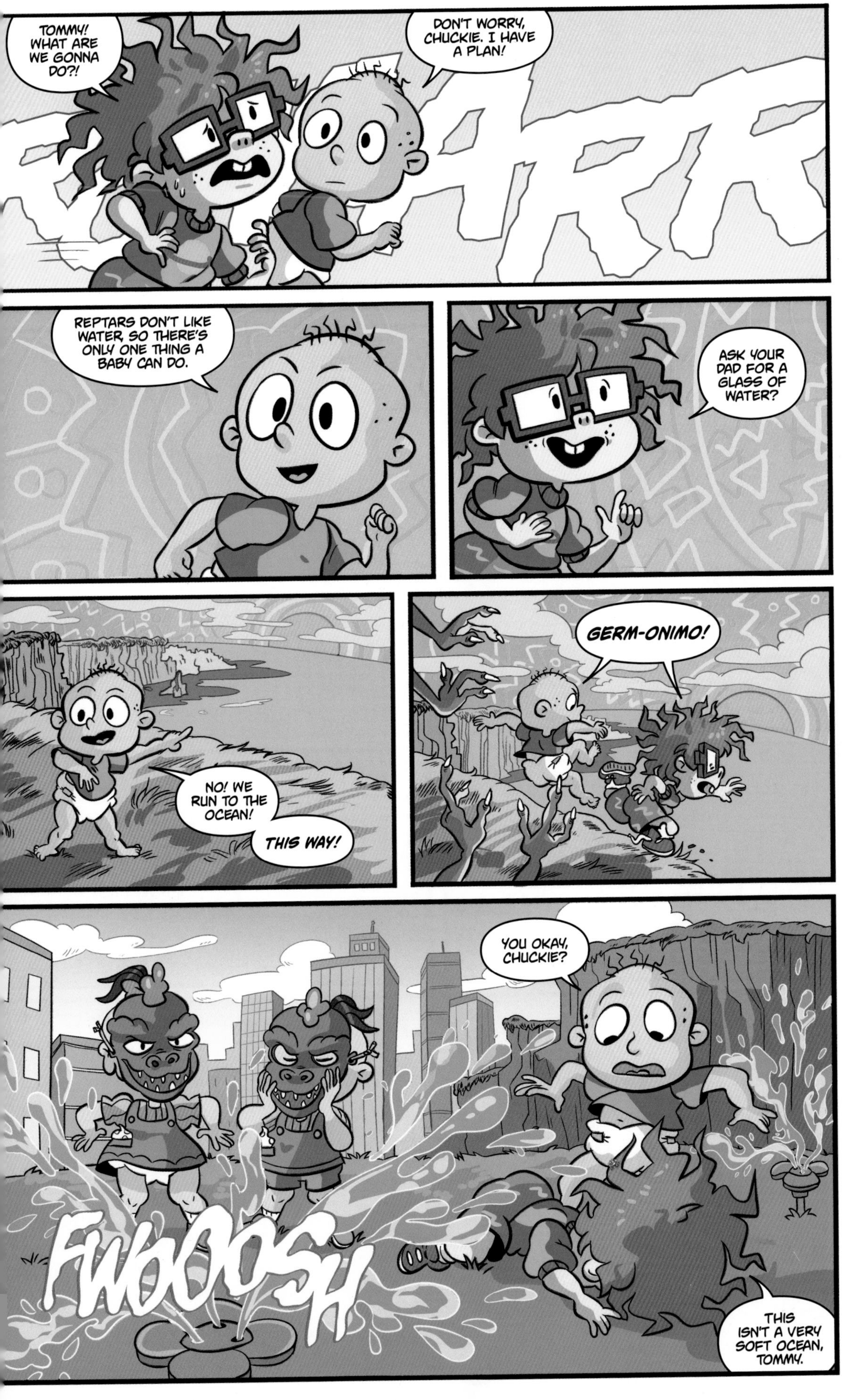
TOMMY! WHAT ARE WE GONNA DO?!
DON'T WORRY, CHUCKIE. I HAVE A PLAN!
REPTARS DON'T LIKE WATER, SO THERE'S ONLY ONE THING A BABY CAN DO.
ASK YOUR DAD FOR A GLASS OF WATER?
NO! WE RUN TO THE OCEAN!
THIS WAY!
GERM-ONIMO!
YOU OKAY, CHUCKIE?
FWOOOSH
THIS ISN'T A VERY SOFT OCEAN, TOMMY.

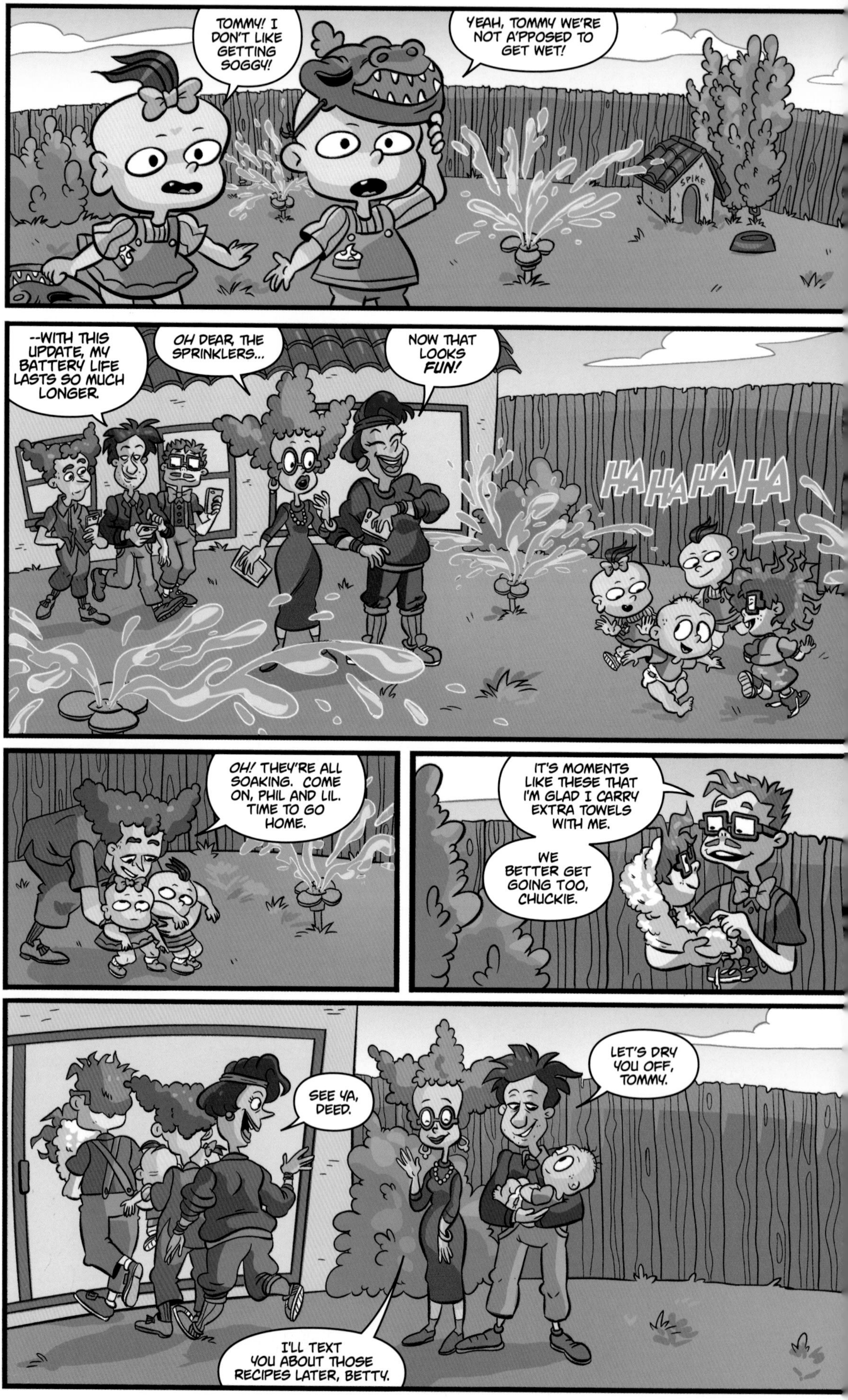
TOMMY! I DON'T LIKE GETTING SOGGY!
YEAH, TOMMY WE'RE NOT A'PPOSED TO GET WET!
SPIKE
--WITH THIS UPDATE, MY BATTERY LIFE LASTS SO MUCH LONGER.
OH DEAR, THE SPRINKLERS...
NOW THAT LOOKS FUN!
HAHAHAHA
OH! THEY'RE ALL SOAKING. COME ON, PHIL AND LIL. TIME TO GO HOME.
IT'S MOMENTS LIKE THESE THAT I'M GLAD I CARRY EXTRA TOWELS WITH ME.
WE BETTER GET GOING TOO, CHUCKIE.
SEE YA, DEED.
LET'S DRY YOU OFF, TOMMY.
I'LL TEXT YOU ABOUT THOSE RECIPES LATER, BETTY.

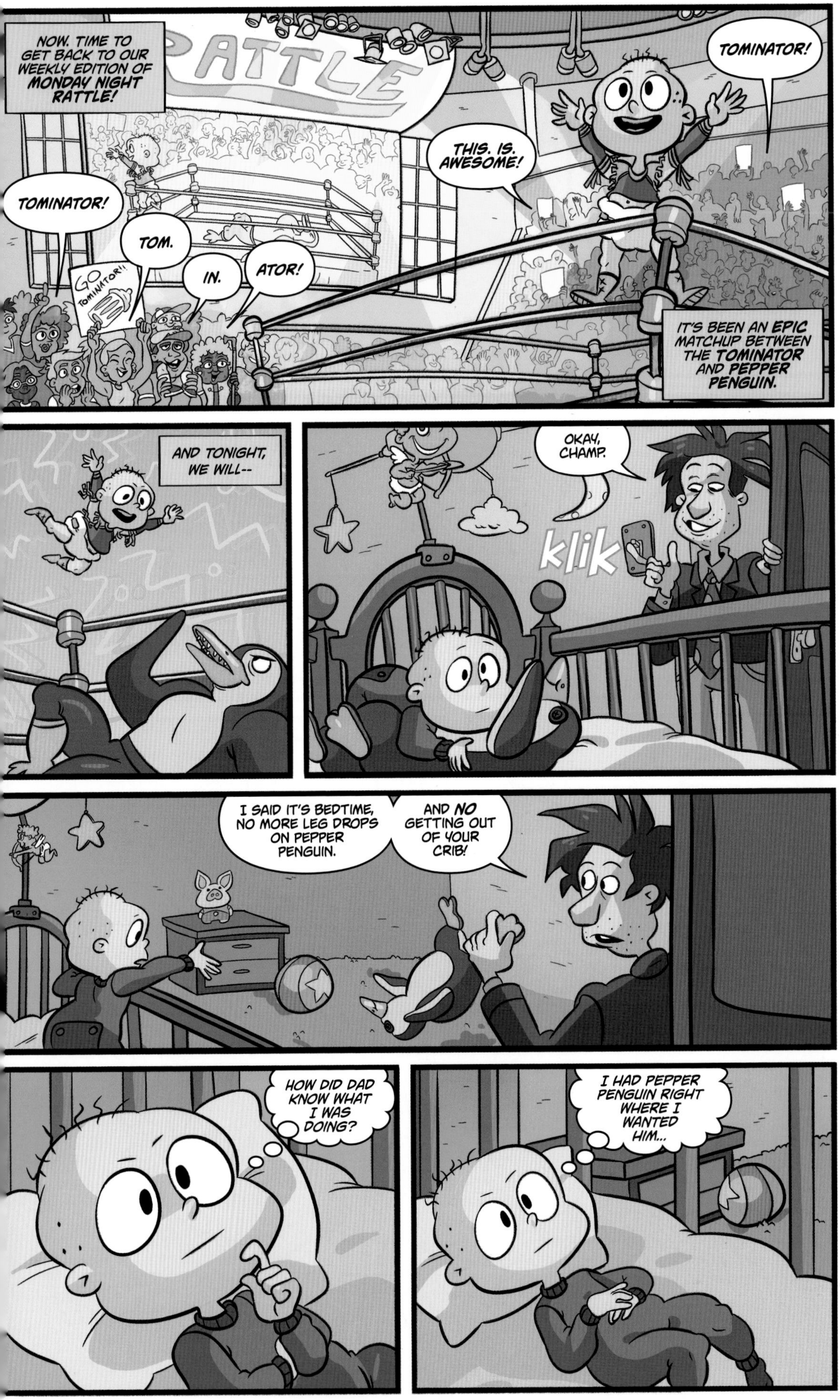
NOW. TIME TO GET BACK TO OUR WEEKLY EDITION OF MONDAY NIGHT RATTLE!
RATTLE
TOMINATOR!
TOM.
GO TOMINATOR!!
IN.
ATOR!
THIS. IS. AWESOME!
TOMINATOR!
IT'S BEEN AN EPIC MATCHUP BETWEEN THE TOMINATOR AND PEPPER PENGUIN.
AND TONIGHT, WE WILL--
OKAY, CHAMP.
klik
I SAID IT'S BEDTIME, NO MORE LEG DROPS ON PEPPER PENGUIN.
AND NO GETTING OUT OF YOUR CRIB!
HOW DID DAD KNOW WHAT I WAS DOING?
I HAD PEPPER PENGUIN RIGHT WHERE I WANTED HIM...

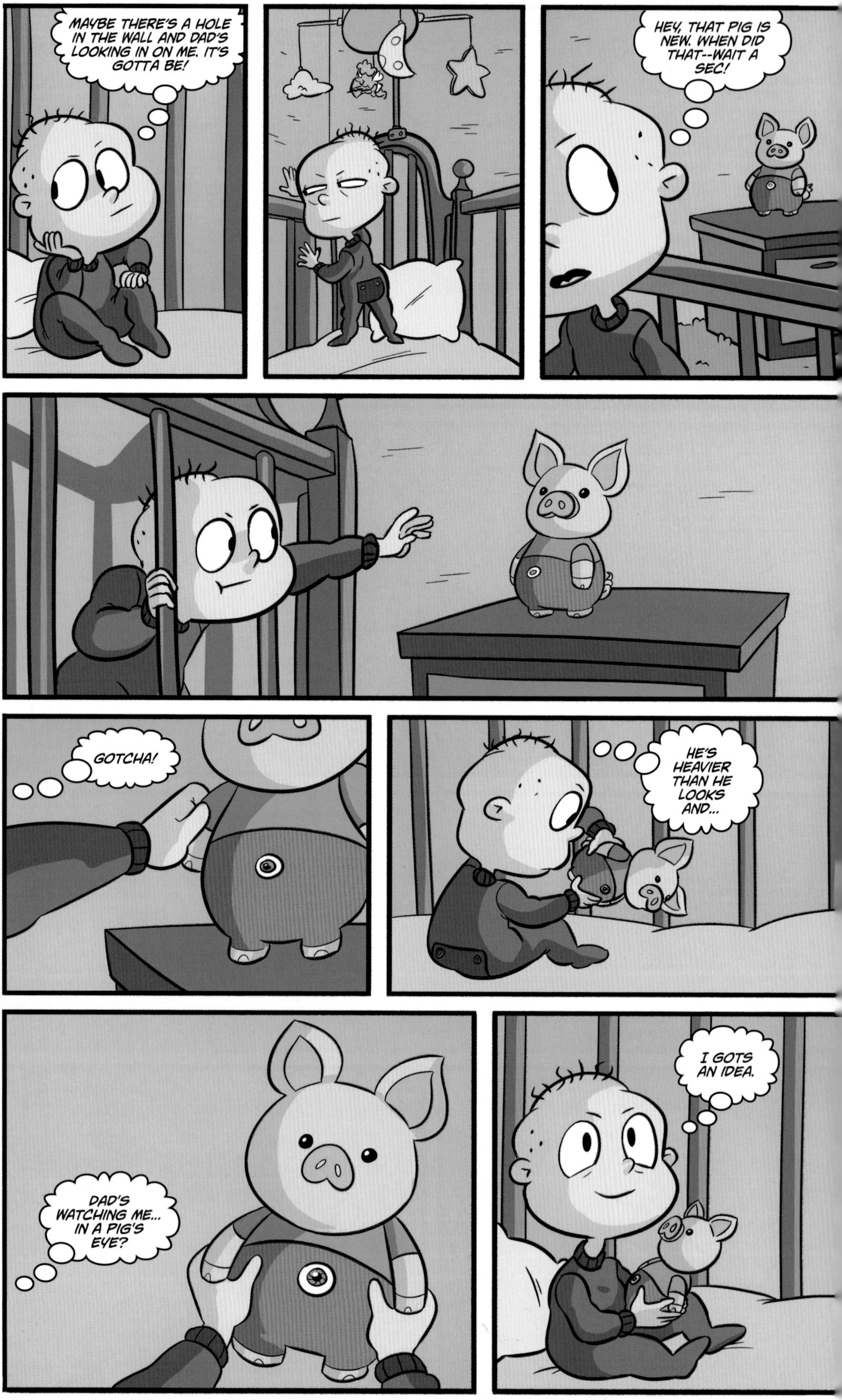
MAYBE THERE'S A HOLE IN THE WALL AND DAD'S LOOKING IN ON ME. IT'S GOTTA BE!
HEY, THAT PIG IS NEW. WHEN DID THAT--WAIT A SEC!
GOTCHA!
HE'S HEAVIER THAN HE LOOKS AND...
DAD'S WATCHING ME... IN A PIG'S EYE?
I GOTS AN IDEA.

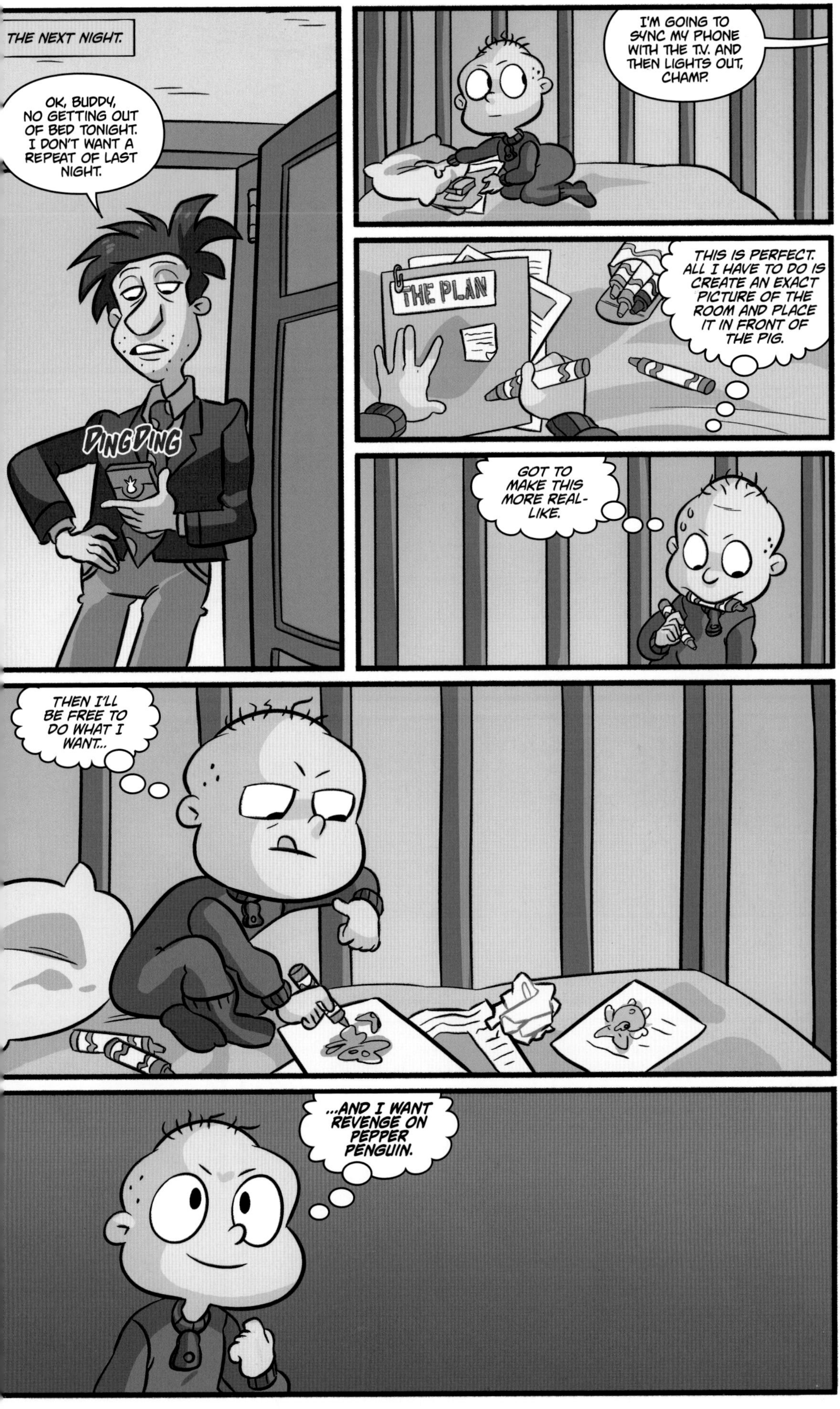
THE NEXT NIGHT.
OK, BUDDY, NO GETTING OUT OF BED TONIGHT. I DON'T WANT A REPEAT OF LAST NIGHT.
DING DING
I'M GOING TO SYNC MY PHONE WITH THE T.V. AND THEN LIGHTS OUT, CHAMP.
THE PLAN
THIS IS PERFECT. ALL I HAVE TO DO IS CREATE AN EXACT PICTURE OF THE ROOM AND PLACE IT IN FRONT OF THE PIG.
GOT TO MAKE THIS MORE REAL-LIKE.
THEN I'LL BE FREE TO DO WHAT I WANT...
...AND I WANT REVENGE ON PEPPER PENGUIN.

FIVE MINUTES LATER.

click

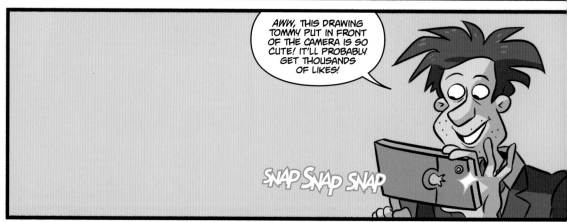

AWW, THIS DRAWING TOMMY PUT IN FRONT OF THE CAMERA IS SO CUTE! IT'LL PROBABLY GET THOUSANDS OF LIKES!

SNAP SNAP SNAP

HOW DID HE KNOW IT WAS A FAKE?

NIGHT, SLUGGER.

click

IT WAS A *PERFICK* REAL-LIKE DRAWING OF ME! NO ONE COULD HAVE KNOWN!

WHAT...WHAT IF I NEVER GET TO HAVE MY REVENGE ON PEPPER PENGUIN CAUSE MOM AND DAD WON'T STOP WATCHING ME ALL THE TIME?

≥GULP≤

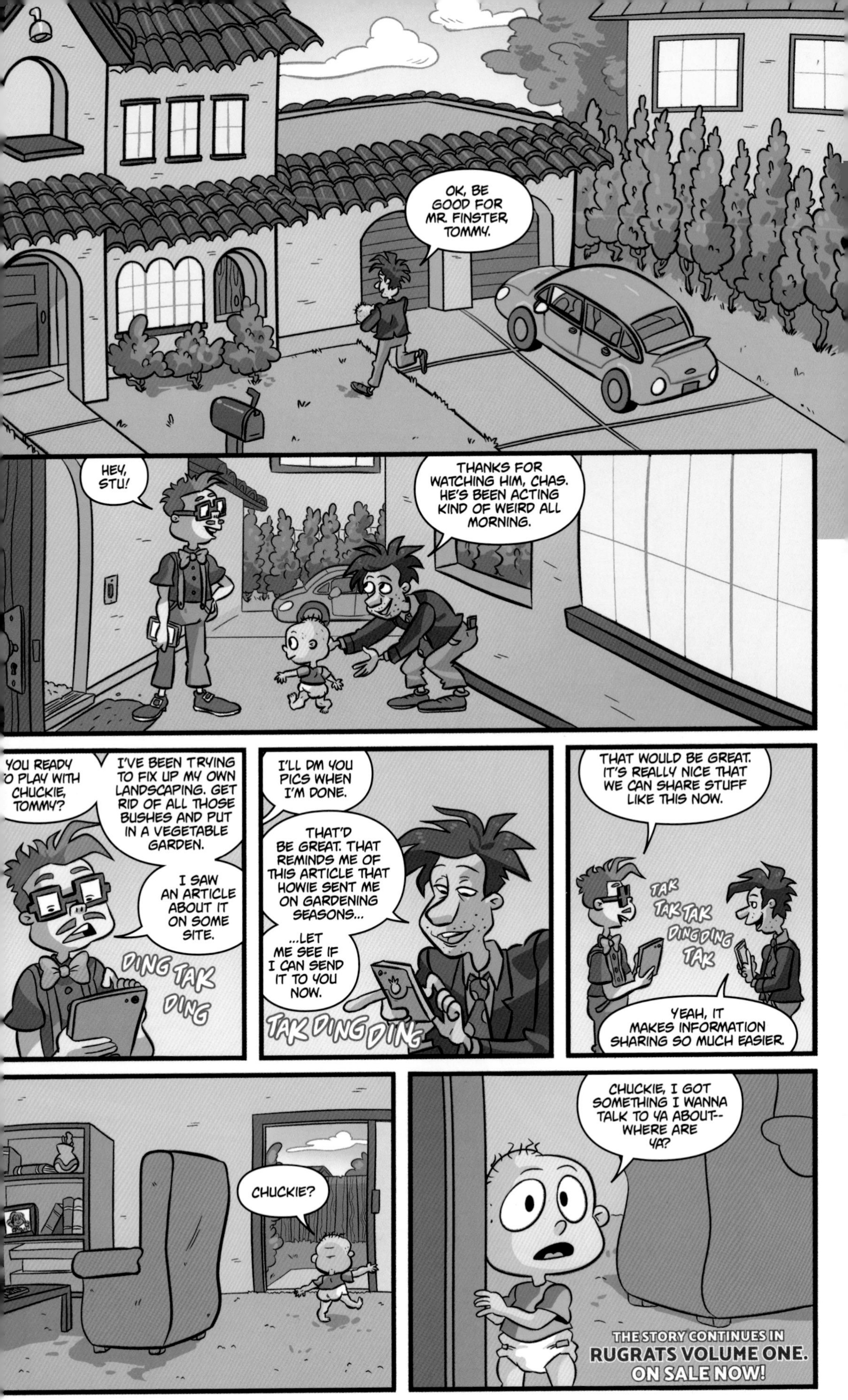
OK, BE GOOD FOR MR. FINSTER, TOMMY.
HEY, STU!
THANKS FOR WATCHING HIM, CHAS. HE'S BEEN ACTING KIND OF WEIRD ALL MORNING.
YOU READY TO PLAY WITH CHUCKIE, TOMMY?
I'VE BEEN TRYING TO FIX UP MY OWN LANDSCAPING. GET RID OF ALL THOSE BUSHES AND PUT IN A VEGETABLE GARDEN.
I SAW AN ARTICLE ABOUT IT ON SOME SITE.
DING TAK DING
I'LL DM YOU PICS WHEN I'M DONE.
THAT'D BE GREAT. THAT REMINDS ME OF THIS ARTICLE THAT HOWIE SENT ME ON GARDENING SEASONS...
...LET ME SEE IF I CAN SEND IT TO YOU NOW.
TAK DING DING
THAT WOULD BE GREAT. IT'S REALLY NICE THAT WE CAN SHARE STUFF LIKE THIS NOW.
TAK TAK TAK DING DING TAK
YEAH, IT MAKES INFORMATION SHARING SO MUCH EASIER.
CHUCKIE?
CHUCKIE, I GOT SOMETHING I WANNA TALK TO YA ABOUT-- WHERE ARE YA?
THE STORY CONTINUES IN RUGRATS VOLUME ONE. ON SALE NOW!

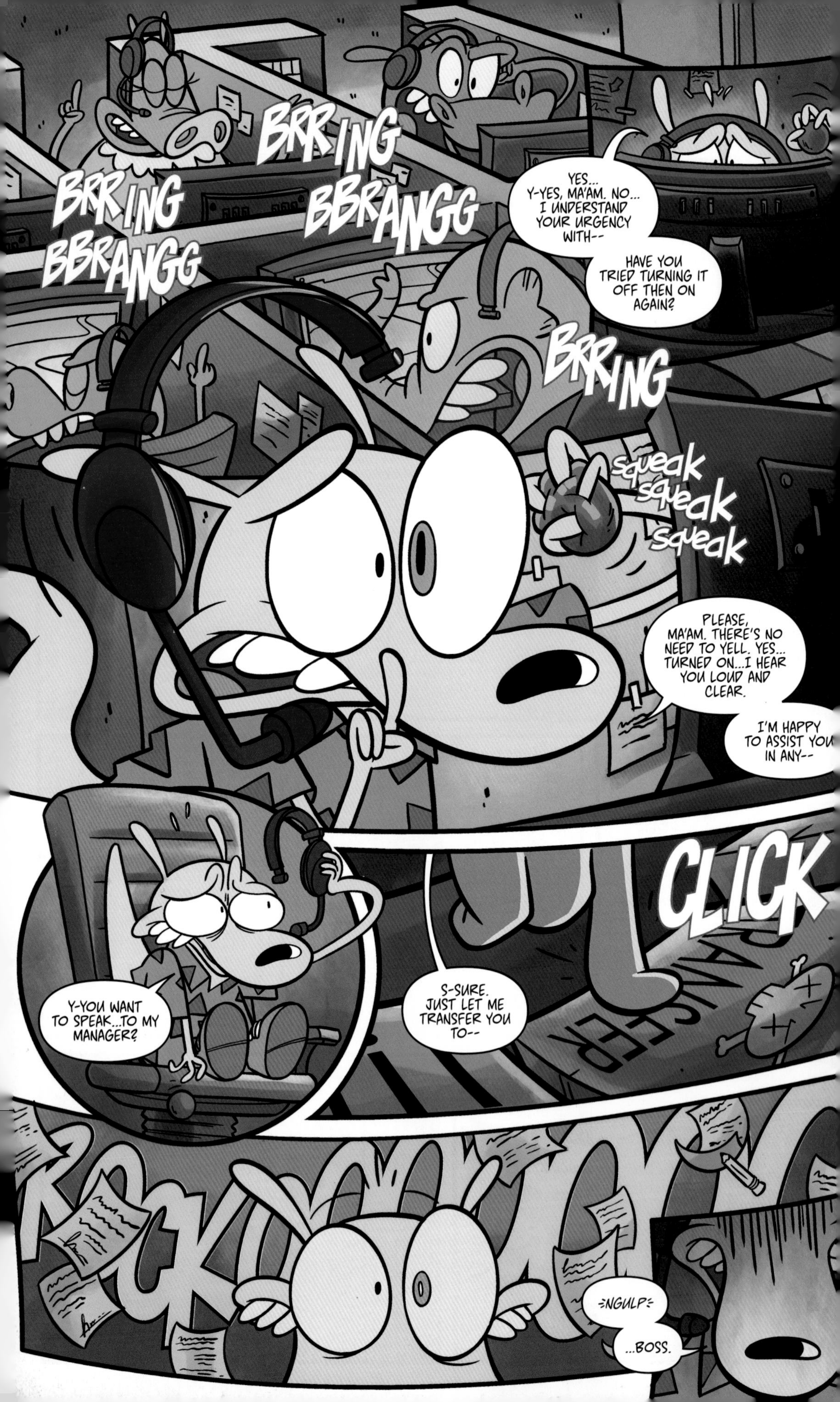
BRRING
BBRANGG
BRRING
BBRANGG
YES... Y-YES, MA'AM. NO... I UNDERSTAND YOUR URGENCY WITH--
HAVE YOU TRIED TURNING IT OFF THEN ON AGAIN?
BRRING
squeak squeak squeak
PLEASE, MA'AM. THERE'S NO NEED TO YELL. YES... TURNED ON...I HEAR YOU LOUD AND CLEAR.
I'M HAPPY TO ASSIST YOU IN ANY--
CLICK
Y-YOU WANT TO SPEAK...TO MY MANAGER?
S-SURE. JUST LET ME TRANSFER YOU TO--
=NGULP=
...BOSS.

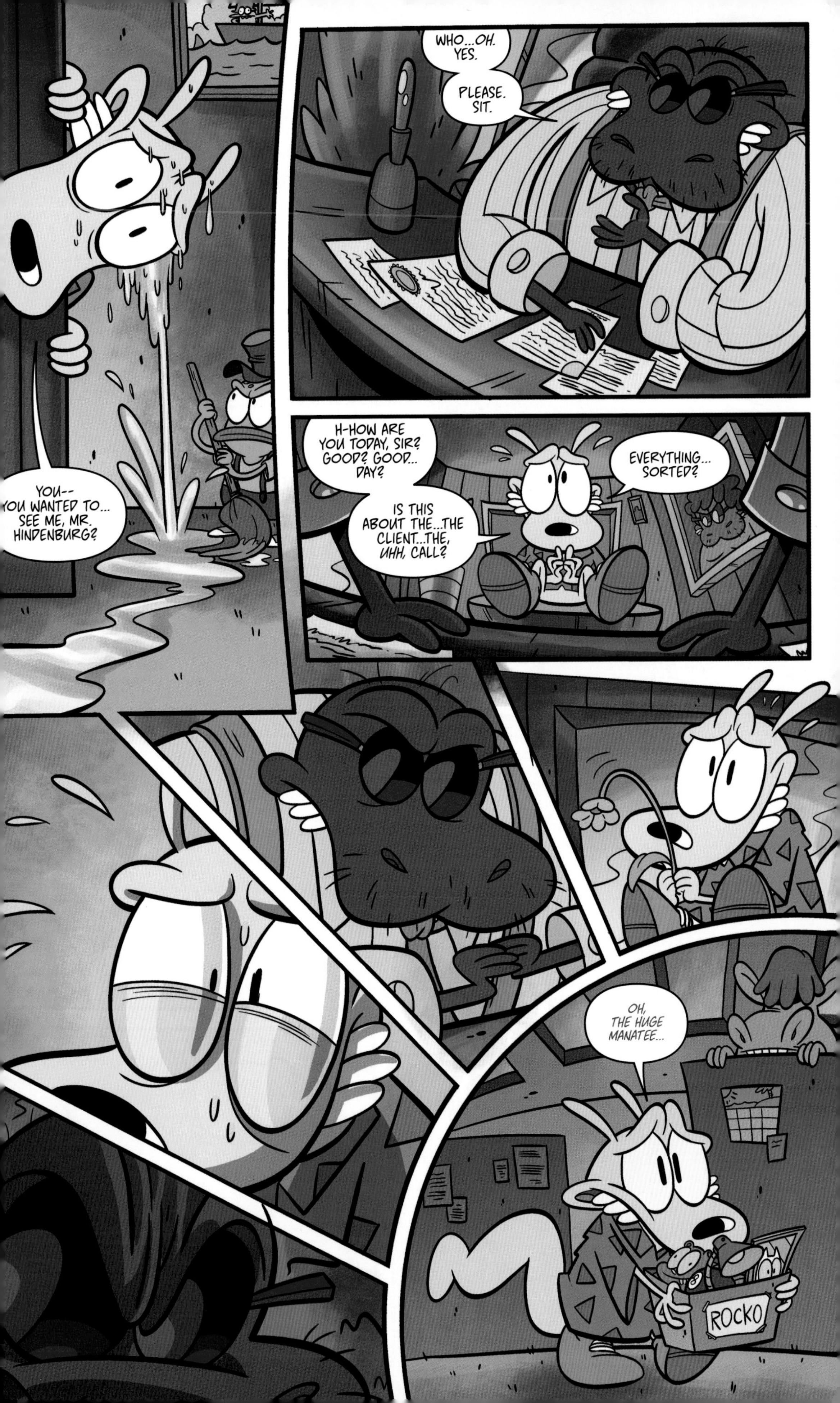
YOU--
YOU WANTED TO... SEE ME, MR. HINDENBURG?
WHO...OH. YES.
PLEASE. SIT.
H-HOW ARE YOU TODAY, SIR? GOOD? GOOD... DAY?
IS THIS ABOUT THE...THE CLIENT...THE, UHH, CALL?
EVERYTHING... SORTED?
OH, THE HUGE MANATEE...
ROCKO

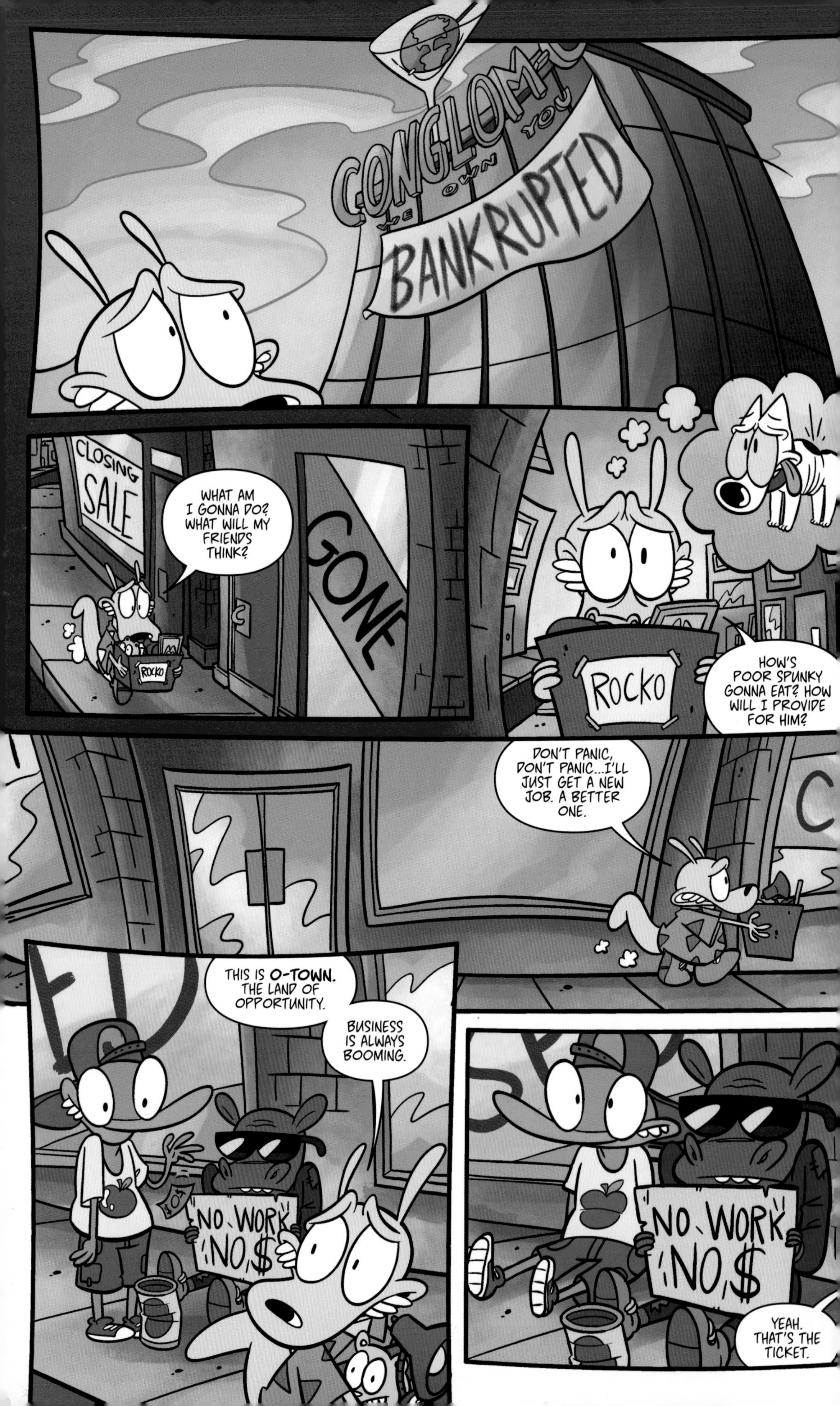
CONGLOM-O
WE OWN YOU
BANKRUPTED
CLOSING SALE
WHAT AM I GONNA DO? WHAT WILL MY FRIENDS THINK?
GONE
ROCKO
HOW'S POOR SPUNKY GONNA EAT? HOW WILL I PROVIDE FOR HIM?
DON'T PANIC, DON'T PANIC...I'LL JUST GET A NEW JOB. A BETTER ONE.
THIS IS O-TOWN. THE LAND OF OPPORTUNITY.
BUSINESS IS ALWAYS BOOMING.
NO WORK NO $
NO WORK NO $
YEAH. THAT'S THE TICKET.

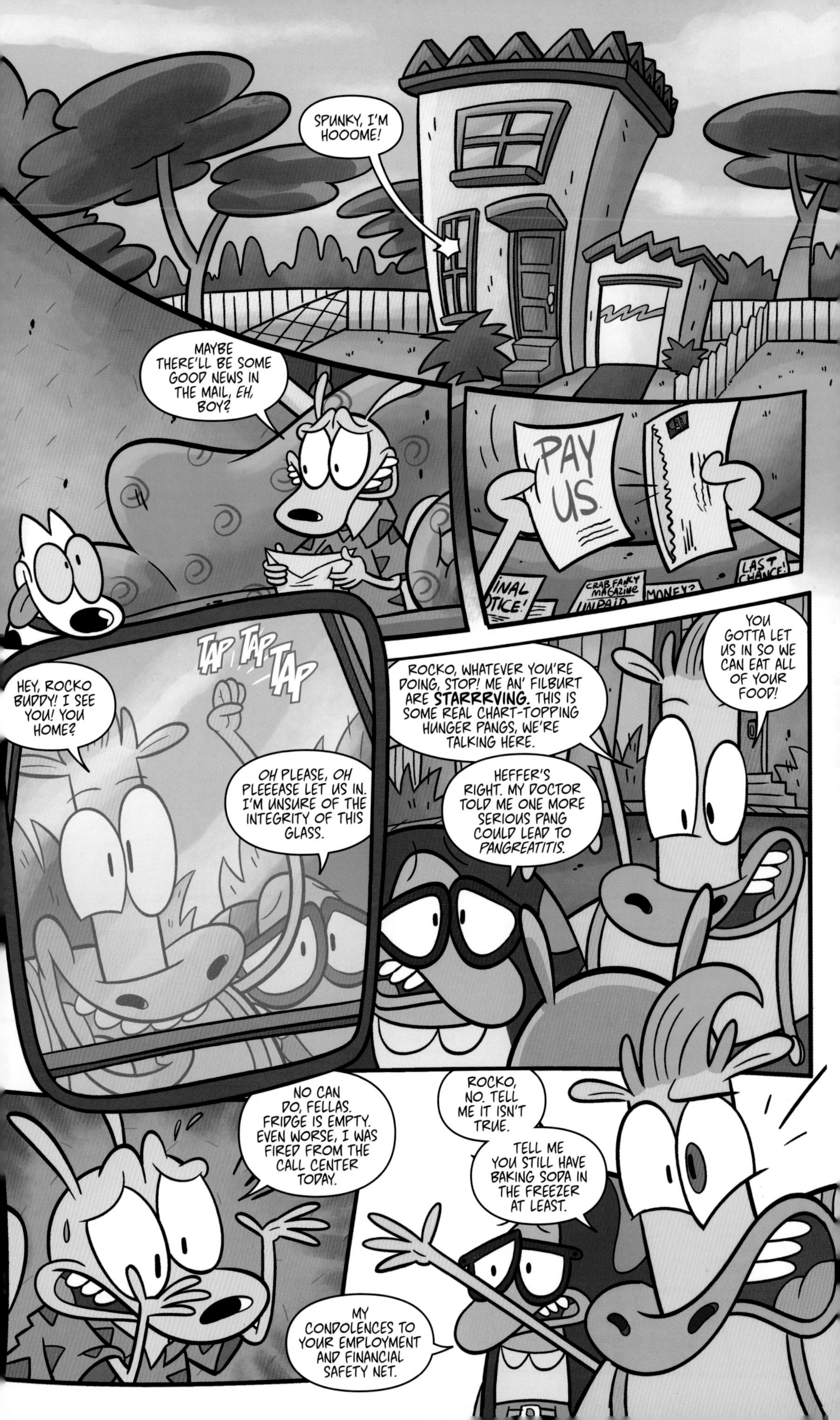
SPUNKY, I'M HOOOME!
MAYBE THERE'LL BE SOME GOOD NEWS IN THE MAIL, EH, BOY?
PAY US
FINAL NOTICE!
CRAB FANCY MAGAZINE UNPAID
MONEY?
LAST CHANCE!
TAP TAP TAP
HEY, ROCKO BUDDY! I SEE YOU! YOU HOME?
OH PLEASE, OH PLEEEASE LET US IN. I'M UNSURE OF THE INTEGRITY OF THIS GLASS.
ROCKO, WHATEVER YOU'RE DOING, STOP! ME AN' FILBURT ARE **STARRRVING.** THIS IS SOME REAL CHART-TOPPING HUNGER PANGS, WE'RE TALKING HERE.
YOU GOTTA LET US IN SO WE CAN EAT ALL OF YOUR FOOD!
HEFFER'S RIGHT. MY DOCTOR TOLD ME ONE MORE SERIOUS PANG COULD LEAD TO *PANGREATITIS.*
NO CAN DO, FELLAS. FRIDGE IS EMPTY. EVEN WORSE, I WAS FIRED FROM THE CALL CENTER TODAY.
ROCKO, NO. TELL ME IT ISN'T TRUE.
TELL ME YOU STILL HAVE BAKING SODA IN THE FREEZER AT LEAST.
MY CONDOLENCES TO YOUR EMPLOYMENT AND FINANCIAL SAFETY NET.

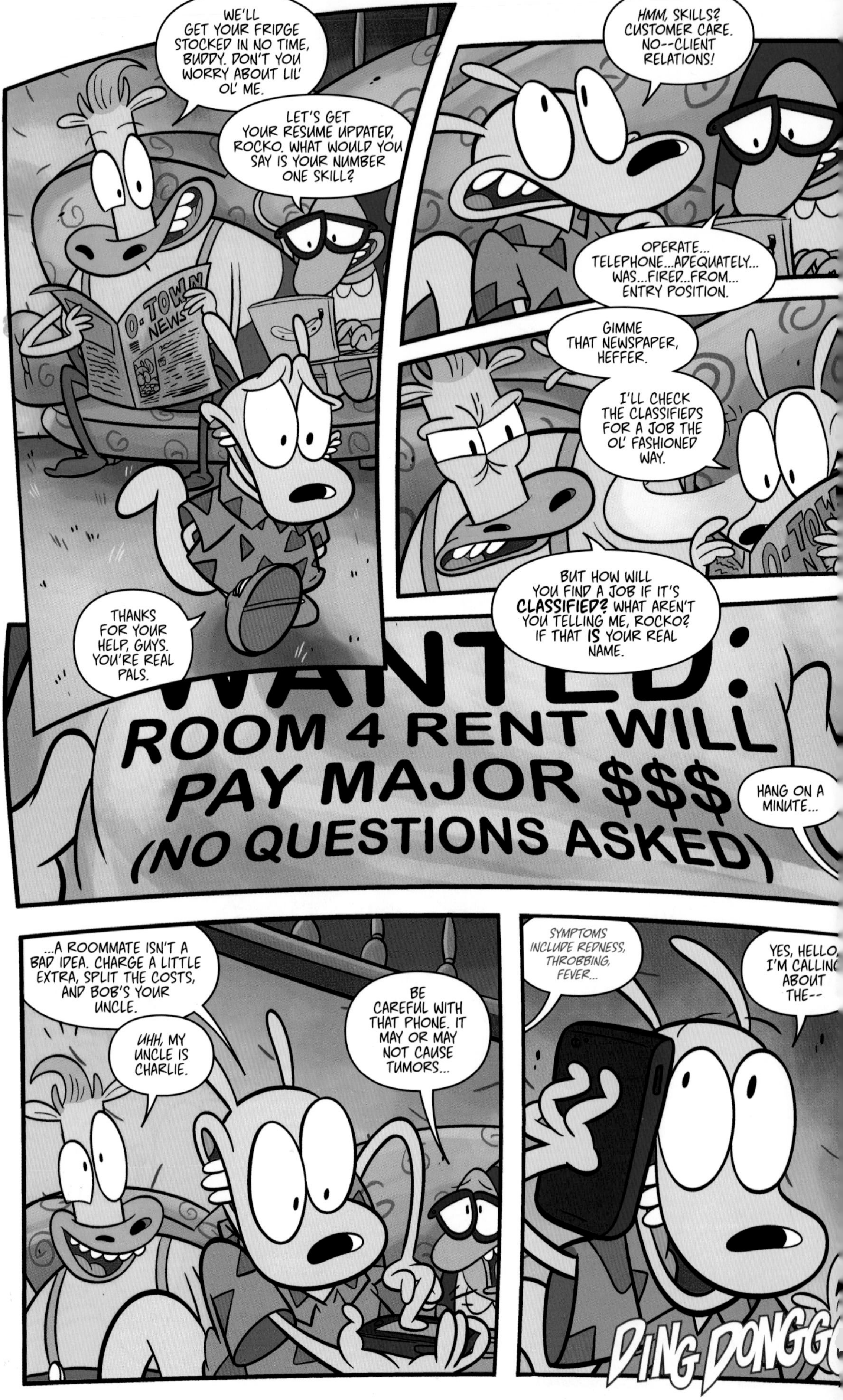
WE'LL GET YOUR FRIDGE STOCKED IN NO TIME, BUDDY. DON'T YOU WORRY ABOUT LIL' OL' ME.
LET'S GET YOUR RESUME UPDATED, ROCKO. WHAT WOULD YOU SAY IS YOUR NUMBER ONE SKILL?
O-TOWN NEWS
THANKS FOR YOUR HELP, GUYS. YOU'RE REAL PALS.
HMM, SKILLS? CUSTOMER CARE. NO--CLIENT RELATIONS!
OPERATE... TELEPHONE...ADEQUATELY... WAS...FIRED...FROM... ENTRY POSITION.
GIMME THAT NEWSPAPER, HEFFER.
I'LL CHECK THE CLASSIFIEDS FOR A JOB THE OL' FASHIONED WAY.
BUT HOW WILL YOU FIND A JOB IF IT'S **CLASSIFIED?** WHAT AREN'T YOU TELLING ME, ROCKO? IF THAT **IS** YOUR REAL NAME.
WANTED: ROOM 4 RENT WILL PAY MAJOR $$$ (NO QUESTIONS ASKED)
HANG ON A MINUTE...
...A ROOMMATE ISN'T A BAD IDEA. CHARGE A LITTLE EXTRA, SPLIT THE COSTS, AND BOB'S YOUR UNCLE.
UHH, MY UNCLE IS CHARLIE.
BE CAREFUL WITH THAT PHONE. IT MAY OR MAY NOT CAUSE TUMORS...
SYMPTOMS INCLUDE REDNESS, THROBBING, FEVER...
YES, HELLO, I'M CALLIN ABOUT THE--
DING DONGG

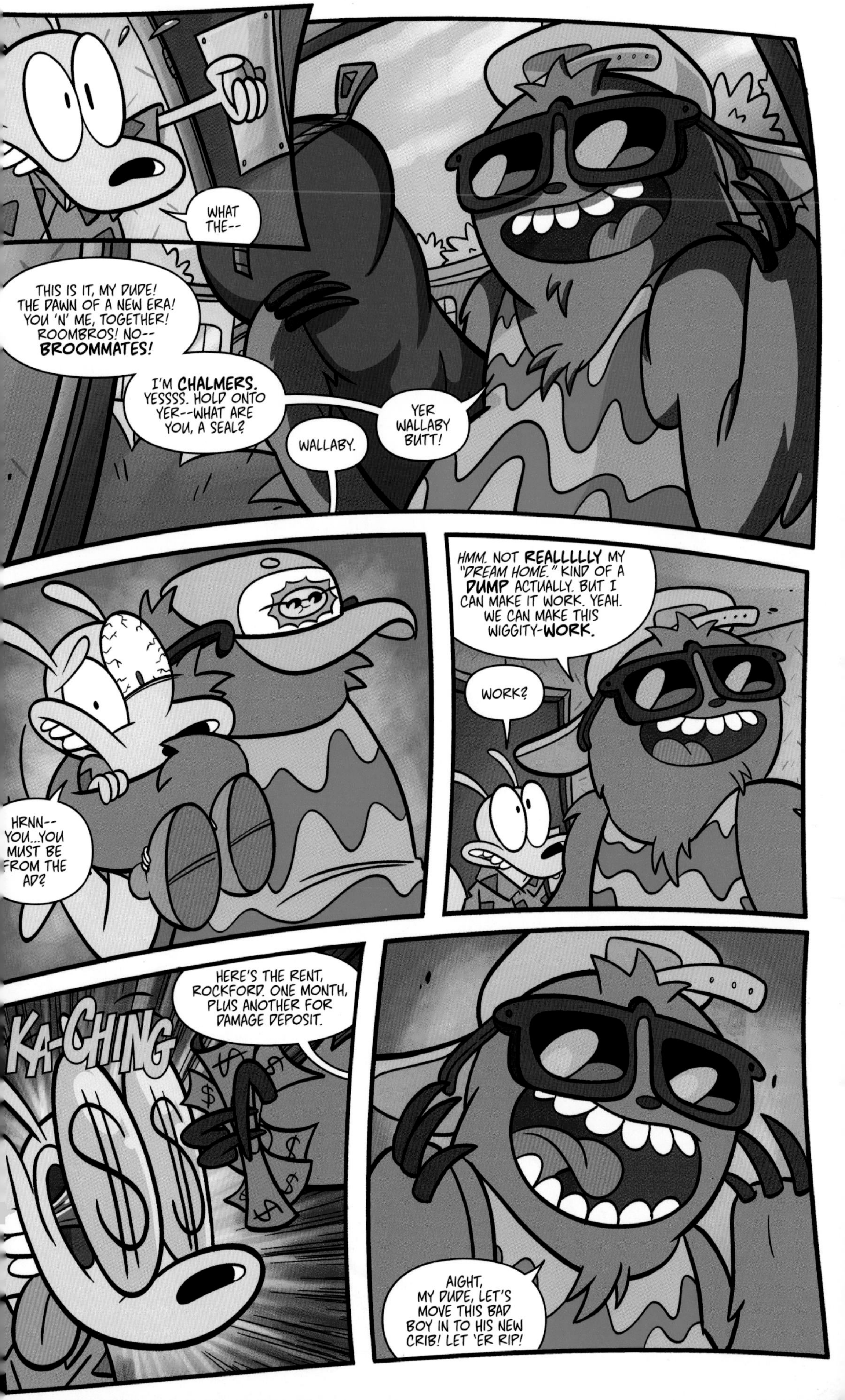
WHAT THE--
THIS IS IT, MY DUDE! THE DAWN OF A NEW ERA! YOU 'N' ME, TOGETHER! ROOMBROS! NO-- BROOMMATES!
I'M CHALMERS. YESSSS. HOLD ONTO YER--WHAT ARE YOU, A SEAL?
WALLABY.
YER WALLABY BUTT!
HRNN-- YOU...YOU MUST BE FROM THE AD?
HMM. NOT REALLLLLY MY "DREAM HOME." KIND OF A DUMP ACTUALLY. BUT I CAN MAKE IT WORK. YEAH. WE CAN MAKE THIS WIGGITY-WORK.
WORK?
KA-CHING
HERE'S THE RENT, ROCKFORD. ONE MONTH, PLUS ANOTHER FOR DAMAGE DEPOSIT.
AIGHT, MY DUDE, LET'S MOVE THIS BAD BOY IN TO HIS NEW CRIB! LET 'ER RIP!

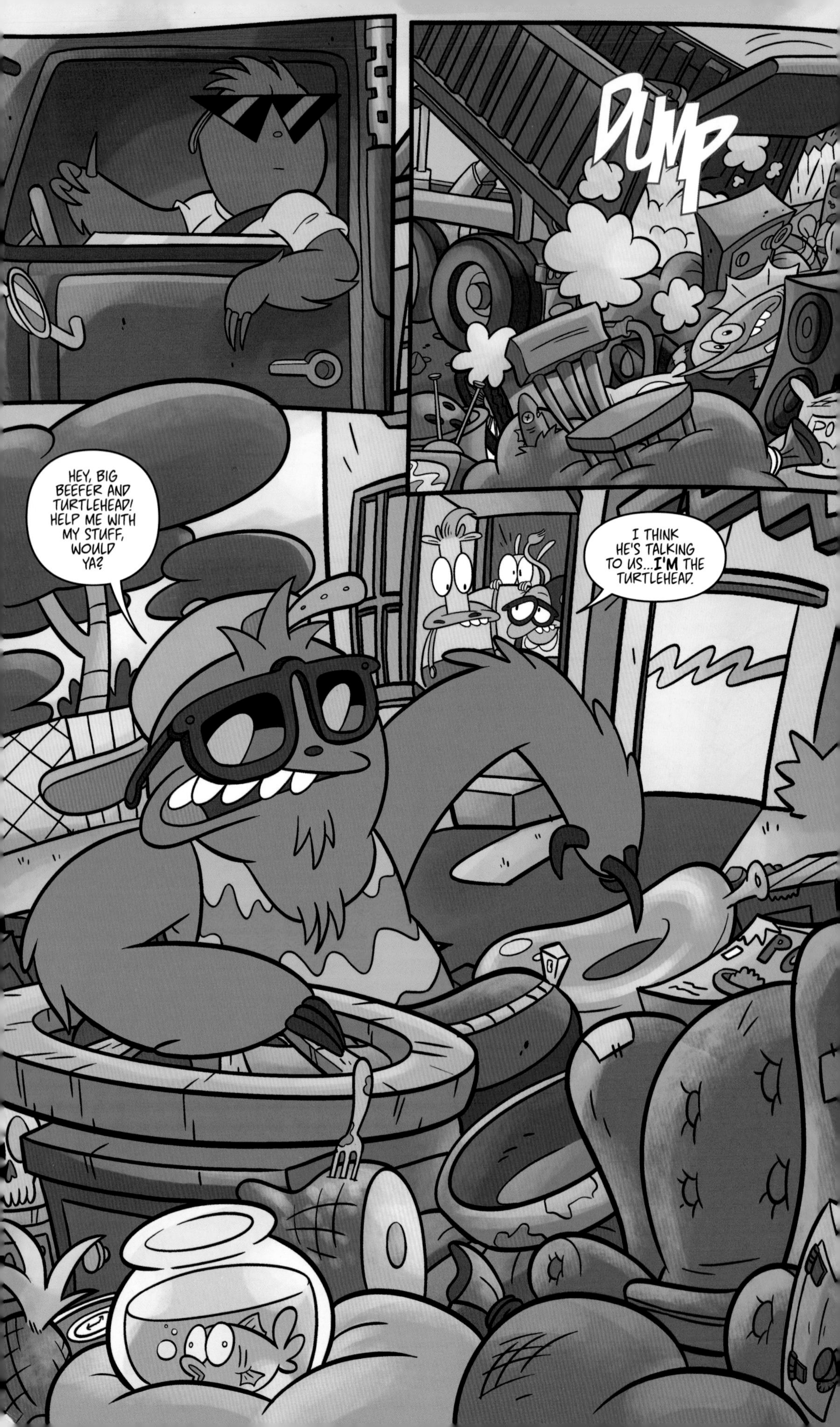
DUMP
HEY, BIG BEEFER AND TURTLEHEAD! HELP ME WITH MY STUFF, WOULD YA?
I THINK HE'S TALKING TO US...**I'M** THE TURTLEHEAD.

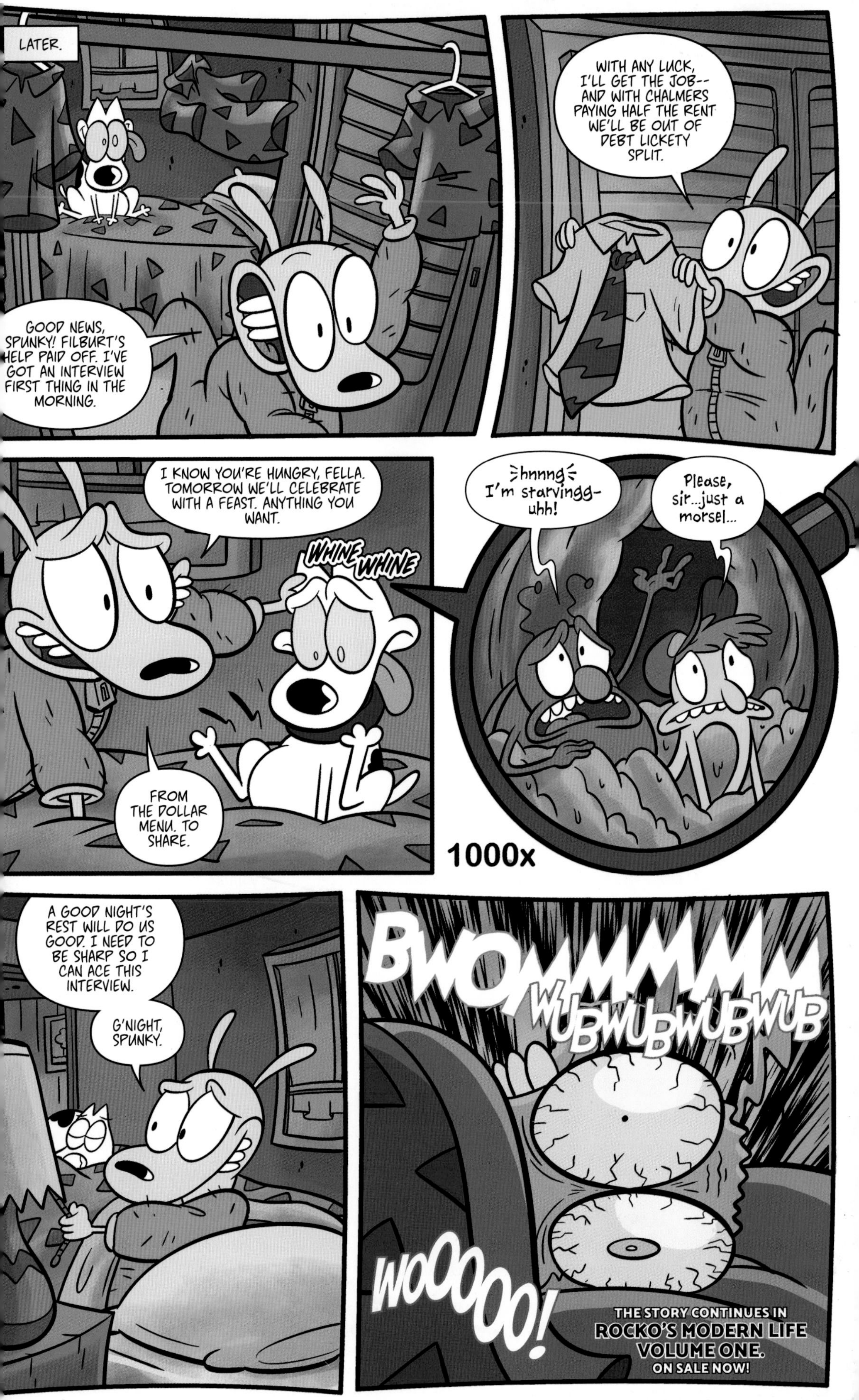

LATER.
GOOD NEWS, SPUNKY! FILBURT'S HELP PAID OFF. I'VE GOT AN INTERVIEW FIRST THING IN THE MORNING.
WITH ANY LUCK, I'LL GET THE JOB-- AND WITH CHALMERS PAYING HALF THE RENT WE'LL BE OUT OF DEBT LICKETY SPLIT.
I KNOW YOU'RE HUNGRY, FELLA. TOMORROW WE'LL CELEBRATE WITH A FEAST. ANYTHING YOU WANT.
WHINE WHINE
FROM THE DOLLAR MENU. TO SHARE.
hnnng I'm starvingg-uhh!
Please, sir...just a morsel...
1000x
A GOOD NIGHT'S REST WILL DO US GOOD. I NEED TO BE SHARP SO I CAN ACE THIS INTERVIEW.
G'NIGHT, SPUNKY.
BWOMMMMM
WUBWUBWUBWUB
WOOOOO!
THE STORY CONTINUES IN ROCKO'S MODERN LIFE VOLUME ONE. ON SALE NOW!

DISCOVER
EXPLOSIVE NEW WORLDS

ADVENTURE TIME

Sam Sykes · Selina Espiritu · Sarah Stern
Brave Chef Brianna

KELLY THOMPSON BRIANNE DROUHARD M. VICTORIA ROBADO
MEGA PRINCESS

THE NOT-SO SECRET SOCIETY
DALEY · CRAFTS · CLARK · BRUNI
KEEP OUT
CAUTION

OVER THE GARDEN WALL

STEVEN UNIVERSE
VOLUME ONE

kaboom!

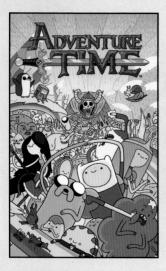

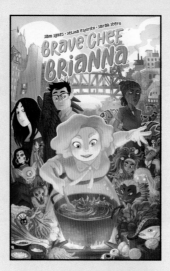

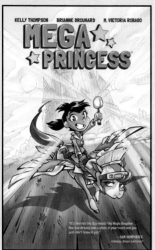

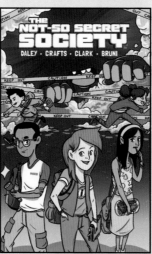

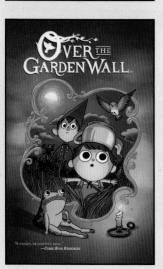

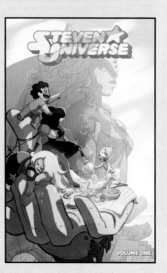

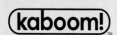

AVAILABLE AT YOUR LOCAL COMICS SHOP AND BOOKSTORE

To find a comics shop in your area, visit www.comicshoplocator.com

WWW.**BOOM-STUDIOS**.COM

Adventure Time
Pendleton Ward and Others
Volume 1
ISBN: 978-1-60886-280-1 | $14.99 US
Volume 2
ISBN: 978-1-60886-323-5 | $14.99 US
Adventure Time: Islands
ISBN: 978-1-60886-972-5 | $9.99 US

The Amazing World of Gumball
Ben Bocquelet and Others
Volume 1
ISBN: 978-1-60886-488-1 | $14.99 US
Volume 2
ISBN: 978-1-60886-793-6 | $14.99 US

Brave Chef Brianna
Sam Sykes, Selina Espiritu
ISBN: 978-1-68415-050-2 | $14.99 US

Mega Princess
Kelly Thompson, Brianne Drouhard
ISBN: 978-1-68415-007-6 | $14.99 US

The Not-So Secret Society
Matthew Daley, Arlene Daley, Wook Jin Clark
ISBN: 978-1-60886-997-8 | $9.99 US

Over the Garden Wall
Patrick McHale, Jim Campbell and Others
Volume 1
ISBN: 978-1-60886-940-4 | $14.99 US
Volume 2
ISBN: 978-1-68415-006-9 | $14.99 US

Steven Universe
Rebecca Sugar and Others
Volume 1
ISBN: 978-1-60886-706-6 | $14.99 US
Volume 2
ISBN: 978-1-60886-796-7 | $14.99 US

Steven Universe & The Crystal Gems
ISBN: 978-1-60886-921-3 | $14.99 US

Steven Universe: Too Cool for School
ISBN: 978-1-60886-771-4 | $14.99 US